EXTINCTIONS

JOSEPHINE WILSON

EXTINCTIONS

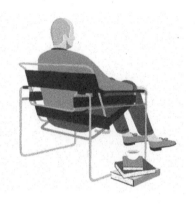

JOSEPHINE WILSON

First published in Great Britain in 2018 by Serpent's Tail,
an imprint of Profile Books Ltd
3 Holford Yard
Bevin Way
London
WC1X 9HD
www.serpentstail.com

1 3 5 7 9 10 8 6 4 2

Designed by sue@lambledesign.demon.co.uk

Typeset in Bembo by MacGuru Ltd

Printed and bound by Clays, St Ives plc

A CIP record for this book can be obtained from the British Library

ISBN 978 1 78816 076 6
eISBN 978 1 78283 461 8

FSC
www.fsc.org
MIX
Paper from
responsible sources
FSC® C018072

For Christopher Hill, who understands

Who is prepared to deprive life of a significant dénouement?

Jean Améry

Tales of extinction often begin near the end. The past is invoked – a prior Eden where wildness reigned and the dark earth was rich and generous, the air thick with the beating of feathers. We all know what will happen next. Over the page, just around the corner, is the massacre.

After the clubbing and shooting and plucking and boiling there is a hiatus, a pause that deepens into a permanent silence. Years, decades later – it is seldom more – that silence is remarked, and there begins a search for the Last Ones. Expeditions are dispatched. Local knowledge is invoked. And when it is documented that all is gone, all but the odd mute captive, writers are conscripted to pen salutary tales. These remains are gathered up. There follows a mourning of the remnants, of the last few metres of a patterned cloth that will never be printed again.

These Last Ones are best captured through image, rendered in painting or etching or photograph – an old bird alone in a wire cage in a Midwestern zoo, a single male beast lowing mournfully in a concrete enclosure in Budapest; or through dramatic reenactment – a cumbersome bird beaten to death on an island off the coast of Newfoundland, a quagga brought to its knees on the African plains.

Some stories are exemplary, propitious, like the American Martha, the last passenger pigeon, whose centenary was marked in 2014 by the Cincinnati Zoo, where the bird died in the same cage used by Incas, a Carolina parakeet. Incas, too, is extinct, but who remembers her?

In the end, all is allegory.

BOOK 1

Columns

Column by column in a cloud of dust
They marched away enduring a belief
Whose logic brought them somewhere else, to grief

W. H. Auden, *The Shield of Achilles*

Sunday, 15 January 2006

OUT THE WINDOW there was nothing that could be called poetry, nothing windswept, billowing, tossing or turning in a streaky sky, nothing other than a taut blue dome and the low drone of air conditioners. In car parks across the city women pulled on soft cotton hats and cowered under brollies. Babies kicked and squalled, itchy with heat rash. Fridges groaned. Water dripped from old rubber seals. Milk soured. Fans turned. The grid strained.

Light, an excess of light, as if there had been some kind of global mistake, a wrongful accounting.

At midday the UV index hovered on perilous, dispensed like a terrible penance. If the man in number 7 could remove the tiled roof of his two-bedroom unit and look up into that vaulted sky, it would not be out of the question for him to spot an evil archangel tumbling through that dreadful gouge and dropping right into the lounge room where Frederick sat, newspaper folded back, pen uncapped, reading the obituary columns.

He picked up the remote and pointed it at the cream cylinder on the wall. Chlorine molecules rose around him, heaven-bent. Unaware of the presence of angels (either avenging or beneficent), he shuffled through the pages. *Ossibus et capiti inhumato.* Fred had returned to Latin around the time of his wife's diagnosis and he still found it a comfort. It had been surprisingly easy to find a tutor with the same passion for a dead language – a call to the university and a consultation with the phone book and he had his man, a retired classics teacher from a private boys' school. They were both Catholic by birth, Frederick lapsed, the professor by nature sceptical, but they had enjoyed their time together, which was largely spent mourning the introduction of Novus Ordo and the abandoning of the Latin Mass.

One Saturday the professor's name appeared in the columns. An aneurysm on the golf course? A stroke in the shower? There were no clues in the columns. If the professor had not been divorced he could have called the man's wife. There were no children either. He believed there was a dog called Minos, but where could you go with that? And what did it matter how you'd died once you were dead?

This was what Frederick Lothian thought on Sunday, 15 January. Or what Frederick thought he thought. What he liked to think he thought.

The phone rang twice and then stopped. *Credo in unum Deum, Patrem omnipotentem factorem caeli et terrae, visibilium omnium et invisibilium.*

Sometime in the 1980s, Martha had dragged him off to pray with a group of Tibetan monks. The similarities between Buddhist and Gregorian chant were astonishing, but when he tried to tell Martha she refused to listen. 'You're ruining it,' she snapped. After Martha's death, he returned briefly to the church and took to hanging around after Mass to discuss his ecumenical epiphany with the parish priest, but the stupid man had glazed over and moved on to a group of parishioners fundraising for a new toilet block at the primary school.

The cistern flushed and filled in the next-door unit. He angled the paper towards the window. Despite the excess of light outside he had no northern aspect to speak of. He blamed his daughter. It was Caroline's fault he was here. He hated the word 'retirement', but not as much as he hated the word 'village', as if ageing made you a peasant or a fool. Herein lives the village idiot. At sixty-nine he was getting on, but did it have to be rammed down his throat? He tried to inhabit only those sections of the complex designed for the more able-bodied citizens of St Sylvan's, but he still managed to run into ancient women on Zimmers and signs reminding him to 'Mind the Step', to go 'This Way for Wheelchair Access' and that way 'For a Courtesy Buggy'. Old age had infiltrated his being, and that had to be the reason his left knee kept giving way and his right eye clouded over in bright light and emitted the odd salty tear, as it was doing right now onto the columns.

He took off his glasses to wipe his eye. Out the window a blurry figure was making its way across the open quadrangle in the direction of the dining room. Was that Tom Chelmsley? Frederick stood up and put on his glasses. What was he doing out there in the heat? Look at the poor old fellow, with his frame and leather braces and his bent old back, hanging on by a thread to his villa. Any minute now Tom would be up for reclassification and bundled out of his two-bedroom semide-tached into a tiny single-brick box with a television, a kettle and a pop-up toaster. Would you look at him? It was a wonder they had ever let Tom buy into the independent area.

Frederick sat down. It was just too painful to watch Tom hobbling on the Zimmer in the fierce heat. Why would you bother going all that way for an indigestible meal? There was no shade out there and the temperature must be well over forty degrees. Fred had been to one or two meals in the dining room and he wouldn't be going again. Tom could have called for a gofer to take him, but that might have given the social workers a leg up when they came to reassess his meds and mobility and tick off boxes and add up the columns and announce that Mr Thomas H. Chelmsley was no longer capable of reaching down to wipe himself or squeeze out his own tea bag, and he and all that was his were to be shrink-wrapped and trolleyed without ado across the green to the supported living units, which were just a hop, step and a jump from the high-care facility, where they were all headed anyway. They might as well have erected the villas over a sawdust pit in the ground, because that was how close death was at St Sylvan's. No archangel beating above you with soft Latin wings, but a dark stinking shithole right beneath your feet.

Fred swept a finger down the narrow columns of type. A name was usually enough to warn you off. You could be pretty sure there were no dead children around named Walter or Enid – or Frederick, for that matter, unless you were French. Frédéric.

It was a name fit for kings and queens when he was born, but now it was more likely to be someone from the television. His name was finished. He could well be the last of the Fredericks – it was hard to imagine celebrities embracing little blond Alfreds or Enochs, although Caroline's best friend had called her first child Camellia and continued the weak theme by calling the second Rose. It was hardly appropriate from the point of view of Australian landscape or character, but then the mother's name was Fleur, so what could you expect? How could a little girl get on in this part of the world when she shared a name with an imported species requiring hand-watering and supplementary feeding?

He heard the metallic *thunk* of an instant gas hot-water system next door. An aged and decrepit body would be stepping across the flat tiled floor into a shower cubicle (no perilously high bathtubs or raised rims to clamber over in this village), gripping the sturdy metal rail on the wall, readying itself for the brisk application of liquid soap to crêpey flesh. Frederick shuddered.

The columns beckoned. The codes were easy once you mastered the iconography. To be avoided at all costs: little pairs of booties, ballet shoes, dummies and motorbikes. Wreaths, logos and Masonic imagery were generally safe – anything that signified late-middle-aged grown-up rule-bound behaviour. His eyes snagged on a line.

Our darling boy, four years old and
lost. Wait for us, sweetheart.
It won't be long. Mummy and
Daddy will be there soon …

Ambushed. There was only one notice for four-year-old 'Thompson, David Michael'. The boy would have died late in the week, on Wednesday or perhaps Thursday. Not Friday, though – today was Saturday and that would be far too soon to come up for air. This would be the first notice, from his mother and father. 'Soon' was a disturbing choice of word. Surely they weren't planning on dying too? And why those three dots at the end of the sentence? What did they mean? Why would you use them in the columns? They should be banned.

Few books had made it out of the boxes stacked around the house, but he had managed to shelve the foreign-language dictionaries and the odd grammar reference. All was not lost. It was a Greek word, of course: ἔλλειψις, *élleipsis*, meaning 'omission' or 'falling short': 'An ellipsis could indicate an unfinished thought … or at the beginning of a sentence, a trailing off into silence … which could also be indicated by a long dash known as an em dash – which was known as aposiopesis …'

Known to whom, he'd like to know. He'd never heard of aposiopesis, and he was certain no one he knew had either. Did anyone use these words any more? What was the point of aposiopesis? He wasn't anti-intellectual – just the opposite. He was himself a respected professor of structural engineering (retired). He had studied Latin. He of all people knew that a specialised language was essential in real-world professions such as engineering. The people who designed and built the world had to have a terminology to deal collectively with challenging structural problems. Without specialised languages, buildings and bridges would simply topple over in a breeze. Aircraft would drop out of the sky. The hulls of ships would split open and sink into the depths of the Atlantic Ocean. People would die.

Could a similar defence be mounted in the case of aposiopesis, which (he flipped pages furiously) according to *The Dictionary of Rhetorical Terms* meant 'becoming silent' and indicated 'the inability or unwillingness to continue'?

The example given was equally baffling: 'But I thought he was ...' What kind of an example was that? Here you have some poor fellow lost for words, unable to go on, and the experts turn up and offer him the use of an obscure word of Greek origin composed of five or six syllables. Wasn't that a contradiction? Or was it irony? Could you call it a conundrum? Whatever it was, ellipses ought not to be allowed in the columns. What were David Michael's parents thinking?

He shook out his paper. Tomorrow there would be a flood of notices from family and friends, playmates, distant relatives, the volume receding gradually over the following days, like the water level of the lake at Saint-Clair.

April 1946, almost sixty years ago.

Young people thought sixty years was a long time, but it was nothing, really. It was like the day before the day before yesterday. Virgil would have been sixty-five in June.

Pasquale, il mio amore,
sempre baci, Carlotta.

You had to hand it to the Italians. There was a community of people who were faithful to their roots, marking the death in print of an ancient lost brother in Calabria, or the tenth anniversary of the passing of Nonna in a stony village in

Piedmont. Neither that stupid parish priest nor his very own wife understood the function of the Latin root, its capacity to illuminate from the grave something alive and vital. He was not ashamed of his attraction to the columns, not at all. *It is animal to die. It is reasonable to face death. Everybody dies. My wife has died. My brother Virgil is dead. My mother died. My father, thank god, has died. My son …*

Frederick sought out the bare wall near the kitchen. He had yet to get around to decoration. Breakfast, lunch, a walk on Mondays and a turn on the bicycle followed by an occasional frozen dinner were about all he could manage. Monday was the keystone of his week. Remove it, and the whole structure would collapse. Every Monday, rain, hail or shine, he walked along the river. If anyone asked Fred Lothian what he'd been up to, Fred Lothian would be ready with a breezy, easy answer. 'Oh, I always walk by the river in the mornings.' They would nod encouragingly: 'Good job, Fred. Up early, keeping active, that's the way.' He studied the cream render and the single photograph hanging from the sole hook in his entire villa. He had inherited the hook from the previous owner – no guesses what happened to her. He walked over and stood right in front of the photo of his daughter and imagined the previous owner standing exactly where he was, gazing at a photo of her own children. The estate agent had swept his arm around and muttered vague nothings when asked why the owner was selling, but the manager let the cat out of the bag. 'It was quick,' she said. 'A coronary in sitting dance' (yes, apparently you can sit and dance), 'in the break between "The Russian Jig" and "The Irish Washerwoman".'

It was a formal portrait of his daughter, no different from millions of others all over the world, a successful young woman in her black gown, glossy hair cascading from under her mortarboard, hand clutching a rolled-up degree tied with a red ribbon. He and Martha flew to meet her in Honolulu for the graduation ceremony. It was a last-minute decision and accommodation was so tight they had to stay at a themed hotel that cost him a fortune. 'I never want to see another hula hoop or lei in my life,' Martha declared in the airport departure lounge. At least she had the good grace to wait until they left to complain. Caroline spent the entire time reminding them that the hotel was an insult to the indigenous Hawaiian culture and he ought never to have booked them in there. She was too embarrassed to ask her student friends to meet her at the bar. 'We've just finished a masters in anthropology. I don't think they want a cocktail in half a coconut served by a barefoot native.' It was tacky, she was right, but did she have to make such a fuss? He told her she could go to the backpackers' hostel if she liked. That shut her up.

He studied the photograph. There was no denying she looked like her mother, his wife, Martha. As Caroline grew older the likeness had taken root, as if physical proximity drove mother and daughter towards resemblance. Wasn't there a word for that? No doubt another Greek obscurity. Caroline's younger brother had taken after him. 'I've been trumped,' Martha said as the boy grew. Frederick was nothing like his own father, thank god, but looked a lot like his mother – pointy, sallow-skinned. But looks were one thing, temperament another. Caroline and her mother were given to smouldering feuds that lasted for days, if not weeks. Caroline's brother had a furious, spiking temper that passed quickly.

He had had a temper, he used to have a temper. Were given, used to be given, shall have been given, he parsed. He was still troubled by the distinction between the perfect – which he understood now to be the tense employed for complete actions in the past – and the imperfect, which was used for unfinished business.

My wife looks like my daughter.
My daughter's brother used to look like his father.
My wife is dead.

My son …

Caroline flashed him a frozen grin. Another lie. Caroline was still sulking after a blow-up with her mother that started on their first day in Hawaii and lasted all the way through the graduation ceremony to the dinner afterwards. What was it about? What did it matter now?

Frederick sat down at the table and smoothed the newspaper with the palm of his hand. David Michael Thompson was only four. Four-year-olds shouldn't be allowed to die. Where was his mother? How did he die? It was an accident, he was sure of it. If it were cancer the parents would thank the hospital and the wonderful doctor who had been with them all along, and no flowers please, but donations to a charity of your choice. An accident then, a summer accident on a summer's day, on a perfect day for drowning in the backyard pool.

David Michael is in the playroom with Thomas the Tank Engine. His mother has her hands full with the washing machine and a blocked drain. That damn plumber will not return her calls. The phone rings somewhere in the house. David Michael looks around and sees the screen door is ajar. He walks out to the wheelbarrow next to the pool safety gate and begins to climb. His father was out there early in the morning, clearing the filter of leaves, and in his rush to get to work he has left the wheelbarrow against the gate. The boy climbs up into the wheelbarrow. The latch lifts up. The gate swings open. A lizard kicks hopelessly in the deep end. The boy leans right over to touch it and the waters part, then close over, as they did for the Israelites.

Above the town of Saint-Clair there are fierce, grey, billowing clouds. A ten-year-old boy stands on the green field, as stiff as a scarecrow, while his coat whips around his frozen body and his father bears down like a tank.

He had stayed at work to finish a lecture, and when he got home Martha was in the kitchen with Caroline propped up on the bench, licking a cake bowl. Martha was pregnant with Callum and was wearing an enormous knitted sweater and wooden Scholl's. Frederick leant forward and brushed her lips. She tasted of flour and butter and sugar and eggs.

'Oh, Fred, you had a call from your aunt in Scotland. She said she'd call back later tonight when the rates are cheaper. I couldn't understand a word she said.'

'She's my great-aunt, not my aunt. She's my mother's mother's sister. My Granny's sister. My aunt is my father's sister. My aunt has dementia and lives in Lincoln.'

Martha shook her head. It was all too confusing for her.

But why was she calling now? Aunt Marjorie called on his birthday. He dreaded her calls. Her voice was like a big old rusty hook that dragged him back into the tangled tongue of his family, to a time no one in his new life would understand, when there was only one place to live and one way to speak, and the rest of the globe was a story you made up in bed for your little brother.

Marjorie lived in Aberfeldy, Scotland, in a sandstone bungalow with a pea-shingle roof. He went there as a boy, when his gran died. When his gran fell out with Pop, she moved up to live with Marjorie. The day after Gran died, his mother came and took him out of school. They caught the bus and the train all day and night as far as Pitlochry, as far as the train would go, and then they walked the last miles holding hands, with their hats pulled down against the jagging wind. He must have been thirteen or fourteen, because Mam was still alive, holding tight to his cold hand. They sat in Marjorie's house with Gran's coffin in the parlour and the fire in the flue heating up the dung they still used to render the inside of chimneys. It was thick and snug and he cried for his gran, even though he was a big boy and she had left him all alone in Lincoln.

He went up to Aberfeldy once more, as a grown man, to tell Marjorie he was getting married and moving to Australia. He went to say goodbye. Back then, goodbye carried more than a chance of for ever. For Aunt Marjorie, it was another word for death. Old people stayed behind with their coupons and their mean coal fires, while the Fredericks of the world took off to the Americas and the Antipodes. Families did not travel back to the other side on summer breaks, or telephone every other day – not unless they were as rich as kings.

'They were my happiest years,' Marjorie told Freddy that last time he saw her, 'those years with your gran. We were like girls again, laughing and knitting.' He sat with Marjorie and held his chipped Willow-pattern teacup. On a shelf there was a row of old books his gran bought in the second-hand shops on the high street.

'She bought them for you, Freddy,' said Marjorie. 'She just never got round to boxing them up and putting them in the post.'

Later, Marjorie sent him the leather-bound copies of Robert Louis Stevenson and Lewis Carroll. They were somewhere in the unit, their front pages marked with Gran's distinctive hand.

Fred wrote to Marjorie twice a year, around his mother's birthday and at Christmas, and always enclosed two twenty-pound notes. She never thanked him for the money, and he never mentioned it. They both knew it was nowhere near enough to make up for what he had taken away. Between birthdays, Christmas and the odd sleepless night, he managed not to think about Great-Aunt Marjorie, about what it might be like for a very old woman cut off and left behind.

'Did Aunt Marjorie say why she called, Martha? Give Daddy a taste of that, young lady.'

'No,' said Caroline, hugging the bowl to her chest. 'It's mine.'

'Just one lick. Daddy's been at work all day. He's hungry for cake!'

'Carrie, give Dad a little taste. Don't be greedy.'

'No. He eats everything.'

'I do not,' he objected. He glanced at Martha. She raised her eyebrows. Their daughter hated to share anything, but food was the worst.

'I think your aunt might have really lost her wits. She said, "Tell Freddy to wake up the bees." I had to ask her to repeat it three times. Do you have any idea what she means?'

'Caroline, hop down and go wash your face.' He lifted her off the bench and watched her leave the kitchen.

'It means my father is dead.'

'What?'

'Alexander is dead. It's something they used to say in my gran's day, a Lincolnshire thing. When the master or mistress dies you must go straight to the hives and whisper to the bees. You have to whisper that the master is dead.'

Martha was studying his face for signs of emotion. He turned from her and ran a finger around the glass cake bowl. His wife's hand touched the back of his neck.

'Poor darling,' she said gently. 'What a terrible shock.'

In truth, Frederick felt the most extraordinary sense of release, like a gull cut free from a fishing line. On the phone, he let Aunty talk and talk, until his ear softened to her voice. 'It was a stroke in the end, Freddy.' So many afflictions beset Alexander it didn't seem to matter how he died, just that he was dead. Martha listened from the couch with her legs tucked under her, madly knitting a jacket for the new baby. Her fingers went to and fro, as if she were conducting a tiny orchestra. Each time she tugged at the fine white wool, the ball jumped off the ground. 'Thank you, Aunty,' he said. 'I'll make all the arrangements.' He was crisp and distant, but his father was dead and he had to shepherd his elation carefully. Yet Aunt Marjorie hated his father too: 'The way he stopped your gran coming down when Virgil died. That was a terrible sin, I tell you.'

When Aunt Marjorie died he arranged for that as well. She

14

left her little cottage to Caroline and Callum. It was worth very little, but it was finally sold and he put the money aside. 'They might want to study overseas,' he said to Martha, 'in America or England, or even Europe. You never know, do you?'

Caroline had spent all her portion on study in Hawaii, but the other half of the money was still somewhere in a bank, rolling over slowly, like a fixed wheel about water.

A sudden screeching made Fred start. His hand slapped the side of his cup, sending it crashing onto the tiled floor. He grabbed a grubby little cushion for his weak knee and sank down into it, as if he were on a wooden pew at church. Damn those birds next door, pretending to be happy in a cage. He was crying now. Crying like a child, crying because he had loved Martha and Martha was dead, and he had broken Martha's cup.

When they were young his children would come home from the supermarket clutching brand-new toys. They would have stamped and whined until Martha gave in at the checkout, mortified by their bad behaviour. Martha was weak that way. Of course, the toys broke as soon as they were unwrapped, or were abandoned under a bush in the front garden just in time for the next trip to the supermarket. Mass-produced rubbish, all of it – a white furry rabbit, a pink furry monkey, some small bug-eyed doll trapped in a plastic bubble. He bought Danish wooden blocks for his son and, later, army-green sturdy Meccano. He had tried so hard to guide his children towards quality wooden toys and insisted that Martha resist their tears, but did she listen? Of course not. He found a craftsman in a catalogue and ordered pieces of doll's furniture for Caroline. The tiny teak wardrobe and chests of drawers arrived in small pine boxes, nestled in straw like bird's eggs. Martha promptly declared the furniture far too good for a little girl to play with and, despite howls of protest from Caroline, boxed them up in a cupboard for when she was older. So what did they end up playing with? The same rubbish as all the other children.

But it was not their tears that had enraged him; he could see that now. It was the private conviction that the whole situation was of his own doing: he ought to have put his foot down.

He craned his neck under the table, looking for pieces. The handle of the cup was stuck right beneath the couch. He would need the broom. People will attach themselves to the most arbitrary of things. He knew that now. Attachment was not a logical business. He was going to have to speak to management about that woman next door and her birds – everyone knew pets weren't permitted. When she waved and smiled at him from across the low hedge that separated their units he was careful to nod, drop his head and head straight indoors. She was just like her awful birds: pretending to be happy in a cage. He cursed as he poked about in the gap beneath the couch and the wall. It was one of Martha's blue-and-white Norwegian oddments. Lotte, the design was called; it had always been Caroline's favourite. He gave her that cup to use the last time she came to stay. She had asked if she could take it with her, but he couldn't have that. 'I like to keep your mother's things together,' he said. If he gave in, bit by bit, there would be nothing left in the end. And now it was broken. After months alone in the house, looking through boxes, turning things over, trying to reach Martha through Martha's things, he knew everything he could know about what was left of Martha. The Lotte set was missing three dinner plates, two side plates and now one cup. If he had known that before, he could have helped her complete the set. Martha always had trouble finishing things. Her energy would dissipate, her focus would wobble and he would have to corral her into action again. Just one more term. Just one more round of chemotherapy.

There it was. He retrieved the handle and clambered up from the floor. His knee throbbed. The cup would go straight out into the large green wheelie bin – the pick-up was in the morning. But how many times had he almost let go of some scrap of Martha's, only to hesitate at the final hour? He had packed up the family home and moved without throwing out a single piece of Martha. Her clothes had to go, of course, along with her shoes and her handbags and all those empty perfume bottles she kept among her bras and pants. There had been no point discussing any of this with Caroline because she would have spent weeks folding and sorting and weeping and wailing and then she would have wanted to take it all home with her and soon she would have started to wear the clothes his wife had once worn. Imagine, dinner at their favourite Japanese restaurant with his daughter in Martha's cardigan, reaching into Martha's leather bag for Martha's lipstick. Unbearable.

He shepherded the broken cup into a large manila envelope and put it on the table. It sat there, bulky and enigmatic.

Fragments of Martha Lothian's Lotte cup, broken by Frederick Lothian, her loving husband, on Sunday 15 January ...

Gone but never forgotten.

Frederick Lothian, you are a liar and a coward. He stood to stretch his throbbing knee. A handful of black and yellow birds were squabbling over a red flower in the ground cover. Wasn't it too hot for birds? And weren't those little bushes supposed to blossom in spring? It was Martha who had learnt the names and habits of plants and animals when they came to Australia. Then, as now, he really had no idea what was going on out there.

'What a wonderful back garden,' visitors said when they saw Martha's show of banksias and grevilleas.

'She's nature, I'm culture,' he liked to quip, until one day Martha asked him not to.

'You have no idea what you're saying, Fred, and until you do I'd like you to stop.'

Sometimes his wife was a mystery to him.

It looked like old Tom had changed his mind about lunch.

Clever man. He was making his way back towards the safety of his villa. Now, where was Martha's sewing basket? It made a perfect footrest for his knee. There it was. Who else but Martha's mother would think this a suitable Christmas present for a daughter in Australia? Apparently English wicker never made it to the Great South Land. When Martha opened the box she sighed that special sigh she reserved for her mother and declared it horrible.

'Of course it's horrible,' he admitted, 'but any minute you'll be ringing Miriam in Hoboken and telling her how much you adore it. "It's *exactly* what I wanted, Mother," you'll say. "How *did* you know?"'

Until he was married he had no idea that women were such terrific liars. It didn't matter where you were – at the shops, at school drop-out, on the phone. 'How are you? Oh, so much better! You loved it? Me too! Did it fit? Perfectly!' Sometimes he would go with Martha to pick up the kids from a friend's place and have to listen to his wife gush over some ghastly addition to the home they were visiting. Family rooms were all the go at the time, and nasty pine spa baths and English cottage gardens spread out beneath a contradictory tropical spray of plumbago, monstera and banana palm.

'How can you say those things?' he would say in the car on the way home. 'How can you look straight in their faces and lie like that?'

Martha shook her head dismissively. 'They're good people, Fred. Their children are our children's friends. What would you like me to do? Tell them they have no taste? That they ought to be planting natives? Employing an architect? "Oh, by the way, Fred's best friend Ralph Orr is a famous architect! Would you like his number? He's a modernist. I'm sure you two would hit it off!"'

'But how will people know if there's anything better out there if you keep pretending you like everything, Martha? Even

that appalling vinyl bar with the gold buttons – and not just like, but adore.'

'Poor Fred,' crowed Martha. 'Do you think it's our job to impose your ideas on them? To ruin their pleasure in their own home? Well, guess what? There are more important things in life than our educated opinions and your careful attention to style.'

Oh, Martha, how right you were.

Fred stood at the window and tried to move his knee. *Would you look at that?* Tom had turned around again and was shuffling back up the path towards the recreation centre. His spine was like a Maillart bridge: one long arch supported at the ends by a metal walking frame.

Should he call someone? He'd give it a few minutes – Tom was such an independent fellow, he wouldn't like the fuss. Fred flipped open Martha's basket and took out the dark-red cable-knit jumper, then settled his bad leg on the closed lid. The instructions had given her hell, but then his wife wasn't much of a pattern reader. Unlike him, Martha liked to make things up as she went along, which might work wonders with the parents of your children's friends, or a stir-fry, but it was really not the go when it came to knitwear. Every so often he took this unfinished jumper out of the basket. The plump yellow number 12s were paused mid-stitch, needles crossed – abandoned *in medias res*. He tugged fitfully at a single loose thread of chunky red wool protruding through the side of the wicker basket. It was the colour of persimmons. On and on went the thread, as if she had laid it there for him, like Ariadne for Theseus.

Though they'd only had five hours in Tokyo on the stop-over, he'd managed to get Martha and the children through Immigration and put them on the Keisei Line to the Naritasan Temple. Once they were off the train they thrust their frozen hands into their down jackets and walked quickly under the archway and up the stairs to the red pagoda. The black branches of the persimmon trees formed spidery lines against the white snow, like ink on paper. The red fruit glowed against the black and white, like a hand-tinted photograph.

When he met Martha he knew nothing of families, and very little of love. A family was something to fear, like a long, dark tunnel cutting through a mountain. Who knew if you would come out the other side alive?

The children ate udon noodles from steaming lacquer bowls in a tearoom near the station, smiling happily and nodding at the woman behind the counter, before returning to the terminal for the long flight to New York. Red-cheeked, wide-eyed, their souls as quiet and steady as stars at night.

Here dwells the monster, hid from human view
Not to be found, but by the faithful clew.

The monster could still paint a pretty picture. He struggled out of the chair and pushed the jumper back in the basket. What was Tom doing now? He had got himself off the concrete path and was in among the ground cover. A telephone call would bring attention to Tom's frailty, and might trigger a review and forced removal – and that would be the end of his neighbour Tom Chelmsley, who was as close a friend as his current life permitted – not that he had actually sat down and talked at length to Tom, just a friendly wave here and there and the odd hello when Tom was reversing his Morris Minor out of the garage, but all in good time. The main thing was, they were there for each other. Martha never appreciated the subtle ways men communicated. She complained that it was she who had to make all the phone calls, she who'd had to write all the letters and send the Christmas cards to keep in touch, she who had to schedule the dinner parties. When Ralph's eldest girl took off to Sydney with that boy, Martha hounded him.

'But Martha, Ralph and I don't need to call each other,' he told her. Ralph was his best friend. They were all best friends. They saw Ralph and Veronica and the kids most weekends. His friend didn't need any more pressure now, not with Katie taking off like that.

'But he's in a terrible way, Fred. Veronica says he won't speak to anyone, just sits in his office chain-smoking and drinking whisky. At least call him.'

'Ralph will contact me when he's ready,' said Fred stiffly. He would not be told when and how to talk to anyone. 'I think I know my own friend, Martha. Men don't like people prying into their private lives, trust me.'

Slowly and deliberately, he twisted the red wool around his index and middle fingers. Tom would be embarrassed if he called for a gofer. And knowing what he did about the woman next door – knowing what he did about women – his neighbour had no doubt stuck her nose in right where it didn't belong and already called management. He was doing everything he could for his elderly neighbour. He watched for Tom's kitchen light to go on at sunset. He listened for the television to go off at night and the radio to start in the morning. He wouldn't want Tom to be lying alone on the floor with a broken hip, unable to reach the emergency buzzer on the wall in the lounge room. Apparently Tom refused to wear one of those necklaces the social workers pushed at you when you moved in. 'No, thank you,' Fred had said to the woman when she suggested it to him, 'I'm not quite at that stage yet.' But he had read the brochure on fall prevention they had left in his villa, in case he needed to have a word with Tom, and then he disposed of both it and the laminated sign on the back wall of his bathroom. He was young, relatively speaking, and Tom was tough as an old boot. He and Tom would be fine.

A light tremor passed over him, like a minor quake. He had turned down the phone, but he could feel its vibration across the wooden table. He examined his fingers. If he left this wool for long enough they would turn blue or black, or whatever colour the body went when the vessels were starved of blood. His fingers would putrefy and drop away and he would be like one of those Roman statues: bloodless, stripped of colour, without fingers, arms or head.

The wool came from down south, from one of those hippie shops that sold hand-knitted beanies and dreamcatchers. It was just the two of them in the car. Caroline had just moved in with Julian, and Callum was staying with his best friend, Aaron Bessell. He and Martha drove down in the new red Peugeot 405, Car of the Year. Miriam left Martha a tidy sum when she died, unlike his own father, who left him nothing but debt and a council flat full of rubbish. Callum had inherited Fred's old Saab. The boy had pestered him ever since he got his licence. He had worn Fred down with his wanting, and in the end he gave it to Callum because it made sense. It was the logical thing to do. It was exactly the kind of car a young man study-ing architecture would want – old-school European design with cracked cherry-red leather seats and engineered for safety, because it was Swedish, and everything they made in Sweden was safe, and he would have got nothing on a trade-in, nothing. Nothing.

His fingers were blue. The wool was red.

It was clear now that that was when Martha began to change. She was always picking up hobbies and causes, but when they got back from that trip she began to act out of character. It was her mother's money, he was sure of it now. First she hired a cleaner – not that they couldn't afford one before, but she had always refused on principle. 'Now I have my own money,' she said firmly, 'that makes all the difference.' At the time it seemed like a reasonable thing to say, but in hindsight he ought to have rebuked her. 'But it's always been our money, darling. Yours as much as mine. We're a team.'

Then Martha went to Melbourne on her own. She had never done that before. She said she wanted to stroll down Brunswick Street and sleep in a bed all by herself. She wanted to think. She came back from Melbourne and announced she was enrolling in a degree in child psychology. Callum was hor-rified. He had only just started the second year of his course and was appalled at the idea of running into his own mother on campus – it was bad enough having a father at the university. 'If you talk to me, I'll kill you,' he said to her.

'A delicate imbalance of power.' That was how the new Martha described their marriage. They were at Ralph and Veronica's when she said it, and if he remembered correctly it was the same night they met Paul Mondale.

With the children almost grown, and with Katie long gone, dinners were few and far between.

Everything was different by then.

'So, Paul,' asked Martha, always prying into other people's business, 'what's a clever young architect from Melbourne doing working with an old codger like Ralph?'

'It's a great project and our company's glad to be on board,' said Paul. 'Ralph Orr has a terrific reputation in urban renewal.'

Martha filled her glass. 'Do you have a family, Paul? Or are you having too much fun being single?'

Fred gritted his teeth. Martha loved to flirt with younger men. It was humiliating for her. And she was drinking more than usual since her trip to Melbourne.

'No family yet, Martha. I've been with my partner for nearly eight years, though. We met in the US when I was doing postgrad studies.'

'Would you like to have children?'

'You don't have to answer that, Paul,' said Fred. 'My wife is always sticking her nose into other people's business.' Besides, he didn't want to mention children. Since Katie died they rarely talked about their children, their achievements, their plans, the lives they had ahead of them.

Martha glared at him. 'My husband has a horror of the personal. Fred rarely starts a conversation. He prefers to communicate telepathically. Apparently it's all the go among blokes of his generation.'

Paul snorted. Yet another man who found Martha amusing. 'I'd love to have ten children,' he said, 'but I'm gay, so I'm not sure how Corey and I are going to manage that. Hopefully we'll find a way. We're thinking of adoption. And what about you, Martha? How many years have you and Fred been married? Did you meet in the States?'

Ralph stood up and gestured towards him, and then clomped down the stairs. Fred followed dutifully. Ralph was wearing those ugly stacked-up R. M. Williams riding boots. 'The footwear of the squattocracy,' Martha called them. Ralph had a thing about being short, although he'd never admit it.

'Well, there you go,' Ralph said as he flicked on the light to the cellar. 'What do you know? He's gay. I've worked with Paul on two projects here and in Melbourne and I had no idea.'

'Architecture's full of gay men, Ralph – not like engineering.'

Take that, Ralph.

The table was vibrating again. Fred waited until it stopped, and then, against his better judgment, turned up the volume. He picked at his nail. Reluctantly, he began to count backwards. The boy was in the second year of his course, so it must have been 1992. He gave a paper at a conference in San Francisco at the end of the 80s. Was it 1989 or 1990? He'd ducked out of a tedious session to buy the weekend papers, then took a coffee up to his hotel room and read the obituaries. Columns and columns of young men were dead, stacked up like tombs. Directors, writers, actors, artists, dancers. He walked up and down the steep streets. He picked up the small magazines on the benches of coffee shops. He read the posters pasted to street poles. He changed his flight and went home early.

In San Francisco he had witnessed something terrible, some-thing everyone should know about, but when he came back to the vacant suburban streets and footpaths of his middle-class Australia and to his carpeted office next door to the Chancel-lery, Frederick forgot what he had learnt. Then a member of his own department lost his son – Professor Lawrence Hardi-gan, from Electrical. Was there an edge of shame in the hushed voices in the photocopy room? 'He was an only child too – imagine losing your only child.' Lawrence and his wife went into early retirement down south somewhere. Why hadn't he contacted Lawrence? Why hadn't he reached out to him? He had no answer.

Paul died a few years later, around 1995. Fred came home from work and found Martha crying, which was nothing unusual. She looked up through her tears. 'Paul's dead. We knew he was HIV-positive, but we didn't even know he was sick. No one told us. Poor Corey.' Who was 'we', Fred wondered briefly. Martha had stayed with Paul and Corey on her trips to Melbourne, but she hadn't been to Melbourne in years.

After the phone call she stopped travelling. She stopped studying. She stopped talking. Everything ended with the phone call.

'Why the pretence?' snapped Ralph that night in the cellar. 'Why did Paul have to pretend?' Ralph shook his head and pulled out two dusty reds from the rack.

When they got back to the table, Martha, Paul and Veronica were head to head.

'Here's Batman and Robin!' said Paul. 'Martha was just telling me about Harry Harlow – the guy who did that monkey experiment?'

'Paul's mother is a psychiatrist in Melbourne,' said Veronica. 'She specialises in the male menopause. You should have told me that, Ralph – we could have got you in.'

Martha laughed. It wasn't like Veronica to make jokes about Ralph.

'I don't think Paul had ever told me about his mother's work,' said Ralph. 'Paul hasn't shared much at all about his personal life.'

Paul studied Ralph's face. 'Oh, god, you're not going to tell me you didn't know I was gay?' He laughed. Veronica and Martha joined in. 'Did you want me to wear an armband with a pink triangle?'

'Now hang on there,' protested Ralph.

'You met Corey at my house, Ralph. He was that good-looking man cooking dinner in our kitchen, the one who kept putting his arm around me?'

'When you said he was your partner, I presumed you meant in business,' sniffled Ralph.

Martha snorted. 'Oh, come on, Ralph, I had no idea you were such a fuddy-duddy.' She looked at her husband and shook her head. 'What a pair.'

Paul turned towards Fred. 'You and Martha must have the most amazing conversations, Fred – telepathically, I mean! Your interests are so different. Engineering and child psychology.'

'Pardon?' said Frederick. He was not listening. It had just dawned on him that his oldest friend, Ralph, was more than a bit like his dead father.

That's when Martha said it. 'Actually, Paul, I like to think of our marriage as a delicate imbalance of power.'

When Martha made some kind of joke, even at his expense, Fred had to make sure he laughed louder than Ralph, which was not always easy because his friend had dedicated himself to appearing more hearty and masculine than any other man at his table. But this time Ralph was silent. He was staring at Martha. Fred looked at his wife. She was looking at Ralph. Her face was flushed. Martha had drunk too much, he decided. It was time to go home.

Fred squeezed his fingers. He could have taken a blowtorch to them, or a hammer and a nail, and he would have felt nothing. The last time he saw Ralph was at Martha's funeral. His former best friend had come in with his pot belly hanging over his tight jeans, a new wife on one arm and a black ribbon on the other, as if there were no such thing as personal history. Frederick had wanted to hit him in the face – he might have killed him if not for his own daughter, if not for Ralph's girls, if this weren't the funeral of his wife.

He held the wool up to his nose. Lanolin? He foraged in the basket and pulled out one of Veronica's clumsy linocut cards. 'Merry Christmas 1983 with love from Ralph, Veronica, Katie, Lucinda and Lauren. *Banksia articulata*, with apologies to Margaret Preston.' Those were the years when Veronica was always in a frenzy of craft and children. She moved quickly through the dominant crafts of the day: weaving, raku pottery, Japanese calligraphy. Before dinner (cannelloni, paprika chicken, steak Diane and, later, spinach pie and chickpea burgers) she would have to clear the vast rough-cut jarrah dining table of wax and paper, copper stencil sets and batik inks.

Frederick caught the tail of the wool and began to wind it back onto the old card.

Veronica called from South Africa when Martha died. She just couldn't get back for the funeral … it was all happening so quickly … it was impossible to get a flight …

While he listened to her sobbing into the phone, Fred became more and more enraged. It was his wife who was dead, the mother of his children, not hers. Veronica had abandoned Martha when she was sick, and after all the support Martha had given her with Katie. Then Veronica began to harp on about how the important community art project in the township was finally starting to gel, how he had no idea of the number of children without any parents, and the statistics on HIV infection were just staggering, and the inability of the World Health Organization to get these American companies to reduce the cost of the antiviral drugs so that at least the pregnant women could give birth without –

'Please, Veronica,' he interrupted. That day on the phone he had no room for tragedy on a grand and anonymous scale.

When it came to grief, Ralph's ex-wife was no different from other people. Martha would have understood perfectly: far less complicated for Veronica to throw herself into helping victims in a faraway tragedy than to come home and face your own damage.

Frederick tied off the tail of the wool. He and his generation had thought they were a different species from their own parents.

They thought their parents would die out and take their petty misery and prejudice with them, and be replaced by a brand-new generation who were free of their blinkers and their leather straps, who would never stand in the way of their girls and boys. They would not damage their children as they had been damaged. Their children would not be expected to make up for their parents' lost opportunities.

He tossed the card in the wicker basket. When it came to grief, everyone had to find their own form, everyone had their own limits – everyone except Ralph Orr. Ralph knew about form, all right. Form always was Ralph's thing. Everything was aesthetics to Ralph – the view out the window, the photo on the wall, the worn-out body of his poor wife Veronica. Ralph knew nothing of limits, of boundaries, with his big new house, his smooth young wife, his ridiculous baby (at his age) and his three lovely daughters – two, two lovely daughters.

Frederick opened the kitchen bin with his toe and paused. He just couldn't do it. The wool and the card went back in the basket. I've made a start, he told himself, and it was never easy to throw things away. He picked up the jumper. The knitting hovered midway between the wicker basket and the rubbish bin. Frederick turned towards the window. Tom was standing on the edge of the path, teetering like a man on a wire, his frame nowhere in sight, then pitched straight forward and cracked his forehead on the concrete. 'Oh, god,' Fred heard himself say. Tom lay perfectly still, face down, like a fallen icon. 'Get up,' Fred whispered. But nothing moved, no bird, no cloud, not a pale finger or a twitching toe. Fred stepped back from the glass. His hand shook as he dialled.

'It's about Tom,' he said faintly into the phone. 'Tom Chelmsley has fallen over.'

'Where?' shouted the woman in the office, assuming he was deaf. 'Exactly where is Tom now?'

'There,' said Frederick faintly, pointing out the window. 'There's Tom.'

He watched as the doors of the administration building opened on the far side of the quadrangle and two figures walked briskly across the lawn. The taller woman knelt down and pressed her finger against Tom's neck, while the other spoke into a mobile phone. A single white square moved fitfully across the green turf. Tom's hanky? At the end of the path, some way from Tom, was the upturned Zimmer frame. It lay on its side, all akimbo. There was no doctor in the village on a Sunday, so they would have called the hospital.

Soon an ambulance would drive in through the open gates, mount the low verge and cross the green. Fred looked up at the clock on the wall. Had anyone else seen Tom fall? Who else was sitting inside their villa, waiting to test the gap between call and response, waiting to see how they might fare if they happened to topple to the ground like a broken pillar?

Up in the dining room, Tom's dining chair would be empty. His cream of chicken soup would be forming a thick skin. Someone at his table would suggest giving Tom a call – just in case, the unspoken on all their lips. No one in the village was late if they could help it.

In the distance a siren wailed. That was the least they could do for old Tom – put on the siren. He had heard of dying men and women loaded quickly into ambulances in the dead of night without even the flashing of a blue light. But then that was how it was when you were old: the whole drama of accidents and emergencies was abandoned for ever, and in its place a familiar script with a mute ending.

An ambulance taxied silently across the open quad, all signs of urgency expunged. The salesman for his unit had made a feature of the open design. 'Every corner of the village is accessible by vehicle,' he announced. At the time Fred had been

unsure of the beneficiaries. Movers? A tree-lopping service? It was all clear now.

The ambulance officers were placing some kind of white padding on the side of Tom's head. Was he bleeding? Was Tom already dead? All around Fred were chairs, but not one was suitable for the kind of sitting he needed to do. The long arms of the Papa Bear Chair reached out to embrace him, but he recoiled. A terrible thing had happened to Hans Wegner's chair. The teal wool had split in deep gashes, and chunks of dense, grey horsehair were bubbling out like brains. A single upholstery button hung by a thread, like an eyeball wrenched from its socket.

Frederick caught a glimpse of chrome under a pile of debris. He pushed aside a heap of crumpled shirts and dusty issues of the *Journal of Civil Engineering* and tugged at the metal arms. The chair was wedged between two white plastic Kartell modular bookcases (one cracked in three places by the idiot movers, the other chipped at the top).

He managed to free the chair, then found a damp tea towel in the kitchen and got down on his good knee to wipe the tubular steel, and set about dusting off the thick rectangular straps of brown leather. You would recognise the silhouette of Marcel Breuer's revolutionary B3 anywhere – the chair was a modern classic, there was no doubt about that, but the leather was crying out for wax.

Would you look at that frame? Martha bought the chair for him at an auction at Sotheby's in 1976, when she took Caroline and the baby home to meet her ancient grandmother in Hoboken. She had chosen this chair because she knew what it meant. This chair represented modernity and resilience. This chair had sat in his study for nearly thirty years, testimony to the distance that he, Frederick Lothian, had put between himself and the stupefied leather armchairs of his father's generation, all pocked and studded and stuffed and weighed down by dark Victorian forces, stinking of cigar smoke and whisky drunk out of cut-crystal tumblers. Martha had bought the chair because she understood its historical context. 'Without historical context,' he always told his wife and children and anyone else who would listen, 'there are only commodities.'

He pulled the chair towards the window to get a better view. There was rust on one leg – he would have to get that looked at by a professional. It was good to see the B3 again, but it troubled him. When Martha began her degree in psychology she started to criticise him for what she called his truisms. 'You and your truisms,' she scoffed. '"Without historical context there are only commodities." Exactly who do you think you are, Fred? Karl Marx? Max Weber? And what would you know about historical context?'

'No comment,' replied Fred.

Like many educated people, Frederick had his opinions, most of which were set in concrete so as to render them more akin to truths, but in reality politics and modern history were

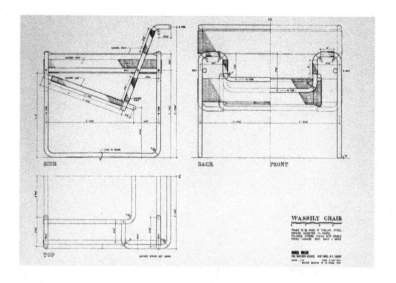

his weak points – along with poetry. Where poetry and politics were concerned he feared a lack of foundation, which left
him vulnerable to challenge. Deep down he knew that opinion
– like concrete – was most resilient when well founded and
reinforced.

When she was little, Caroline was always begging him to
read her poems. 'Show your mother,' he muttered, keeping
his head bent towards a stack of assignments, 'I have to get
this marking done.' What was he supposed to do? Pretend that
a whole series of sentences ending in question marks meant
something to him?

> Who am I?
> Where am I?
> What am I?
> Do I mean?
> Do I?

He took a step back to study the chair. Such simplicity. In contrast, could there be anything in the world as complicated and useless as poetry? What function did it serve? What did it do? A chair meant what it was – or was what it meant. It was indisputably, irrevocably here. It was not pretending to be something it was not, which seemed to be the whole point of poetry. Here, in the most unlikely of contexts, in number 7, St Sylvan's Estate, was an original Marcel Breuer masterpiece, the first chair made of tubular bent steel. This very chair had formed the basis of his famous first-year lectures for the introductory course 'Shock and Stress in the Twentieth Century: An Engineer's Perspective'.

'Good afternoon, ladies and gentlemen, and welcome to the first in a series of lectures that introduces you to engineering concepts through the examination of ordinary objects.' He pushed the round black button of the slide carousel. 'Before you is a chair, but it is no ordinary chair. The Wassily Chair, or B3, is an example of what we engineers call the minimax solution: the minimum use of material for maximum outcome. Nature abounds in examples: the head of the femur (*push*), seeds (*push*), kites (*push*), dinghies (*push*) and tents (*push*). Only with the invention of continuous steel extrusion was such a chair possible.'

The last picture was taken camping at Walpole. Callum was standing to attention in front of the tent, wearing a silly hat on his head and holding a tennis racquet. The brim of the hat cast a long shadow over his face, but Frederick liked to imagine his son was smiling.

Driving to and from camping trips, Frederick always tried to keep the children engaged. 'Did you know that the invention of the highway and the car changed the design of bridges for ever, Callum? There was no need for a span to support the weight of a train, so the bridges could be lighter, and dispense with heavy iron and steel and instead use ... guess what? Reinforced concrete, of course, which is able to deal with both compression and tension. Are you listening, Caroline? Caroline?'

Fred turned the chair upside down. The chair was genuine, he was sure of that, but this latest fashion for cheap reproductions of mid-century classics had unsettled him. He had been shocked to see copies of his pieces advertised in home-decorating magazines. You couldn't tell from far away what they really were, but up close there was no mistaking the original. Just to be sure, he ran his finger over the faded label: 'Thonet Möbel'.

One Saturday morning he brought the children up into the study. Katie was there too – Ralph and Veronica's eldest girl must have been babysitting and stayed the night. Callum was wearing his hockey gear, ready for the game, and Caroline was still in her pyjamas, as usual.

He checked the stairs to make sure his wife was out of earshot. 'You're not lecturing them again, are you, Fred?' Martha yelled up the stairwell. 'I need them in the kitchen to wipe up the breakfast things.' He closed the study door and took up position behind his desk, then decided to stand so he could bring the focus back to the chair.

'So what we have here is the Wassily Chair, B3, designed by Marcel Breuer in 1925, just seven years after the end of the First World War, eleven years before I was born.'

'That makes you a hundred and ten, right, Dad?' said Callum.

'Is that where Pop lost his arm, World War I?'

'That's right, Caroline. In the trenches.' Caroline had always been more interested than Callum in family history.

'How did Pop get dressed with only one arm, Dad?'

'I'm not sure, Callum.'

'Where did his arm go? Did the Germans get it?'

'I don't know, Callum.'

'Imagine if one of the Germans lost his arm, and this other arm comes flying through the air and lands in his lap. Or he catches it and takes it home. Can they stitch an arm back on, Dad? They can, can't they?'

'Shut up, Callum,' said Caroline. 'You're being stupid.'

'That's enough, both of you,' Fred snapped.

Fred was occupied with the problem of how best to convey to the children the moment when something altogether different and unexpected appears. 'Right, I want you all to imagine an infant growing into a toddler. The baby has been unable to express himself, until one miraculous day he discovers he can talk. Can you imagine that day? You don't have to put your hand up, Caroline, we're not in school. What is it?'

'Dad, what's this got to do with Pop's lost arm?'

'What if it's a girl?' asked Katie.

'Thank you, Katie. And I'm not talking about Pop's lost

arm now, Caroline, I'm talking about the exact moment when a child first learns to talk. I'm talking about this chair, and I'm asking you to liken the design of this chair to the moment when a toddler learns to talk. Is that clear?'

'Are you talking about the entire finished chair, Dad? Because if you are and if you're comparing a whole chair to a baby who can't talk and you're saying that all of a sudden the baby just starts saying whole words and sentences, then that doesn't make sense.'

'What do you mean, Caroline?' He preferred not to stop in the middle of an analogy that was already strained. Analogies were another of his weaknesses. Years of lecturing had taught him that if you stray too far from the object you might lose sight of it completely.

'What I mean is that this B3 is a whole chair, but babies learn to talk in bits and pieces. I can remember when Katie's little sister was starting to talk and mostly she grunted out garbled stuff. Mum said that's how she learns to talk and it takes a long time. Do you remember that, Katie?'

'So what?' said the boy.

'That's enough,' Frederick said, glaring at Callum but really aiming for his daughter. 'It's just an analogy, Caroline, or a metaphor, which is a word that as a budding young poet you might like to investigate. Look it up when I finish.' He nodded towards the two volumes of the *Shorter Oxford English Dictionary* sitting on his shelf, wishing he could reach for them himself.

'We did that at school, Mr Lothian. A metaphor is like a simile but without the "like".'

'Thank you, Katie, and I've told you, you can call me Fred. This is the 1980s. Adults are not ogres. Now, have a look. Come closer. Can you see that this chair is inspired by a bicycle? This was the very first chair to be made of tubular bent steel, which is remarkably strong and can also absorb shock. What have you got on your hands, Callum? Is that chocolate? Don't touch the leather – go and wash in the bathroom. This is the era of the invention of flight and skyscrapers, and the discovery of new materials like steel and ferroconcrete, all of which bend and flex and absorb stress – what is it now, Callum? I told you to go and clean your hands.'

'Dad, what's stress?'

'Stress is an expression of force, either internal or external. Now go and wash those hands.'

'Mum says that Dad makes her stressed,' said Katie.

'And Dad, maybe a new language would be better?'

'Better than what, Caroline?' Was there no end to the interruptions?

'Better than your anal-logic.'

'*Analogy*, the word is *analogy*.'

'It's like the maker of the chair – and Dad, I'm pretty sure you were just making a simile, not an analogy or a metaphor, about the design and the ways babies talk?'

'Please get to the point.'

'What's his name? The maker?'

'The designer's name was Marcel Breuer.'

'It's like Moselle Brower had to use all the things around him to make something different. He could already speak because he wasn't a baby, so he didn't have to make up actual words like "metal" or "leather" because they were already out there in bikes and planes and skyscrapers, but he had to look around and find all the words and bring them all together to make a new sentence that had never been put together that way, but which made sense.'

Caroline was thinking very deeply, and it annoyed the hell out of Frederick. Katie was looking at Caroline as if she were onto something when Callum came tearing through the door, his arms flailing.

'Yeehaa! Go get 'em, cowboy!'

'Callum! Stop it! That's a good analogy, Caroline, or simile.

Whatever it is, this chair is like a succinct sentence made of bits of other words. Excellent. Now, how about you get out of your pyjamas and do some homework? Katie might give you some help with it before we take her home. I hear from your father that you're a whiz at maths, Katie. As for you, Callum Lothian, you have the attention span of a flea.'

The nickel-chrome plating was cold to the touch. He knew now that he ought to have let the children sit in the chair. But it was too late. It was too late for everything. How old would Katie be now? Katie was about three years older than Caroline. Caroline was thirty-seven now, which would make Katie forty. It was just over twenty years ago. He ought to know the year. Martha would have known the year, and the month, and the day. She would have known the hour. How is it that we live these lives of such intense detail, where moment to moment we have people we love all around us, and we have to act and think about and decide so many things, and then it is all gone? All that detail is lost, and we return to dirt.

Humus, from the Latin, meaning 'earth' or 'ground'.

Martha was always worrying about Katie. Katie wafted through the glassy ambiguous spaces of Ralph's open-plan house in crop tops and little bikini bottoms, with pieces of orange and red raffia plaited into her hair like tropical butter-flies. She carried a sheaf of paper under her arm. Like Callum, she loved to draw.

'She's far too old to be wandering around dressed like that when there's visitors,' Martha said on the way back from a Friday-night barbecue. It was summer, because Callum was asleep on the back seat with a beach towel over him. Caroline was wide awake and pretending not to listen. 'I don't know what Ralph and Veronica are thinking. Ralph always has a house full of men.'

'She's only fifteen, Martha, let the girl be. It's perfectly normal. You've become so proper, you know. I see young people every day at work. I know how they dress – or don't dress.'

Martha raised her eyebrows at him.

Fred had to be loyal to Ralph. Ralph was his best friend. But in truth he didn't like the way Ralph spoke about his daughter. 'Look at her,' said Ralph with a nudge when Katie came in from the swimming pool, sleek and long. 'Hard to believe she's just a teenager.'

'I don't believe you notice anything about your students, Fred. All I know is she shouldn't be sitting on her father's knee. Did you see them tonight?' Martha said. 'It makes me very uncomfortable.'

Fred had seen Ralph grab Katie by the waist and pull her onto his lap. She draped herself over him and tickled his neck.

'Get off the couch,' said Veronica quickly. 'Your bathers are still damp.'

'They should rein that girl in,' Martha said. 'Veronica needs to step up and challenge Ralph. He's such a bull, that man.'

'Not now,' he said quickly, looking in the rear-view mirror. Caroline was clearly listening.

'Watch the road,' said Martha. He had veered to the left and come close to a parked car. 'Are you sure you're all right to drive? How much have you had to drink? Take the back route, just to be safe.'

Even when the children were little there was too much drinking at Ralph's place, and they were careful to drive home the back way. Ralph kept a cellar and had an encyclopedic knowledge of wine. Evenings began with the host announcing he was going downstairs to find something special, and would any of the men like to join him? Fred would follow dutifully and they would return with a clutch of bottles, which Ralph would present with a lecture on the regions and winemakers, stopping just short of telling them exactly how much each bottle had cost.

Towards the end they all drank far too much and argued bitterly. Australians had become too dependent on welfare, announced Ralph. Where was the incentive to work? Salaries were too high in the construction business. Unions had far too much influence. And we seemed to be letting an awful number of these migrants come in.

'I do worry about foreign influence ...' Ralph said, shaking his head and leaving aposiopesis to say all the things he was not quite willing to say.

But Martha wouldn't let it go. 'You forget, we're all foreigners here, Ralph, except for Indigenous Australians. What exactly do you worry about, Ralph? Is it the calibre of these migrants? Or is it their colour? Perhaps you think they might be gay? Or are you concerned about their lack of appreciation for modernist architecture?'

'Martha!' admonished Fred. She was drunk again. And he certainly didn't want Ralph to think he had been talking about him to his wife.

'Well, excuse me, Martha!' retorted Ralph loudly. Veronica sat up and touched Ralph's arm.

Ralph pushed her away. 'It's all right, Veronica, I'm not going to hit anyone.'

Veronica got up from the table. 'I'm going to the kitchen.'

'Not till I finish, you're not,' said Ralph loudly. Fred glanced at Martha. But Ralph was not stopping there. 'Fred, back me up here. You've seen these two-storey monstrosities going up everywhere. None of them are architect-built. They're rezoning and battle-axing the entire city. These so-called economic migrants are coming down here all cashed up and they haven't got an aesthetic bone in their bodies. You know what I'm talking about, Fred. Corbusier would turn in his grave. They'd never allow this in a European city.'

'We're not in Europe,' snapped Martha. 'We're in Australia, remember? And just up there is Asia. Come on, Veronica.'

★

When Ralph left her, Veronica went off to South Africa with barely a word to anyone. They got a letter in the mail, addressed to them both. 'I've been very unhappy for many years,' she wrote. 'The house is too sad to live in. I'll always remember the years my girls were together with Callum and Caroline. We all had such dreams for our two families. Martha, I'm sorry to leave you like this. I'll call when I am sorted out. The girls will keep in touch with you for now. Give my love to Caroline. You're so lucky to have her. Fred, you must face what has happened, for everyone's sake.'

At the time he was incensed. 'Just like she's faced it all,' he said to Martha, 'running away to South Africa.'

'It wasn't easy for Veronica either,' said Martha tightly, and left the room.

Martha was right. Ralph was a bully, and Veronica had put up with him for years, raising those children while he dreamed up his open-plan spaces, and then Katie dies and he up and leaves her. At their family dinners she was always ferrying plates to the kitchen, or rinsing off glasses and checking on the dessert with Martha in tow. He could not remember a single occasion in all those years when he and Ralph had cleared the table or done the dishes – and they never worried about what the children were up to while the adults were upstairs drinking and eating. As far as the men were concerned, the children were doing their own thing well out of sight of the adults, which was just what children ought to be doing.

Caroline would have been about twelve when she sidled up to him at the dinner table.

'Where's Mum?'

'In the kitchen, helping Veronica with the dishes,' Fred said. 'What do you want her for?' Ralph had unrolled a draft of the new city plaza and wanted Fred's input on a pedestrian overpass.

'I just need her,' Caroline said under her breath. 'Can you please come, Dad?'

'What's wrong, Caroline? I'm busy here. Don't tell me you and Callum are at each other again?'

'I need you,' she hissed and pointed towards the cantilevered wooden staircase. He followed Caroline downstairs and into Katie's room, where he found the girl face down on the bed. Fred rolled her over. She was breathing.

'She sculled heaps of red wine from the cellar. I think she drank two whole bottles. She kept saying, "It serves Dad right."'

Fred picked up an empty bottle from the floor. He righted a second bottle on the bed. A pink stain was spreading across the white sheet. The first thing Frederick thought was, *Ralph will be livid.* And then, *We have to wake her up.*

He carried Katie into her en suite bathroom and propped her up on the toilet seat. She slipped forward, but he managed to get between her skull and the tiled floor.

'Go get a bucket from the laundry and a cup from the bathroom or kitchen,' he said. 'Don't let your mother or anyone else see you. Where are the little girls? Where's Callum?' It was important that no one know what Katie had done, especially Martha and Veronica.

'They're watching TV,' said Caroline as she ran off to the laundry.

'Katie,' he said urgently, slapping her lightly on the face. 'Katie, wake up. You've drunk too much. You have to vomit.'

When Caroline came back he told her to turn on the shower and fill the bucket with cold water. 'Watch out,' he said. He stepped back and threw the bucket of cold water over the girl's head.

'Dad!' said Caroline. The bathroom floor flooded and Fred's clothes were damp, but it worked. Katie flung her head upwards, and opened her eyes. Frederick helped her down to the ground and threw back the lid to the toilet.

'Hold her hair back,' he said.

Caroline held Katie's long hair in two hands.

'Katie, I want you to make yourself sick. Do you under-stand? Or else we have to get your parents and take you to the hospital. You need to get rid of the alcohol. Can you hear me, Katie?'

Katie lifted her face to look at him through strands of wet hair. She jammed her fingers down her throat, her glassy eyes staring at Fred. Then with a violent turn she leant into the toilet and threw up an ocean of stinking red liquid.

Frederick waited till she was dry-retching, then he turned on the shower and flushed the toilet. 'I'm going to leave you with Caroline now,' he began to say, but Katie staggered up, wiping her mouth with her hand. She stepped right into the shower fully clothed and slid to the floor. Her black hair fell across her face.

'Should I go get Mum?' asked Caroline, urgently. 'We need Mum.'

Katie helped herself upright and began to take off her top.

'There's no reason for your mother to know about this,' said Frederick quickly. 'Or Katie's mother either. You make sure she gets out okay and dries off. Then get her some clothes and make her drink as much water as you can and then put her to bed.'

'But why, Dad?' Caroline said in a furious whisper, although no one could have heard her over the shower. 'Why can't I tell Mum and Veronica? Katie needs her mum. Why is this a secret?'

Frederick stripped off the stained cotton bedspread and pushed it into the washing machine in the laundry. He carried the empty bottles out to the bin near the pool and hid them under a bag of kitchen waste. One night, years in the future, he thought grimly, Ralph would go to the cellar looking for the '55. They would be celebrating something big – Katie's engage-ment, Callum's latest commission, Caroline's first child, forty years of happy marriage – and that's when he would tell Ralph about the night Katie drank two bottles of his Penfolds Grange Hermitage, and what could he do but laugh?

As he came back into the house he looked through the window into the den where the little ones were watching a video. Not *E. T.* again?

The phone was ringing in the villa next door. Would it have made any difference if he had gone to get Ralph and Veronica? What if it had been Caroline who was drunk, and Ralph who hadn't told them? Why wouldn't he let Caroline get Veronica that night? It had something to do with protecting Ralph. Ralph was very drunk that night, and when he drank he became argumentative and mean to his wife. Martha would try to protect her friend, and there would have been a terrible scene with Ralph and Fred would have had to stand up for him, because Ralph was his friend, and then Martha would use that in her campaign against Ralph. If he hadn't done what he had done, then Martha would have won.

Clearly, he had been wrong. Ralph had never been his friend. And Katie was dead.

Katie began to lose weight in high school, after the incident with the wine. Around the same time Caroline went on a diet, refusing to eat dinner for a whole week until Martha told her if she didn't eat she would have to go on the school trip to Europe. Caroline hated school trips. Martha spent hours on the phone in the evening talking to Veronica about Katie, nodding and sighing, and dropping hints about family therapy.

'Poor Veronica. Ralph is so pig-headed,' she said when she put down the phone. 'He thinks these kinds of problems can solve themselves. He's told Veronica he doesn't believe in therapy.'

'Neither do I,' said Fred. 'These therapists are all charlatans. Do you know what they're charging per hour? No child of mine is ever going to therapy. Not that they'll ever need to.'

Then Katie no longer wanted to babysit for them. She began to sneak out of her house when everyone was asleep to meet her boyfriends and drink at parties. She left school weeks before her final-year exams and moved in with an older boy who played in a local band.

Martha was furious with Ralph. 'Apparently he keeps saying the boy's a creative genius – takes one to know one. Veronica says he's actually lending the boy cash for new amplifiers and keyboards. Can you believe that? You need to talk to him, Fred.'

'I agree with Ralph on this one, Martha. The boy is talented. He's not the no-hoper you make him out to be. His parents were clients of Ralph's – you remember the Buckler House? He went to an excellent private school. Unlike our children, he stuck at his instrument and was in the youth orchestra until he struck out on his own. His band is apparently doing very well.'

'What has the Buckler House and sticking at clarinet got to do with anything, Fred? I can't believe you.'

Over the next twelve months Katie disappeared; she was replaced by a thin, pale girl who couldn't sit still and wouldn't look you in the eye. She couldn't be left alone in the house because she would steal your money or camera and anything else she could hock. It was Caroline who found out it was heroin – someone at school was a cousin of the musician – and Martha told Fred. He had to break the news to Ralph because Ralph and Veronica weren't speaking, and because Martha said she would leave him if he didn't tell Ralph the truth.

'Your so-called best friend has a daughter using heroin and what does the so-called best friend do? Absolutely nothing.'

In the end, he went to Ralph, who refused to believe him. 'Leave now!' he bellowed. 'And you and your precious wife keep your nose out of our family, do you hear me? We'll deal with this our way. Now leave.'

There were no more Friday meals, no more dinner-table consultations on design briefs. They finally got Katie into a private centre for girls with eating disorders, which was hardly the main problem by then. One day she checked out and took off for Kings Cross, and a year or two later she was dead.

He got up off the ground to inspect the chair. It was cleaner, but that rust would not budge. And a phone was ringing again. He opened his front door. It was coming from Tom Chelmsley's place. Where was Tom now? Being trolleyed into the emergency ward of the public hospital? People didn't belong in hospitals, just as this chair didn't belong here in this villa. This chair should be in the lobby of the Seagram Building in New York, in front of the vast curtain of amber glass.

Thoughts do strike a person. It was not a metaphor at all. The sudden realisation that he was unlikely to see New York City again propelled Fred forward onto the chrome arms of the B3. He fell clumsily into the leather sling and lay half in, half out, like a broken jack-in-the-box. In any other chair he would have damaged the discs in the base of his spine; he would be confined to a wheelchair and transferred out of his villa into the independent area, from where it would be just a trolley ride to high-care. A poorly paid woman would hold his dick when he pissed and wipe his arse when he shat. He would be confined to a bed. He would develop bedsores and his lungs would fill with fluid and he would contract pneumonia. Over the following days his breathing would become laboured. He would be transferred to another ward. There would be further infections. All of this would be very difficult for his only daughter, and she would often leave the room in tears. After several rounds of IV antibiotics there would be a stroke. It would happen in the night, when no one was near, and if he was lucky he might never have to know that a vast part of his function had been swept away, like so much paper after a tickertape parade. There would be a meeting with the palliative care team – a quiet discussion in a room, where more tears would be shed – and then, without much of a fight (there is such inevitability in these stories), there would be acquiescence and agreement.

Over a number of days, with the help of the wonder drug morphine, Fred Lothian would give up the struggle against the rising fluid in his lungs. His breathing rate would grow shallow and fast, and then he would cease to be.

Martha had ceased on a Sunday.

Died peacefully in her sleep. Beloved
wife of _____. Mother of _____.

Two or three hours ago Tom Chelmsley had been on his way to chicken soup at the dining room.

A well-designed structure could absorb the shock of earthquakes, bombs, even a small tsunami. Frank Lloyd Wright had balanced Tokyo's Imperial Hotel on subsoil. Frederick had used

IMPERIAL HOTEL· TOKYO· JAPAN·   ルテホ國帝京東

the example of the Lloyd Wright hotel in 'Engineering 2.01: Managing Disaster', but then had taken it out after a student complained. Lloyd Wright had floated the building on expansion joints above an underground lake to protect the structure from quakes and shudders, and it alone was still standing after the Great Kanto Earthquake of 1923.

But what would protect the human body? Who had protected Linda Yu?

He had never meant to think of Linda Yu, the student who complained. He invoked her name gingerly, as if lifting the lid off something perishable that had been left out in the sun, and had become so much worse over time.

When the girl arrived in his office in tears, he had sat her down and closed the door. This was new territory for Fred. Girls were still an anomaly among engineering students, but with some gentle coaxing, she spoke up.

'Professor Lothian, I want to talk with you about the lecture on the Frank Lloyd Wright building in Tokyo. The hotel?'

'Yes? Did you find it hard to understand? Did I speak too fast for you? Please, be honest. I won't bite your head off.'

The girl was playing with a flat, blue leather wallet, turning it over and over in her right hand.

'Actually, Professor, I found the lecture cruel. It was cruel and narrow in focus.'

Frederick was dumbstruck. Cruel? Narrow? 'What exactly do you mean?'

'Thousands of people died in that earthquake, almost one hundred thousand. It is strange to speak of only one building that has succeeded when so many failed, when so many are dead. What good did one building do for all those people who were burnt to death? Many buildings in Tokyo were wooden. There were terrible fires.'

Frederick lifted up his hand, his palm facing Linda Yu. *Enough*, his hand said, *enough of this nonsense*. 'I think it's time you took a deep breath –'

'I've been researching in the library, Professor Lothian. People became stuck in the melting tarmac on the roads when they were trying to get away from the fires. They sank into the roads. Imagine the children …'

Frederick placed his palms on the desk and leant in towards his student. The girl spoke with a Chinese accent, but her English was almost faultless. It was time to set her on the right path. 'Good building codes are what save lives in a disaster, Miss …' He had checked her enrolment when she made the appointment, but he had forgotten her name. These Chinese names were impossible to remember.

'Linda. Linda Yu.'

'Miss Yu – Linda, you must understand that in many countries, including your own, a combination of poor design, weak regulation of building codes and corruption in the industry has led to millions of people dying in earthquakes of far less magnitude than the Japanese earthquake of 1923.' He spoke slowly and deliberately, giving his words time to sink in. 'Japan now has engineering practices second to none. Frank Lloyd Wright stood up to the developers and insisted on building redundancy into the design when they wanted to cut costs. That is why the building survived. That was the central point of my lecture. As an engineer you will have to be tough enough to stand up to all kinds of overt and covert pressures in design and budget. Do you think you can be tough enough, Miss Yu?' He paused, changed tack. 'Do you intend to return to China to work?'

'Of course. I am Chinese.' She was crying again.

'Then you'll certainly have your work cut out for you.' He handed her a tissue and checked his watch. It was unnerving to have tears in his office. Male students tended towards either mute insolence or repressed rage. 'Can I get you a cup of tea?' He hoped she would refuse; there was a lunch in the Staff Club starting any minute.

She sniffed and blew her nose. 'I'm sorry, Professor. No, thank you. Sometimes I'm not certain I am going to be a good engineer.'

'Rubbish,' said Fred, beaming in what he imagined to be an avuncular fashion. 'I checked your grades when you booked this appointment. You're doing brilliantly. Flying through. Almost top of the class.' He looked meaningfully towards the office door, in what he hoped would be interpreted as a sign.

She played with the tissue. 'I find the course itself man-ageable, but it's not easy when there are so few other female students.' She swallowed, then bit her lip and flipped the wallet in her hand.

Frederick waited impatiently. Something was clearly expected of him, but he had no idea what it was. He glanced at his watch. He would miss a seat at his favourite table if he didn't leave now.

She pressed on. 'It's not easy in engineering for a girl, for a woman at this university,' she said. 'Particularly a woman from overseas.' She stopped again. 'A woman from Asia. For an Asian woman the Australian boys can be …' She paused. 'This is difficult.'

Frederick rubbed his hands together slowly. 'You're absolutely right, Linda. The department is aware of the need to attract more girls – young women. We're doing our best to change the' – he didn't want to say it, but he would – 'culture.' Frederick stood up. 'And now, Linda, if you don't mind I have another appointment. I expect to see you applying to do a doctorate when the time comes. I hope I can interest you in staying with concrete structures.'

He walked around his desk and gestured towards the door. 'Thank you so much for coming to see me. I always appreciate feedback from students, particularly talented ones.'

He waited as Linda picked up her backpack. 'A word of advice, Linda?'

The girl looked at him. Even without hindsight, there was no denying it was a desperate look.

'Linda, get involved in a club or a sport. These young lads are all bark and no bite. If you get invited to something, don't be shy. Promise the professor?'

Linda nodded and closed the door behind her.

Fred changed the lecture before the repeat on the Wednesday, not because he doubted the significance of the Lloyd Wright design in the development of earthquake-resistant buildings or because he was cold-hearted (the idea!), but because one detail kept returning to the surface, like a stubborn infection. He could not stop thinking about molten bitumen and children running barefoot from the inferno, sinking into the burning roads and sticking like tiny flies on glue paper.

His phone screeched and he jumped. Who could that be? He and his daughter had set times to call. Other calls he ignored, just as he ignored the letters from the university requesting the

former professor's presence at _____; the invitation from the Royal Institute asking if he might attend the opening of_____; endless letters from Roger Wu wondering if he might consider reading his recent paper on _____; and finally a request from the editors of _____ to contribute to a special edition of _____. The machine beeped and he pushed replay.

'Fred, it's Roger Wu calling –'

Not again. His former student was now running the workshops at the university and was doing all kinds of things with concrete, but none of it interested Fred. He deleted the message.

Not quite a week after Linda Yu came to his office, her face appeared on a flyer on the concrete column outside the department. 'HAVE YOU SEEN LINDA YU?' it asked, in English and Mandarin. Fred was summoned to an urgent meeting.

The dean was in a state. Linda was not normally in his tutorials, Fred explained, but yes, she had made an appointment with the departmental secretary and he had met with her for a short time in his office, just over a week ago.

'Nothing like this has ever happened under my watch,' said

the dean. 'Did the student indicate any kind of trauma, Fred? Was there any sense that she was struggling with her studies or with her tutors? Were there any personal issues? Did she try to reach out to you?'

Fred shook his head slowly, considering the dean's question. 'Nothing, Rob, nothing like that.'

Fred was stuck in the visitor's chair while Rob paced up and down the space between the wall and his desk. 'No one has seen her for more than three days, Fred. She hasn't been back to her room at the college. The police are involved and her parents are flying in from Beijing. They're understandably distraught, plus we've got the Chinese consulate on our backs. Her parents are VIPs over there. The vice-chancellor is furious at the department for not looking after our overseas students.'

Fred wished Rob would sit down in his chair like a normal professor. But Rob was far from normal. He wore blue denim jeans to work and had started an interdepartmental marathon club. Rob Bartholomew had come from America at the beginning of the year and brought with him a whole new jargon. There were meetings every other week to discuss gender equity, positive discrimination, the faculty culture and how to counter the dominant image of engineering. All the staff were being asked to get out into the community, to speak to Year 12 students, to sell engineering to talented girls. Rob helped himself to a tall glass of water and offered one to Fred. Fred shook his head. Rob was lean and stringy, with not an ounce of fat on him. He made Fred feel soggy and stodgy, like the winter puddings his mother used to make.

'The issue is this: we know for a fact there has been overt racism and harassment. Linda Yu had been receiving notes.' Rob looked at him, narrowing his brows.

Fred felt the colour leave his face. 'What kind of notes?'

'I think you'd call them racist, Fred. Racist and sexist. We found some in her room – unsigned, of course, but handwritten, so we're working on it. Terrible. A few nights ago she was lured into the Tavern by a group of students. I say "lured" because I mean "lured". They lied to her, Fred. They invited her under the pretence of a club sporting event – an international table tennis tournament.'

'But there's no table tennis in the Tavern.'

'Pardon? Speak up.'

'There is no table tennis at the Tavern.'

'Exactly. Linda Yu spoke superb English. Her parents are some kind of aeronautical engineers responsible for the entire Chinese space programme. They're national heroes. They have travelled all over the world. She's their only child, of course. She must have been totally humiliated when she realised what was going on. One of the boys has come forward now. He's not the ringleader, but he went along with it. We've got names, and we're interviewing them all. This boy told us she arrived at the Tavern on her own and she was distraught when she realised there were no tables set up and no other competitors. They bullied her into drinking a few glasses of beer and then she left in tears. This particular boy went outside to look for her and she was being sick in the garden. He says she went back to the college, but we can't confirm what happened after that. We suspect they took her somewhere, and then – well, we can only imagine. Are you okay, Fred? You look a little pale. It's a terrible situation for all of us, I know.'

He handed Fred a glass of water and patted him on the back. Fred drank it in one gulp.

'Parents entrust us with their children's education,' continued Rob. 'The situation is delicate. The university bent over backwards to get Linda Yu here after she was accepted into all the major American universities. She's a star recruit. As you know, we're really pushing the department in Asia. It's the new market for us. Things have to change, Fred. Would you want your daughter to come into this faculty? It's neanderthal. Now, what exactly did she want when she came to see you?'

Fred cleared his throat. 'It was about my lecture, Rob. Linda was upset about the lecture I had just given in 2.01. I always use documentary photographs – I find they humanise the issues. We saw slides of the 1923 Tokyo earthquake and then I moved on to the subsoil solutions proposed by Lloyd Wright in the Imperial Hotel. Linda came to me and said that she felt there ought to be more focus on the human side of the story.'

'What do you mean, Fred? I don't follow you.'

'She had clearly become obsessed with the Tokyo disaster. She knew the death toll, and some of the more graphic details of how people died, and she wanted me to bring that into the lecture. I was very sympathetic, of course, if a little puzzled. I explained that the purpose of structural engineering in earthquake zones is to save lives. I was quite clear that this is an engineering faculty, not an emergency department.'

The dean nodded slowly. He looked at Fred intently. 'I don't want to put you under any pressure here, Fred.' He jiggled his sneakered foot. 'Linda was fragile, then? Would you say she had any kind of predisposition to – I'm not sure how to phrase this …'

'She was definitely very sensitive, Rob, there's no doubt about that. She was in a fragile state when she arrived in my office.'

'Was she, Fred? Are you sure? Did she say anything to that effect?'

Fred looked at his hands. He thought of Eichmann in his glass box. The dean had turned his back to him and was staring out the glass window behind the desk, into the Great Court.

'I believe she did, Rob – in fact, she said something to that very effect.'

The dean swung around to face him.

'Is that right? If you had to summarise, if you had to bring it down to its essence …'The dean paused. Did Professor Lothian have that special word the dean was looking for?

Fred reached deep into his repertoire of specialist terms and emerged with something in hand. 'There is no doubt in my mind that Linda Yu arrived in my office in a depressed and unstable state and was inordinately concerned about issues well beyond the reach of the engineering faculty and course.'

Rob lowered himself into his leather chair.

'Thank you, Fred, thank you very much. You've made an invaluable contribution. Let's hope we can get Linda back in class. I'll see she gets some counselling. You've been most supportive, and I'll be sure to let the VC know.'

He reached his large, strong hand across his desk, and Fred shook it manfully.

He was shaking right now. Why had Linda Yu returned, after all these years? Three days after his meeting with the dean a horticulturalist found Linda's body in Kings Park. The girl had taken an overdose of sleeping pills and walked into the bush, not far off the long drive lined with old eucalyptus that marked the dead in the First World War. There was an autopsy, where it was confirmed that Linda Yu had severe bruising, cuts and abrasions in the genital area, consistent with forceful penetration, but as no semen was recovered, no charges could be brought, and, for the sake of the family, wrote the dean in his personal note to Fred, we have asked that these details be kept out of the press.

A careful note from her parents arrived some weeks later, thanking the famous professor for teaching their only daughter:

Dear Professor Lothian,

We thank you for your respected work in the field of engineering, and for caring for our daughter Zhu Zhu, who you would have known as Linda.

My husband was born in Tangshan, in Hebei Province. In 1976 an earthquake struck his hometown, killing over 250,000 people. Among those killed were my husband's mother and father and grandparents, as well as many aunts, uncles, cousins and childhood friends. Our daughter's dream was to design and build strong, safe buildings in China's earthquake zones, and to protect the Chinese people.

In the bathroom mirror he caught the wild eyes and lined face of an old man who could not be Frederick Lothian. How could anyone have loved such a monster? He opened the cabinet and took out Martha's pink toilet bag. As a rule, Fred did not take medicine. As a rule, medicine was for the sick and the very old. Fred swallowed two Valium and zipped up the bag.

Something very odd was happening to Frederick Lothian. His head had been severed from his body and had rolled onto the ground, mute and still, like the abandoned egg of some giant bird. He had taken drugs and fallen asleep on the couch and he was trapped at the bottom of a giant aviary, surrounded by high-pitched screeching.

Fred struggled to pull himself upright. It wasn't a dream – it was those fucking budgerigars next door. He sent a message to his toes, but they ignored him. He loathed birds in cages. He might have welcomed Tom Chelmsley into his life, but he had done everything he could to ignore his neighbour on the other side, mainly because she was a woman and women always want to talk, but also because she kept budgerigars in cages. His aunt in Lincoln had kept budgerigars in cages and she was his father's sister and he hated his father, so he hated budgerigars. And it wasn't right to keep birds in cages. His villa was squashed in so close to his neighbour's that he could almost hear the little hooked beaks cracking open the tiny seeds in their special budgie mix to extract whatever it was the stupid things liked to eat. He experimented with lifting his head – nothing.

Caroline's budgie was blue with black spots … but did budgies have spots?

He had resisted her pleas for as long as he could – pets were a burden and children never looked after them properly – but then Theodore arrived from a neighbour whose bird had chicks, and he gave in. He was a chirpy little chap. Caroline put a bowl of warm water at the bottom of his cage and watched him primp and preen and flap about in the shallows. Then Martha decided the damn budgie should be allowed to fly around the house in the mornings, which meant they had to close all the curtains and lower the blinds in case Theodore flew straight into the glass.

Theodore. What a ridiculous name. One day he flew into Fred's study and dropped a message right on the B3.

'Martha!'

Caroline would stand in the middle of the lounge room with her index finger in the air, waving it from side to side like a juicy bone and whistling lightly until the bird came. One windy morning Callum came rushing in from the garden and threw open the flyscreen door just as Theodore was swooping through the lounge and into the kitchen. Out went Theodore. The whole family drove around looking for him. They put notices on telephone poles and signs at the local deli: 'Theodore is missing.' Caroline sat in the front seat weeping and wailing while they drove up and down the streets. 'Theodore! Come home, Theodore!' Caroline called out the window, ever the drama queen. Even Martha had to stifle a smile. Their daughter loved to blow things completely out of proportion, and blamed Callum for the whole thing. Alas, Theodore was gone for ever.

More tweeting from the neighbour's direction. Fred's usual defence was to pull the screen door shut, slamming it hard so the woman next door would hear, but at the moment he couldn't move his body. It didn't really matter, because slamming the door was a symbolic action. Door open or door closed, it made no difference to the volume of the twitters since there was not even so much as a proper cavity wall between him and his neighbour. It struck him (at least his brain was functioning) that it was men like his former friend Ralph the architect (why were they always men?) who had paved the way for the compression of space in places like the village. Everything was quick-built and multipurpose and flexible by design. There was a time when he had thrown his weight behind the promulgators of open-plan houses and schools and offices, when he had sided with trendy 'visionaries' like Ralph who insisted on one function bleeding easily into another – overlapping even, like his wives. But once you accepted the logic of living in a glass cube with flexible walls, it was just a short distance to the container box, and then the empty refrigerator carton, and the end of homes for ever. You were left with the Community Living Centre (the 'Gerry', as it was affectionately known), where the dining room doubled as a games room (just stack the chairs and fold the tables!) and should you require a smaller space (bingo, or a great-grandson's birthday party?), simply slide the retractable stacking wall panels across the concealed floor tracking, like *so*!

Frederick was now a firm believer in mandatory gaps and impermeable boundaries, and these beliefs placed him in direct conflict with the designers and builders of the villages of the Western world.

At least he had his things to keep him busy. When he was able to move his body he planned to shift this couch and carry the clean B3 chair to the lounge-room window. He might even unpack a box from the garage and give everything a good wipe.

Caroline had been horrified when she realised he was bringing the lot with him, but he was only doing it for her. If she would just finish with her dead animals in Europe, he would give her the Saarinen table and chairs and the Minotti lounge and his two George Nelson clocks and the Eileen Gray table and all his other beautiful objects that stood for something. But what to do with his precious Dieter Rams collection, which was packed into six large wooden crates in the back of the carport/garage? They were more of a boy's thing. *Good design is as little design as possible.* How could anyone disagree with Dieter, who over at Braun had single-handedly designed Germany back into the postwar small-electronics market?

Frederick and Ralph had spent many pleasurable evenings with the Braun collection. When a box arrived from Europe or America, Fred would call Ralph and they would take their drinks into the huge garage and set up a trestle table for the box. Callum stood to one side while Fred wielded the Stanley knife and Ralph shook the Braun from the packing foam. The pride of his collection was the Braun SK6 Record Player.

'Just look at this, Callum! All the way from Germany. What a beauty.'

'It looks okay, Dad, but what's so great about it? It's not like it's a Walkman or anything. Am I going to get a Walkman for Christmas?'

'What? Before these arrived on the scene, record players and radios were in huge wooden cabinets and took up half the house. Remember that, Ralph?'

'I certainly do,' said Ralph. 'Strictly speaking, they were furniture, not electronics.'

Fred ran his hand along the metal and wooden case. 'What do you think, Callum? It's hard to believe it was designed nearly forty years ago.'

'Can we play a record on it?'

'Of course not, the voltage and plugs are different in Europe.'

'Can't you change it? What about an adaptor?'

'It's possible,' said Ralph thoughtfully. 'As long as the drive belt can be adjusted.'

'We're not changing it. This is in original mint condition. No one is going to be using this record player, Callum.'

'Please, Dad?' whined the boy. 'I could put it in my room.'

'Enough, Callum. Help me pick up these plastic bubbles.'

He tried his toes again. A little bit of movement. Caroline might not be able to see the beauty in a thirty-year-old electric men's shaver, but surely she would appreciate the record player? He struggled to lift his eyelids, but they were so heavy he had to let them fall all the way down again. And then he slept.

He is in the Old Woods at Skellingthorpe, running down a path covered with briar and brambles. Dieter Rams is far ahead of him, walking between birch trees. Dieter is wearing black-rimmed glasses, fawn slacks and a dark polo neck jumper. He is moving so fast that Fred cannot reach him, which makes Fred angry, because Dieter has something that Fred desperately wants. Dieter stops and kneels down. Fred comes up behind him, breathing heavily. He leans over Dieter's shoulder. It is the SK6, but it is so much bigger than he remembers. He begins to cry, but his tears will not flow. A single tear is blocking the duct in the corner of his eye. The more he cries, the more the tear expands, until he can no longer see Dieter, or the record player, or the path in the Skellingthorpe Woods. Why, he wonders, do the twin influences of surface tension and gravity not sever the tear suspended from the corner of his eye? He shakes his head from side to side, until the huge sphere breaks away and crashes down to the lid of the record player. Dieter Rams is furious. He is speaking in German and moving his hands in the air. He tells Dieter he is sorry, but Dieter does not hear. He takes out a cloth and wipes the lid clean, and now Fred sees what is trapped under the cover of the SK6. It is his son Callum, aged twenty years and ten months, dressed in his blue-and-white hockey socks, shin guards, shorts and club shirt, asleep with his arms folded across his body, just like Snow White.

'Callum, guess what they nicknamed the SK6 at the Braun factory?'
    'What?' said Callum.
    'What?' said Ralph.
    'What?' said Callum, a little louder.
    'What?' yelled Ralph.
    They were both laughing at him.
    'Have you finished?' said Fred.
    'Sorry, Fred,' said Ralph.
    'Sorry, Dad,' said Callum.
    '*Schneewittchensarg.*'
    'What?'
    'Snow White's coffin.'
    'I get it,' said Callum. 'That's a good movie – but not as good as *E. T.*'
    'Of course not,' said Fred.
    'Of course not,' said Ralph.

He would never take a Valium again. *E. T.* was to Callum as *Snow White* was to Frederick. He would have been seven or eight when the film came to Lincoln. Up until then the only movies he had ever seen were black-and-white show reels that cost a penny or two, but *Snow White* was a whole hour and a half of Technicolor. His father would never have paid for him to see it, but then a miracle happened at church. Just as the congregation were picking up their coats and hats and gloves and missals, Father McMahon scrambled up to the pulpit. St Hugh's had received a small bequest, he announced, and the parish would pay for all the children to go to the cinema in Lincoln to see *Snow White* as long as the children were over six – 'not five, not six, but seven and over.' Virgil bawled because he was only four, but the chosen ones covered their mouths with their hands to stop themselves shouting in church, and then said a quick 'Our Father'.

At the theatre, the boys pressed up together in one long line, pinching and kicking and laughing and sucking on bullseye sweeties, right up to when the velvet curtain lifted and the gorgeous credits began. How is it that an image can press itself so firmly into the mind of a child? Fred was terrified of the Wicked Queen and her evil green transubstantiation. He was delighted by the dwarfs and charmed by Snow White, who was not only beautiful and kind, but also had the gift of turning a ramshackle house full of very small men into a proper home. If only he had a mother like Snow White. His mother was too sad to be happily tidying up the house. She was always picking things up and putting things away, and urging the boys to get it all done before their father came home from the Lord Nelson, but even with all that hurrying, she never seemed to arrive at the moment when it was finished.

His sherbet fountain was gone by the time Snow White fell to the ground, but even if he had another, he would have had to stop eating. He could hardly look at the screen. Snow White lay inside a glass sarcophagus with a tiny piece of apple wedged inside her mouth. When the prince finally bent down to kiss the red lips of Snow White and dislodge the poisonous wedge,

Frederick trembled and swallowed hard. Snow White was alive. She was back from the dead. Life could begin again.

Fred walked home down Steep Hill in a daze of Disney marketing. *Snow White* had taken over every shop window on the main street of Lincoln. *Snow White* wallpaper hung in long rolls in the drapers'. *Snow White* record albums were propped up next to *Snow White* calendars. There were *Snow White* colouring books, toothbrushes, train sets, pencil boxes, Bakelite lamps, jigsaw puzzles, and ceramic figurines of the seven dwarfs. At school they made masks of the seven dwarfs. They coloured in pictures of the pumpkin carriage. They hummed along to the songs. They were encased and enfolded by *Snow White*.

Fred wiggled his toes, then his fingers, then sat up and turned off the air conditioning. It was cold in the villa, cold like a coffin. He squeezed past the couch and stepped outside into the furnace. The quadrangle was deserted, but he could feel the full weight of his boxes and chairs and seats and tables pressing up behind him, like a wave behind a sea wall. 'Just leave all this furniture in the house,' Caroline had said when he was moving. 'Just rent the house semi-furnished. You'll never get all this into the villa.'

But he was keeping it for her. It was only a matter of time before she came begging. He would give her the Knoll Tulip chairs and the matching oval table by Eero Saarinen. The marble tabletop was far too big and heavy for his kitchen/ dining/lounge area, and far too difficult to explain to the residents of St Sylvan's, whose taste in dining settings swung between Olde Tudor England and what Martha called 'Balinese chunky-wood'. The foot of the upended table functioned quite nicely as a bedside table and was at present piled high with dirty teacups in need of washing.

Frederick set off in search of the chairs that went with the table. He found them stacked top-to-toe under wool blankets in the covered alcove outside the back door. They ought to be inside in a stable environment, but there was just no room in his villa. The seats needed reupholstering, but what would you expect after all this time? They had been sat upon all those years, hadn't they? This was what Caroline and all her friends would never understand – even modernism wore out, like everything else. He inspected the upholstery. The navy wool had faded and the rubber padding was degraded into bunchy mounds. At one stage the boy had got to the chairs with black Dymo tape. 'CHAR' he pressed out in red tape. 'TAIBL' he stuck on the pedestal. For years Martha refused to remove the tape because she was ridiculously sentimental. Everything the children made she would cut out, fold and store, or put in an album. 'That tape will ruin the plastic,' he protested. But she would not budge. He tiptoed downstairs when Martha was asleep and found the sponge he had left soaking in solvent. He dabbed it on the tape until it lifted off without a mark. Martha didn't even notice they were gone, which was so Martha – a huge fuss, and then all was forgotten.

The table and chairs were fine examples of plastic organic design, but they were much more than that. They marked the real beginning of his life. Each time his family sat for dinner – daughter, son, mother, father – he looked around the white laminated ellipse and saw his future in the shape of a fresh, white egg, warm with hope. He tried not to dwell upon the unease he felt as he set the bottom chair on top and shook out the plastic tarp he used to protect them.

'Do not stand on that couch, Callum! How many times have I told you?'

'Caroline, get that hot cup off that marble table! Use the cork mats.'

'You're not planning on getting out those paints on my marble, are you?'

He watched Martha picking up dirty cups, scrambling for

the coasters, wiping up the spills, shaking her head, tightening her lips, trying to juggle the insatiable, imperious needs of her children with the demands of her husband's precious things.

He had just managed to get the one good Tulip chair to the ground when the phone screamed. It was after midnight in England, so it couldn't be Caroline. Phones ring, he told himself. There was no need to panic. That's what telephones do. They ring for no reason – a wrong number, a mechanically generated fault. He was here in his unit on a Sunday just like every other Sunday. He had eaten breakfast and survived the columns. It was probably Roger Wu hounding him again about some research project he had on the go. But the day was only half over, and a four-year-old was dead, and Tom Chelmsley had toppled over right before his eyes. And now the phone was ringing all over the place.

The seat of the chair wobbled on its stem. It needed tightening, but he had no screwdriver.

Once upon a time there were no problems, only solutions. Theoretical solutions. 'Work backwards from a problem,' he told his students. Model every possible solution until you come up with an answer. He and Martha had emigrated with the idea that he would establish his own practice. He would consult to the public infrastructure for the booming primary industries of this remote Australian state. Martha would run the office. But the recession arrived and poverty terrified him. For a few years he struggled as a private consultant. Then they had a daughter, and he wanted to buy a house. He wanted to give his family what he had never had. When he took the offer of a teaching position at the university and time off to complete his doctorate, he knew he would never leave. He stepped right out of a world where things could fall down and kill someone, into a far, far safer place.

At the university every problem had an answer – in theory. Take the problem of the past: the past shimmered on the other side of a vast swirling expanse and appeared to be out of reach, like Shangri La. But for an engineer there was a bridge for every situation, be it arch, beam, cantilever or cable. The first step was to identify the topological and geological conditions – river, gorge, valley, mountain range. Then he, Professor Frederick Lothian PhD, master of reinforced concrete and thin-shell structures, would determine an appropriate method of spanning the chasm with a structure of logical simplicity and elegance. He would locate a point at which to anchor the bridge. Why go abroad? Why go anywhere at all? Why not start right here at number 7? He would locate the other anchor point somewhere easily recognisable – the airport at New York City where he first set eyes on the lovely Miss Martha Salomon.

For this particular bridge he would ignore the modern clichés – steel, silica, superplasticisers – and return to the basics. For the underwater sections he would employ the ancient and primal material of pozzolan cement. He had the Roman Vitruvius to thank for the unforgettable recipe: 'One part lime, four parts sand and an admixture of milk, blood and animal fat.'

Since it was a bridge for only one person (Frederick Lothian), the question of structural efficiency (the load-to-weight ratio) would not be of concern. Once it was completed, he would step out of his village-prison and stride with singular purpose across his one-man bridge, all the way back to TWA Terminal, New York.

Once again, it is 16 December 1966. He has just bought a pastrami sandwich and a copy of the *New York Times* from a kiosk in the transfer terminal. As he enters the stupendous concrete curves of the terminal he is reading the obituary of Walter Elias 'Walt' Disney. Approaching the information pod he thinks of *Snow White* – the film, not the record player.

He looks up and spies a dark-haired beauty (this would be Martha, of course – it would be inappropriate to abandon reality completely) staring at the information pod. He stands next to her and searches for his flight. There is no hint of simulation, no air of stagey re-enactment.

He steals a glance. This time he will play hard to get. He pretends not to see the slight woman in the yellow cotton sleeveless seersucker shift. He does not stare at her thick dark hair, or admire her tanned legs and the fine bones of her wrists. Her arms are folded in front of her and the tips of her fingers are tap, tap, tapping on her forearms, like a healthy pulse. Side by side they stand, gazing at the announcements of arrivals and departures.

'How was London?' she says suddenly, turning towards him with a stunning smile.

'How did you guess?' he replies, enthralled once more by the idea that a woman – a gorgeous American woman with snow-white teeth – can be bothered trying to determine his origins. She winks and looks back up at the board.

The first time they met, Martha had tapped the logo on his silly BOAC travel bag. 'That's how I knew,' she said, and made him feel like a little boy whose game had been penetrated by a higher order being. It is different this time. This time he concentrates on the board, searching for his connection to Chicago, where he is going to a conference on trussed-tube and X-bracing. Fazlur Khan himself is speaking. This time he will not try to explain to Martha the centrality of lateral load to Khan's innovations in trussed concrete steel. On the complex subject of tubing he will remain absolutely silent.

It is his first trip to America. He is thirty years old. He has never been married. He has had sex with a woman exactly seven times: four times with the wife of the chief architect of the new Liverpool Cathedral, and twice with a nice young woman in the construction office who was seeing another man and in the end decided to go for humour over prospects (her words, not his), and once when he was at university with a woman he met at the pub. Monica. Her name was Monica.

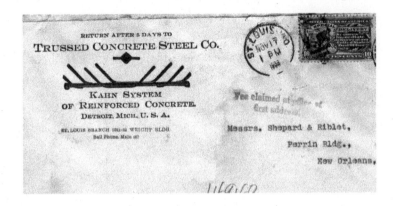

'So, how was London?'

'London was cold,' he says with a slight smile, 'cold and old, the truth be told.'

She laughs at his spontaneous attempt at rhyme, which she had not done the first time they met. This time around Martha finds him irresistibly witty, which (in his view) Martha failed to do throughout most of their marriage.

'First trip to the USA?'

'Indeed,' he said in 1966 and immediately regretted it. He'd never wanted to be the sort of man who said 'indeed'. His father had tried to become that sort of man, and Frederick was hell-bent on avoiding any of his father's dreams. 'Sure is,' he replies instead, upbeat, American, modern, and off the cuff.

'Nice tie,' Martha said in 1966, flicking the tight navy knot at his neck, smiling that amused smile he would come to fear. This time there is no navy tie with little anvils to signify his membership of the Royal College of Engineers; this time he is wearing his egg-blue paisley silk shirt from King's Road, Chelsea, which he wears loose and nonchalantly unbuttoned.

'Architect?' asks Martha Salomon.

'Engineer,' he replies, with a knowing nod to her assumption. This time he will save the details for later. He should have learnt from Liverpool that nothing kills a woman's interest in a man quicker than concrete. He had almost lost Martha in 1966, but he would not make the same mistake.

'Bridges,' he says, narrowing his eyes and looking up in the vague direction of the elliptical departure board, his mind turned towards matters of far greater import than an arrival and departure pod. 'And thin-shell structures.'

It was a miracle he had seen Martha at all in 1966, given he was so completely absorbed by the extraordinary Saarinen terminal. It was a concrete-lover's heaven. Even the ventilators were a utopian mutation of nature and concrete formed into an organic paroxysm of simulated growth. A creamy, smooth, concrete forest, with walls like the skin of a mushroom.

Then he remembered *E. T.*

Caroline was in his study looking through the shelves. She took down a hardcover book bound in cloth, an old Thames & Hudson in the *Masters of Modern Architecture* series. It had been a birthday present from Ralph and Veronica.

'Look at this, Dad,' she said, walking over to his desk. 'It's that airport in New York. *The TWA Terminal, New York,*' she began to read. '*Japanese mosaic tiles cover the cantilevered desk and departure board in the ticket lobby. Photo by Yu-kio Fu-ta-ga-wa.* Take it, Dad.'

Frederick took the book.

'It's E.T., Dad.'

She was right. The huge elliptical information pod at the TWA Terminal mounted on top of the elongated concrete neck bore an uncanny resemblance to E.T.

'I'm going to show Callum. He'll love this picture. Do you think Steven Spielberg copied the idea for E.T. from this airport? Do you think he was looking for his flight time on his way back to Hollywood and he got the idea? What do you think? Is that how it could have happened?'

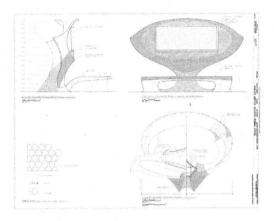

Fred studied the photograph. He was having his own thoughts. 'I'm not sure, Caroline. E.T. is organic in design, meaning it looks like some kind of plant or living matter, and so is the architecture in this airport, so there's a connection, but whether we can ever know if one thing caused another, well, we just don't know, but it seems unlikely.'

'But what about chance, Dad? Can't good things come by chance? Steven Spielberg could just have looked up and got the idea, like *that*!' She snapped her long fingers. 'And there's something else, Dad. *E. T.* is Callum's all-time favourite film, and this is where you and Mum met. Mum told me. She said I should come up here and find this book. She said to remind you that E.T. came to earth in search of seedpods, just like you. What's that about?'

Why would Martha have made some kind of bizarre reference to him being on a seed hunt? He stole a glance at his daughter. 'What else did she tell you?'

But she had gone to find her brother.

Where was that book now? Before he moved to the villa, Caroline had labelled a few boxes before giving up. *Modern US Architecture 1950/60/70* was on top of a stack of boxes in his bedroom cupboard. Why did mothers think they had the right to tell their daughters everything? Was nothing private? He opened the box. Martha should never have told Caroline that they had met and fallen in love and married and parented because they both happened to be standing in front of an arrivals and departures board that resembled the fabricated extraterrestrial star of a children's film. Children shouldn't be exposed to the arbitrariness of beginnings, and especially not adopted children. When he confronted Martha about it later, she was dismissive.

'Well, how would you describe how we met, Fred? An act of god?'

'What the hell was all that stuff about seedpods? Where did that come from?'

'You've got no sense of humour, Fred, do you know that? Try thinking of it as irony. I was hardly the fertility god, was I?'

'Why are you bringing that up now, Martha? We've got two perfect children. What more could we want?'

A brisk knock on the front door and Frederick froze, like a setter with a bird in the bush. Another knock.

'Anyone home?' A woman's voice. He didn't know any women.

'Who is it?' He heard the voice of a scared old man.

'It's Jan Venturi, from next door?'

The budgerigar woman. What could she possibly want? He left the box of books on the table and went over to open the door, leaving the security chain in place.

'Fred? Hello, how are you? It's good to finally see you close up — or at least a bit of you. Hello, nose.'

He unchained the door and pulled it ajar, leaving his body in the narrow gap.

'I can't get the wheel of my recycling bin out of the gutter. I've been at it ten minutes and it's stinking hot. I was wondering if you'd mind giving me a hand. I'm sorry to bother you.'

'Of course, Janet,' muttered Fred, meaning of course he minded and of course she wouldn't have any idea that he minded. He fiddled with the door and found his slip-on shoes, then made his way out to his neighbour, who was standing on the other side of the driveway, wrangling a large bin that was pitched sideways in the gutter.

'Terrible weather, isn't it,' Jan called. She was tugging at the bin with one arm while keeping another hand on the stack of empty yoghurt containers spilling out of the top.

'Awful,' agreed Frederick, hurrying over to help. How could anyone eat that much yoghurt? He hated yoghurt. As he walked towards her his left knee gave out and he stumbled.

'Are you all right there, Fred? Do you need a hand?'

'I'm fine, I just tripped on something.'

'Really? What was it?'

'A stick, I believe.'

'A stick?' Jan said, casting around. 'We should get rid of that. It's dangerous. Where is it?'

'I kicked it over there,' said Frederick, gesturing vaguely towards the grass next to the driveway.

'I'll just make sure no one else trips over it, then,' she said, scanning the open space. 'The driveway, you say?' Jan left the bin and let yoghurt containers spill down onto the path. She walked slowly across the driveway with her arms behind her back and her eyes on the ground.

'No, the lawn, but please Janet, let me find it later,' he said. 'Don't you bother.'

'Call me Jan. No one calls me Janet except my budgerigars. That's a joke, by the way. And it's no bother. A large stick, you say? Over this way?'

'Actually, it was a small- to medium-sized stick – and greeny-coloured. Like grass.' Oh, god.

'Hmm,' she said, head bowed, looking left to right, 'a small to medium grass-coloured stick …'

'Please, leave the stick to me and let's deal with this bin. If you could just pick up those yoghurt containers.'

'Fine, Fred,' she said. 'I was just trying to help.'

What an infuriating woman. Only his closest friends called him Fred, but he could hardly ask her to lengthen his own name straight after she had told him to shorten hers. He tried out her name in his head: *Jan. Hi, Jan!* There were many reasons not to chat to Janet – Jan – but the main one was she might want to become his friend, and Frederick did not want any friends. Jan tugged at her headscarf while Fred dragged the bin out of the gutter. He desperately wanted to ask her if she had seen Tom fall, and if she knew how he was, but he didn't want Jan to know he had been standing inside watching Tom tottering around in the heat.

After all, it was a fine line between watching and doing.

It was called Mogumber when they went, but before that it was Moore River Native Settlement, where they brought what they called half-castes after they took them away from their families. Later they set some of that film there, the one about the Aboriginal girls who walked all the way back to Jigalong. He hadn't wanted to bring Caroline to visit the mission, but Martha insisted; she had arranged it all and found a guide to meet them there, and they weren't changing their plans now. They followed the woman around the compound and through the abandoned wooden cottages where they once housed the children. Had they checked the registers for relatives, the guide asked, all the while looking at Caroline. Martha shook her head, and they all fell in behind the guide. They stopped to look at old black-and-white photographs on a display board: well-to-do women in hats and gloves standing behind rows of barefoot Aboriginal children. It looked to him like the 1930s, but he wasn't about to ask either the guide or his wife.

'Christians,' said the guide. 'They drove up from Perth once a month to check on the children.'

'At least there were some white people back then who showed concern,' said Fred. 'I suppose not all of them were heartless.'

Martha glared at him. Their guide shrugged. 'It's a fine line between watching and doing,' she said.

'Can we go?' whispered Caroline. 'I don't like it here.'

'Watch yourself,' said Jan, pulling at her scarf. Her hair was presumably tucked in somewhere underneath it, as if she were halfway through spring-cleaning. Or perhaps she was recovering from an illness. Not cancer, surely? He couldn't manage that. He wheeled the bin down the side of her unit.

Jan gestured to the uneven paving at their feet. 'Never mind the sticks, look at that! You could break your hip and that would be the end of it. I reported this to management weeks ago,' she continued, 'and still no action, the cheapskates.' Frederick nodded in agreement. At least his neighbour thought the village was poorly run. This might be a good time to mention Tom.

'Speaking of sticks –' she began again.

'Did you get the letter about the latest extraordinary levy?' he interrupted.

'For retiling the pool, you mean? I prefer the beach. Tell me, Fred, where have you been since we last met? We were in the library, I think? Have you been back? I haven't seen you there.'

And she never would. What they called 'the library' was a dim alcove with a low teak table for the local rag and two small bookcases with his-and-hers Tom Clancys and Georgette Heyers.

Rather than answer, he set to work helping Jan reposition the paving stone.

'How are you enjoying the *village*?' Jan asked, rolling her eyes and laughing.

He smiled. So Jan saw what this place really was; it was not a village at all. A village was a small town in England surrounded by woods. A village was a remote community of weavers in the foothills of Nepal. This was a detention centre. They were all refugees from youth and middle age who had been cut off from the normal ebb and flow of life and were being prepared for a slow and painful death. 'I've been busy moving in, actually, Jan. It takes time to settle.'

'It certainly does,' she said quietly. 'It takes some getting used to.' She stood with her hands on her hips, looking at him. 'Thanks so much for the help,' she said. 'I really appreciate it.'

Fred shuffled in his slip-ons and eyed his front door. 'Well,' he said, 'I suppose it's time for me to –'

'Why don't you come in, Fred? I've made a chicken pie and coleslaw and it's not the sort of thing a woman should eat alone.' Jan patted her belly, which appeared to be a small firm mound.

'Oh no, I couldn't,' he said hurriedly. Couldn't, and wouldn't.

'Oh, but you have to,' said Jan carefully. 'It was hard enough for me to ask, let alone having you turn me down.'

Frederick ran his tongue around his lips.

'You have to come in, Fred, or else I will be unhappy all afternoon, and when I get unhappy I stamp my feet and flap my wings and cry very loudly.' She paused for effect. 'And then the little fellows get upset and we wouldn't want that, would we? You know how thin the walls on these places are.'

'Little fellows?' said Fred weakly.

'The birds,' she said, smiling. 'Don't look so terrified. You can at least take some pie home with you, can't you?'

There was no way out of it now. Frederick waited as Jan fiddled with her keys. As the front door opened he heard an appalling flapping and screeching. The budgerigars. Frederick remained rooted on the spot. Once he crossed the threshold all would be lost.

'I think I hear my phone,' he said.

'Really? I'm amazed you can hear anything over my birds.'

'There it is again,' said Fred, cocking his head slightly. 'Do you mind if I duck back?'

'I'll take the pie out of the oven and let it cool. I'm pleased my birds don't bother you. I was worried when you moved in that you might complain. I'm not supposed to have so many birds, but how will they know if no one tells them? Off you go now, big ears.'

'It's stopped,' said Fred. He was defeated. It was pointless to either take offence or refuse the pie. And he did have rather large ears, and he had always hated them.

'Has it? Haven't you got good hearing!'

Jan's house was not at all what he expected. He had imagined a fussy, female kind of place, with doilies and mass-produced figurines in the sentimental genre, but his neighbour had a preference for simple, well-made wooden furniture and Asian art. There was a lovely mahogany Buddha on the floor near the sliding door, and scrolls of Japanese and Chinese paintings on the walls. On the face of her windows Jan had hung thin bamboo blinds, which filtered subdued light into the lounge room, where the one longer wall was covered with books.

'It's nice,' he said, without thinking.

'Not what you'd expect from an old woman. No doilies and antimacassars? I do have the budgerigars, though.'

His neck reddened.

'My husband and I lived in South-East Asia on and off for over fifteen years … Singapore, Bangkok, China. China was Sam's last job. He was with a Japanese manufacturer who relocated their parts factory from here and needed a supervisor. I taught English at the local school and did volunteer work. We had a wonderful time. We travelled all over Asia – Vietnam, Mongolia, Japan, and then he got sick and we had to come home, and then, well, then Samuel died.'

Fred watched Jan's face carefully. He waited for death to pass over and depart. Samuel. A biblical name, like Martha. 'I'm sorry,' he said finally.

'Never mind,' said Jan. She sat very still. She was waiting for him to say the right thing. He could reach inside and pull out some words, just like he had done for the dean, or he could say nothing, as he'd done when he met Linda Yu.

'I want to see if you can guess my secret ingredients. Start, please, before it gets cold. Help yourself to salad.'

Jan's pie was positively aromatic. It was absolutely perfect. He could not fault it. The crust was buttery yet crisp and melted away on his tongue, and the chicken filling was dense and juicy and firm and succulent.

'Well?' prompted Jan.

'Fantastic.'

'No, I mean the secret ingredients.'

'Onion?' he suggested.

'Hardly a secret.'

'Garlic?'

'Again, too obvious.'

'Parsley?'

'Closer, but no, there's no parsley. You've dropped some pie on your shirt.' She handed him a napkin.

Fred dabbed at his shirt, keen to return to his food. He had never tasted a pie like this. Martha was a wonderful cook, but after all those years even the best recipes wear out. 'Sage?'

'You'll be going for rosemary and thyme next.'

'I give up.'

'There are two secret ingredients – three if you count ground cashew nut.'

'Cashews? I think I can taste them now. And?'

'Fresh tarragon – dried is too overwhelming and kills the other ingredients. And finally, saffron.'

'It's very good, Jan.' He was trying to hide his hunger. It was as if he hadn't eaten a real meal since Martha died.

'Another slice?'

'Please!'

'Next week it's your turn.'

'I beg your pardon?'

'Next week it's your turn to cook.'

Fred masked his alarm with a fixed smile. 'I'm afraid I'm not much of a cook, Jan. I was always the sous-chef for my wife – the assistant.' A bald lie. Martha ran the kitchen with Caroline in tow, and he had happily accepted the division of labour.

'I know what a sous-chef is, Fred. Are you telling me that a big boy like you can't cook? Samuel was what I call a book cook – someone who needs a book in order to cook. I'm more of an improviser in the kitchen, more of a Charlie Parker.'

'A book cook – I'll have to remember that. My wife never allowed me to take the helm in the kitchen – you know what women are like. She insisted on cooking every meal. Of course, I can open things and mix them together.'

He did not like the way Jan was looking at him.

'So what do you eat over there, Fred? At number 7?'

What did he eat? 'Well, I have a toasted-sandwich maker and plenty of cereal. Healthy cereal, like muesli, with fresh fruit and yoghurt. I love yoghurt. Like you! And I have … I have beans.'

'Beans?' said Jan quizzically. 'What sort of beans?'

'Large beans,' said Fred weakly. 'And small beans.'

'Can you read, Frederick?'

'Pardon?' he said.

'Can you read?'

'Of course I can read.' Did she have to be so blunt?

'Because cooking is as straightforward as reading and following instructions. I heard from Tom Chelmsley that you were an engineer? You should be fine with the technical side of cooking.'

'Tom had an accident. I saw him fall.' It came out like a confession to Father McMahon.

Jan set down her fork. 'I didn't want to mention it until after the pie. Is that wrong of me? I'm very upset about it. Actually, that's why I asked you in; I didn't want to be here alone. I'm very fond of Tom. We have coffee most mornings. I cook for him: the poor man misses his wife terribly and he's too old for cookbooks – not like you, Fred. Tom was married for sixty years. Can you imagine that? Poor Tom.'

Jan's eyes were watering. Fred had a large, juicy piece of chicken on the end of his fork, just ready to pop in his mouth. He was starving. He lowered his fork and tried to concentrate on Jan's face.

'Even though I complain, I like it here, in spite of the management. There's no maintenance, I feel safe and I've got friends if I need company. I can come and go as I please. But there's no escaping what's around the corner, and it gets me down.'

He nodded, and glanced quickly at the buttery pie on the end of his fork. Was it too soon to eat? Could he eat and listen?

'I think I must have been in the shower when he fell. They'd taken him away by the time I came out – I had the radio going and I had to wash my hair and, what with the birds, I missed the whole thing. Then Bernadette from number 10 called from the dining room to see if I'd go and check on Tom because he was late for lunch and they'd started on the soup. What's wrong? Are you all right, Fred? It's upsetting, I know.'

Fred jerked his head up. His gaze had fallen down to the pie again. 'I'm fine,' he said.

'I usually go in and see Tom in the late afternoon. I take him a plate of food if he's not up to going to the dining room. We have a cup of tea and I put on a load of washing. He really can't look after himself, but we don't want the bosses to know that. They'll have him out of there before you can say Jack Robinson. When he didn't answer his door I called the office, and they told me he'd had a bad fall and that it was you who called.'

Fred nodded.

'Thank god you happened to look in the quad at just the right time. He could have been out there in the heat for hours. That's the best thing about this place – you've got people looking out for you.'

Fred pushed his knife and fork into the finished position. He would not be able to eat his pie now.

'You can't be full? You can't leave it on the plate.'

'How is Tom? Have you heard anything?'

'Nothing. I hope he hasn't broken his hip. That would be the end of him in his villa. At his age you're never the same after an anaesthetic.'

'I think it was his head,' muttered Fred. He really needed to go home and lie down. 'I think he hit his head when he fell.'

'That doesn't sound good. What was he doing out there all by himself? Where was everyone? I can't believe no one saw him. He's not exactly the fastest man on a Zimmer; it must have taken him hours to get across the quadrangle. Why didn't someone go and help him, or call a gofer to pick him up? I'll put some plastic wrap on what's left of that pie. Just bring the plate back when you can.'

He sat while Jan cleared the plates and wiped down the table.

'Would you like tea?'

'No, thank you, Jan. I really have to go. Lunch was very nice.'

'You are most welcome. Next time I want to hear all about your engineering. What was your area? Structural? Mechanical? Electrical?'

'I was at the university. Concrete.'

'Concrete? Well, that must have been hard!'

'Pardon? Oh, I see. I'm a bit slow at jokes.'

'Obviously – not that it was particularly funny. I blame Sam – it didn't matter what I said, the man laughed. He thought I was a real comedienne. I can't tell you how much I miss that. Here's your plate, Fred – watch the edges, I don't think the plastic is stuck down properly. What I miss most is having someone who likes me to make them laugh, someone who thinks I'm funny. What about you, Fred?'

'Pardon?'

'Your wife's gone too, hasn't she? I hope you don't mind my asking.'

'Not at all. Martha, that was my wife's name. Martha Salomon. Until she married me, and then it was Lothian. Martha Lothian.'

'Martha. What a lovely name. I'm sure she was a wonderful woman.'

'Yes, she was. She was a wonderful woman.'

'How long has it been?'

'Two years or so.'

'Only yesterday, really. Samuel has been dead for four years, three months and twenty-two days. Tell me, what do you miss most?'

Something had set the budgies off again. It would be polite to ask about them – they obviously played a large part in Jan's life – but he wasn't really up to it. 'I miss it all, Jan.'

'Fair enough,' said Jan, as if she didn't mean it.

There were two photos on the wall near the front door. A fat baby was lying on its stomach on a sheepskin, stark naked except for a blue beanie with a logo from a football team Fred could not name. The second was the same boy, Fred guessed, aged about three. He was wearing oversized football shorts and holding a Sherrin ball.

'He's a mad Eagles fan. That's my only grandson, Morrison. He's five now.'

'Your daughter's child?' Fred wished he had missed the pictures completely, because soon the conversation would fold back towards him. He would be circled and targeted.

'My only son's boy.' She paused. 'He's dead.'

'Morrison is dead?' His voice sounded shrill and hysterical.

'No, not Morrison; my son, Paul.'

'Your son is dead?' What could he do but repeat her misery?

'A year ago on Friday. He was dead for a week and I didn't even know. He was a heroin addict. In the end I had to draw the line, for the sake of my sanity. We sent him to boarding school when we lived in Bangkok and Hubei. It was a terrible mistake. He fell in with the wrong crowd.'

'I understand,' said Fred. He thought of Katie.

'We should never have left him in that school.'

He ought to say more, but what could he say? 'It happened to our best friends' eldest daughter – many years ago. Her name was Katie. Katie Orr. It was a sad time for all of us.'

To his horror Jan's eyes welled with tears. 'Thank you,' she said quietly and opened the front door. 'The boy is with his mother now. But not for long.' She raised her eyebrows.

There was clearly more to the story, but it was definitely time for him to exit. 'Thank you again, Jan,' he said stiffly.

'You are most welcome, Fred. I look forward to our next meal. And I want to thank you.'

'Please,' said Fred. *Don't thank me,* he wanted to say. *I don't want to be thanked. I don't want us to owe each other anything.*

Jan waited at the door as Fred crossed the driveway towards his villa.

'Fred?' she called out.

He gave a little wave without looking back.

'Watch out for medium-sized grass-coloured sticks!'

Lunch had left him feeling undone. He stood at his front door, holding the plate with the slice of pie in one hand, his keys in the other. Jan's unit was the mirror image of his own, but they could not have been more different. He braced himself and opened the door.

It rose up to meet him as he stepped inside – his furniture, his books, his papers, the half-sorted boxes, the unwashed cups, clothes that needed washing, shirts that needed putting away. He fought his way into the laundry to retrieve the remote for the split. He hated reverse-cycle air conditioning; it was bad in summer, but far worse in winter. Warmth, he and Martha had always believed, emanated; it did not blow.

There was barely enough room in his small fridge for Jan's pie. The shelves and door were stacked with half-eaten jars of jam and pickles and spreads and chutneys. He kept buying condiments to dress up his slices of ham and cheese, but could never find one he really liked. The chicken in the meat drawer was out of date. There were cans of beetroot and jars of gherkins and prunes that Martha had bought and he had ferried across to his new fridge. He thought, *When those prunes were picked Martha was still alive.*

He was losing his marbles. He pushed the pie in on top of some jars. By his reckoning Jan would be in her late sixties or early seventies. Did he look older than her? 'You and the lady next door, you're our youngsters.' That's what the manager said when he moved in. Was it true, or do they say that to everyone to make them feel better? What time was it? He had lost track of time.

A giant cockroach climbed out of the cardboard box. Frederick slammed his foot down on the hard shell and wiped it off on the carpet. The damn thing was stuck to his shoe. He tried again, and managed to dislodge it. Soft, grey sludge was hanging out the side of the insect, but it was still alive. It was crawling away in desperation, like a mortally wounded adversary in a cowboy movie. He grabbed the paper off the table, rolled it up and brought it straight down on top of the filthy thing.

Martha wanted to have at least four children. He had wanted only one – so they could travel, he explained, and still have flexibility in their lives. Before she agreed to marry him she made him promise not to stand in her way. Four it was. After a barrage of tests and one terrible late-term miscarriage, they adopted Caroline. Two years later she was pregnant.

He turned the pages of the Saarinen book. He did not remember the mosaic tiles – he ought to remember something like that – and he could not recall any colour either, although in this photo the tiles around the pod were orange or yellow. His whole memory of the TWA Terminal was in black and white, as if it had been filtered through an abstract idea of the past.

He brought the book up to his face, in case there was a date on the information pod. It wasn't a pod at all. There was absolutely no relationship between the display board and a pod. There was a small vase of orange flowers on the counter near the two attendants in the photo, but that hardly justified calling it a pod. People stood in lines beneath a sign saying 'Ticket Lobby'. Above the atrium there was a coffee shop called the Paris Café. On another level was a restaurant and cocktail bar – the Lisbon Lounge. He looked very closely. How extraordinary. The seats were white with tulip bases. They were his seats. He and Martha had had a coffee there together, and then moved to the bar for a drink. He had a gin and tonic; she had a Manhattan.

Later, they had hamburgers. He changed his flight to Chicago and they spent the night at a hotel near the terminal. The radio station played Dylan's new album, *Blonde on Blonde*, from beginning to end, and then all over again. All night long. In the morning she left for her mother, and he went on to his conference.

Caroline heard a different version.

'So what did you do when you met, Dad? Did you kiss straight away, like in the movies?' Caroline giggled.

'We exchanged addresses – in those days you were more likely to write a letter than make a phone call. On my way back to England I stopped in New York to see her again.'

'What did you do, Dad?'

Sex. They had sex and sex and sex.

'I took your mother to dinner at the Four Seasons Restaurant, in the Seagram Building.'

'Wow. So I bet it was summer – or spring?'

'Pardon? Oh, I see.'

'Was meeting Mum exciting? Was it romantic?'

'Of course it was exciting. Now get ready for dinner. Go help your mother. Go.'

He looked at the clock. He wondered what Jan would make of his original George Nelson wall clock. The giant eyeball had always made him nervous. It was a parting gift from the chief architect when he finished the cathedral. Had the man suspected he had slept with his wife? Was it a message? Caroline hated it. She always said it gave her the creeps. If nobody really liked it, why didn't he just get rid of it?

How could he explain his loyalty to objects? Yes, his pieces were classics, but holding on to them was also some kind of penance, something to be endured, like crawling on your knees at the Shrine of Our Lady of Fatima. He needed to talk to someone about this, but who? Caroline? Why didn't he just call her? Nothing felt right. Tom had fallen over. The woman next door had given him pie. But he couldn't call Caroline, because it was her turn to call. If he called her now it would disturb the precarious balance of things. Caroline needed him at least as much as he needed her, and a break in routine might signify a shift, and at his age any shift had to mean a decline. That was why he refused to move out of the family home for so long. A whole year and a quarter he held out, enduring Caroline's phone calls and whirlwind visits. She swept by and whisked him off to see coastal developments aimed at the over-55s, all of them a series of worn-out nouns modified by exhausted adjectives – Secret Harbour, Hidden Sanctuary, Golden Sands, Sunset Strip. After forty minutes or so she would slow down, pull in for a coffee, and wait for him to insist it was too far away.

Deep down his daughter was in agreement: why would you move to the end of the earth to die when you could do it in the convenience of your own home? That was what he was doing now, here in his unit: he was dying. The villa was a bridge between his real life, which had ended, and death, which waited behind a wall of paperbacks on the other side of the quadrangle. He had finished accumulating experiences, and now he was shuffling around in the past, peeking inside boxes and then closing them quickly. Moving to St Sylvan's had cemented his fate.

In the end, Caroline gave up on the drives and sent him

brochures and websites for new developments, begging him to look at the plans and choose. He read them to find out what they were up to in the retirement village game. Maximising profits and putting a strong case for three- and four-storey developments. Secure, easy-care. Most of the newer apartments had two bedrooms, each with their own ensuite bathroom. He had assumed that this was to allow for visits from friends and family, but then a salesman explained that at his age most couples were more comfortable with a room of their own.

'Lets everyone get a good night's sleep,' he explained. Was it true? Was this what older couples wanted? To leave each other alone?

He was out cycling when he saw this place for sale – single level, mature trees out the front, a little older than most, but close to the family home, which he wasn't quite ready to sell. Not yet. He would have the house painted and recarpeted and rent it out, he explained to Caroline. He would keep an eye on the place, and if she ever were to, you know ...

'What? Settle down? Have a family?'

'Caroline, it's not out of the question. Don't look at me like that.'

'Dad, I'm single and on my way to forty. I don't like men any more.'

For a long time there was Julian. In the end he left her for a twenty-six-year-old postgrad. Julian was a theorist, whatever that was. Good-looking idiot, if you liked a man who wore 'product' in his hair. With this new research project it could only get worse. How would Caroline ever meet anyone, flying around the world in search of stuffed animals? And what if she met someone overseas? She might never come back; he might never see his daughter again, which was exactly what Miriam had said when Martha announced she was marrying an Englishman and migrating to Australia. 'Migration? Americans don't migrate. We're the place people migrate *to*. Why would anyone want to leave America? I'll never see my daughter again!'

Great-Aunt Marjorie must have felt like that when he left her that afternoon in Aberfeldy. He bought her lunch at the Palace Hotel and helped her home in the rain. She was tiny and frail, like a little canary, and when he finally said goodbye, she wrapped her knobbly fingers around his hand and held on for a very long time.

'Freddy, when you have all those little babies, you bring them back to me, won't you?'

He promised, and he broke his promise.

The past was rattling its bones and ringing its jangly bells. Residents at St Sylvan's were scared witless of losing their memory, but wasn't it so much more terrifying to put up with its eternal return?

They had the same picture in all the brochures: a still-handsome older man sits in the shade of a generous verandah, smiling contentedly as his grandchildren play in the large garden. On one side of him sits his trim, well-preserved wife (good teeth, modern haircut), on the other the faithful golden retriever. The children are tearing barefoot across the grass, rushing towards the future, while the older couple are centre frame, like the sun, happy to sit there all day long doing a bit of straightforward remembering. *Darling, remember when …?*

But memory did not work that way. The path back to the TWA Terminal and to Martha Salomon was not a road or a bridge, or any kind of straight line. Memory was more Russian than that; it was more like Vladimir Shukhov's hyperbolic paraboloid. He had seen this for himself in Moscow, in the bustling neighbourhood of Shabolovka. Shukhov's structure was thin and light. Like the tube walls of Fazlur Khan's skyscrapers, their strength came from interconnectedness and dependency, from the mesh, not from the two static pillars of the present and the

Башня системы пин.В.Г.Шухова для безпроволоч. телеграфа высокаго 350 m.

past pretending to hold the whole thing up. *Terminus a quo, terminus ad quem.* The starting point and the end point.

'If man were to live and work in cities in the sky,' he told his students at the start of his lecture on tubing and skyscrapers, 'then he had to learn to manage lateral load.'

But how was a man to withstand forces you could not measure?

Fred pulled back the curtain. Tom's Zimmer frame was still lying on its side in the grass. You could land a small plane on that grass – not a jet, although he would like to see that, but some kind of nimble biplane. It could almost taxi right up to his window. He would pick up his navy-blue overnight bag and duck past the beating propellers, climb in and fly all the way back to Martha. But he would do it differently this time.

Were there really people in the world who could say 'No, I

wouldn't change a thing'? He would give anything to be one of those people.

Soon he would ring the hospital for news of Tom. Tom was the first, but all of his merry band of villagers were passengers in transit. After lifetimes of consuming and hoarding they had set off on their final journey and were travelling light. They had sold their family homes and redistributed the cash to help the kids with their ill-advised mortgages, freeing up leafy older suburbs for rezoning and battle-axing. They were moving on so that others might move on in. It was the sort of altruism championed by estate agents. His fellow travellers were making life easy for the kids, ruthlessly culling and cataloguing, and turning the debris out on the verge for the bi-annual council pick-up. 'We'd never want to be a burden,' was the smug mantra over lunch and a few white wines at the Gerry.

But not Frederick Lothian. Oh no, no, no. He was digging in with his Breuer and his Braun and the books and the pictures and the paintings and the letters and the filing cabinets and the Samoan bark paintings, not to mention the flokatis and the kilims and Rose Levy Beranbaum's *Cake Bible* and the Boda ironware and Martha's mother's copy of Blu Greenberg's classic *How to Run a Traditional Jewish Household* and the chipped orange Le Creuset set that was a wedding present from Martha's mother. The past was right here in front of him, piling up under the bed, along the walls, stacked one box on top of the other, and woe betide anyone who tried to take it away. Occasionally a brave traveller from the committee would stick their head in to see if that new fellow in number 7 was up for a bit of OT in the function room – 'just to keep the joints oiled!' 'How about a minibus to the casino, Fred?' They got a quick look at the furniture and the boxes, and their brows would knit and they would think the better of saying anything because, really, it was none of their business if Fred Lothian had a crock of funny furniture, all of it the worse for wear, and if Fred didn't want to play dominoes or blackjack that was fine too, because it was his house and it was a free country. 'Tooroo, Fred!'

It would not be by bridge or plane that he would depart, but by an ambulance travelling well within the speed limit, its siren discreetly muted. He would not go quietly, though. He had made quite sure of that.

Fred folded the paper on the table and put it near the front door. Poor little David Michael. He lifted last week's newspaper off the answering machine and turned the machine on. The light began to flash. He pushed the button. 'You have five messages.'

'Fred, it's Roger Wu from the department. I can't believe you've actually got your machine on. You're a hard man to reach. I'm wondering if you could give me a call. We're running a project for the graduate workshop and we'd love your input. Plus, the department's got a very exciting proposal for you. We won't let you say no!'

'Mr Lothian, this is Nathan Hamilton from Mateera Realty. I've been trying to reach you in person but I'm not having much luck. I wanted to let you know that your tenants have broken their lease. I wonder if you could come into the office to sort out the bond and sign some papers to get it back on the market? Give me a call and we'll make a time.'

'Nathan Hamilton here –'

'Mr Lothian, hello, it's Jane from Mateera Realty. Nathan asked me –'

'Hello, Fred, it's me again, Roger. I'm going to –' Delete. Delete. Delete.

Almost immediately the phone rang. Should he pick it up? Roger had been his last PhD student before he left the university, and even after all these years he liked to surprise Fred with a query about some technical issue. But that Nathan Hamilton was the last person in the world he wanted to talk to. Apparently he had once been a famous football player, but Fred had never heard of him. The phone persisted. *It might be about Tom*, he thought suddenly. He picked it up.

'Frederick Lothian.'

'Mr Lothian?'

'Speaking.' He heard a shuffle of papers. 'Is this about Tom?' he asked.

'Tom? I'm sorry?'

'Tom Chelmsley? The man who fell? I made the initial call.'

'This is Nicola Masterson, Mr Lothian. I'm the manager of the Sir Charles Court Care Facility. I'm calling with regard to Callum.'

'Callum,' he repeated.

'Your son is Callum Lothian? I have you here as the emergency contact.'

'Emergency,' Fred repeated.

'I don't mean to alarm you. Emergency is a technical term only –'

'Caroline,' he interrupted. 'You must call Caroline.'

'Let me explain, please. I have a note on file from Caroline saying that you should be contacted. It says here, let me see, "Next of kin is in London."'

'London, that's correct. My daughter has a laptop computer with her and a phone. I have the details.' Frederick cradled the earpiece between his shoulder and neck and opened the kitchen drawer. He rummaged frantically through peelers and scissors and old video rental cards for his address book.

'Are you ready? Here's her number.' He opened the back cover and read off the twelve digits.

'But Mr Lothian –'

'Thank you for calling, Ms Masterson,' he said.

'Mr Lothian, your son is –'

He pulled the socket out of the wall. Soon it would be dark and he could turn off the air conditioner and open the window. Jan's birdies would go home to their perches for the night. The villagers would pair up for their suburban walks. Over on the decrepit ward the nurses would be sorting out the evening meds.

He looked up at the metal eye. In London it would soon be morning.

'Ring, ring,' he whispered. And then he closed his eyes.

BOOK 2

Bridges

Monday, 16 January 2006

MONDAY WAS THE DAY Fred always walked along the fore-shore, so he managed to get out of bed before midday. He had hardly slept a wink. *Thinking* had usurped sleeping, although you could hardly call it thought. Thinking was not supposed to be disconnected from the person doing it. In Frederick's profession thought had to be marshalled by the thinker and carefully directed at something in particular, like an arrow at a target. Engineers were trained to think in context, to imagine in situ, but now renegade thoughts had infiltrated his brain. They were masked insurgents, hooded terrorists who came ashore under the cover of darkness, paddling in quietly with their bombs deep in their pockets and their bullets on their belts.

At the river he found a parking space under a tree. A pale-blue VW Kombi pulled up right next to him and the door flew open to release a large black dog. It was the sort of dog a family should own – a loping, smiling, licking dog – a Labrador-cross? A girl and a boy climbed down, and then leant against the car door. She took a packet of tobacco from her pocket and began to roll a cigarette. Ralph used to smoke cigarettes like that, and Fred always suspected him of being a secret pot smoker. Towards the end of a four-bottle night his former friend would make a big fuss about heading off to find the 'baccy', defusing its toxic reality with a bit of chummy vernacular. He would come back to the table with the leather pouch and fiddle around with the papers, turning the tobacco round and round until it was just right, and then running his tongue down the length of the white stick. 'You're not thinking of smoking that in here,' Martha would say, and Ralph would just lean back in his chair and strike a match. Martha's father had died of lung cancer when she was nineteen. She hated smoking.

The boy came up behind the girl and took the cigarette, running his hand inside the back of her T-shirt. Fred caught sight of a band of pale flesh and the edge of a black bra strap. She laughed and stole a quick look at him, then pressed herself into the boy. Fred turned away and saw the dog race to the edge of the limestone wall and brace itself, as if it were about to leap into the shallow water.

Warm, smooth, elastic skin. When was the last time he touched the skin of another human being? His own flaking epidermis was more like parchment than skin, more like the dry and yellowed pages of a textbook that no one would ever read again about a country that no longer existed. But you couldn't compare the human body to a country, could you? The disappearance of a country was a good thing, at least in the late twentieth century. Why would anyone want to bring back Rhodesia? That was another thing he couldn't stand – the way everyone acted as if the past were *golden*. Most of the books he read as a child were cruel, stupid stories full of gollies and blackies and huge boiling pots ringed by naked cannibals, readying themselves for the arrival of a delicious European. Dead and gone for ever – and good riddance too. Of course, Martha had never agreed with expunging the record. 'That's what they do in communist countries,' she said when the local library sent a circular announcing they were going through the collection with a fine-tooth comb to rid themselves of offensive titles. 'It's a whiteout. You've read Milan Kundera – or pretended to read him. This is how totalitarian dictatorships function – they just pretend it didn't happen!'

Frederick disagreed. He didn't want his daughter going

to the library and coming home with some book that had 'piccaninnies' playing in lily ponds, and 'natives' tossing their boomerangs into the sunset. He didn't want her to see those terrible words underneath the pen-and-ink drawings: 'gin', 'lubra', 'half-caste'.

'That's all very well, Martha, if you're reading those old books with the intention of talking about them in a class, putting them in context, so to speak, but what about when children go and choose their own books? What happens when they stumble across this material?'

'Don't "so to speak" me, Fred Lothian. Don't "context" me. I'm going to complain, and that's that.'

The couple had dragged a large branch to the edge of the river. The boy heaved it into the water, and they both clapped and whistled when the dog launched itself off the wall and paddled madly after it, then tried to scramble up the steps with the log in its mouth. The boy took off his T-shirt and stretched towards the sky. He was lean and thin and loose in the joints, as young men were meant to be. When he held his arms above his head, his board shorts slid down his narrow hips. When Martha was dying her skin began to soften and separate from her body in soft folds and drapes, like muslin, as if it were getting ready to shroud her body.

As if, as if, as if – was there some genetic connection between old age and 'as if'? He'd had about enough of 'as if'. It had begun when Martha died. It was *as if* he began to drift, *as if* he could no longer see things as they really were, but only through the fog of what they were not. At first he thought his turn from reality might be a *paradox*. Or was it a *metaphor*? He spent hours in the reference section of the library and emerged none the wiser. Engineers were not supposed to concern themselves with figures of speech. The entire profession had sworn off it and devoted itself to the literal business of getting things done. They had handed the whole sticky business of metaphor – or whatever it was – over to the architects, who took to it like fish to bait.

'We're employing the metaphor of flight in the concept drawing for the new airport administration wing,' Ralph announced at one of his Friday dinners. Fred was aware that architects loved to grab hold of the closest metaphor at hand to give their projects a bit of lift, but this time Ralph had gone too far.

'But why is that a metaphor, Ralph? It's an airport. Flight is what airports are about. It's obvious. Why do you think they call it a *new wing*? These so-called metaphors are just a cheap way of translating complex briefs into something the client can drop into their PR material. Surely a great building speaks for itself through its design and structural resolve.'

'Poor old Fred, you're such a grinch. Isn't he, Martha? I don't know how he makes you happy. The idea of a wing has got nothing to do with airports. You should know that, Fred. It's Roman – Vitruvius. It comes from the theatre. I don't recall there being any large airports in the first century BC, but correct me if I'm wrong. A glass of Pommery, anyone?'

How could you actually use metaphors to *think* if you ended up thinking about something altogether different from what you started with? A metaphor was like the end of an electrical bundle that had lost its plastic coating: instead of nice thick, red lines of wire leading to a socket or another circuit you had a chaos of fraying ends writhing about one another, like the tentacles of a giant squid. There you go, he'd done it again – a simile this time. The field was laden with cliché. Even he could see that.

The young couple were just ahead of him on the path, arm in arm, falling about each other like puppies. Their dog was meaningfully engaged in chasing down a tiny white poodle on a long lead, sending the poodle into a dizzy frenzy. The poodle was indistinct, *like a cloud, like a dandelion in a breeze.*

Stalked by the ghost of his own unoriginality. Every day it was the same. He woke up – if he had slept at all – with an uneasy feeling in the pit of his stomach, and the distinct sense that there was something obscure, malevolent and obsessive lying in wait for him, ready to ambush him when he was at his weakest. Thoughts were ghosts. They were zombies. They wafted about in the white heat and dark stillness of St Sylvan's Retirement Village, tapping on windows, whispering forgotten lines, staging scenes that were supposed to have been deleted from the script long ago.

Once upon a time he would never have been without a pencil and paper, in case he was called upon to calculate the axial and buckling compression of a column, or to devise an algorithm for the distribution of weight across a span. In the field of engineering thought led to action, at least somewhere down the line. But his pencil was gone. The House of Frederick was empty, hollow, osteoporotic. Was that a word? It was now. He stole a glance behind him. The only way of knowing there had even been a real thought anywhere near was the feeling left behind, like mud on a boot proving there was a walk in the rain, or the imprint of a finger on a glass proving the presence of an intruder.

The couple from the Kombi were lying on the grass in the

fitful shade of a casuarina tree. He threw his leg across her and they hinged into each other, like a giant clam on the ocean floor. Their mouths opened and she ran her tongue over his lips. Frederick quickened his pace.

Sex. Sex was like New York: never again.

Sex with Martha had always been troubling. After the children were older (who had time for anything when you had very young children?), she would go through periods of studied passion. After working late he would come home exhausted and tiptoe into the bedroom in the darkness, trying not to disturb her. Just as he sank his head onto the pillow in relief, she would throw on the reading light to reveal elaborate pink panties and lacy padded bras that elevated and exaggerated her small breasts. Where did women find such things? But these intermittent periods of erotic hijacking would give way to months of unbroken droughts, where she would pull away from him and dismiss his attempts at foreplay.

'I just feel like talking,' she would say. 'We never talk any more.' Talking was the last thing Fred felt like doing after a day with his postgrads.

'We never *stop* talking, Martha.'

'I don't mean about the children, or Ralph and Veronica, or my mother, or the fucking pool and how the Kreepy Krauly keeps getting stuck on the bottom so the filter fills up with leaves from that tree you were supposed to trim last autumn, I mean *really* talk.'

Some nights he would find her awake in the dark. When he reached for her, she would flinch.

'I'm sorry, Fred, do you mind? I'm thinking.'

A large March fly would not leave him alone. He pulled a strand of bark off a peppermint tree. Who says things like that? Martha always had trouble with her thinking. But then women were so easily distracted. Martha loved to think, and there was absolutely no doubt that she was a clever woman, but she had never been able to *apply* her thinking in a sustained way. If engineering had taught him anything, it was that thinking had to be firmly laminated to the project at hand. Martha had never been able to finish that degree. She was incapable of attaining the focus and application necessary to complete anything of significance.

'I can't think straight, Fred,' she called out from the kitchen table where she was working on an assignment. She had left her books to stand at the door of his study. 'It's chaos in this house. Didn't you hear the washing machine beeping? Couldn't you just go and open the door? One of us has to pick up Callum from the Bessells'. Did you even remember he was going back there after hockey? They can't drop him off because their car is being serviced. Do I have to remember everything? Do I have to worry about it all?'

But Martha liked to worry; worry was what Martha did best. If it wasn't the washing or the cooking, she would worry about the entire world. 'Oh, Frederick, the world is such a terrible place,' she would say mournfully, putting down her books and her papers.

'Could you be more specific, darling?'

The giant fly moved as slowly as a zeppelin, but still he couldn't manage to dispatch it. If Martha had been a writer of fiction, or some kind of poet (god forbid), she might have found something to do with all those ideas that scrambled around in her head and came pouring out willy-nilly. She did it to spite him, he was sure of it. He would be in the living room, absorbed in reading a journal or writing a lecture, while Martha was in the kitchen and then all of a sudden a thought – any thought – would pop into her head and she would have to think it out loud.

'I think I'll do a roast chicken for dinner, Fred. What do you think? Or maybe we should have pasta? But do we have any pasta? Let me see … No, all gone. We do have tortillas, though. Chicken tortillas … but are there any cans of tomato?'

'Do you have to think out loud?'

'Pardon?'

He gathered up his papers and put them in his briefcase.

'I think I'll go into work for a while. I have to finish the paper for the Brisbane conference and I need to send it off. What time's dinner?'

'You have your own office here at home, you know. You have a room all to yourself upstairs. I've never understood why you have to work in the lounge, right next to where I'm cooking. I can't even listen to my radio because you're *just there*. I hate you sitting *just there*, thinking about pre-stressed concrete or hyperbolic structures or global fault lines while I'm over here chopping capsicums.'

'It's *hyperboloid*, not *hyperbolic*, and am I really disturbing you, Martha? Am I doing a single thing to disrupt you, just sitting over here quietly, working away?'

'It's the juxtaposition of you and me, Fred, and the hierarchy implicit in that juxtaposition.'

'I have no idea what you're talking about, Martha. None whatsoever. Did you hear that in your latest psychology lecture?'

He squinted into the sun. He should have brought his hat with him. It was already far too hot for walking. It ought to be too hot for thinking too, but the thought had already landed heavily and stopped him in his tracks: why hadn't he got up to chop the capsicums? Why hadn't he offered to go to the shops for the tomatoes? Why hadn't he gone up to his study to work?

Why the truth? Why now?

The truth was, he hated being alone. That was the real reason he was in the lounge room and not in his study. He found it almost impossible to work upstairs. He felt lonely in his study. He left the door ajar to hear what they were all saying, and then yelled at them to keep it down. He hated sleeping alone too. When Martha went to Melbourne he was bereft.

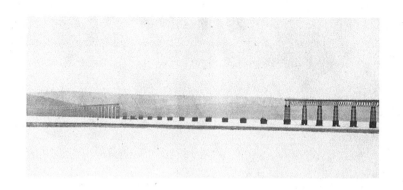

When he was little he had always slept with Virgil, and when Virgil was no longer there, he pretended he was. He continued to tell Virgil off when he didn't wash his hands before dinner. He kept two pillows on his bed and slept right up against the wall, so Virgil would have enough room. He held Virgil's hand when he walked to school. 'Look and look again,' he whispered as they stepped across a road. He couldn't remember when the imaginary Virgil left for good, but one day he woke up and the bed was empty.

He picked up a plastic water bottle and looked for a bin. Martha connected him to the earth, like a button to a jacket. *That's what a family is for,* he thought. *A family pins a man's thoughts to the earth, like a pylon grounds a bridge.*

Frederick wiped his face. He was covered in sweat. One more terrible thought was slowly taking shape, a figure in the distance advancing on the path. And there it was, as clear as the dark lines on a plan drawing: what use are thoughts without someone specific to think about?

Despite the heat, despite the fly he began to walk. It was a high tide, and rust-coloured water lapped listlessly at the cap of the limestone wall. A pod of brown jellyfish pulsed in the shallows.

The black dog tore past him on its way to retrieve yet

another stick. A pile of dried blow fish was stacked up on the edge of the path, left over from a failed fishing expedition. Another fly went up his left nostril. Two women came storming past in their black Lycra gear, red-faced, arms pumping.

'I said to her homeroom teacher, can you please give her some extra work? When clever kids get bored, they're bound to act up.'

'Good on you, Emma. Poor Hannah, she's struggling. I'm not sure what to do next.'

'Even with a full-time aide? I don't know how you manage, Kathy. I'm sure I couldn't.'

A concentration of quivering water in the shallows at the edge, then a dark, elongated mass.

An enormous dolphin swam in a sinusoid wave along the wall, its fin just breaking the surface, so close he could have reached out and touched the sleek skin. The dolphin began to pick up speed and Frederick followed, keeping pace until it slid to a sudden stop and lifted up its snub nose. The viscous eye kept watch as he sunk first to his knees and then onto his belly with his head and shoulders protruding just over the edge of the parapet. 'Hello,' he said, close enough to kiss the animal on the snout.

The dolphin blinked, raising and lowering its eyelids. Dolphins had eyelids? It blinked again, to prove its point. The dolphin held its mouth ajar in a half-smile, revealing a row of small, conical teeth, like blunt splinters. What was it thinking? Dolphins were clever, but did they stop to think? The dolphin shook its head, declining a conference on the subject. Perhaps it was waiting for him to do the talking. But what do you say to a dolphin you've only just met?

The dolphin pressed onward. Frederick clambered to his feet. He kept up in a stiff-legged jog, ligaments aching, lungs burning, his efforts punctuated by the puff and whoop of the animal's breath. Its tail pulsed up and down, up and down. From

the camber of its backbone he saw that a dolphin bends verti-
cally, like a dog or a horse, not at all like the tail of a fish that
moves sideways to give it lateral thrust. Why had engineering
taught him nothing about dolphins?

Just as Fred could go on no more, the animal leapt into
the air in a sleek, plastic-laminated arch and headed into deep
water, leaving him too exhausted to think but nevertheless
feeling something altogether original. Fred had glimpsed perfection. He looked out into deep water, in case the dolphin
surfaced, and managed to pick out a curved fin in the distance.
It was heading west, towards the river mouth and the Indian
Ocean. That animal knew where it was going. If only he did
too.

It was mid-afternoon when he got home. Jan was standing at
her front door. What was she doing out in the heat? He waved
as he drove in and waited impatiently for the garage door. He
needed water. He parked and got out of the car, and when he
turned around she was still there.

'I've been waiting for you,' she called out, coming towards
him. 'You're all red in the face. You should wear a hat in this
weather.'

Fred did not like the idea of Jan waiting for him. She
wouldn't expect him to cook for her, would she? That was the
trouble with gifts and friends – they got you all caught up with
returning the favour.

'Tom Chelmsley's dead.'

'What?' he said faintly, walking from the garage towards
Jan's front door. How could Tom be dead when only yesterday
he was alive? How could he die when Fred was planning to
visit him this afternoon? He was going to stop at the shops and
pick up a tin of Walker's shortbread. He was going to read Tom
something he would like. *The Thirty-Nine Steps*. 'Clancy of the
Overflow'.

Jan met him halfway to her house. 'Tom and I spent most of last week playing euchre. I can't believe he's gone.'

'Pardon? Shall we have a cup of tea?'

'Can we go to your place? Do you mind? I think I need to be away from old memories.'

'Of course,' said Fred, turning around. Of course I mind. Did he have fresh milk? Sugar? Was the kitchen table clear? It was impossible not to imagine the interior of his unit through Jan's eyes: the house of a madman.

'Your poor wife,' Jan said with a smile, as she looked around his lounge room

What the hell did that mean? He ignored her and carried the newspapers and cups from the table.

'You have too many things in here. It's much worse than I imagined. You've got to cull – dreadful word, I know, but this kind of furniture is just not suited to this style of unit. You need to think compact in these small spaces. Think Japanese.'

'My wife collected modern furniture, mostly Danish,' he said stiffly. 'I'm not quite ready to let it all go.' That should keep her quiet. And what did she mean, 'worse than I imagined'? Why was she imagining the interior of his house at all? He hated the idea of anyone imagining his house. Let her imagine her own house.

Jan ran her hand along the top of his Børge Mogensen cabinet.

'There's a strong Japanese influence in this modern furniture, isn't there? It's a pity all the pieces are so large.'

She looked at her palm and rubbed it against her skirt. No, he hadn't dusted lately.

'My husband and I loved Japan, but you wouldn't find this clutter in a Japanese home. Yes, please, milk and sugar. And look at all these boxes! What's in them? Books? A professor must have his books. You've even brought your old filing cabinet. Is it full of old papers from work? We're retired now, Fred. That part of our lives is over. Filing cabinets are like tombs. Metal tombs. Sarcophagi. Is that the plural?'

'I have no idea,' said Fred tightly. He carried a tray to the table. The milk was on the edge. He hoped she wouldn't notice.

'So many boxes. Buddhists say you have to be careful your possessions don't end up possessing you. What have you got in all those cartons out in the garage? There are dozens of them. More books?'

'Most of that belongs to my daughter. She's overseas at the moment. The rest of it is Martha's collections.'

'What kind of things did your wife collect, besides furniture?'

'Postwar electrical appliances, actually. Mainly German. They're becoming very sought after.'

'Is that right, Fred? What kind of things are we talking about? What brands?'

'Braun is the most famous.' He would prefer to get off the topic.

'How valuable? I must tell the women down at the Salvos. I volunteer once a month and we see all kinds of things. We're not allowed to sell electrical goods, so if they're donated we have to throw them away. You do mean Braun as in the Braun men's shaver? They made a good coffee grinder, too.'

Fred nodded. That kettle was taking for ever.

'Samuel had one of their shavers, I'm sure of it. What a pity I threw it out. I could have sold it to the highest bidder. I couldn't stand the blunt little hairs it sprayed all over the bathroom, so I got him on to disposables. I know they're not good for the environment, but at least they don't leave a mess.'

'Would you like something with your tea?' Not that he had anything to offer.

'Your wife must have been an interesting woman. The things she collected! Electrical appliances …'

'Martha had broad interests.'

'I'd love a yoghurt, actually.'

'A yoghurt?'

'I remember you saying you lived on yoghurt. Yoghurt and beans, I think it was. It's a bit early in the day for a bean, so it will have to be a yoghurt.'

'I'm so sorry, Jan, but it's shopping day and I've run out of yoghurt. And beans.'

'What a pity.' Jan smiled at him like a cat.

The woman was unbearable. 'When did you hear about Tom?'

'This morning, very early. I asked Eileen to let me know if she heard anything. You did know that she and Tom were brother and sister?'

'I had no idea.' He had no idea who Eileen was, but he would rather keep that from Jan.

'That's strange, what with you and Tom being next-door neighbours. He never mentioned her? She lives down the other end in number 16.'

'He might have said he had a sister; yes, I'm sure he did. He said it was wonderful to have family here.'

'How odd. Neither of them could say a good word about the other. Mortal enemies. You do know Eileen, don't you? Small woman with a walking stick, wears houndstooth skirts and flouncy nylon shirts with floppy bows at the neck?'

Fred moved his head in an ambiguous circular direction.

'Is that a yes or a no? She's always neat as a pin. She and Tom came in together, but they didn't see eye to eye so she stayed at one end of the village, he at the other, and they never spoke. They had a lot to say about each other, though. Apparently there was an uncle with money. He had sheep and wheat properties out past Morawa. When he died he bypassed the niece – that was Eileen – and left it to his only nephew, Tom. Eileen was a very promising ballet dancer, but the family couldn't afford to send her to Sydney for more training so she had to quit and get married instead. She never forgave the family and always blamed Tom.'

'Fascinating,' said Fred.

Jan laughed. 'You are droll, aren't you? Eileen is inconsolable now, of course. It's all forgiven and forgotten. I'll go over there this evening and take her some dinner. Why don't you come with me? She has a passion for crochet unparalleled in the village. Personally, I hate crochet, but Eileen lifts it to a whole other level.' She paused to take a sip of tea. 'I think your milk's on the way out. Eileen has a wonderful photo of herself as a young woman in pointe shoes and a tutu. It took me a while, but you can see it's Eileen, even though it was more than seventy-five years ago. She's over ninety, you know. Eileen has crocheted a pair of ballet shoes and then done something with starch to make them stiff and had one of the old fellows with a garage make a plinth to display them on. She's done the same thing for some of the residents. She's starching up tiny jackets and newborn booties that they knitted for their grandchildren, and mounting them on plinths. Can you imagine?'

No, he could not imagine. His head was spinning.

'I'm sorry if I talk too much. That's what happens when you live alone – as soon as you get company you can't shut up. At least I can't.'

'Tom?' he said weakly.

'Poor Tom. I called you to tell you but the phone rang out. Where were you at 6 am? Unplugged? I thought you might have had a fall, but then I thought, *If I go and knock he might be sleeping, or on the toilet.* I'd be so embarrassed if you were sitting on the loo – when you get to our age I know how long it can take to –'

For god's sake. 'Did he suffer? Did Tom suffer?'

'He was in a coma when I first rang, so I suppose he didn't *suffer*, no, but that doesn't make it any easier for the people who cared about him. I call that a "palliative statement". Most people suffer, one way or another. Did your wife suffer?'

'Yes,' he said defensively, 'Martha suffered a great deal.'

'I'm sorry to hear that, Fred. Was it cancer?'

'A brain tumour.'

'Samuel was cancer of the stomach, but he'd had dementia for some years. It was worse because he didn't understand why he was in pain.'

They drank their tea in silence.

'You know, Fred, I hope you don't mind me saying this ...' Jan paused.

Would he have to respond? He was exhausted.

'I just can't imagine a woman collecting this furniture. It seems so masculine, more like office furniture. It belongs in some New York apartment, not in a family home. It's so impractical with children. It seems so unlike a woman. How many children do you have, Fred?'

'Do women always have to be practical, Jan? Don't you think that's a bit old-fashioned? Of course, as well as her collections of furniture and, er ...'

'Shavers?'

'Electronics, she collected ceramics. Martha loved knitting and cooking too.'

Jan raised an eyebrow. 'A real woman then, despite being impractical.' She put down her empty cup and rubbed her temples. 'I'm sorry, Fred, I'm being rude. I'm not myself today.'

Fred cleared the cups off the table, hoping Jan would see this as a sign she should leave.

'Do you want me to go?'

'Of course not, Jan, stay as long as you like.'

'I can't stay long because I have an appointment this afternoon.'

Fred rinsed the teacups and stacked them upside down in the drainer. The strainer in the sink was blocked with the remains of last night's dinner – two chops and boiled peas. At the super-market he had been ashamed of his basket. If he'd had a cloth he would have draped it across the top, like Father McMahon would do when he finished with the transubstantiation and was left once more with red wine and a bit of flat bread. Last week at the supermarket checkout he had been surrounded by women with little children whining and pulling and pleading for Kinder Surprises while their mothers navigated vast shopping trolleys of giant cereal boxes and strawberry-swirl ice-cream and shampoo and disposable nappies and watermelon and a new copy of *Nemo* because the other one had worn out, and goodness me, what do we have here – an old man holding up the queue, fumbling for his wallet, with a basket half-full of one loaf of white toasting bread, a bag of frozen peas, a single roll of toilet paper, a small square of low-fat mince covered with cling wrap, and two lamb chops, trimmed of excess fat.

He tapped the peas out in the bin, replaced the strainer and began to wipe the cups.

'It's in the city. I have to be there by 2 pm.'

One of the pair had a chip. This afternoon he would go up to the Lakes and buy two new mugs.

'I have to be at the Law Courts.'

The underground parking at the Lakes was always full on hot days. It might be better to wait until the morning and get there early.

'It's about Morrison. My son's boy – my grandson.'

Weren't there some loose cups in one of Martha's boxes? Wouldn't it be better to use them than have them sitting there?

'I took a DNA test.'

But which box was it? The laundry or the bedroom? Or was it in the garage?

'What kind of person are you?'

Frederick jumped. Jan's face was flushed, and her mouth was open. Her chest was rising and falling.

He stepped past her towards the B3. His knees gave out ten centimetres above the leather seat and he landed hard. 'What DNA?' he said.

'To prove I am who I say I am – Morrison's grandmother. His mother took off to Bangkok and left the boy at home. He was left all alone, Fred. He's only five. Five years old.'

'When was this?'

'Just last week. On Tuesday. They found him after I called the police when I couldn't get hold of them. I'd tried for two days. Her mobile phone was always out of credit or hocked, and she used to head off down south with Morrison to see her sister, but this time I had a feeling, and thank god, I went with it. They had to break the lock to get in. She must have owed money and got scared. I should have gone over there myself as soon as I couldn't reach them, but I'd turned my ankle on that step outside and couldn't take a bus. Tom wasn't up to driving me and I didn't know who to ask.'

Jan looked like she was on the verge of tears. Fred could not bear it when women cried. It was so – *demanding*.

'I was too embarrassed to ask for a lift. Can you believe that? I could have taken a taxi, but I have this ridiculous thing about them. As soon as I get in a taxi I start thinking about murder. Do you remember when all those girls were murdered? They've never found the person who did it, but they always thought it was a taxi driver. Every time I get in a taxi and look at the driver I know that he didn't do it, but then I think of their parents, and how they must feel after all these years. They must be getting on now – they'll need a daughter to look after them. My son died, but that was different; he murdered himself. But that poor girl. Can you imagine losing a child like that?'

Frederick rubbed his kneecaps. Perhaps. Perhaps he could imagine it.

'I was too ashamed to even ask a friend to drive me. I didn't want anyone to know what had happened to Paul, and now my grandson. The Stokeses in number 2 would have done it. They're big in Rotary, and she's got a knitting charity that makes dolls for Africa. Mind you, I'm not so sure that woollen dolls is what they need most – I sponsor two kids, but it's for the basics so they can get to school and eat.'

Frederick massaged his shins.

'He was there for two days, all by himself. He lived on a block of cheese and dried pasta. He tried to add water to the pasta to get it to soften, and apparently it does begin to absorb water. He's quite the scientist. Luckily there was no gas on, or he might have tried to cook something. She hadn't paid the gas bill and they'd turned it off. The toilet was all blocked up and the place stank to high heaven. The police said it looked like he'd tried to make his bed.'

Jan wore black mascara around her very green eyes. Martha never wore make-up. 'A waste of money,' she said, but then Martha was very beautiful. It was easy for beautiful women to say things like that.

'I think I might use the bathroom, Fred. I know where it is. I'd love another cup of tea – black is fine.'

'I'll put the kettle on.'

Frederick heaved himself out of his chair. His thighs and calves ached from his morning exertions. *I'll put the kettle on.* That was the first thing his mother said when his father came home from the pub. He would burst through the front door like a Mark IV tank and Frederick would be shooed into the bedroom with Virgil. They listened to their mother in the kitchen, her leather heels clipping on the cold flagstones, as she tried to placate Alexander with fat rashers of bacon and mugs of sweet tea. If they were lucky his father would pass right out on the couch, and he and Virgil would creep in and eat the crisp bacon between two slabs of buttered bread. But there were times when their father would not sleep, when he would eat hunched over the table and then rise up like a bull in a box and strike whoever was within reach. He and Virgil would get off the bed and into the wardrobe and pull the door shut, cowering among the scratchy hems of woollen duffel coats, shoes and cold rubber wellingtons, seeking out each other's hands. Virgil would squeeze his fingers, and Frederick would pump them like a heart, and once or twice he felt the warm wet release of urine soak into his pants.

When Jan came back she filled her cup with fresh tea. 'If I'd known you a little better last week I could have asked you to drive me.'

'It's not your fault, Jan,' he said. He cleared his throat. 'You weren't to know the boy was there all alone.' He was having trouble speaking. 'So how was he? Morrison – the boy. How is he?'

'That's the amazing thing,' she said, 'once they got the door open he demanded he see their badges. That's my boy! The social worker found my number in a letter on the fridge. They had to take him to the Children's Hospital. He was such a brave little boy. I took a cab in that night. He was very pale and thin but so happy to see me. I brought him a new teddy. I'm not sure why I'm telling you all this. I hope you don't mind.'

Fred shook his head.

'They kept him in overnight on fluids because he was so dehydrated. He's in temporary foster care now out in the boon-docks. There was no record of me as a living relative, so the police and the services had to take me off to give blood and do a swab. The hearing is today.'

'The hearing?'

'To present the DNA and to file for custody.'

'Custody?'

'Of Morrison. I'm taking Morrison.'

Fred stared at her. 'You're going to have a child live with you? A five-year-old child?'

Jan sighed. 'I've wrestled with this. I struggle with it. I ask myself, at my age, how can I do this? I've already raised a son. I saw my husband through dementia and then cancer – not that I regret it for a moment. He would have done the same for me. I lost and found my son so many times and then I lost him altogether. I'm seventy years old, Fred. I thought maybe Morrison should go to a real family. Maybe he'd be better off. He'd be adopted and have brothers and sisters. But they told me that more than likely he won't be adopted while the mother is still around, even if she's out of the country, so that leaves long-term fostering and temporary care. I can't have that. I'm his grandmother.'

'A five-year-old boy.' The idea of it.

'You're right, Fred. At first I didn't want to do it. I wanted to be selfish. I was so angry with my son. I like my home here, even with the management. I have friends in the village. I feel safe. I can stay up all night listening to the radio or reading a book. I can lie in bed just *thinking* if I want to. It's such a luxury, to be able to think. I love the way thoughts just breeze across you and you don't have to do anything with them, just let them come and go. And now I have to leave.'

'What? Why are you leaving?' Jan couldn't go; she had only just arrived. She was direct and to the point and she never stopped talking, but there was something very reassuring about Jan. She was like those loose cross-stitches Martha would sew onto fabric to show where the buttonhole should go.

'I can't stay here, Fred. They don't even allow dogs or cats. Samuel's budgerigars were pushing it, so I hardly think a boisterous five-year-old is on the agenda.'

'But these are our homes,' said Fred, indignantly. 'This is where we live. We own them.' How dare management dictate how they live the last years of their lives? How dare they?

'We don't own them really – not like you own the family home. You know that. They're expensive holding pens for us oldies. There are rules we agreed to when we bought. Now, I have to get going if I'm going to get that bus to town. Don't get up if you can't.'

With difficulty, Fred hoisted himself up out of the chair, refusing Jan's offer of a hand. When he opened the door a wall of heat pressed into the unit. He stood aside to let Jan pass.

'I saw a dolphin in the river today,' he said quickly, half-hoping she would not hear.

She turned to look at him. 'They're quite common, I think.'

'No, I mean it was really close, as close as you are. So close I could have touched it.'

'You weren't in the water, were you? Were you swimming in the river?'

Fred shook his head. 'I think it was trying to talk to me.' He reddened. 'No, really, Jan, it was extraordinary. I was walking along the path by the river wall and suddenly there was a giant dolphin in less than a metre of water, right in front of me. It was huge. It was like it had decided to find me and follow me, or to lead me along the walkway. At one stage it stopped and looked right at me.'

'Did it wink?'

'You think I'm silly.'

'Au contraire, that's the best story I've heard from you. Admittedly, it's the only one so far, but it's a good one. Talking dolphins are a sign, Fred.'

'A sign of what?'

'You're the professor. I'll leave that to you.'

'Do you think it's a metaphor? A real animal can't be a metaphor, can it?'

Jan laughed. 'You remind me of my Grade 4s. Where did I put my front door key?'

'It must be a symbol, then, or a sign. I get confused.'

'It means something, Fred, because it's got you thinking.

Here they are, right where I left them.' Jan picked up her keys and was gone.

Fred ran an eye down a shelf of old hardbacks that had come straight from his study and never made it into a box, and there it was, the one with the blue-green spine and a painted dolphin on the cover. Frederick went back to the B3, but this time he placed a pillow from his bed between his stiff hips and the leather base. He tried to read, but he couldn't concentrate.

The kitchen bench was recycled pine. The cupboards and shelves were orange Laminex. When she was preparing food, Martha would cut straight onto the wood benchtop, round up the scraps with her hand and toss them into the guinea pig's bucket on the windowsill. A heavy orange casserole sat on the gas hob. Next to the hob was a tin of olive oil and a yellow saltbox. The shelf to the right of the hob held her cookbooks. Along the top of the shelf was a line of aluminium Italian espresso machines, from two cups to ten. A small black transistor was playing Bach. *Ich Habe Genug.* 'I have enough.'

But it was not enough. It had never been enough. He ought to have cut the capsicums.

Whether or not a man of his age was capable of leaping out of a Marcel Breuer chair is in dispute, but Frederick was up and out of the house in seconds, clutching his keys, his wallet and his book. He banged on Jan's front door but the curtains were already drawn. Damn. He opened the garage and reversed out, and then swung the car in the direction of the main road and the bus stop, cursing at the stop sign and the oncoming traffic. As he turned the corner into the two lanes he strained to see if she was still there, at the bus stop, waiting.

If there were a god in heaven, he would have offered up a year of rosaries and a thousand candles, or some Buddhist equivalent. When he pulled up and wound down the window, Jan looked at him in astonishment.

'Get in,' he said. 'Quick, before I hold up the traffic.' Neither of them said a word as they crossed the freeway.

He stole a sideways look at the river. Would he ever see his dolphin again?

As they crossed the bridge into the city, Jan took out a compact road directory. 'Left at the interchange, Fred, and then you need to go around the block because it's a one-way street.'

Frederick found a loading zone near the Central Courts. Jan leant towards him. She was wearing some kind of perfume he associated with meditation and yoga. Martha had taken to essential oils in the late 1970s, and he had wallowed in her heavy, sweet smell until Caroline developed chronic sinusitis.

'I'll catch the bus back. I can't thank you enough, Fred.'

'I'm going to wait for you to finish. I've got nothing to do today.'

'What about your shopping? What about your beans and yoghurt?'

'Pardon? I'll park the car in the multistorey and wait for you over there.' He gestured towards a small shaded square in front of a park, where office workers were eating lunch.

'But I have no idea if I'll be half an hour or three hours.'

'I have this,' he said, holding up the book.

'*A Book of Dolphins*,' she read. 'You have a book of everything, Fred. Are you sure you can wait?'

'I'll be fine. Good luck, Jan.'

'How can I repay you?'

I'm well in arrears, he thought. And then, to his horror, he began to cry. 'I loved Martha the moment I saw her,' he blurted out. 'Go, please,' he said, gripping the wheel of the car. 'You'll be late.'

Jan put her hand across his. 'The trouble is, it's not enough. I loved my son, and look what happened to us. Love is a feeling.

But it's also like yoga. You have to do it over and over again, and then you have to accept that you'll never be perfect. Stay out of the sun. I'll be back as soon as I can.'

Ich habe genug. I have enough. I am enough. I had enough, but it wasn't enough. God was not enough. My wife was not enough. I was not enough to my wife. My daughter was not enough. My son was not enough. I am not enough. I am not anything close to enough. And I didn't do enough.

I ought to have cut the capsicums.

> It was said that Dionysos, the god of wine and frenzy, engaged a vessel to take him from the island of Ikaria to the island of Naxos; but the sailors were a crew of pirates and, not knowing that he was a god, they formed a plot to abduct him. Sailing past Naxos they made for Asia, where they intended to sell him as a slave. When he realized what they were doing he called on his magical powers. He changed the oars into snakes and filled the ship with vines and ivy and the sound of flutes. The sailors felt madness coming on them and all dived into the sea where they were changed into dolphins and made incapable of doing any harm.

Frederick sat on a bench with his book. He would like to be made incapable of doing any harm. Every now and then he sipped his water. Men in suits rushed past on their phones, sweating in the heat. Office girls stopped to light cigarettes and dragged on them hungrily, flicking ash to the ground before heading down the Terrace. A council worker in a bright safety vest and a wide-brimmed hat pushed butts and litter into a dustpan. The red arm of a giant crane swept a steel girder across the blue-white sky. He closed his eyes and picked out from the din of cars and buses the deep repetitive beat of a pile being driven into the ground. Once upon a time he had felt connected to the upward thrust of the city. Even for a professor who had never built a thing there was a deep pleasure in construction. At its purest level it was mathematical, abstract, even in its concrete form. He opened his eyes. One day all these buildings would fall to the ground. All his thin-shell structures would crumble, like hollow bones in a grave or shells on a beach.

> Before that time there had been no dolphins. After it, they
> stood for kindness and virtue in the sea; and the first to learn of
> their usefulness was the god of the ocean himself, Poseidon, or
> Neptune, as the Romans called him.

Behind the square was a fenced park backing on to the Governor's Residence. 'Open 12 to 2 daily, except Sunday', said the sign on the gate. Frederick walked towards a shaded grove of old trees. He recognised the oaks and elms from his childhood. Martha carried little botanical reference books wherever she went, but he had never been interested in nature. She was always writing letters to the local council, asking them to replace exotics with natives. Despite the traffic and the heat behind him, he could have been in Old Hag Wood, in the ancient forest, playing hide and seek with Virgil. There was a theatrical sleight to the park; in the bucolic shade of this vast canopy the invader could go on pretending they were right at home.

Jan was fanning her face as she came towards him. 'There you are! I thought you might be here. Look at these trees. Aren't they wonderful? I suppose they remind you of jolly old England.'

Jan had been successful; he could see that straight away.

'He's mine,' she said carefully, holding a thick manila file.

'That's wonderful,' said Fred. What else could he say? 'It was so quick.'

'I know, it took no time at all. I can't believe it, really.'

'So what's next, Jan? Where is he? Where is – Morrison?' Saying his name was difficult. It made him real.

'He wasn't at the hearing – it wouldn't have been appropriate. I have to wait for documentation from the department. He's with the foster family. I'll see him this week and tell him what's happening. He can come out with me for the day on Friday, and then again on Saturday night, but I won't have him permanently for at least three weeks, until I work out where we're going to live. I'm going to talk to management this afternoon, and hopefully they'll have someone on the waiting list ready to buy. It's all happening so quickly. I'll have to pack again. And then there are the budgerigars … they were Sam's, you know.'

'He has to go to school!' said Fred, registering for the first time the practicalities of Jan's situation. 'You'll have to find him a good school. When's his birthday? Does he start this year coming?'

'He can enrol in pre-primary, thank goodness. I don't know what I'd do with a five-year-old all day, every day. But I'm going to have to go further afield if I want to buy. Imagine me at the school canteen. I'll be the oldest mum by fifty years. Have you ever kept a budgerigar, Fred?'

'Pardon? I'm sure it will be fine at school,' he said. But it didn't sound fine. It sounded difficult and exhausting and not at all what a woman of Jan's age should be doing.

'Do you think we could go now? I'm exhausted. My ankle's sore from standing for so long.'

Fred led Jan out of the park to the bench in the square. 'Sit here. I'll find somewhere to pull up. I'll beep when I get back. I should be about fifteen minutes. Will you be all right?'

'Where's that book of yours – the dolphin book? Thanks, Fred. Really, I mean it.'

Jan read to him for the whole trip back. The traffic was heavy and the air conditioner strained to keep the car cool.

'Listen to this: "When Poseidon was looking for the dark-eyed Amphitrite, to make her his bride, it was a dolphin that found her for him. She had been hiding from him in a cavern by the sea. For this service, Poseidon conferred the highest of all honours, setting in the sky the constellation of the Dolphin. If you live in the northern hemisphere you can see it in July, over in the south-east sky between Aquila and Pegasus." Do you have any knowledge of astronomy, Fred? "The very word for *dolphin*, or *dolphins* as the Greeks wrote it, is itself a beautiful representation of the animal's twirling motion through the water" – I can't read the Greek.'

'I think you say it *delphis*. It means "womb". There's an index in the back.'

'Womb? How beautiful. So is that a sign, a symbol, a metaphor or just a strange coincidence? What do you think?'

Fred kept his eyes on the road. 'I'm not sure, Jan. Here we are, home at last.'

'I'm going straight to see management. Do you have plans?'

'Plans? For when?'

'As in, would you like to go out to dinner tonight? My treat, but you'd have to drive. I used to love to go to the beach in the late afternoon for a dip, so we could do that and shower in the changing rooms, and then go straight to dinner. The saltwater is good for my ankle.'

Fred hadn't been to the beach in years. He was not sure he had any bathers he would dare to be seen in. Did he have the time and energy to go to the department store and get some new trunks? *Trunks.* Another stupid English word.

'I'm sure you swim like a dolphin, Fred. What about we go at about a quarter to six, after the traffic? I know a very good Vietnamese restaurant. And don't buy the wine, that's on me too. One thing, though, if you don't mind me saying?'

What now? He wanted to get out of the heat.

'Get out the Braun. Have a shave. I'll be at your place at about five-thirty?'

'But what about Tom's sister?' he called after her. 'Don't you have to see her tonight?'

'I'll call her now and tell her I'm busy. I've got something in the freezer she can have.' She laughed and shook her head.

Fred went straight to the bathroom and looked in the mirror. How long since he'd been in a rush? Or had a decent shave? Or a haircut? He still had hair, didn't he? He would go over to the shopping centre right now and buy new bathers and get one of those long-sleeved Lycra tops to cover up his parchment. He would floss. He would scrub. He would iron and he would polish.

And with that, he flicked his tail and disappeared into the shower.

BOOK 3

Eggs

As you walk the length of the darkened corridor towards the illuminated wooden case you hear sounds that are difficult to place.

'A few low croaks,' wrote Newton in 1861. 'A rough and hoarse scream,' noted Fabricius in 1842. 'The captive bird utters a gurgling noise when expressing anxiety,' wrote Fleming in 1821. These sounds collide and amplify as you draw near. You are listening to the guttural choking of a single creature cut off for ever from the millions of heavy-bodied birds that once nested side by side on Funk Island. It is a sound that marries an Arctic tern sheared off from its flock by a winter storm with the insatiable cry of a foundling. Blind hope: could this be an incubator and the mottled egg inside not some cold booty lifted out from under the smashed and bloodied bones of its mother, not some egg abandoned on a cliff face, but something warm and alive, something that might, with care and attention – with what might even be called love – become a living thing?

Pl. XXXX.

1. EGG OF DINORNIS MAXIMUS.   2. EGG OF APTERYX AUSTRALIS.

Sunday evening, 22 January 2006

IT WAS FREEZING IN LONDON, but at least it wasn't raining. Caroline Lothian had spent the night wondering what to do until six in the morning, when she could begin to get ready for her flight. At one point she considered the club down the road. How long since she'd had sex? She could still put on tight jeans and boots and a leather jacket and don some war paint and, with a bit of luck and a bottle or two of white wine, snare a local Romeo, but why bother? For a woman close to extinction, sex was merely palliative.

People didn't understand loneliness; they thought it was something to be overcome by moving to a table with more people. But loneliness could not be chased out of the room by a crowd, at least not the kind that Caroline felt. She had always felt as if something essential had been ripped out of her and taken away, leaving a raw selvedge, but since Martha died the edges were smooth and cold to the touch, like polished concrete.

Perhaps it was because she was thirty-seven, perhaps it was because she was adopted, but Caroline could not stop thinking about *a child of her own*. Her mother would have disapproved of the expression, with its assumption of motherhood as possession by birth alone, but when she imagined being pregnant she felt such a mixture of terror and longing it left her breathless. When she dreamed about her baby it was always a girl who looked just like her. *Such undisguised narcissism*, thought

Caroline. So much braver to dream of a child who looked nothing like you.

She heard a faint mechanical whirring on the street, like a windup toy. Through the narrow pane of glass that ran the length of the basement flat she saw the rim of a wheelchair and the torso of a man. The chair came to a sudden halt, rotated 360 degrees, and stopped. Was he waiting for friends? No one came trailing after him. The man turned to face the wall of her building. He was wearing long Ugg boots. What was he doing? Why was he out there alone?

She returned to her emails. The flight for Aberdeen was still departing at 8.20 am. There had been a forecast of snow, but it had been usurped by an icy wind from the North Sea. She printed out her ticket and then spun on her chair. He was still there. Why didn't he move on?

The screen went black and the room fell into darkness. When she was little she hid in the cupboard in her room, holding the door shut tight while her mother tried to coax her out.

'There's a lovely piece of chocolate fudge just out here on a plate. I wonder who's going to eat it?'

'Not me.'

'Well, I'll just leave it here for when you get hungry. How would that be?'

'I'm not coming out. Ever.'

She tapped the keyboard and the pale egg floated back out on the screen, like an uninhabited planet. The Aberdeen auk egg was not the only specimen left in the world, but it was the one she wanted for her exhibition. The first encounter with the egg in its glass nest would connect her visitors to a primal scene in what Caroline had called in her funding application 'the drama of extinction'. An unmarked egg was the beginning of a story, but a marked egg the final word. The dutiful members of the public, having paid their ten euros or fifteen dollars to enter the exhibition, would stand exactly where the high-browed scientists, gentlemen collectors, tomb robbers and the profiteers had once stood, slack-jawed at nature's preposterous and exaggerated ways, staring as she herself had stared at the large speckled egg of the extinct auk. They would read for the first time the word written across the egg in Indian ink: *Pingouin.* She imagined the visitor taking a metaphorical step backward at the sight of the marks on the egg, and turning their attention towards the label. A contemporary font for all the labels and panels in the exhibition, reasoned Caroline, sans serif, global. Helvetica? *Egg of the Great Auk, Pinguinus impennis. c. 1844.*

BRITISH BIRDS. 405

THE GREAT AUK.

NORTHERN PENGUIN, OR GAIR-FOWL.

SUMMER PLUMAGE.

(Alca Impennis, Linn.—*Pingouin brachiptère,* Temm.)

Insurance and shipping for all the other exhibits were sorted, but this one little university museum was digging in its heels. She ran through her letters to the vice-chancellor. Small museums were always tricky; they were just not used to lending their collections. Tomorrow she would meet the curator and take her to lunch – what do you eat in Aberdeen? Some kind of fish? Herring? She would show them the draft catalogue and explain the importance of the egg to the whole exhibition.

Against Horace's advice, she would begin *ab ovo*. 'It all begins with the egg,' she would say.

Why had she stayed with Julian for so long? All those wasted years. Julian had lived in a squalid theoretical pile, jumping from one mound to another. She had followed him – or rather, led him – to postcolonial theory, from where he quickly hopped over to trauma theory. All by himself he tiptoed gingerly across to queer theory, where he got quite comfortable until one of his young postgrad students shook her posthumanist booty at him and he left for ever.

He and the posthumanist had twins now. Identical twins who looked just like their father.

'Don't tell me you're still upset about that man?' her father said when she told him about the twins. 'Look on the bright side for once, Caroline. He was a complete narcissist.'

Takes one to know one. But her father was right about one thing: she had always found it hard to see the bright side of anything. 'Glass half-empty,' he liked to say when she was a teenager, mooning about the house in her slippers and pyjamas.

A feeling is more than just a question of point of view, Dad. It is not just a matter of changing the place you sit. Her father preferred not to think about that. He preferred not to think about anything difficult, not even his own son. She was furious with him over Callum's prescription. All he had to do was verbally okay it with the care facility and they could have gone ahead, but no, he had to put down the phone on them and pull the plug, so they had to contact her on the other side of the world.

No one asked where it had come from, this *extinction* thing. She rarely spoke to her father about her work, and he avoided questions that might have a complicated answer. She went along with him, as she always had. If he ever got around to asking, she would say something vague, like, 'I have my finger on the pulse. We live on an anxious planet, Dad.'

But right now, her project seemed neither prescient nor apotropaic (a word from anthropology that she loved).

Her phone beckoned from the bedside table, but Caroline resisted the urge to turn it on. In the morning she would be gone, and her father would be left waiting. Let him stew in his juices. Let him sort out Callum. Let him bitch to himself about the village. She had heard his complaints a million times: the food, the people, the management, the view – actually, the view was the best thing about his place. St Sylvan's was set surprisingly high up. Her little London flat was a boggy depression in the ground. She was like Mole, down, down, down in her dark and lowly little house, scrabbling and scratching and scraping and scrooging.

'Hang spring-cleaning!' A yellow wool blanket so scratchy her mother had to turn back the cotton sheet to make a soft cuff for her chin. It was one of Aunt Marjorie's books, *The Wind in the Willows*, Methuen and Co., London, 1908, old green cloth, frayed edges, gilt spine, on the cover the horned Piper at the Gates of Dawn squatting in the rushes and reeds of the River Thames. The cover of the book was mysterious and terrifying, and reminded her of the stories her father's granny used to tell him about small river creatures and rows of shiny stones arranged in wheels.

> Hang spring-cleaning! … Something up above was calling him imperiously, and he made for the steep little tunnel which answered in his case to the gravelled carriage-drive owned by animals whose residences are nearer to the sun and air. So he scraped and scratched and scrabbled and scrooged and then he scrooged again and scrabbled and scratched and scraped, working busily with his little paws and muttering to himself, 'Up we go! Up we go!' till at last, pop! his snout came out into the sunlight, and he found himself rolling in the warm grass of a great meadow.

Caroline picked up her coat and keys and ran up the stairs. It was wrong to leave that man out there in the cold; he might need help. She stopped well behind him and cleared her throat, and saw that the chair was one of those new high-tech ones.

'Excuse me?' she said. 'Are you okay? I live downstairs. I saw you through the window. It's pretty cold out here.'

He was black, in his thirties. His thick hair was pulled back in a band. A few coils twisted in the light coming off the lamp across the road. He wore gloves and pushed a knob to turn himself towards her. Thank goodness, she thought. Around his neck he wore a fine dove-coloured scarf, as if to distinguish the soft part of himself from the metal armour of his chair.

'I thought you might have fallen asleep ...'

He looked up at her. 'What are you doing out on this chilly night.' His words had a fine slur, like those soft edges of the River Thames. 'I'm fine, actually. As fine as can be expected.'

'Was it an accident?' she asked, angry with him. He had no right to self-pity, not with a complete stranger.

'I was on my motorbike,' he said evenly. 'Not my fault, which explains the glamorous mode of transportation I now enjoy. Insurance is such a blessing. I was the unwitting target of a twenty-three-year-old drunk out for the evening in his daddy's BMW.' He paused. 'You have to excuse me, I've been at the pub and I've had a few too many pints. I don't usually wallow.'

'You're fine,' she said. 'My brother had an accident too.' The words just came out.

'So we have something in common,' he said. 'Para or quad?'

'Neither.'

'Lucky man,' he said evenly.

'He has brain damage. Severe brain damage.'

'Not so lucky then.' He paused. 'My brain is fine. I'm a C7: "full elbow and wrist extension and flexion".' He had an accent she could not place. 'I lack strength, hence the electric chair. But no fine motor to speak of. But you're not from here.'

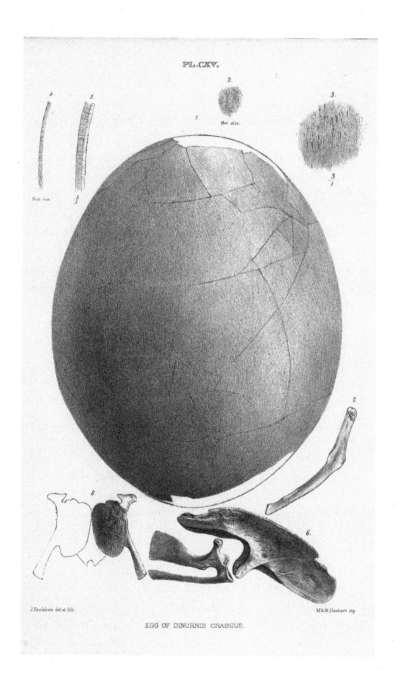

EGG OF DINORNIS CRASSUS.

'No,' she said. 'I'm Australian.'

'Are you black? You are, aren't you? Black like me. Are you one of those real Australian Aborigines they're always writing about in the *Guardian*?' He smiled.

She was glad he smiled, because she wanted to be able to like him.

Glass broke outside the Bull and Boar. The wind dropped, and silence rushed in to expel cars and people, to give back the city to slow, burrowing creatures, like Rat and Badger and Toad and Mole. Why, she wondered, did the English so love their animals, and so hate her people? The skies parted and the moon appeared. Had she ever seen stars like this in London? She searched in vain for Alpha and Beta Centauri and Lupus the wolf, while the man manoeuvred his chair to see the sky.

'You have different stars in the southern hemisphere, don't you? You rarely see this in London. There's usually too much pollution.'

'I'm from Liverpool originally,' he continued. He was breathing heavily. 'The air is clearer there. What we need is a telescope. I don't suppose you have one on you, tucked in your back pocket?'

'Not on me, no. When my brother was little my father made him a telescope. He was an engineer — my dad. They were both so proud of it. Actually, it was my mother's idea, but my father got naming rights.' How much would she tell him? she wondered.

'Well, naturally,' said the man in the chair. 'De man must dominate de woman.'

Caroline smiled. It was a habit of a lifetime that her father still could not break — to assume that he thought of everything and her mother merely followed. Both her parents had gone to that conference in California. At a faculty dinner her mother sat next to a woman whose child was on a school trip to the desert. 'They're taking their own telescopes,' the woman had told Martha, 'that they made in school with cheap materials.'

Martha came home with a sheaf of paper. 'All eyes on Mommy! I hold in my hand Xeroxes for the construction of a Dobsonian telescope.' She read from the inventor's form letter, in her best imitation of Martin Luther King: 'It is my hope and dream that every child in every house in every block of America will have the means to build their own telescope.'

'Is your father still making telescopes? Hello? Are you still here?'

'Pardon?'

'Your parents, are they in Australia? Does your dad still make telescopes?'

'My mother died two years ago, but yes, he's still around. He lives over there. And no, no more telescopes. What about you? Do you have family?' *What about children?* That was what she really wanted to know.

'I have my mother,' he replied. 'And one sister. She lives near my mum, with her husband and kids. She's got four of them. They're a gorgeous, rowdy lot.'

'Are you the doting uncle?'

He sucked his lip. 'I can't see them, not yet. They don't understand why their uncle doesn't want to come and I can't explain it to them. My therapist – I have my very own therapist – tells me I'm being selfish. It seems I'm punishing myself and everyone else I love. She says that's why I won't go back to my work.'

'I don't know about that. But I think I understand.'

'Which part?'

'Pardon?'

'Which part do you think you understand?'

It seemed important to meet his gaze evenly. He looked away.

'So, since we're into the book of revelations, what about your brother? When did it happen?'

'What's your work?' she asked. 'What do you do?'

'I'm a musician – a composer. That is, I used to be. And you?'

A double-decker bus pulled up across the road. A group of teenagers tumbled out and threw their skateboards onto the footpath and took off, scratching and scraping the underbellies of their boards on the concrete kerb.

'It happened a long time ago now, nearly fifteen years. My brother was in his final year of university. Architecture.' The final weeks of his last month.

Caroline pulled her down jacket closer at the neck and stamped her feet. It was very cold, but she would continue. 'My father had wanted to be an architect, but his own father wouldn't let him. My father always pretended engineering was his *destiny*, but my mother never believed it and neither do I. In the end I think he chose to pretend that it was meant to be. It was his way of dealing with how his life turned out.' *There it is: my bitter edge.*

'Destiny is an easy god,' he said. 'Saves you from the burden of choice, or the tragedy of having no choice at all. How's that? Am I *profound* enough for you?'

'It happened on a Saturday evening. Callum was driving my father's old car. It was a Saab.' She paused. She was going to tell someone she didn't know and would never see again. 'There was just him in the car.'

He had turned away from her, towards the street, and she was grateful for that. She preferred not to see his face. Everything now depended on how the words came out. She would have to be very careful: it could only be told in short sentences, cut to length.

'It was a grey Saab with leather seats.' Thick, red leather seats. She had to crop, to rely on tight close-ups, so she didn't have to see too much at once.

★

The back of the car with Callum, coming home from Ralph and Veronica's, late on a Friday night. Callum has dropped his chewing gum on the red leather and they are trying to get it off without their parents seeing, but the more they pick at it the more it heats up and stretches, like toffee, sticking them together.

In the back seat with her mother, under the unzipped sleeping bag, Callum and Dad in the fields with the telescope. The stitched seam of the leather presses a line into her cheek, leaving a scar when she wakes up.

Two dollars for cleaning the outside of the Saab, and another dollar for the red leather seats.

'Was he drunk?' the man said quietly.
    'What? Yes, he was drunk.' But not drunk enough not to know.

She was in the living room with her mother when her father came storming home from Callum's hockey final. 'He lost his nerve. I tell you, he missed the crucial pass. He let the whole team down.' Her father spoke under his breath to Martha, but Caroline heard him. 'We had words.' Martha caught Caroline's eye, and raised an eyebrow. Neither of them understood the fury in his voice, and why it mattered so much. Later, just before Caroline left to have dinner with Fleur, Callum called from the club. Martha picked up the phone.
    'Callum, are you all right, darling? Have you been drinking?' She cupped the mouthpiece and pointed towards the study. 'Go get your father,' she hissed. 'Listen to me, Callum, calm down. Your father was just upset about the game, that's all. I don't want you driving home tonight. Do you hear? Who are you with? Is Aaron with you? Dad will come and pick you up. Just a moment.'

Caroline returned with her father and she watched her mother press the phone into her breast.

'He sounds very upset, Fred, I'm sure he's drunk. He can't drive home. I don't know if Aaron's still there or not, but maybe you should call the Bessells too. What did you say to him after the game? I don't want you to upset him any more. It's just a game, Fred –'

'Give it to me,' her father said, and snatched the phone. 'Don't you talk to me like that. It was pathetic play and then you go off snivelling, like a baby. I was ashamed of you, hear me? Don't you use that language –'

'He and my father had a blowup after a sports game –' She could not go on.

'I'm sorry,' he said. 'Look, I have to go. I can't stay out here in the cold. I'm Richard Waterford, by the way.'

'Caroline Lothian. It wasn't about the game, though.' That was not why her father was angry with Callum. Callum wasn't good enough. None of them were.

Her friend Fleur had been renting near the university, and Caroline went there to help with the new baby – not that Fleur needed help; she and her girlfriend were perfect parents. Caroline just poured the wine and stacked the dishes and marvelled at the way the baby's mouth formed a perfect letter *K* around Fleur's long nipple.

When they heard the crash they all stopped what they were doing, all but the baby, who kept on sucking as if nothing had happened.

'That was close,' said Fleur, taking the baby off her breast.

'It sounded bad,' said Kate. 'It was down the hill, near the hockey club.'

'Should we call someone?'

'Someone already would have,' said Fleur, but she picked up the phone.

'I'm going to walk down,' said Kate quickly. She disappeared and came back with a stack of folded towels.

'But why?' said Caroline. 'Why would you want to see that?'

'I don't want to see it,' snapped Kate. 'I'm almost a doctor, remember?'

When Kate left, Caroline wiped the table and cleared the glasses. She listened to the police sirens, and then the ambulance, while Fleur put the baby down.

When Kate returned she had a policeman by her side.

Richard moved his chair forward. 'At least he didn't hurt anyone else.'

'What?'

'Your brother. At least he was alone. The truth is, Caroline Lothian, it's fucking cold and I'm not allowed to get cold. My lungs are not great.'

He hurt lots of people, she wanted to say. Who have you hurt? she wondered. She reached out and placed her hands on his cheeks. He took her fingers with his mouth. She closed her eyes as he drew her warm, wet hand from his lips.

'I hope this isn't pity,' he said quietly.

'What about self-pity? Is that allowed?'

'I'll have to go away and think about that. You're a beautiful woman. Too thin, but beautiful.'

'I don't feel beautiful,' she said, and then regretted it.

'I suppose you think I'm telling you you're beautiful because I'm desperate?'

'I don't know,' she said. 'Are you desperate?'

'Sometimes,' he said, 'but not in the way people think. It's not sex I'm desperate for. It's touch. I crave touch.'

'I'm sorry,' she said.

'Don't be. You should be grateful for your perfect beauty

and your lovely body. You can run downstairs after I leave and take off your clothes and put your hands between your legs and come all by yourself if you want to.'

She thought, *If he wasn't in a chair I would run away fast from this man. Or I might fuck him.* When she got down the stairs she looked back through the window and he was gone. She was left with nothing but her little brother, and he refused to leave her alone.

Callum traipsed into her bedroom and flopped onto the bed to announce every breakthrough, every setback. 'We got the lens in okay,' he reported, 'but now the hinges are too small. Are you listening? Guess where we got the lens? Guess?'

'The zoo?'

'Don't be a retard. We went down the coast to where they build the boats, to a marine salvage yard. I bet you've never been to one of them – a marine salvage yard? Have you?'

'I have, actually. Millions of times.'

'Liar.'

'Don't call me a liar.'

'It's from a porthole, actually.'

'What's from a porthole?'

'The lens. Dad says it's got the right *curvachar*.'

'Curvature,' Caroline mocked.

'Yep,' Callum continued. 'It has to be convex. Which, in case you didn't know, is the opposite of concave.'

Callum was so earnest it was unbearable. He never got the joke because he wasn't looking for the funny line. He didn't need to put anyone down, which made him fragile, in need of protection, and open to abuse. She knew that even as a teenager.

'And Caro? Dad's even bringing home a piece of Sonotube from one of the labs at the School.' He chewed his gum, waited for her to bite.

'So, Albert Einstein, what's a Sonotube and why is he bringing it home?'

Callum launched into his explanation, punctuating his words with short chopping movements of his left hand. Unlike her, Callum was left-handed. Used to be left-handed. 'It's an empty tube made of thick cardboard. They're used in the formwork when they're pouring concrete columns.' The chopping hand paused in mid-air. 'Do you want me to tell you what formwork is?'

'I already know that,' said Caroline airily.

'You do not.'

'Dad told me.'

'He did not.'

'He did so.'

It ended, as always, in a ritualistic battle over their father. Who owned him most, who loved him most, who he loved most. From the very beginning Callum had made it clear that only he and his father truly understood the telescope. 'It's not for looking at things you can already see,' he said dismissively when she asked if they'd be able to observe the moon from the back garden. 'It's for deep space, for observing nebulae, star clusters, galaxies – that kind of stuff.'

Callum would watch the lunar cycles and announce that it was a full moon or gibbous or waxing or waning – she never could get a handle on the moon – and then they would all have to rush around getting the sleeping bags and the tent and pile into the Saab and head out into the Wheatbelt to pitch a tent at a campground in a one-pub town like Goomalling, Dumbleyung, Wandering. When camp was set up they would drive into the cold, silent wheat fields and search for a hill. The land was so flat it was almost impossible to find any kind of gradient, so eventually her mother would put a stop to it. 'This'll do right here, Fred,' she would say. 'Just pull over and get on with it.'

She and her mother would lift the telescope out of the

back seat where it had been wedged between them for the two-hour drive. Her father would get underneath the tube and hoist it onto his shoulders, like it was a small ground-to-air missile, while Callum came up next to him with a backpack stuffed with a sleeping bag, biscuits and a thermos of hot milk, leaving Caroline and her mother to cocoon inside the car. They watched the boys climb the fence and cross the stubble into the freezing wheat field. Caroline wound down the window.

'Callum!'

She could see him now with his striped beanie pulled down over his ears, paused on the flank of the hill with one hand on his hip, swinging his torch to and fro like a beacon.

'What now?' he yelled.

'E. T. PHONE HOME!'

She had stayed with her father on her trip back from Melbourne, almost ready to forgive him for throwing out Martha's clothes. The first night it was impossible to sleep and she worked until past midnight, then put on her coat and went out into the quadrangle. He caught her by surprise. She turned and saw her father as she had never seen him before: a deranged old man in flannelette pyjamas, his thick grey hair standing to attention and his dressing gown half-on, half-off.

'What are you doing out here in the middle of the night?' he said. 'You woke me up. You've left the side door wide open. It's freezing inside the house.'

'I can't sleep.' She returned to her study of the stars. 'Do you remember the Dobsonian?' She needed to hurt him that night.

'The what?' he asked, but he knew exactly what she was talking about.

'That telescope you built for Callum. You bought the lens at a marine salvage yard. The tube had something to do with concrete.'

'Such a simple design,' he said quietly. 'I got the plans in the US.' He took a step backward.

'Actually, Mum ordered the plans after she got back from California.'

'I don't think so, Caroline. Not that it matters now. It was Sonotube,' he added, 'used to form concrete columns. I'm going back to bed now. Shall I close the door behind me?'

She would have liked to take up a knife and plunge it in his back. But instead she came in and locked the door. With her cup of tea, she scrolled aimlessly through her bookmarks to check online collections. She was having trouble with her proposal for her first major exhibition. 'I am interested in the cultural boundaries of nature,' she had written. 'I believe we are hopelessly allegorical.' But what did that mean? Then she found the egg.

It had always troubled her that she had not arrived at the beginning by any of the approved academic routes, and that it happened because she had been with her father: it had been luck, not rigour. Serendipity.

But it had been a mistake to stay with him. He'd brought everything from their family home before he put it up for rent – the leather couch and the sideboards and the dining table and chairs, and all those boxes and buffets. The chairs were piled top to bottom on the outside patio – she had to turn sideways just to get to the back door. 'Sell it all,' she said, 'or put it on the verge', but he took no notice.

That first day with him she listened to a documentary on the radio, about an earthquake in a city in New Zealand: 'Old people cannot go out for walks, even now that the debris is cleared and order restored. They can no longer remember their way home. They have no markers, no familiar visual signs to help them move through the places they have grown up with.'

It was as if the waters of the Indian Ocean had heaved themselves at her life and taken away everything that was not nailed to the ground, leaving the remains strewn across her

Josephine Wilson

father's villa. Familiar paintings were stacked in corners, framed photographs of the family poked out from under beds, books flowed from boxes, her mother's vases protruded from their newspaper wrapping, rolls of Turkish rugs were doubled up over the tops of wardrobes, and chipped brown Arabia plates were stacked on the laundry floor.

The only thing left fully intact was a brass menorah on top of the fridge. Caroline had never been told where it had come from, and she had never asked. Death robbed you of beginnings as well as endings. 'We were cultural Jews,' Caroline heard her mother say to Veronica at a family dinner. What did that mean? she wondered as a nine-year-old. Cultured? The dictionary led her to a microscopic organism in a glass Petri dish and to pearls in a viscous shell. She was left to cobble together her own story of the candles, which featured steel-capped boots on stairs, Alsatian dogs, small pale-faced children who miracu-lously survived by hiding in cupboards and then sneaked away under the cover of night to travel through bombed-out cities in threadbare red woollen coats, carrying a creased Agfa colour of Mama and Papa, twenty US dollars, and a brass menorah, heading for America.

And now she was in London. Richard Waterford. Could that be his real name? Had Richard made it home okay? If he fell over, who would pick him up?

Her egg hovered on the screen. Soon she would travel to Scotland. One hundred and seventy years ago a Monsieur Dufresne, Keeper of the King's Cabinet in Paris, had taken up a quill and lowered it into a pool of Indian ink. He leant over the auk egg and wrote the word *Pingouin* across its curved surface before placing it in a cabinet with the rare and curious. You would never do that now – mark a specimen like that. You would never sully the mute purity of nature with the indelible mark of the human hand.

A pair of high black stilettos and lace-up Dockers stumbled into the elongated frame of her window. They stopped and got their shoes and legs all tangled up in each other and then they left. *How perilous to be a bird*, she thought, *to arrive on earth half-formed and unfinished inside a thin veneer of shell, to have to wait beneath the feathers of your mother or father until you were ready to hatch.* How exactly did they remove the living matter from inside the eggs? They used a needle, but there must have been a technique. She put a yellow sticky note on her screen to remind her to find out.

The door to the hallway opened. Her father threw on the main light.

'I thought you were going to sleep, Caroline.'

'Am I keeping you awake? I'll turn off the overhead light and put on the reading lamp.'

'You can stay up as long as you like. It's your house too,' he said.

'No, it's not,' she replied.

He fussed in the kitchen with the kettle and the tin of malted chocolate.

She watched him spoon chocolate into a mug and crush it against the edges before adding cold milk.

'You should put hot water in first to dissolve it.'

'Why?'

Because that's the way Mum did it, that's why. She began to gather up her papers.

'Can I see?' he asked. He carried his drink to the table where her printer was set up.

'There's nothing much to see, just a few things I found on the internet.'

He put down his cup and picked up the image of the egg. 'What is this?' he asked.

'An egg.'

Her father took a steadying breath. '*Egg of the Great Auk, circa 1844*,' he read, and then placed the paper on the table in front of him, smoothing it as if it were creased. 'Is the creature extinct? That's what you're working on, isn't it – extinction? Another one of your uplifting subjects … The writing on the shell is striking. Just wait a moment.' He disappeared into his room. She could hear boxes being moved, chaos descending. He returned with a small book.

'Here it is,' he said after running through some pages. '*Nec gemino bellum Troianum orditur ab ovo.*'

'Meaning?'

He held up the book. Horace, *Ars Poetica*. He gazed into the distance, head inclined upward, the incarnation of knowledge. Her father loved to gather up his own clever thoughts and take them off into a corner to examine, like ancient runes inscribed with a secret script.

'Horace is describing his ideal epic poet, who tells the story of the Trojan War not from the beginning – not *ab ovo*, "from the egg" – but *in medias res*, "in the middle of the action". "*Ab ovo*" is a reference to the twin eggs, from one of which Helen of Troy hatched. Helen sets off the chain of events that leads to the fall of Troy and the death of Agamemnon.'

'Remind me how Helen got to be an egg?'

'There are many versions of the story. Leda, the Queen of Sparta, is pursued by Zeus, the god of thunder and lightning and the ruler of the sky, who disguises himself as a swan and descends upon Leda and impregnates her, as a consequence of which she gives birth to twin eggs, one of which is Helen.'

'It was rape. I remember the poem by Yeats. But why does Horace prefer stories that start in the middle?'

'I'm not that familiar with the text. I'll have a good look at it and let you know, if you like. It's not one that we spent much time on in Latin. Are you going to use this auk egg?'

'I don't know yet – I just found it. I have to get the

institution to lend it.' Her hand flicked the air dismissively as she spoke.

'Well, good night, Caroline. Don't stay up too late.'

In her other life she would have opened up to her father. She would have called him every other day from overseas. 'Use me as a sounding board,' he told her when she was doing her degree. Use me to refract and amplify your thoughts. Let me be your mirror.

'Dad?'

'Yes?' He turned back towards her, holding his cup. He was lit from behind by the soft yellow of the light in his bedroom.

'You should never have thrown out Mum's things.'

He took a deep breath. 'There's plenty of your mother's belongings here, Caroline. They're all in boxes, just waiting for you to take them.'

'You know I'm not talking about saucepans or cookbooks or the Danish crockery collection that you started for her and she could never be bothered finishing. I mean her clothes – her suits, her jackets, her shoes, her handbags, even her underwear. How could you have done that? How?'

'I can't believe you're still going on about this. Why do you keep on about it? There was nothing valuable there, Caroline. You got all the jewellery.'

'This isn't about value, Dad. Do you get that? I don't care about the fucking value. You keep all your fucking furniture as if it means something, and it means nothing at all. Keeping isn't just about value.'

She should not have screamed at him. It was a mistake.

His mouth was twitching. 'I just can't have you using that language, Caroline. I can't have you screaming at me any more. Do you hear me? We have neighbours now. And stop that crying. Stop right now.' His face was bright red.

'That's what we do, Dad. That's what we're supposed to do.'

'What are you talking about now? Please, I can't stand the hysterics. What's this about? What is it we're supposed to do?'

'Not *we*, Dad, not you – *me*. That's what daughters are supposed to do. We sort out our mother's things when our mothers die. You knew Mum asked me to do it. She asked me when you were busy trying to get her into some fucking experimental trial when she was just about dead anyway. Do you remember that, Dad? Do you remember how you were when Mum was dying? Do you remember how you treated that poor nurse? Daughters are supposed to go through their mother's things and decide what to throw out and what to keep. They get time to think about when their mother wore something, or where she bought it, or how much she loved it. That's a daughter's job. Did you know that?'

She was crying even now, in London. He had taken away her right to be a daughter, a right she had had to fight for all her life.

When her father came out in the morning she was already dressed and at the computer, her suitcase at the front door. When he stood behind her and put one hand on her shoulder, she closed her eyes and let it be.

'I'm sorry about what happened with your mother's things. I should have waited.'

Caroline continued to type her email to the curator of the museum in Scotland.

He leant over and touched her shoulder. 'Are you sure that egg is authentic? Could it be an ersatz egg?'

Caroline gritted her teeth and shook her shoulder. 'Give it a break, Dad.'

Should she take her down vest to Scotland? She put it in her case on top of the large white envelope. Her father had an obsession with 'the correct terminology'. He preferred the word *terminology* to *language*. Because of him she knew all the synonyms for *fake*, as well as all the other terms in dictionaries of vernacular, be they English, American, Australian. She knew the words designed to separate skin from meat. *Coconut, Oreo.* She herself preferred *inauthentic*, a disinterested and formal word that best expressed an internal state without bluntly asking you to imagine yourself skinned alive and hung up on a hook. Where was her Gore-Tex jacket? Why wasn't it on the hanger in the cupboard?

To be inauthentic was to exist in the negative. 'I am nothing. I'm rubbish,' she screamed at her mother when she was six or seven. Martha had written these things down and now Caroline had those journals. She took them with her when she travelled, not because she wanted to read them again – she had read them so many times since her mother died she knew the words by heart – but because she was afraid of losing them. She had a photocopy in Melbourne, and one in a box in the garage at her father's house, but the imprint of her mother's hand on the page could never be copied, and she needed it with her. Whenever she was packing to travel she had to debate the relative probability of losing her carry-on luggage in the departure lounge over losing her suitcase in the hold. Since she had not slept and sleeplessness made her forgetful, it was far more likely, she reasoned, that she would lose her own leather backpack than that the airline would lose her suitcase. So they were in her suitcase this time.

Fred,

These are for Caroline. Please pass them directly to her. They do not concern you at all. You are not mentioned, nor is our marriage. They were written when she was young. They might help her understand. I hope she can forgive me.

There was no note for her, just three small notebooks with

During their passage the sun was darkened and the moon refused to give her light. The beating of their wings was like the thunder and their steady on-coming like the continuous roar of Niagara. Where they roosted great branches, and even trees two feet in diameter, were broken down beneath their weight, and where they nested a hundred square miles of timber groaned with the weight of the nest or lay buried in ordure.

W. L. Dawson, *The Birds of Ohio*, 1903

intermittent entries from the time Caroline was adopted to around the age of twelve. Her mother wrote in a small, neat hand in fine black pen. She had thin fingers and the very tip of her right index finger was missing. According to Callum, she lost it when her brother chopped it off with the kindling axe when they were playing in the woodshed, but when she asked her mother if it was true, she just laughed.

April 197–

Caroline was very angry with me from the moment she woke up. She has so much trouble getting to sleep she wakes up moody and tired, but today was a bad one. She started by kicking her bedroom door and when I tried to stop her she scratched my face and made it bleed. I must remember to cut her nails regularly. I am still struggling to stay calm when she touches me and hurts me. Then she started to pull her own hair. She was covered in sweat and throwing herself on the ground. I'm rubbish, she screamed. When I tried to stop her pulling her hair she pinched me very hard on the face. She said, I hate you. I wish you would die. It was hard to hear those words but I tried to do my breathing and stay calm. Then Callum was woken up by her screams and he started to cry and I got really angry. I picked Caroline up and threw her on the bed. I did not hurt her but I wanted to. I am not a good mother. I know that now.

Her only pair of woollen socks was still damp. She put them in the dryer and turned it on low, then she took off her clothes and turned on the shower. She stepped in and let the water run over her head and down her back. She could not remember her mother or father ever asking her to pretend or to forget or to do any of those damaging things scattered throughout the pages of the adoption memoirs and handbooks that Martha gave her, and which she read in binges and purges throughout adolescence and beyond. But pretend and forget and deny she had. Some things were too big for a child to imagine. By the time she was ten or eleven everyone else knew there had been a catastrophe, and by the time she was twelve or thirteen she knew about it too. Caroline slid down the tiles and sat on the floor of the shower. Water pooled about her. She found a flannel and squeezed liquid soap into it. She began to rub her skin.

At first the catastrophe was personal, so it was not really a catastrophe at all, not at the time. At the time it was just something that happened to one little girl on 17 January 1969, the date on her birth certificate.

> Caroline came home from school crying again. When I asked her what was wrong she said, 'I am the only one in the whole school who doesn't look like her mother and father.' I felt so bad for her. All I could do was hug her and tell her how sorry I was, and I wished I could take that away. Then I produced my famous chocolate cake and all was forgotten. Children are resilient. I have to remember that.

She scrubbed the soles of her feet, the palest part of her body. They were impossibly long, thin feet, difficult to fit in shoes. They were nothing like her mother's feet, which were small and soft, with high arches and blunt toes and well-formed nails that she filed and clipped but never painted. Caroline's were not like her father's and brother's feet, with their narrow heel and broad front and those prominent metatarsals. She turned off the water. She found a towel and began to dry her very own skinny body.

Her father always pretended she was well-adjusted, unlike so many of the other Aboriginal children in the historical tragedy that unfolded in front of their family, but her mother struggled with the truth.

It was clear now — her parents' confusion about their role in the catastrophe, the ways they were at odds with each other — but at seven or eight she just felt different and she hated it.

She was a poor copy, a fake. At primary school it was hard to be surrounded by pale mums and their miniature offspring, but she thought the feelings would disappear. At thirteen, fourteen, fifteen, though, she realised they would never pass.

'Mum, am I a half-caste?'

'What?' said her mother sharply. 'Where did you hear that word? There's no such thing. We don't use that language in this family, Caroline. Those words are for animals, not people.'

'Then what am I, Mum?'

She knew she was Aboriginal. She had been adopted right at the tail end. Officially, the forced removals were over, and yet they continued in a haphazard way. The odd baby somewhere in the system intersected with the kindness of a well-placed doctor helping an infertile young couple. Her parents distinguished themselves from those who pretended that nothing had happened. They tried to meet history's stony glower with equanimity, or so they believed. They were liberal, educated. They watched movies with Sidney Poitier and Gregory Peck. Martha taught her children all about slavery, and about the Ku Klux Klan and the riots in Chicago. Caroline listened to Eartha Kitt and Nina Simone, just like her mother. Soul and funk. She read the speeches of Martin Luther King Jr and, late at night with a torch under the covers, Malcolm X. She loved Maya Angelou. She idolised Aretha Franklin and Etta James. All her mother's American heroes were her heroes too.

'Two peas in a pod,' her father liked to say.

Fleur had told her a story about the time she went to stay with her aunty in north Queensland. Her aunt had had a miserable marriage to a man who lived under the house with his gemstone polisher and his home brew, while she lived upstairs with the Aga and the TV. She and Fleur watched game-show television every evening, until Fleur asked if she could turn on SBS News.

'What's that, then?' asked her aunt. '*The Cosby Show* is

On permanent display in that room, there is a very large Audubon book of birds. It is in a glass case, and is opened to this beautiful page of the Carolina Parakeet. This now extinct species was found in very great numbers in the Millcreek valley by early white farmers in Cincinnati. John James Audubon describes their slaughter:

> ... the Parakeets are destroyed in great numbers, for whilst busily engaged in plucking off the fruits or tearing the grain from the stacks, the husbandman approaches them with perfect ease, and commits great slaughter among them. All the survivors rise, shriek, fly round about for a few minutes, and again alight on the very place of most imminent danger. The gun is kept at work; eight or ten, or even twenty, are killed at every discharge. The living birds, as if conscious of the death of their companions, sweep over their bodies, screaming as loud as ever, but still return to the stack to be shot at, until so few remain alive, that the farmer does not consider it worth his while to spend more of his ammunition. I have seen several hundreds destroyed in this manner in the course of a few hours, and have procured a basketful of these birds at a few shots, in order to make choice of good specimens for drawing the figures by which this species is represented in the plate now under your consideration.

John J. Audubon, *Birds of America*, 1843

coming on. I don't want to miss the beginning. If only our black fellas could be that funny.'

They offered her forms of compensation she could not accept. Her mother ticked the boxes for 'Indigenous' at school and on the census, insisting on Caroline's Aboriginality, even though many refused to see it.

'She doesn't really look it, does she?'

'I can see it now.'

'You'd never know, would you?'

'She could be from anywhere.'

From anywhere, from nowhere. Martha insisted on ticking the box, claiming the higher ground of unavoidable truth. But what were the odds of Caroline being in the nursery at Ngala Home for Single Mothers on the very weekend that nice Mr and Mrs Frederick Lothian came in for a visit? What if she had been back in the hospital that weekend, where she was regularly subjected to inquiries into the possible reasons for her continued 'failure to thrive'? What if the car had had a flat tyre? What if another nice white family had done the rounds that day, coming in early because of the weather, or the rain, or a family birthday?

But her mother was right; it was not by chance that children were removed, that her birth mother (the careful terms, the fine discriminations) walked away. Closer to home there was the local tragedy of Martha's miscarriages and the more oblique drama of her modern, liberal American family married to the Lincolnshire Lothians' family business of perpetual misery. A baby in the family was meant to be a replacement for all the things that did not happen to Martha and Frederick, and a reparation for the past.

When the lens of Australian history began to grind and turn towards the adoptive mother in the story – the collaborator – Martha's response was to lower her eyes, to accept the judgment and embrace the sentence. Her mother followed the inquiries into black deaths in custody like a penitent on her knees. She attended hearings and returned in tears and went to bed for days on end. Sometimes she heard her father argue with her mother.

'Why go, Martha? Why put yourself through this?'

She must have seen how others saw her: a blackbirder, a thief, a nester. Her mother put up her hand and passed out leaflets. She spoke up. Single-handedly she would make up for the things that were done to her daughter's people, the people her daughter never had. She returned to university and enrolled in child psychology. She would turn a cool, scientific eye towards the damage she had done.

There was her mother's catastrophe, and there was her own, and for a very long time there was no telling the two apart.

And there came a time to step away. 'We're not the same,' she screamed at her mother, 'in any way whatsoever.' That was before she discovered their conspiracy, well before Martha got sick.

Why did she have to carry this thing? She might have taken back some of the terrible words she said as a teenager and young woman had her parents told her the truth, but her father believed his daughter's tragedy happened long ago, in the past; they had dealt with all that and it was time for everyone to move on. 'Look at you,' he would say. 'Such a success.'

Caroline put her toothbrush in a ziplock bag and ran her fingers through her hair. Her dark, straight hair.

She buried herself in school and university. She studied and she smiled. She neither avoided nor looked for Aboriginal friends. She was like Switzerland: neutral and safe. She was careful to avoid the malls of Fremantle and Perth, where her folk hung out and liked to stop her, asking questions about her country, her people, wanting more than she could give.

Martha went to work in a soup kitchen in Fremantle. She became a prison visitor. She took phone calls in the evening. Caroline ignored her.

There were two other Indigenous kids in her high school, both of them boarders from up north, neither of them adopted. She hung out with the Indians and the Koreans and Chinese – they were studious, like her. Their parents had their own local prejudices, no doubt, but they hadn't been in Australia long enough to absorb the dominant view of her people. My people.

At university she joined a support group for Aboriginal students. She helped girls and boys in from the country to find their classes and borrow books from the library and structure their first-year essays. She gave them her lecture notes. She lent them small amounts of money she did not need. She tried to talk them into staying in Perth when all they wanted to do was go home. But she refused their invitations to parties and she shied away from questions of country and people.

There was an award from the dean, an invitation to join a committee. She declined, citing study commitments.

When she left school she began to talk about 'my real mother,' not because she wanted to hurt Martha, although that was part of it, but to set the record straight, to let them know that terminology was no match for the truth. She was at university when she accessed her medical records. She could remember sitting on the verandah of a friend's house, drinking red wine, smoking a cigarette, and thinking, *Enough. I can't take any more.*

But even the records were not enough, not in London at 4.56 am fully dressed, ready to leave for the airport.

She used to wish she were one of those children adopted from Russia, pale children with straw-coloured hair and dark rings under their eyes, children who could disappear into their families. No doubt they were damaged – all children who were abandoned are damaged – but at least they could hide away. But Caroline could never disappear. Her mark made her different

THE EXTERMINATION OF THE AMERICAN BISON.

BY

WILLIAM T. HORNADAY,

Superintendent of the National Zoological Park.

It seemed as if Providence had ordained that this splendid animal, perfect in limb, noble in size, should be saved to serve as a monument to the greatness of his race, that once roamed the prairies in myriads. Bullets found in his body showed that he had been chased and hunted before, but fate preserved him for the immortality of a Museum exhibit. His vertical height at the shoulders is 5 feet 8 inches. The thick hair adds enough to his height to make it full 6 feet. The length of his head and body is 9 feet 2 inches, his girth 8 feet 4 inches and his weight is, or was, about 1,600 pounds.

from her family, but it was not even written in a script that could be clearly read.

In public her mother tried to buffer and shield her with an explanation out of earshot, or an early announcement designed to silence any questions.

'And this is our daughter, Caroline. And our son, Caroline's younger brother, Callum.'

'Oh, she's nothing like you, is she? Is she ad – ?'

'She looks Ab –'

'Do you know who her – ?'

'You look just like your mother,' her father liked to say. When she was little she loved to hear it, but as she got older it drove her crazy. At seven she was thrilled and gratified when, after begging and begging, her mother finally dyed her grey-streaked hair a glossy dark brown, just like her own. Now she matched. 'You and me are the same, Mummy. Exactly the same.'

'Promise me something,' Martha said, crimping the edge of her dark quilt. It was an American mourning quilt, made by women whose men had failed to come home from the Civil War. The tight black-and-white print was called Shaker grey. How did it come to be on her mother's bed? It belonged in a box in the attic, carefully folded over acid-free tubes so the creases did not age and crack. At the time Caroline thought, *How like her, how like my mother to clothe herself in someone else's mourning.* And then she thought, *Soon that quilt will be mine.*

'I want you to promise me something.'

Her mother was only sixty-three. She was a lean, agile woman. When she was not in bed in one of her moods, she walked in the early morning, a brisk thirty minutes along the river. Twice a week she went to hatha yoga. She was in her second term of Arabic at TAFE. She was teaching English to refugees. The university degree had never been completed. It was a subject to be avoided in their family, one among many. After Callum's accident there was no potential in the future, no profession for Martha. There was devotion, and loathing.

When they finally found a cause for the terrible headaches and the clouded vision, once they had a picture of the thing in her brain, Frederick swung into action. He ignored Martha's weak protests and Caroline's strong opposition, and moved Martha into the downstairs bedroom. He employed a nurse he barely tolerated. He called Martha's only brother in Jersey City and asked him to come. Uncle Sam declined as always, this time citing high blood pressure. But Martha's women friends rallied around, arriving one by one with the sort of soft, wet food that goes in and out easily – pumpkin soup, tuna mornay, cauliflower cheese.

They came with pinched faces and left with swollen eyes, throwing themselves one after another at Caroline, unable, even at this terrible time, to imagine either offering comfort to or seeking it from Frederick Lothian, who stood to attention by the front door, holding out their handbags and their coats and their empty Tupperware containers, as if he couldn't wait to get them out of the house.

'Caroline?'

'Yes, Mum, I'm here.'

'There's some things in the gunmetal chest upstairs, some notebooks. They're for you.'

'Don't speak, Mum.' Martha needed morphine for the pain, and it left her struggling for air.

'I want you to sort my things – only you, not your father. My clothes, everything. There are some letters under the quilts. I want you to get rid of the letters.'

'Letters from Dad?' Caroline began to cry. 'Love letters?' She didn't want to get rid of her parents' letters. There had been love, and it was not to be thrown away.

'No. No.' Her eyes were closing as the drugs took over. 'Not your father.'

Caroline waited to see if her mother would return. It was minutes before she opened her eyes and spoke.

'Ralph.'

She heard her mother, but waited to hear it again.

'Ralph.'

She found them that afternoon, a small bundle in her mother's writing inside a blank yellow envelope.

R.

F. leaves on Friday for Helsinki. Saturday? Sunday? Monday? I'll wait for your call.

M.

Her father's best friend. The man her mother could hardly stand. The last envelope was pale blue. It was from Ralph.

M.

Veronica knows everything. I am returning your notes. Please, Martha, do not tell F. There is nothing to be gained now. Veronica will say nothing because of Callum. Everything is different now. You and Fred must have each other.

R.

She stared at the date at the top of the thick pale-blue paper. October 1995, a few months after the accident. When her father left, she found some newspaper and matches and lit a fire in the brick barbecue next to the swimming pool. Brown leaves carpeted the bottom of the pool and the filter was clogged with decomposing flowers and insects. As a child she spent her summers on patrol, rescuing lizards, a lifeguard for the unguarded of the world. Her mother's beautiful yellow grevillea had run woody and wild. It had been years since Martha had gardened with passion; not since the accident. Caroline pushed the letters into the fire and waited until the words were gone.

That was long ago. She was about to take the train to Heathrow and fly to Scotland. She had money in her wallet and thousands of frequent-flyer points. She had a career. But it was not the career she had wanted as a young woman. She had wanted a career where evenings were spent in a book-lined study, poring over papers and doing battle with the fax machine while your lovely wife and clever children hovered below you on the ground floor, like iron filings. She had wanted a man's career.

'Your father is teaching tonight,' her mother would tell them when they ate dinner without him. Overnight he might disappear to Amsterdam or Buenos Aires, called to wherever a major idea had developed theoretical cracks.

'Your father is giving a paper in Helsinki,' Martha would announce at breakfast. 'Callum, eat your porridge.'

'E. T. doesn't eat porridge and neither do I,' replied Callum.

Before he had taken early retirement, Frederick had had his own laboratory at the university and students who came from all over the world seeking his supervision. His colleagues wondered why a man of his stature and talent would sink himself out of sight in a minor Australian city at the end of the world.

'Your father is the J. D. Salinger of concrete,' Ralph told her once.

She and Callum had laughed, even though neither knew what he meant. 'My father is the smartest man in the world,' she told her classmates in Grade 7.

It was clear to her now that his distance from the old centres lent him an aura of eccentricity, but as development turned from London and Zurich to Kuala Lumpur and Singapore, Mumbai and Shanghai, Frederick Lothian was deemed prescient. Architects and reps from engineering companies flew down to consult on the early stages of their projects for the booming economies of Asia. Her father, the brilliant Frederick Lothian, would spin the mathematics and help them demonstrate the structural feasibility of their new design for the parliament or law courts, and with his invaluable expertise and innate empathy for design they would achieve the flexibility and cost-effectiveness of concrete but, more crucially, they would bypass brutalism in favour of a more organic monumentalism. 'A practical poetry,' one article said of his designs for concrete shells.

Such lives no longer existed. There were too many students, too little prestige, and too little money. Young academics now were harried and exhausted, struggling to move from casual teaching to a short-term contract. Caroline wandered around the world with a small suitcase and a laptop.

She heard laughter on the street. The clubs had closed. Soon she would fly to Aberdeen, but she would never have a real career. A real career was launched like a missile at a target, and travelled towards it, true and unswerving. A real career was not initiated by a chance encounter with an egg on the internet. She learnt from watching her mother that in the absence of a real career, a woman had to make things up for herself. Martha had abandoned her first degree when she married Frederick. She threw herself into motherhood, running the tuck shop at their primary school, teaching quilting at summer school, working part-time as a teacher's assistant, at the soup kitchen, caring for little Callum and moody Caroline. Martha had gone in the first convoy to Noonkanbah, to protest mining on Aboriginal land. She wanted Caroline to come too, but Caroline had a piano competition she could not miss.

At thirty-seven Caroline had been to Broome and the Kimberley only twice, for conferences on museums and Aboriginal collections. At the first she delivered an impassioned paper on the repatriation of cultural materials to a round of applause, and then went back to her hotel to consider suicide. The town was awash with tourists and faux architecture and themed shops with their mock-historic fonts. She hated seeing young

Aboriginal girls on the streets and ruined men at the bar. She met locals and leaders who had mothers and fathers and aunties and uncles and nieces and nephews, but in Broome she kept looking for the sad folk, because she was sad too.

It ended. Her father's career was shot down by a phone call in the evening.

Her mother's life ended on a Monday.

'Promise me,' her mother repeated.

'I promise,' Caroline replied, dreading what was coming. She wanted no more deathbed revelations. How could her mother betray her father? How could she tell her this now?

'Say it to me,' her mother whispered fiercely, her frail hand tightening around her wrist. 'Say out loud what it is you promise.'

'Mum, please.'

'Say it to me. I implore you.'

Caroline winced. *Implore* was not a word her mother would ever use. It was the drugs, she was sure.

'Caroline?'

'I promise I'll try …'

Damp strands of grey hair stuck to her mother's nose and upper lip.

'I'll contact my real mother's family.'

The correct word was *biological*. That was Martha's word for the other mother; that was the word they had always used when they had their talks. Martha always kept abreast of current thinking on adoption. Caroline had no doubt that the woman who lay dying under the quilt was her mother. But Martha had known what was in her letter at the hospital, and had kept it from her. Both her parents knew from the day of the adoption that her mother had a first name and a last name, that she came from a town on a map, and they both knew exactly when she died.

Mixed-race female, born King Edward Memorial Hospital, approximately eight weeks premature, with severe respiratory trauma. 4 lb 1 oz.

They put her in a box with a warm light, like a battery egg. Her real mother came back when the baby was fat and healthy and took her for two years and one month.

Part-Aboriginal female, two years and four months, removed by Department of Community Welfare after child presented at Princess Margaret Hospital with multiple small burns and broken leg after domestic between mother and partner. X-rays show prior fractures of arm, legs and skull, consistent with prior abuse. Evidence of malnutrition.

She had thought it would take for ever to locate her family, but she was wrong. When she first received the handwritten letter from a woman who said she was her mother's sister, she had scanned it and saved it to her desktop. Sometimes she would open the jpeg and stare at the document, then zoom in until two words filled the screen: *Aunty Maureen*. Was this how her mother had written too, with looping l's and f's, and fine long tails on the ends of every word?

'Next time you are in town, we would love to see you,' her

aunt wrote, 'we're only a couple of hours north on a sealed road', as if Kalgoorlie was a place she visited often.

When she turned on her phone there were five voicemails. The first was from her father. She could see that he had phoned on Sunday morning, Perth time, which was unusual, because it was her turn to call. 'Caroline,' he began. 'It's your father here –'

Later, she thought, and closed her eyes.

BOOK 4

Trench

Monday evening, 16 January 2006

AS HE WALKED TOWARDS the water, Fred dug his bare feet into the sand to hide the thick yellow nails on the end of his ugly old toes. Jan might not be a strong swimmer, but there was no doubting her buoyancy. She had been floating on her back for at least twenty minutes. The beach was crowded after the hot day. Most people had stripped down to their swimsuits, but just up the beach was a group of women covered head to toe in soft, dark fabric. They swayed left to right, like silent bells, catching the cool air coming off the water. Their children bobbed around the shallows inside transparent inflatable rings, *spluthering* and *jauping* the water about them – Granny's words, dredged up from the dead. Hiding in the cupboard from the Mester Pig, he and Virgil would pretend to count up sheep in Granny's tongue to keep them from crying: *yan, tan, tethera, fethera, pethera, lethera, sethera, hovera, covera, dik, yanadik, tanadik, tetheradik, fetheradik, bumfits*. Bumfits? That old local word for the number fifteen twisted their terror until it torqued into laughter that loosened back up quick enough when they remembered what would happen if Dadda heard. *Bumfits*?

A group of Asian tourists were struggling to settle a tripod in the sand and adjusting their cameras, getting ready to catch the sunset, repeating the same mistake he and all first-time visitors to the Indian Ocean had made. A sunset could not be captured. There were boxes and boxes of slides under his bed at the villa, testament to the failure of photography. He passed a family who had brought their Esky. They lay around it plunging sticks of celery and carrot into green and pink dips and drinking Coke. A young woman in a bikini ran an icy can down her neck and between her breasts, rolling it into her deep cleavage. Frederick looked away. Some young lads were tossing a Frisbee, diving after it and landing heavily in the sand. They came up laughing and dusting off their legs. A thin, stringy boy with a head of dark hair and a little nub of fluff under his lip leapt sideways and missed. He met the ground not as you would meet an adversary – hardened and eager to hurt – but like a member of the family who had been gone just a little too long: a quick embrace, an easier release. What would he be – eighteen, nineteen?

Fred let the water cover his hairy toes. He could count on one hand the number of times he had been in the ocean in the last thirty years. His children laughed at him when he stayed on a towel under his cricket hat while they skidded across the shallows on their foam boards, or rose up on the crest of a dumper and disappeared under its cruel lip. Fred would dash to the edge, casting about anxiously until they staggered up in the churning white water with a thatch of sandy hair hanging over their faces. 'You'll be fine,' he would call out. 'Just breathe, Callum. Don't rub your eyes, Caroline.' Martha didn't like him taking the children to the beach without her. What if they got into trouble? What if they needed to be rescued? But they were perfectly safe. He always stayed between the flags where the lifeguards were on duty.

'I can swim quite well,' he said to Jan in the car on the way to the beach, 'I really just prefer not to.' He told her about when he had been forced to learn in school, in a fetid indoor public pool in Lincoln.

'You have no idea how filthy those English pools were. I can still remember the horrible black-green mould in the gaps between the tiles.'

'Strange how a little detail from childhood has affected you so much,' she said. 'Would you turn down the air conditioning?'

But that was only the half of it. The mould brought back Grandpa's description of living filth that nested in the skin and under the toes and fingers of men in the trenches. 'You'd try to pick it off, to get it out. Pick and pick. Get a stick, a piddle of wire. Wouldn't want to come, would it? Put a bit of meat in front of it and it'd all crawl on out. Least you had your supper, hey, Freddy?'

Young Fred learnt to swim in jagged, desperate grabs, feet paddling wildly, his neck straining to keep his head up above the waterline to avoid the scraps of snot and brown stuff that floated past, and to save his eyes from the fierce antiseptic they tipped into the pool from grey tin buckets each time a new group arrived. The boys were made to wait on the edge of the pool in their saggy jersey trunks, blue-white and rigid with cold, while the attendants took up long wooden poles and stirred the water to and fro, like Macbeth's witches.

Eye of newt, and toe of frog,
Wool of bat, and tongue of dog.

Mr Chandish sneaked up behind him and pushed. Frederick went in as stiff as a statue and sank, then kicked his way up for air. Through stinging eyes and mouthfuls of acid water he saw his hated teacher's thick glasses and small eyes. The bright patch of red hair above his mouth moved up and down, up and down, like a signal flag: 'Stroke, Lothian, stroke!'

The detail was small, yes, but it had an unstoppable tread. It rolled straight over the top of the pool and up the green hill to his father and Pop, staggering home from the pub.

He had always been afraid of grown-up men. Granny said that Pop was different before the war, when he started out as a lad at Foster's Engineering on Waterloo Street, after they set him down in the foundry to make tractors and harvesters. When war broke out, the company made a tank, which was just a pair of metal boxes stacked one on the other, like tin coffins. It had small eyes with little flaps, just like Mr Chandish. They named it Little Willie, and it scared the pants off the children in town. 'I'll lock you in Little Willie and leave you there to rot,' mothers told their boys when they misbehaved. The next tanks were just converted tractors, but then they made the Mark IV, a categorical leap in engineering terms. By then Pop had laid down his tools and volunteered. He was too old for the war, well over forty, but they took him anyway, and when they brought him back he was missing one arm, half a leg, and all of his sense of humour, or so Granny said before she packed up and went to live with her sister Marjorie in Aberfeldy, Scotland.

'Don't you go, Granny,' he cried.

'Oh, no, no,' sobbed Virgil.

'Stop your kebbing,' said Granny, but she was crying too.

Granny was the only warm, sweet, constant thing that he and Virgil had ever had – he didn't count his mother, because she was too wrapped up in fear of his father to be putting out love to her boys. You couldn't blame Gran for going. When he came back from battle, Pop retired to the Hare and the Fox,

where you still only needed one arm to lift a pint. It was too much for Gran, so she left for good. She never forgot her two boys, though. There were little bits of money on birthdays, and postcards of the Falls of Moness and Edinburgh Castle. 'Write me, Freddy, and tell me, is your Pop still at the pub?'

When Virgil died, she wrote to their dad. 'Alexander, I'm coming down for Freddy.'

But his father wouldn't have it. 'She left Pop of her own free will. She's laid down on her own bed up there, so don't go thinking she can *sneell* back now.'

His father was at the foundry from fourteen. By the war he was almost old enough to join with his pa, but they dismissed him outright on account of a buckle in the spine. Without the older men to beat him back and with only women on the factory floor, he climbed up to foreman. Well after the machines were forged and riveted and readied and the Mark IV rolled off the line and out to Mesopotamia, his father kept rising, like dough on top of a warm oven, going up an imaginary run to be a floor manager of sorts, from where he got the occasional glimpse of Sir William and Lady Isobel in their suits and furs, preparing for true posterity.

Fred looked out to sea. The Indian Ocean was oily and firm, like the rind of a tropical fruit or the sleek body of his dolphin. *He is out there somewhere*, he thought nervously. Towards dusk a fin could go either way. The wrong sort of fin could rise up and take you down. Of all the stories of sharks and shark attacks, none scared him more than those about people who disappeared. Weeks later a pair of trunks might wash up on a beach, or, even worse, a small part of the missing person: a remainder – a reminder – like a leg or a torso. He imagined being called in to identify the missing person.

'Mr Lothian, is this the leg?'

A solemn nod. 'I'd recognise that kneecap anywhere.'

He was being silly now. Jan lifted her head and waved.

'Are you coming in?' she called. 'It'll be dark soon.'

She was using her hands as rudders and paddles, turning herself around and around in the water, like the arms of a large railway clock. You could never be sure if Dad was coming home as a dolphin or a shark. He balanced work with an equal weight of lager and Scotch, which he took at the bar with Pa and a toast to the fallen, but when Virgil died those scales tipped right over and he took them all down with him.

Fred stepped in up to his knees and felt his feet sink into the soft, sucking sand. He and Virgil had been prepared for the likelihood of quicksand in Sarawak and the Congo.

'Always carry a length of good rope,' Fred advised his little brother, 'and be tied together around the waist, like they do on the Matterhorn.'

'What about a plank of wood, Freddy?' said Virgil. 'I can throw it across the quicksand and pull you out. Hey, Freddy, how quick is that quicksand?'

He planned it all. He and Virgil would stow away on a

boat to Port Said, then it was on to Hong Kong and the East Indies, where they would be adopted by a pair of intelligent orangutans (they both loved Kipling) before being discovered by a distant uncle with a private income and a vast library of old books. Uncle would give them brass telescopes and make them dugout canoes from fallen tree trunks. After a series of adventures with pirates, they would find buried treasure and settle down in the British Enclosure in Canton, which Frederick had read about in his encyclopedia. He was going to give up French, which he hated, and learn to speak Mandarin and Cantonese. He would study the architecture of the Great Wall and travel to the Forbidden City, while Virgil would do whatever Virgil wanted to do, which at four – nearly five – was eat sugary cakes and dig large holes in the garden with his bare hands. They would be leaving from Liverpool in the spring of 1948. But Virgil wanted to leave from Southampton, because, he said, the *Mayflower* had gone from Southampton. (How did Virgil know this? Had he imagined it all?) He tried his best to change his brother's mind, because Southampton had farewelled the *Titanic* and Fred was superstitious, but Virgil whined and stamped like a baby.

'But, Freddy' – was he really only four? – 'Southampton was where them flying boats is from.' Frederick gave in – Southampton it was. The plan was broad in scope, short on detail. Through careful thievery from the pocket of his father's jacket when he was passed out on the couch, along with money earnt by fairer means (delivering milk early on Friday mornings for Mr Smith's dairy), he managed to save up three pounds and ten shillings, which was tied up in a sock and stuffed under his mattress. He never told Virgil about the money. Virgil was bound to get overexcited and go tell Mam. He could hardly be trusted with a stolen sugar cube, let alone the great escape.

Fred stepped in up to his thighs. It was freezing. Why was he digging up what was done when he'd just have to go bury it again? After they put Virgil in his new woollen pants and jacket and dropped him in his pine box and covered him up with dirt, Fred stole the old metal stirring spoon from his mother's kitchen drawer and dug out a hole near the grave and dropped the sock right in. Three pounds ten shillings, and all that was left of that.

He took a deep breath. This would be the time to turn and head for his towel, but he would not be doing that today. Today he was wearing a new black Lycra rashie and navy trunks that were itching the insides of his thighs. Today he took a breath of fresh air into his lungs, stepped forward into the cold water and dived right in.

Stroke, Lothian, stroke.

He came up and breaststroked slowly by Jan, who was passing through ten o'clock on her way to twelve. He would not think about the incalculable volume of water below him, or the immeasurable volume of air above him, or of the endless capacity of the ocean to swallow and digest all who entered. He pushed his face forward, letting his chin skim the water, then pulled his arms apart and tucked them in tight, like chicken wings, and raised his head to breathe. His knees said goodbye

and his feet said hello as he frogged his legs up, out and back together in a nice long snap, driving his arms and hands forward in a straight line, just as he had been taught to do more than sixty years before. The waters parted in front of him and closed over behind him. On and on he swam, towards another place altogether, aiming straight for that fierce orange sun ball slipping down behind the world. As he swam a red curtain was dragged right across the sky, and then it too began to drop away, leaving only a grey sky and a single star.

'Fred! Fred!'

He turned. He was far from the shore, out in the middle of the ocean. A figure on the beach was zigzagging in diminishing zeds until it came to a full stop. Clouds descended and the water rose up. He paddled furiously in tight circles, like a lost dog, looking for Virgil. He dived down and grabbed at the sea, desperate to feel his brother's worsted jacket, but instead he met something greasy and entangling. He fought it off and swam upward for air and met neither storm clouds nor driving rain, but a benign Venus in a clear sky. He tugged at the long thread of sea grass that had wrapped itself around his legs. This was not the lake at Saint-Clair. That was not his mother on the shore worrying her heavy grey wool skirt, but Jan, wrapped in a pale-blue towel, calling him in.

His legs shook when he stumbled ashore. He had not swum that far since he was a child. Jan held up the towel, spread wide, as if he were a little boy coming in from the cold. She had been worried. He had given her a fright. He waited for the fountain of concern, the overflow of words, like down from a pillow, but he was met instead with silence. She snapped the towel about her and picked up her bag. He found his own towel and dried himself carefully, measuring the widening silence. As he bent down to dry between his toes, the Frisbee struck him square on the cheek.

'God!' he said, standing up and clutching his face.

'I'm so sorry – are you okay?' It was the skinny young man with curly black hair, all out of breath from running. 'Are you all right? I missed it. We should have stopped playing, it's too dark.'

'I'm fine,' said Fred, 'it's nothing.' He rubbed his cheek. It hurt like hell.

Two more of the boys came running up. One was very fair and blond, like a Swede or a Dane. The other had freckles and unruly brown hair, like the head of a duster. None of them were laughing now. They were all too worried about the poor old man who'd been felled by their Frisbee.

'He's not hurt,' said Jan brusquely. 'Are you? There'll be a bit of a bruise, but that's it.'

They both watched the boys trying to trip each other up as they walked up the beach. The curly-headed one turned and waved. Jan lifted a hand.

'Lovely boys,' she murmured. 'My boy looked a bit like that one with the freckles. He was all teeth and smiles. He had more of the build of the tall one who threw the Frisbee.'

Fred rubbed his cheek. He cleared his throat. He waited and waited, and then he understood.

'Mine had dark hair,' he said quickly. 'Lots of it. He got it from his mother. You can see he didn't get it from me.'

Jan shot him a dismissive look and put her beach bag over her shoulder.

'Let me get that,' said Fred.

'I can manage,' she said sharply. 'I'm going to the showers.'

He was breathing heavily, straining to keep up. Jan was a fast walker. She had remarkably strong, well-formed calves. It was almost dark, and the tall lights in the car park had been switched on. Seagulls were circling the white beacons, screaming and cawing. The first time he saw seagulls around streetlights he could not get past the idea that they ought to be moths, and that the birds were engaged in some kind of exaggerated animal mimicry. Why would seagulls circle streetlights? But of course it was the bugs. The birds were after the insects that were drawn to the lights. He had missed a whole step in understanding because he could not see the insects.

He went into the men's changing room, where he wrestled with his wet rashie. Why had he bought the smaller size? He could barely get it over his head. Vanity, that's why. It held in his little paunch, tugged at the loose flesh. He thought of the boys on the beach, of the lean, long muscles of his son at twenty.

When he was dressed he sat down on a bench outside to wait for Jan. It was getting late. Where was she? Women always took so much longer than men to change. It wasn't the make-up, because Martha didn't wear it. For a long time he thought it was the bras – those tiny hooks behind your back, the finicky shoulder straps – but then Martha stopped wearing bras and instead wore stretchy black singlets, and he was still left waiting. He watched a man bring a little boy up from the beach on his shoulders. He held him under the head of the shower, turning him back and forth like a plate being rinsed under a tap. His mother held out a towel and wrapped the boy up tight like a roly-poly pudding, binding his arms to his body. The boy squealed and squirmed, like poor Tom Kitten in the clutches of fat Samuel Whiskers and skinny Anna Maria.

But Martha had wanted to keep him waiting. She would rather be in the shower than with her husband in the car, driving to the cinema, where she would have to sit next to him for the entire film and pretend not to like salty popcorn. She would do anything to avoid him. It had been like that since the accident. *Tolerance*, their book would be called, if it were ever written. He checked his watch. What the hell was Jan doing in there? He hated waiting for women. He hated waiting, full stop. He could not bear being left with nothing to do. He needed a pencil and paper, or a torch and a *Women's Weekly*. When he went to the doctor he liked to arrive early so he could read the women's magazines piled up in the waiting room. They kept his mind off the pending examination. The closer you got to death, the more likely you were to be dying. He began with the advice columns. The idea of asking anyone – a stranger – for advice on anything other than a mathematical calculation or superannuation was mystifying. 'My wife of thirty-seven years loathes me. I have trouble sleeping at night. My daughter is adopted. What should I do?'

Jan walked straight past him towards the car. He hurried after her with the keys.

'How was the shower, Jan? Mine was a bit cold.' He fumbled with the remote. 'Have you got everything? It's difficult to see in those showers in the dark. The lights are hopeless. I could hardly get my underpants on the right way. Ha! How were yours? Your lights I mean, not your …'

Something was wrong. There was a vacuum that ought to be filled by words – Jan's words – and in the absence of those words Fred was floundering. He pushed the remote. The boot popped up and Jan tossed her wet things in. He went around to open the door for her, but she pushed past him.

'I can open my own door, thank you,' she said.

Fred started the car and switched on the headlights, but left it in neutral. He turned to look at her. She was staring straight ahead.

'Is everything all right, Jan?'

'Why do you ask?'

'You seem quiet, that's all. I thought I might have done something to upset you.'

'What do you think that might be?'

'Pardon?'

'What do you think you might have done to upset me? I'd be interested to know.'

'I don't know. You just seem – different.'

'Different?'

Fred turned on the car and put it into drive.

Jan took hold of the gearstick and pushed it back to park. 'Is that because I'm not providing the light relief you're accustomed to?'

'What do you mean, Jan? What's this light relief – ?'

'You think I'm one of those kind, chatty older widows who just can't wait to get her hands on another man to look after, who dreams of spending her last days providing comfort and company for a former professor who hates swimming, can't cook and isn't man enough to tell the truth.'

Fred turned off the car. 'I have no idea what to say, Jan. I've never lied to you.' He was about to say, 'I've only known you one day', but thought better of it.

Jan undid her seatbelt with purpose and shifted in her seat to face him. He had not thought that Jan was capable of anger – sadness, yes, of course, women were always sad – but anger was not something he had associated with Jan. Clearly, he had been wrong.

'Why did you swim out so far when you can hardly swim? I was about to call the lifeguards – or the police. You tell me on the way to the beach that you never swim because of some childhood trauma involving mould – which, frankly, I didn't buy, but that's your business – and then you head off into the sunset. How do you think I felt? Do you have any idea what I was thinking?'

Frederick wasn't used to imagining what others might be feeling or thinking. He wasn't sure he was even capable of it. But he had an inkling. 'I don't know what came over me, Jan. I just felt like I could go on for ever.'

The car park was filling up with patrons of the new beach-side restaurant. A stretch limousine pulled up and released a gaggle of girls in short, tight dresses and sparkly high heels. An eighteenth birthday?

'I'm so sorry if I upset you,' he said. 'It wasn't intentional.'

Jan's thick curls were retracting as they dried. He licked his lips.

'I'm not suicidal, if that's what you think.'

It is a strange thing to take possession of a word for the first time. *Suicide*. Fred had never before placed the first-person pronoun and that particular noun in the same sentence; he had never before thought, *my* suicide, but once he took possession of the idea it turned on him, as the turret on a tank rotates the muzzle to find its target. Suddenly suicide had an inexorable logic.

'Then tell me, what's happened to your son. And where's your daughter? You think talk is a one-way street? Good old Jan will manage all the traffic while you sit at home in that ridiculous excuse for a chair and watch the world go by? I saw the way you looked at those boys. I know that look, Fred.' She stopped to gather herself up. 'Is your son dead too?'

Defeated. 'My daughter Caroline lives in Melbourne, but right now she's in London for work. My son was in a car accident. It was almost twelve years ago. He's in a high-care facility. He has an acquired brain injury.'

He watched Jan's face carefully, waiting for sympathy to

soften her unflinching gaze. But she did not soften. If anything, she tightened and drew back, like an arrow in a bow.

'Where?'

'What?'

'Where is this place? Is it in Perth?'

He nodded. It was easier to nod than speak.

'How often do you visit him? When did you last see him?'

The girls were standing under the light, taking long swigs from a bottle of champagne, skidding about on silly heels. Every so often their long, thin legs gave way, like those of baby giraffes learning to stand. Small, shiny evening bags hung down from their shoulders. He focused on the glittery rectangles, hoping they would do something to save him.

'Not very often. He doesn't know who I am.'

Jan laughed, or whatever it is you do when you make a sound like a laugh about something that is the opposite of funny. 'Is that your definition of a person worth visiting? Someone who knows who *you are*?'

This was not how he had imagined the evening. He had imagined a nice little out-of-the-way restaurant, with spicy Vietnamese food in white bowls and tiny glasses of green tea, him eating with chopsticks and nodding and chewing as Jan filled the air about him with comforting, feathery, feminine words.

Jan slumped back in her seat. She shook her head slowly.

He looked past her to the blackening ocean. His dolphin was out there waiting for him, with a smiling face and a winking eye.

'How long has it been, Fred?'

The answer was getting ready to climb out of his mouth and write itself up in the air, in neon, flashing on and off, on and off. 'I saw him just over two years ago, when Martha died.'

'Two years ago.'

A concrete time frame seemed to energise Jan. She turned

to him, with one finger raised. 'You cannot leave this one more day. You must go. I'll come in the car if that helps. I can wait outside. I have to see Morrison, and then you can go to see your boy. Does he have a name?'

'Callum, his name is Callum. We called him Callum.' He should have said 'This is none of your business', but it was too late for that.

Jan opened her door to release her seatbelt strap. 'I need to eat. I can't go to a restaurant now. There's a burger place just off the highway and that'll have to do. Drive as if we're heading home, and I'll tell you when to turn. How do I loosen this belt?'

'You press that button up near your shoulder. See it?'

The car was idling gently. He put it in drive and kept his foot on the brake to wait for Jan. The girls were climbing back into the limo. One of them tripped as she walked after her friends and went down on both kneecaps, like a camel, and began to laugh and cry at the same time. Her friends pulled her into the car. The car door closed.

'Actually, they called yesterday,' said Fred.

'Who called? I'm all buckled in, you can go now.'

'The care facility called last night. I gave them Caroline's number.'

'Why? Is that unusual – that they call, I mean?'

'They don't have my number. They always call Caroline.'

'But I thought Caroline lived in Melbourne? Or London?'

'She comes back regularly to see Callum. She manages things. I pay for the flights.'

This was not completely true. She had been back only two or three times since Martha died, although he knew she spoke to them every week. And she had refused to let him pay for the flights. He looked at Jan. He saw that he should not have mentioned money.

'So they never call you? Normally, I mean?'

Frederick did not answer. Jan had tipped her face away from

him so he could see only the outline of her jaw and the crown of curls. It was like confession, but there was no one left to absolve him of his sins.

Is it a sin of thought or a sin of action, my son?

A sin of thought, Father.

And what are your thoughts? Come, come, laddie, the Lord Jesus will understand.

I want to kill my father. I want to kill him dead.

'What did they want? Why did they call?'

Fred could taste saltwater at the back of his throat.

'Are you going to make me squeeze every little word out of you?'

Jan had clearly had enough of him. Could you blame her?

'They just said it was about Callum, and that my daughter had given them my number while she was out of the country. I passed on her contact details in London.'

'I see,' said Jan.

But she didn't see. She didn't see at all.

'So have you spoken to Caroline? Is Callum all right?'

'I put the phone down. Then I pulled out the plug. That's why you couldn't contact me about Tom. It's still unplugged.'

He was pathetic. He was crawling across the floor like a cockroach.

'But what if it's an emergency?' Jan exhaled heavily. 'I'm trying, I really am. I know you probably think this is none of my business, but anything could have happened, don't you see? He could be dead. How have you managed to live like this? I think I might go straight home.'

He spoke in desperation, just before the truth swallowed him completely. His words rose up slowly like a glacier in front of an ocean liner, cold and hard and unavoidable. 'But Jan, you did it to your son. You said it yourself. You stopped seeing him.'

There was the sound of glass shattering. A girl had thrown an empty bottle out of the window of the limousine.

'What did I do? What did Sam and I do? Turn our backs on our son? Is that what you're saying? You think it's the same? Something equal, two wrongs that cancel each other out? Well, I don't think so, Fred. I've had enough of this. I want to go home.'

'I shouldn't have said that. I'm sorry.' A headlight from a parking car spun around and struck the back of Fred's head, casting his face into darkness. Ahead of him was a giant clock with great big metal arms. He was climbing up onto the clock and trying to push the minute hand back, but it would not budge. He looked at Jan. My god, she was crying. He had made Jan cry.

'You have no feelings. My son was an addict. He robbed us clean. He broke our hearts so many times I could not begin to tell you. We took him back over and over again. We had him in counselling, and rehab, we took him around the world twice to get away from his so-called friends, we bought him a flat, and we put him in new courses and each time he did it again and again. In the end we had no choice. Do you hear me, Fred? We had no choice.'

'I'm sorry, Jan.'

She ignored him. 'But you're right in a way. We always thought it was our fault. And it was. It still is, as far as I'm concerned. Somewhere, sometime, we did something wrong. That's what I believe, deep down. But it's not the same. You can't say it's the same.'

Fred watched the driver of the limousine get out of the car. He walked over to the rear door and opened it. He was angry. Two girls got out and began to pick up broken glass and carry it to the bin. Jan was crying softly. He had known Jan only one day and he had made her cry.

'I know it's not the same,' he said. 'Can you forgive me?' In books and films, moments like these come closer to the end than the beginning. Fred had only just met Jan. It was far too soon for the fog to lift. It was too soon for dawn to break. But there you have it, unlikely, unprecedented and hard to believe: an epiphany early on in the story, at night, in the car park of Leighton Beach.

Jan wiped her eyes and sighed. She reached across and put the car in park. 'I think you'd better turn it off, Fred. We'll run out of petrol next. And the headlights too.'

Fred turned off the car. He fumbled in a compartment on the side of the door for a small packet of tissues and blew his nose loudly, then offered one to Jan.

'No, thanks. Look, I'm not the angel here – or the priest. I'm not here to save you from yourself, or absolve you of your sins. I guess you were brought up Catholic?'

'How did you know?' sniffed Fred.

'This isn't some romantic comedy set in a retirement home … *And then he met chatty Jan, the widow next door with the budgerigars, dot, dot, dot.*'

'Ellipsis,' muttered Fred. 'Those three dots are called ellipses.'

Fred blew his nose. Vast amounts of seawater were coming out of his nostrils. And he was having trouble hearing. He should never go underwater. It was the shape of his ears; they were like funnels. He had run out of tissues, so he doubled them up and blew again. What should he do with the sodden tissues? He had no pockets and he didn't like to drop them on the floor. His house might be a mess, but he kept his car spotless. He saw a bin near the showers.

'I know what an ellipsis is, Fred. I'm a teacher. What are you looking for? Don't tell me you're worried about that tissue, are you? Open your window. Open it!'

Fred pushed the button.

'Now throw the tissue out.'

'What? You can't do that.'

'Why? Because it's littering? Because it wouldn't be the right thing to do? Look, you seem like a good person – or at least capable of good. You have potential. You don't like throwing rubbish out of car windows, for a start. So I don't give much weight to the monster line. You just have to get on with it now. You have to go home and clean it all up – and I don't just mean your villa.'

'I have to change,' said Fred as passionately as he could. He only half-believed his delivery, so he said it again. 'I have to change.' He could do it, he could. But he still didn't know what to do with the tissues. He screwed them up tight in his fist, compressing them into a tiny, wet ball. 'Do you believe that people can change, Jan? The trouble is I've never believed it. How can you change when you don't believe in change?'

'Why is it about belief? It isn't a miracle you need. It's not like you have to assume another identity or do anything monumental. You're not in a thriller where you wake up as, what's his name? Jason Bourne. The good thing about your situation is that you have room for improvement. Lucky you. What are you doing with your hand? Was that the tissue you just pushed out the window?'

His face was hot. He opened his door and plucked the damp ball from the bitumen. He refused to look at Jan. 'I think we should get that burger,' he said stiffly. He turned the key. Nothing. He turned it again. 'I think the battery's flat,' he said meekly. He tried it once more.

'Oh, for goodness sake, it's those effing lights. I told you to turn off the lights. Are you a member of the RAC? I'm going to die of hunger here – if I'm not already dead from frustration. We need to find a phone.'

He left Jan in the car and walked to the front of the restaurant. Two huge panels of glass parted and the cold neon of the car park gave way to the deep blue of an underwater cavern. As he waded towards a long bench he met the languid gaze of a tall, red-headed woman in a nacreous sheath. Between her scalloped breasts hung a length of creamy pearls.

'Good evening, sir, my name is Ariel. Welcome to Le Marin Japonais. Are you here for the degustation? Under what name is the booking?'

A light pulsed on the counter. The girl held up her palm to excuse herself and stepped away to take the call.

Frederick looked along the bench for a menu. Polished concrete. He ran his hand along the surface. *Few people understand the beauty of concrete.* He peered at it closely. His glasses were in the car, but it looked like it had been poured with an aggregate of shell grit and some kind of local curly worm shell, and then ground back at least three times with different grades.

It was a lovely job. He read the menu: 'Chef Yuko De Burge, formerly of Le Buffon Japonais in the Bund, Shanghai, welcomes you. Four-course degustation with matching wines, $150 per head.'

'I'm sorry, sir. What name is your booking under?'

'I don't have a booking, Ariel. My car has broken down. Is there any chance you have a table for two?'

Ariel opened and closed her cornflower-blue eyes.

'Oh my goodness,' she said, clutching her bosom, 'this is your lucky night! What have you been doing to deserve this? We're absolutely fully booked and normally we have a three-month wait, but I've just this very moment had a telephone cancellation for two. Their car has also broken down, but in the northern suburbs! What a coincidence. I think you'll enjoy your table. We've slid back the glass doors onto the beach.'

Ariel gestured into the aqueous depths of the restaurant, past a row of clear tanks filled with heads of purple and pink coral, to the outer shoals of Le Marin. There in the distance was a glowing square, heavy with silver tableware and sparkling glass, opening right onto the pale sand dunes and the waxy ocean.

'That is your table, sir. But you said there were two guests?'

'Could I possibly use your phone?'

'Of course,' said Ariel.

'Do you still have a phone book?'

'Naturally, sir.'

'And then I'll bring my guest from the car.'

Jan point-blank refused. 'I just couldn't, not after everything. And I'm not dressed. It looks very formal in there.'

'Please, Jan, it's my treat,' he said. 'And it's so dark no one can see what you're wearing. I'm so sorry about what I said. It's at least a two-hour wait for the RAC, so why not enjoy it?'

He could offer to put Jan in a taxi and she would be home in less than twenty minutes. But if he was going to change, then he had to do things he would never normally do, like spend $300 on a degustation.

'Why were you so long? I'm not in the best of moods, you know.'

'I realise that,' said Fred, 'and I'm very sorry. That was a terrible thing to say.'

Fred cast his gaze to the ground. He was humbled before Jan. Humble, a state of humility. Humility, from the Latin *humus*, meaning earth. He was truly contrite. Contrition, from the Latin *contritus*, 'ground to pieces' or crushed by guilt. Could there be a link with concrete? He'd have to look that up.

'It was weak,' said Jan.

Fred cleared his throat. 'I called the care facility from the restaurant. Callum has had a chest infection. I couldn't find out much more. They got hold of Caroline in London, and they have him on IV antibiotics but they're not altogether happy with his progress. I'm going in there tomorrow after lunch, to meet with the doctor.'

Jan did not move. Did she think he was making it up? The weekend staff had tried to call him to authorise the drug and they were not at all happy about having to call Europe. 'That was an expensive phone call, Mr Lothian. We won't be doing that again.' He had been very formal on the phone, not at all like a father calling about his son. He could not think about the actual visit. The last time he saw Callum was when Martha died; before that it had been four years. Before that …

'I'll come to dinner,' said Jan suddenly, 'but only because I'm starving. I'm not doing all the talking, though. I'm going to be listening to you.'

She pulled the rear-view mirror towards herself and fossicked in her handbag. Frederick found a pen and paper to write a note to the RAC.

'Moisturiser?'

'Thank you,' said Frederick, accepting a squeeze of pink cream in his open palm.

'Lipstick? I don't normally like degustation menus.'

'Me neither,' said Fred, 'but it's a lovely setting. And I'm paying.'

'If you insist,' said Jan, snapping her lipstick back into its sheath.

Fred rubbed the cream into his face and then got out of the car. It was a perfectly still evening. You could snap your fingers at one end of the galaxy and you'd hear it at the other. This was going better than he could ever have expected. Jan was coming to dinner. He watched her swing out of her seat and close the car door, then together they walked through the car park towards the restaurant. Was it possible that a monster could still live some kind of normal life?

'What's that?' said Jan suddenly. She was pointing towards the small white ball that Fred had tossed behind the wheel of a stationary car when he went to the restaurant to find a phone.

'Oh, thanks,' said Fred. 'My tissue. It must have dropped out of my pocket.'

'Of course it did,' said Jan.

Jan gasped as she stepped inside. She nodded towards Ariel. 'Look at that, our very own little mermaid. Are those seahorses in the tanks? I'm going to use their bathroom.'

Fred waited to be seated, holding on to the concrete bench in case he floated away. He was not feeling himself. The walls of Le Marin were carpeted floor to ceiling in heavy olive-green wool shag, like shreds of nori in miso. An aquatic blue-green light filtered down from the ceiling. Long threads of wool dangled idly from the walls, like sea grass buffeted in the inter-tidal zone. The floor was covered in a nubbly carpet with an uneven twist, the colour of sand at Moggs Eye Beach. Fred felt himself disperse and soften.

'Your table is ready, sir.'

He was led through the restaurant by a young man in oyster-grey pants and shirt who was wearing those ridicu-lous round black-rimmed spectacles, à la Corbusier. Another modern affectation, another one of those short-hand ways of signalling you wanted to belong to some tradition or move-ment or context or country you have no right to claim as your own.

Fred sat down and looked out into the dunes, waiting for his eyes to adjust. It would be a full moon in less than a week. Granny always said a full moon was bad luck. For years he had stayed inside with the curtains drawn on full moons. He peered into the restaurant. Where was Jan? He needed Jan right now, because the moon had just returned his son to him.

Callum was standing among the club rush.

He was wearing one of Martha's knitted beanies, and he was holding a brown metal thermos filled with hot chocolate. He was smiling. He had a bent smile because his second teeth were coming out crooked. He would need braces; they knew that already when he was ten. Frederick stepped out onto the narrow wooden deck abutting the dunes. The moon and the beanie and flask and the crooked smile put the boy up on a hill past Wandering, where they were camping out in search of the Aurora Borealis. Caroline and Martha were asleep in the back of the Saab and there was a fox in the lower paddock, on the hunt for meat. They both heard the lambs mewling nervously in the dark, calling for their mothers.

'Are you coming, Dad? Hurry up! The battery on my torch has just gone.'

'Sir?'

Frederick turned back to the table.

'Can I offer you and your guest a complimentary champagne cocktail?' Ariel carefully lowered two flutes.

Fred sat in his chair and watched thousands of industrious gold and silver bubbles scramble up the tunnel of his glass. The night Callum was conceived, millions of sperm jousted and tussled to meet Martha's lovely egg. What were the chances of his boy being made whole and perfect in that single moment? He picked up his glass and drained the contents. When he put down the glass, Callum had gone and in his place was a clump of coastal sedge. Or was it a myrtle? After working his way through all of Martha's things, he had finally come to the plant books. He could now identify a few of the plants on the dunes: cotton head, snake bush, dune mosses and club rush. Martha had several titles devoted to the grevillea: 'This plant is easily hybridised through a simple cutting, but is given to woodiness if not kept in check.' Martha was right; it was a remarkably beautiful species, especially in spring, when it unfurled its long, sticky-sweet pistil.

Spring was Martha's favourite time to walk along the river. In the first months after the accident, when it was still possible that Callum might regain some semblance of intention and order in his thinking, before he had the seizures that erased all hope, when Fred still prayed to his lost god that his perfect boy might be returned to him whole and intact, Martha would take Callum along the river for walks. With the help of Martha's books, Fred could now conjure these promenades in detail.

'That's hardenbergia, Callum, the creeper with the purple flowers. That beautiful orange plant is a Chapman River creeper

– it's quite a rare plant from up north, and I have no idea how it found its way here. See how it spirals in one direction? Those Carnaby's cockatoos probably flew the seed down from Geraldton. And look at that grevillea with the orange flowers – a "Honey Gem".'

He caught the waiter's eye and pointed at his empty flute. As soon as the waiter had left Fred picked up Jan's glass and drained it in one gulp. Caroline had told him all about their walks. She made a point of talking about everything Martha did with Callum, rubbing it in his face until it hurt. Martha visited Callum every day, and when Caroline was still in town she went with her.

Would he be telling Jan that after the seizures he always made sure he was out of the house when Martha left to see Callum, and up in his study with the door closed when she got home? That he always gave it a good half an hour before he came downstairs, in case Martha was crying again? Or that when he finally appeared he would carry a sheaf of paper in his arms in case he needed an excuse to get back to work?

Martha would be in the laundry doing a load of Callum's washing, even though they did it at the hospital, or she would have her wicker basket open for some kind of stitching job, though nothing of Callum's ever wore out.

'How are things?' he would say.

Once in a blue moon Martha would surprise him with an answer. 'I'm worried about his feet. We need to get a new podiatrist – a specialist. The one they have is hopeless.'

Fred would nod slowly, clear his throat. If she asked, he would help her shake out a wet sheet. He would take hold of his corners and bring them towards her, then bend down and pick up the lower edges and bring them in towards his wife, as if they were dancing a courtly pavane. Then he would step away, leaving her to carry the sheet to the line.

'Any ideas for dinner, Martha? Would you like to eat out?'

On rare occasions she would let him take her to dinner. They would eat Indian food, or pasta, and drink their wine. He would talk endlessly about Caroline, only ever about Caroline. Why was she still with Julian? Was she really going to move to Melbourne? Would Julian go too? He'd have to give up his tenure, and he'd never do that.

The truth is, Jan, there were two different worlds in our house. Martha stayed up at night listening to the radio and cooking vegetable broths, while I was in bed sneaking looks at the books she was reading. In the morning she was up early boiling and mashing the same soft foods Callum ate as a baby – pumpkin, avocado and banana – as if Callum were still teething. I stayed out in the garage with my collection, or closed the door to my study, pretending to keep up with concrete.

Fred was sinking deep into the Mariana Trench, eleven thousand metres below sea level. The pressure on his lungs was enormous. He needed air. He caught the waiter's eye and watched the oyster scuttle over for his empty flute and then swim off in the direction of the mermaid. When it became too hard to manage Callum on the walks, even with Caroline's help, Martha took CDs and books to his room. She would pop on a fugue or a sonata, and then she would open a book. For the first few years Martha read him the books she thought an intelligent young man ought to be reading: *All the Pretty Horses, Midnight's Children, Atonement*. After Callum was finished with these books, Fred tried to read them. But what use was literature to a monster? Monsters had no need of poetic language. Metaphor was lost on monsters.

Martha then read Callum the books she liked to read, the ones by *women writers*, heavily embroidered with female grief and children and trauma. She left them by her bed with little strips of yellow paper marking where she was up to. Sometimes Fred opened them up, looking for the fine pencil lines next to particular passages, desperate to know what was going on inside his wife's head, but terrified of finding out.

When all the children started reading *Harry Potter*, she and Callum read it too.

Mr and Mrs Dursley, of number four, Privet Drive, were proud to say that they were perfectly normal, thank you very much. They were the last people you'd expect to be involved in anything strange or mysterious, because they just didn't hold with such nonsense.

'I'm sorry I took so long. There was a queue.'

Fred stood up while Jan seated herself. She'd done something with her eyes. They were deep green, like sea grass, and rimmed in black, like an elliptical banded fish.

'Where did that come from? Have you looked at the menu?' When the waiter returned with Fred's champagne, Jan reached out to take it.

'Where's yours, Fred? Aren't you having a drink?'

Fred nodded at the waiter. *Another, please, sir.* 'Martha read *Harry Potter* to Callum. She read him all of them as they came out.'

Jan looked at him steadily. 'That's remarkable,' she said. 'Cognitively, how is he?'

'He can't follow stories,' he said. 'He can't follow anything. He can't speak. He makes sounds. He can hear, but we're not sure how much he understands. For the first year we thought he might recover some function, but then there were seizures. He was never going to be the same, but we thought there could be more.'

Jan nodded. 'I'm sorry,' she said.

For seven years Martha and Callum followed Harry and his struggles with Voldemort. Then she began to sweep further back, to *Stuart Little* and *The Velveteen Rabbit*. He never liked that book about the mouse, which she'd bought for Caroline when she was little. 'What exactly is the message, Martha? Is Caroline supposed to think she's as different from us as a white mouse?'

'It's allegorical, Frederick. Look it up.'

Towards the end, she went to the attic and brought down all the children's books. It was during *The Roly-Poly Pudding* that Callum spoke.

'He said, "whiskers", Fred. I heard him.'

She had rushed in from the garage after parking the car. Her eyes were shining and her cheeks were flushed, like St Teresa of Avila. He thought, *Martha's gone mad.* Through all the hell of their marriage — because that was what it had become since Callum's accident — neither could acknowledge the other's version of reality. Their lives were like a Venn diagram with two circles sharing only one small area in common: Caroline.

'He said, "whiskers". I heard him, Fred. I heard Callum speak.' Her look was *beseeching*.

In return, Fred's was *withering*, a look to kill the vine on the trellis. 'Whiskers?' he repeated, curling his lip. Martha nodded dumbly.

'Whiskers?' he repeated.

She began to cry.

'For god's sake, Martha, get a grip,' he shouted, then went up to his study and slammed the door.

The oyster came by with a glass of champagne and a carafe of water.

'Salute!' said Jan, lifting up her glass.

'Santé,' said Fred.

'So, go on,' she said, setting down her glass. 'Please.'

Fred took a mouthful of bubbles and descended another thousand metres into the trench. 'Martha kept up with all the latest therapies. She was the one who kept pushing for more tests. She was always onto them to increase Callum's physio and OT, and to get them to play more classical music and whatever. She wanted them to make sure Callum was *engaged*.'

Fred paused to leave a space for Jan to let him know that she was on his side, that his wife Martha was living a delusion.

'I can understand that,' said Jan carefully. She took a sip of water.

'What, that he had to be *stimulated*?'

'Why would you have a problem with that, Fred? Why?'

All around the restaurant, well-dressed couples were holding hands across their tables. Friends were laughing at shared jokes. *I have none of that*, thought Fred. *I have neither love nor friendship.*

Martha and Caroline read all the books – and there were many – about damaged people trapped inside their hard shells. They scoured the shelves of the university library. They met with academic staff from the Medical Department. They joined the Neurological Society. They wrote letters to America and England to see if there might be some radical therapy to stimulate brain growth and help reconnect ruptured neurons. But Virgil's death had taught Fred everything he knew about hope. Life was not hopeful. Life wore an implacable face, and its disposition was brutal, idle and cruel.

'I knew it wouldn't make a difference, of course. In real terms.'

'Hmm,' said Jan, looking down at the menu. Fred's blood vessels were expanding rapidly.

'Do you disagree? Do you really think that deluding yourself that therapy can make a difference was the right way to live? Do you think I should have lied to my wife so she could keep lying to herself and my daughter?'

He had raised his voice. He hadn't meant to do that. He took a gulp of champagne. His hand shook.

Jan put down her menu. 'I don't know, but it made a difference to your wife, and to Caroline too. It helped them deal with what had happened – to accept that Callum had changed. To have hope.'

'Changed?' Fred picked up the menu. He could not read, but he had to do something other than look at Jan's face. He hated her face. He hated her startling green eyes with their black rims, gazing at him like some kind of sea anemone, its tentacles opened to the entire world, unafraid and unflinching.

When Martha died he had gone to the care facility with Caroline. Caroline had not asked him to come but he knew he had to do it. All the way in the car he had been thinking monstrous thoughts, thoughts he would now desperately like to confess, if he still believed in confession. But Jan had made it clear that she was not here to save him. She would not listen to his terrible thoughts, or absolve him of his mortal sins. *Father, why should it matter to Callum if Martha is gone? He couldn't recognise her when she was here, so why should he care if she's gone?*

Jan looked up from the menu. 'I don't think we have any choice. The courses arrive and we use this document to interpret the dishes. It's like foreign travel. Some of it's in French, which I suppose you speak fluently, what with being a professor, but the food is actually very Japanese, which is my territory.'

The waiter arrived with white wine from somewhere in New Zealand. He tipped the pale fluid into their glasses. Jan picked up the enormous glass bowl and swung her wine around the perimeter.

'Just checking to see if there's a goldfish in it,' she said, and went back to reading the menu.

She had let him off the hook lightly. He could come up a little, release the pressure. But Callum was still down at the bottom of the sea, strapped in his chair like a stone, and to reach him he had to go deeper.

One of the carers was about to feed him. He watched Callum open his mouth to chew. Caroline asked the carer to leave them alone. She took a cloth and wiped her brother's face, and then sat on the bed next to his chair, spooning the soft food into his mouth. Frederick was standing near the door, so he could leave quickly if he had to. Caroline looked over at him with loathing. She put down the plate and took Callum's soft hands in her own.

'Callum, Mum's dead. Our mother has died, Callum. I'm so sorry.'

Callum used to have thin, expressive fingers, like his mother's, but now he had two limp paws that were liable to jerk away from him unless they were held in place. Frederick was concentrating on the blades of the ceiling fan. They were turning so slowly it was hard to see how they could make any difference to the flow of air in the room. Caroline climbed into her brother's lap and wrapped her arms around him. She began to sob. They were loud, terrible sobs. The blades went round and round, round and round. Callum let out one long sound, like air released under pressure, like a calf lost in a storm. Frederick squeezed his fists against his thighs. Round and round went the fan.

'Oh god,' he said involuntarily. 'What have I done?'

Jan started and spilt her water. 'What's wrong, Fred?'

'I have to see Callum. I have to talk to him.'

'Calm down. Here, have some water.' She dabbed the damp spot on the tablecloth with her napkin. 'Your poor wife.'

The waiter arrived with two large oval plates, inflected like a bivalve.

'Bêche-de-mer gunkan sushi,' he said, 'with chocolate-infused nori and a lemon-ginger mousse.' He inspected the damp spot.

'Would you like me to change the tablecloth, Madam?'

'It's fine,' said Fred. He looked at the delicate green and black and orange arrangement on his plate. He took a large swig of wine. He hovered over the silver chopsticks resting across the arched spine of a sardine, then picked up his knife and fork.

'Sea cucumber,' said Jan. 'Eat! We both need food. And when you've eaten, tell me what happened to Callum, if you're up to it. And then I want to hear about Caroline.' Jan popped a tiny orange pearl of roe into her mouth.

'She's adopted,' said Fred. He hacked noisily at the nori with his knife and fork, leaving plenty of room for Jan to do some of her imaginative embroidery around his bombshell.

Jan held another tiny orange roe between the tips of her silver sticks.

'Caroline is adopted,' he repeated. He put some food in his mouth, waiting for Jan to respond. Jan took a piece of nori and popped it in her mouth. She chewed slowly and then put down her chopsticks.

'And that explains what, exactly? Is that going to be it for Caroline?'

'Of course not,' said Fred tightly. Why was he even having dinner with this woman? 'Have you heard of the Stolen Generation? Caroline is Aboriginal. She's Indigenous – well, her mother was. Of course, she wasn't really stolen – not that there isn't a Stolen Generation. We adopted at the end of that period, in the early 1970s, when they stopped taking children away just because they were of mixed heritage. They used to call them half-castes.'

'Look at that!' said Jan, pointing her silver chopstick at the dunes. 'I just saw a fox. At the beach!'

'That wasn't a fox, it was a rabbit. There are no foxes here.'

'I was sure it was a fox. Isn't this dish wonderful? I'm just going to pretend there's no contradiction between our dialogue and our food. Go on. I was a teacher, remember? I know all about Australian history – the real Australian history.'

'Martha's doctor told her about the children's centre and the adoption service. Martha had been trying to get pregnant for years. There were … miscarriages.' The word was itself a miscarriage of justice. 'We went together, and we were allowed to choose a baby. It sounds terrible now, looking back, but that was how it was.'

'And so you chose Caroline. How old was she?'

'She was about two and a half.'

'Poor little girl,' said Jan.

'She'd been brought into the public hospital and went into care from there.'

'That's quite old to relinquish a child. Did her mother actually give her up?'

'Yes, of course,' said Fred. He didn't like those kinds of questions. 'We had all the signed documents.'

Jan played with her chopsticks. 'Mothers didn't have much say then. Especially not if they were young or poor. Or Aboriginal.'

'She was in a bad way. She hadn't been cared for well.' Fred pushed back his chair. 'I need to use the bathroom. Excuse me.' He could not sit there one more moment.

Someone was in the first cubicle so he went into the second one and flipped down the lid and sat with his head cradled in his hands. He was very deep now. There was very little light filtering down from above, but he could see it all.

They both looked into the cot at the sleeping child, taking in her skinny body and the damp cloth nappy and rubber pants. Then Martha spoke.

'What are those marks, Fred?' She leant right over the sleeping child, knowing full well what they were, but unable, as always, to leave things alone. The child's skin was a dull colour, dappled with purple bruises and small, round circles of angry skin.

'These look like burns. Are these some kind of cigarette burn?'

Martha looked across the cot to the woman who was walking them through the nursery. Fred took hold of Martha's forearm. She should be moving along to the far corner, where he had seen a tiny, plump baby asleep in a crib. That was where the Lothian family was meant to be, with that other child, the one with the orange hair and pink cheeks.

'What are you doing?' Martha snapped, pulling away from

him. 'Matron,' Martha called out, 'what happened to her? Did someone hurt this little girl?'

'This little one was in the Children's Hospital before she came to us. A case of chicken pox, I think. I haven't seen her file yet.' The Matron adjusted the edges of her white veil. 'The scars will fade with time.'

Fred flushed the toilet and came out of the cubicle. He turned on the cold tap. Was it any wonder people killed themselves? In the mirror he saw his father's mouth, his mother's cheeks, and the high forehead and sharp nose of his gran. One day he would go to Lincoln and Aberfeldy. He would visit their graves and pull the weeds and clean the headstones with a hard wire brush.

Mimesis – that was the word he had been searching for on Sunday, which seemed a lifetime ago. The insect disguises itself as a stick. The chameleon dissolves into the world around it – so much safer that way. By the end of her second year at home, Caroline had disappeared into the family. She no longer woke up every night with her eyes wide open, screaming in terror but unable to be roused. She no longer hated her mother. He had been ordered to stand by while Martha tried to save her face and arms from the nails and kicks and bites of their screaming, sweating daughter.

'I'm her mother,' Martha told him. 'I have to be able to hold her fear.' She had been consulting her Californian psychology books. 'America is way ahead on trauma,' she had said. 'Our job is to contain her anger, to hold it and make it safe for her to grieve.'

But who would contain *his* anger, he wondered. Who would make it safe for him? Sometimes he would snatch up the screaming, red-eyed child and wrap his arms around her like a vice, with so much fury in his hold and so much wanting to hurt this child who was ruining their lives. And Martha screaming at him not to hurt the child, to 'let her go right now'.

'I can't stand by and let her hit you,' he said when the child was finally asleep and he and Martha were in bed together, shaken and exhausted.

'You have to, Fred. That's our job.'

After a year he rarely noticed that her skin was marked. The nurse was right: the scars had faded. And then Callum arrived.

The toilet flushed and a man came out and looked in the mirror.

'Fred? Fred Lothian?'

Fred looked blankly at the man in the mirror.

'It's Peter Bessell. I thought I saw you walking in tonight. I said to Lisa, "Isn't that Fred Lothian?"'

'Of course,' said Fred, 'how are you, Peter? And how are Lisa and Aaron and Stephen?' The younger son's name had come back to him, like the Creed at Mass.

'Lisa and I are both older, as you can see, but apart from that, excellent, excellent. It's so good to see you, Fred. Lisa will be thrilled. We're having dinner with Sanjay and Leila. You remember them? He's the orthodontist? They had Raji in the year above our boys? Why don't you join us? Please!'

Fred held his tight smile. Aaron Bessell was Callum's best friend at high school and university. They had sleepovers. Aaron came on holidays with them. The boys played hockey together. They were together the night of the final.

Peter rinsed his hands, dried them thoroughly with the paper towel and then reached out and clasped Fred's forearms. 'I'm so sorry about Martha, Fred. We would have contacted you, but we were overseas. We didn't know she'd been sick until we got back. I had a contract with the bank in London, and we were out of the country for nearly three years. I've retired now, but we were out of touch.'

Eventually everyone was out of touch. He had been bitter about that for a very long time, but could you blame them? He had been out of touch too. He took a long, deep mouthful of

air before he went underwater and asked again. 'And how is
Aaron?'

'Excellent, excellent. He's based in Tokyo with my bank –
he's north Asia manager in fact, so Lisa doesn't get to see enough
of him or the grandchildren, which makes her a bit grumpy. He
married a Japanese girl. We've got four grandchildren now, but
only two in Perth. Stephen and his wife have had twins.'

'Twins! Wonderful.'

'A lot of work for Lisa, though – not that she's complaining.'

When Fred was moving house he came across a paper bag
with two tiny cardigans and two pairs of booties wrapped in
tissue. He recognised the wool, but he couldn't recall Martha
knitting them. He had examined the booties in detail. So much
work for something that would fit only for a few months. It
had struck him that knitting for babies was a kind of ephemeral
engineering; there was design and labour and materiality and
technique. It was love-work.

Would Peter ask about Caroline? Perhaps he had forgotten
that he still had a daughter who could give him grandchildren.
Only last month he spotted a notice in the death columns:
'John leaves two children, Sarah and Brian, an adopted daughter Fiona, and seven great-grandchildren.' How could they?

'Caroline's in London at the moment,' he said more loudly
than he meant, 'on an international museum project. She's very
well respected in her field.'

'That's absolutely marvellous,' said Peter. 'Is she married
yet?'

'Any minute,' he said.

One of the staff came in to check the toilets. Peter and
Frederick stood in silence until he left.

'So, how's Callum, Fred?'

It was difficult for Peter to ask that question. His voice was
two threads straining to make one rope; the first was trying to
be even-handed and steady, while the other was already fraying.

'I'm going to see him in the morning, actually. He's had an infection.'

Peter nodded. 'So, no real change then?' Fred clenched his teeth and shook his head.

'You know, Fred, Lisa and I were heartbroken about Callum. It's been terrible for Aaron. He still feels guilty about letting Callum drive off that night. He still talks about it. We told him how important it is to let go of guilt. You'd know all about this, I'm sure.'

'It wasn't Aaron's fault, Peter.' *It was my fault.* 'I'm at St Sylvan's. It's a retirement place not far from the old house. Ask Aaron to come and see me when he's next in town.'

Peter's mouth wobbled. He tightened his grip on Fred's arm. Fred wanted to shake him off, like you would a big, hairy spider.

'That's very good of you, Fred. None of us knew what to do after the accident. Aaron did try to see you. We knew you'd left the university. Lisa spoke to Martha and she said you'd had a breakdown and didn't want any visitors. Martha said you couldn't manage to see Callum at all. I'm so glad you're all right now, Fred. Is that a lady I saw at the table with you?'

Don't wink, thought Fred, *or I'll have to hit you.* But instead Peter lunged at Fred and held him in a tight hug. As they parted Peter reached for his wallet and pulled out his card.

'You must come for dinner, Fred. We've sold up and we've bought a great apartment on the river. Top floor. It's so much easier in a smaller place now that the kids are gone. Lock up and leave! In April we're off to Provence for three months, so make sure it's before then. We've taken a large house in the mountains. The kids are coming with all their children.'

Fred put the card in his shirt pocket and held out his hand.

'Peter.'

'Fred.'

And then Peter was gone.

On the way back to his table he saw Peter leaning in towards his wife and friends. You'll never guess who I just saw! They stole a quick look in his direction. Lisa waved furiously and beamed.

Sanjay nodded – a kindly, mournful nod.

A breakdown was for engines, not engineers. Is that what people thought? That he'd had a breakdown?

Jan was absorbed in the dunes. 'You were right, it was a rabbit. I saw it again. You look terribly pale, Fred. Did something happen? Or is it all this talking? You're not used to it, are you? Drink some water. It might be the champagne. There's never enough food at these places.'

Fred held up his hand. *Stop, please stop.* He felt a light weight on his shoulder. He looked up and saw a carefully manicured hand with long pearly nails.

'Fred? I had to come over in person. I hope you don't mind.' Lisa Bessell ran her palm across a perfect helmet of blonde hair and adjusted the fine silk wrap at her neck. Please, thought Fred, not another round of sympathy.

'Oh, Fred, Peter and I are so sorry about Martha, we really are. She was such a wonderful woman. The way she devoted herself to Callum. And Caroline. She never lost hope, did she? Hello,' she said, thrusting out a hand, 'I'm an old friend of Fred's – Lisa Bessell.'

'Jan Venturi.'

The women touched hands.

'Peter and I want Fred to come to dinner.' She turned to Fred. 'You will bring this lovely lady with the fabulous eyes, won't you?' She wagged a finger at Fred. 'Make sure you call us, or we'll track you down and drag you out.'

'What a glamorous woman,' said Jan after she left. 'Is her husband a colleague from work?'

'Their son was Callum's best friend in high school. They went to university together. I haven't seen them for years. I ran into him in the bathroom. Martha told them I'd had a break-down. I don't even know what a breakdown is.'

Jan shrugged her shoulders. 'You must have been devastated when it happened.'

He said nothing because he had nothing to say. When it happened there was nothing. Nothing.

'You couldn't accept what had happened to Callum.'

'No, I couldn't. Is that a breakdown?'

'Perhaps, back then, when it happened, yes. But it's definitely something else now.'

'What? What is it now? Go on, Jan.' Here she goes again, telling him what's what.

'Not accepting what's happened. Continuing to deny it. It's selfish, Fred. It's unethical.'

'I doubt that's the right word, Jan.'

'You doubt it, do you? Doctors have to have ethics, and so do teachers and priests, so why not parents? I have no idea about engineers. What you're doing isn't right for Caroline, let alone Callum.'

Fred waved at the waiter. He needed more alcohol.

'Slow down. Why don't you have a sparkling water?'

'We'll have a Perrier water and another glass of that New Zealand white,' he told the waiter.

'Perhaps I should tell you a story now, Fred. And look, just in time, more food.'

Paper-thin ribbons of seared beef fillet rose up from the dish in ever-diminishing circles, like a pink hooped skirt abandoned in the centre of a huge white room. At the edge of the dish was a pair of fierce, round, black-spiked sea urchins.

'Rubans de boeuf à la Pernod, with wasabi gelato in a liquorice case.' The waiter turned his open palm towards the small black sputnik. 'Snap-frozen on the outside, warm on the inside.' He took out a silver spoon and gave each spiked ball a sharp crack. The balls broke apart and released a gooey green froth onto their plates.

Jan took up her chopsticks and shook out a long length of pink fillet, dangled it in the green gelato, and then lowered it into her mouth. She groaned. 'How utterly decadent. So, are you listening, Fred?'

Fred nodded.

'My mother was South African. Her father was Scottish and her mother was what they called a Cape Coloured, a local girl. They both died when my mother was fifteen, in a plane crash. Her father was an administrative officer. He'd taken his wife with him over the Drakensberg Mountains from Johannesburg to Mozambique, in a Junkers Ju – a type of small plane quite common in those days. Sam researched it all for me. They'd left my mother at boarding school. This was in the late 30s, before the National Party brought in apartheid, before the ANC and well before Mandela. But my mother still had to endure segregation. She came to Australia with the money left to her by her parents. She enrolled to train as a nurse. She'd always wanted to be a midwife and work in South Africa. She met the man who became my father in the hospital. He was a well-known doctor, a heart specialist – I always thought that was so ironic. Broken-heart specialist, more like. He was older and very married. My mother was only eighteen – just a baby. She was very beautiful and she thought they were in love. He took her to the Adelphi Hotel, in St George's Terrace. It's long gone now. Do you remember it, Fred, or was it before your time? I know it was the Adelphi because she stole a plate from the restaurant at the hotel. I still have that plate – remind me to show it to you.'

She shook out another ribbon of beef. He liked the way Jan ate. She revelled in her food. Martha was a good cook, but pushed and picked her way around a plate and would end up covering it with plastic and putting it in the fridge. 'Cooking and eating don't go together,' she always said. He pushed Martha aside.

'Go on, Jan.'

215

'When she found out she was pregnant, he arranged for her to go to a place up in North Fremantle. I used to drive up there to look at it. It was called Hillcrest. It's all different now. They've knocked down the old buildings – I think it's aged care, but up until the 1970s it was a place for unmarried girls. They arranged adoptions from there too. In the end I went to a couple who did their best, but they had no other children and it was hard. I was such a lonely kid. Back then everyone had to pretend I wasn't adopted and looked no different from my parents, although I did. There was so much people wouldn't talk about – or couldn't. My mother and father were such a pink and white couple it must have been hard for them too, having a little olive-skinned girl with crazy hair. They had a little business in Fremantle selling adding machines and business stationery, but they didn't have much formal education themselves, and I was a quick, smart girl who loved reading and writing. I gave them hell.'

'I'm sure they understood,' he said.

'No, I don't think they did, Fred. Nobody did, back then. Adoption was shameful. It was a big secret. They were kind people, just very drawn inwards. I think I completely confounded them. I was loud and talkative and I loved to laugh. But I hated my skin and my curly hair. I liked my green eyes, though.'

'Your eyes are very striking,' he said. So Jan was adopted. What were the chances of such a thing?

Jan took another mouthful. 'Incredible,' she muttered.

Fred nibbled at his food. He wanted to hear more.

'Did you get on with them in the end?'

'Oh, long before the end. We had to; they were all I had and I was all they had. They've been dead a very long time now. I became a primary teacher, which I loved. I met my husband at a dance and almost straight away he asked me to marry him. We decided never to have children, but just to have fun. And we had so much fun. Too much fun. My parents loved Sam, and Sam loved them, even though they always wanted a grandchild. Sam was an Aussie, but his family was originally from Italy, so he knew how to talk and how to cook. I was close to forty when my son was born, and we were thrilled, but shocked, as you are. But there you are, you got me talking again.'

'So you located your birth mother?'

Jan laughed. 'All these words you've got now, to keep things clear. I didn't have those words when I was young. My *birth mother* didn't have a good life. She never went back to finish her studies after the baby. It just gutted her. I finally tracked her down in Queensland. Sam helped me again. He was really good with research. My poor mother had been through some bad times with the wrong kind of men. She drank.'

Fred nodded.

'She was stuck in a groove, or a ditch more like it, and she kept getting out and falling right back in.'

Fred didn't answer. He took a mouthful of green mousse and quickly reached for the water.

Jan laughed. 'They've used fresh wasabi, not the powder. We kept in touch. I sent her money. She always wrote me little thank you notes. I know it was very painful for her to give me up like that, but she really had no choice. All those years she had no idea if I was dead or alive. The first time we met she was so upset I had to leave and come back the next day.'

'Did you find your father? Did you ever contact him?'

'I knew his name, she told me that much. He was retired by then, but he was easy to find. He had an old colonial house up on the river overlooking the Yacht Club. I went there in my car and waited. Eventually he drove up in a big grey Mercedes-Benz. One weekend I parked around the corner and stood outside his house, right near the driveway. When he drove in I stared straight at him. I saw him do a double take. I could see his wife looking over at me, wondering why I was there. I like to imagine she knew as soon as she saw me. He knew, of course. I look just like my mother. He had children too, so I suppose I could have confronted him and forced a connection. But I had no truck with him. I just wanted to make him acknowledge me. He ruined my mother's life, and I wanted to put a stone in his shoe for the rest of his life. In a different kind of story I might have got a gun and shot him, or demanded money or something, but no, I never actually met him. I sent him a note, though, with some pictures of me as a baby and a toddler, just to make sure he couldn't do that thing that men do.'

'Which is what?'

'Pretend something didn't happen when it did.'

'Right,' said Fred. 'I suppose you mean me.'

Jan picked at the fillet and shook out another long thread, like a bird determined to get the worm.

'It's a sad story,' he said.

'All adoption stories are sad. How can they not be? My parents were good to me. They were just too quiet. Quiet people are hard work.'

'What happened to your mother? Your birth mother?'

'I find that a bit hard to talk about. Give me a moment.' The waiter came for their plates.

'Thank you,' said Jan, 'that was wonderful.' She rolled her wine around her glass. 'I don't know how it was for your daughter, but the hardest thing about not knowing your biological mother or father is that you feel so alone. It's like being the first of a brand-new species – or the last. One of those sad, old beasts in some horrible zoo with a plaque saying "The Last of the Something or Others". Jeanette – that was my mother's name – she had cancer, but she didn't tell me. I was overseas with Sam for a few months. It was very quick, only six weeks from when she was diagnosed. I was contacted when they went through her things and found my name. They wanted someone to collect her body and pay for the funeral. She had no one of her own. It was so terrible, Fred.'

'Pardon, Jan, what did you just say?'

'I said there was no one with her when she died. Are you even listening?'

'No, not that; what did you just say, about being the last one?'

'Being adopted, you're the last of your kind – you know, the thylacine, and the dodo.'

'It's something my daughter's working on. What you just said about animals made me think of it.' Could that be it? Was this exhibition really all about adoption?

Jan tossed her napkin on the table and laughed. It was another of those laughs that meant the opposite of funny. 'You're incredible. I don't think I've ever met a man like you. I just shared something with you that was very painful for me. My mother died and I wasn't there. She was completely alone. I even stopped talking because I didn't want to cry in front of you. Do you remember a little pause in the conversation? Or were you too busy working out how my story could help you work out your story?'

Silence had always been Fred's best line of defence. When he and Martha disagreed he would argue right up to the point where she worked herself into a frenzy, and then he would stop talking and wait. Eventually she would calm down and apologise and he would forgive her. But it wasn't working now. Jan called the waiter and ordered steamed rice. She looked out into the dunes. When the rice came, she turned to her meal with purpose. He was going to have to try something different this time.

'Caroline is working on an exhibition about extinct animals. I never understood why it was so important to her. What you said made me see a connection. I'm sorry I was so caught up when you were speaking about Jennifer.'

'Jeanette. My mother's name was Jeanette.'

'What a coincidence – your names, I mean.'

'It's not a coincidence at all. My parents knew my mother's name. They gave me her name – almost. I loved them for that.' Jan sighed loudly. 'Do you want rice? And I stand by what I said about you. This dinner is doing my head in, as my son used to say. How does Caroline feel about her birth mother? Has she had contact?'

'Actually, for years she never wanted to contact her or find out anything about her birth mother. Unfortunately she died when Caroline was in her last year of school. The woman had a difficult life. We always encouraged her to contact her mother, but she always said she was quite content with us.'

None of this was true. He would explain it all to Jan later, when she was feeling better.

'Really? I find that hard to believe, given the things we know now about forced removals and broken families. I know how it feels; if you don't know your mother you have no one to measure yourself against. When I met my mother I looked at her and saw myself. I grew up hating my hair and my skin and my big mouth. Those things made me stand out from the people who raised me. But if you grow up loving your birth mother, you grow up loving yourself. It's not rocket science, is it? Could you pass the rice? You spend all those baby years staring into her face, it must make it so much easier to love yourself – most of the work has been done for you. Do you see what I mean?'

He saw exactly what she meant. He passed the rice to Jan. 'I suppose Caroline has had a difficult time liking herself,' he said slowly. 'Not only is she adopted, but she's Indigenous. Some people don't see that she's Aboriginal; they think she's some exotic mix, or they don't want to see it because of her light skin, and they think she doesn't have the right to call herself Indigenous. She held herself apart because of it. Will you excuse me, Jan, I'm just going to remind Ariel to look out for the RAC van.'

Fred walked quickly in the direction of the polished cement bench. He would never have admitted anything like this to Martha. He had refused to go along with her when she started on about Caroline's background and about her birth mother, about having contact and finding her Aboriginal identity, and now here he was claiming his wife's position as his own. He was a monster.

Ariel was not at the concrete bench. He would wait.

'Let's just wait until she's got through high school, Martha. She's not ready to absorb any more than what she already knows.'

'But she's nearly thirteen, Fred. She's a teenager. She has to know more about her mother sometime. She's a clever girl, and she has such strong emotions. She knows she's Aboriginal. She knows she's from out east. She's always known that. But she keeps asking me these roundabout questions, skirting about the subject as if it's off-limits. It's like she thinks we don't want her to talk about it, and that she'll upset us if she does. I can't keep not talking about her mother. Soon she'll be wanting to contact her.'

'And what makes you think that? You're making that up now – projecting, I think they call it in your Californian psychology books. Why would she want to contact her? She's perfectly happy with us. And we've never hidden anything from her. She's always known she's adopted. And yes, her mother is Aboriginal, but how else is Caroline different from us? Is it her skin colour? For god's sake, Martha, you and I both believe that the colour of your skin should make no difference to anything. What good comes from dividing people up on the basis of colour? Isn't that what racism is? Look at South Africa, and look where the business of race got your blessed America? We treat her just like any child, no better, no worse.'

'This is about more than colour, Frederick. We've gone over and over this and you just refuse to listen. I'm the one who bothers to educate myself so I can help Caroline. *Colour*, as you call it, means something, Fred. It's history. It's what she means in the eyes of other people – other Australians. White Australians. Black Australians.' Martha was angry. She was spitting out her words.

Fred got up off the couch. 'You're getting yourself worked up again, darling. Can't we have just one discussion without you getting upset? And what you're talking about is not history, it's genetics. Frankly, I can't believe you of all people would say that the fate of a little girl should be determined by her genes. You're always going on about nature and nurture, and gender roles. What is it you always say: "Women are made, not born"?'

'I'm not talking about genes, Frederick, or gender. I'm talking about culture. Black America has its own history and culture, and so does Aboriginal Australia.'

'And Caroline's mother? What culture does she have, wherever she is, living in some godforsaken country town with no real identity of her own, pissing her life away, then going home to a boyfriend to do god-knows-what to her infant daughter? What kind of culture is that?'

The veins were standing out around Martha's neck. 'We don't know that. We don't know anything for certain about who did what. Never repeat that, do you hear me?'

'You want to tell your daughter the truth? Which bit of the truth, Martha? We've told her the truth. She's adopted. Her mother was Aboriginal. Her birth mother couldn't look after her.'

'What about the sin of omission, Frederick? What about the sin of silence? All those times we change the subject, distract her from asking where her mother is, why exactly she might have given her up, where she lived, if she has any relatives?'

'But what about her physical state when she was removed,

222

Martha? What about those things in her file that you never mention, the things you pretend don't exist? If a grown woman can't face the truth, how can a girl of Caroline's age? Suppose we tell her that her mother was a poor, young, innocent girl who got herself in far over her head and committed no wrong other than trusting the handsome Lothario she met at the local dance? Suppose we tell her how brave her mother was, giving up her own baby so she could have a better life? Do we tell her a bit of the truth, Martha, or all of the truth? Which part should we start with? The bits we can see? The scars? The burns?'

Martha looked down. When she lifted her head it was not love or acceptance that he saw, but blunt contempt. 'All right, Fred, you win again. They're like fucking stones, your words. You throw them down in front of me, one on top of the other, and soon I can't see you and I can't touch you. But then you always liked the idea of building things, Frederick, I'll grant you that.'

When he came back to the table, two clean plates had arrived and the waiter was arranging a slab of cast iron between them.

'Careful, sir,' he said, 'this is very hot.' He returned with a tray and placed a dozen scallops on the sizzling plate, waited for a few seconds, and then flipped them over.

'Scallops in a ginger and cherry jus. Just give them a minute or so. The sommelier will be here with your wine.'

'Oh, no more wine for me,' said Jan.

'Yes, please,' said Fred.

Jan bent over the cherry-pink scallops. 'Does this all feel a little strange to you, Fred? A little *bourgeois*, as they say, talking about such sad things in a luxurious, decadent setting? It's like one of those French movies, where beautiful rich people run around the Champs-Élysées having elaborate traumas.'

'It's the blue lights I'm finding most off-putting. I feel as if

223

I should be in a snorkel and mask. But it's not like it's a regular occurrence, is it?'

'What? The food or the conversation – or the lighting?'

'All of it.'

'I'm not sure I can eat much more after this. Are we up to dessert yet?'

'I don't know,' said Fred. 'I don't know what we're up to.'

'Callum. We're up to Callum. When did you adopt Callum?'

'Oh, Callum's not adopted. He's our …' He almost said it, the 'real' word. It had been drummed out of him by Martha and finally defeated by his own recognition of the injury. Caroline was as real as any child could be. But still he had slipped. 'He's our biological son. It was very unexpected.'

'How did Caroline feel about that? How old was she?'

'She was five years old. She was so excited when he came along. She adored her little brother. Does that look like some kind of candied Blackpool rock at the other table? What about these scallops? Do you think that's a minute?'

'I think so. No more talking for a while. Let's eat.'

There was no question that Caroline was their first child, and that she was loved, no question at all. When Martha found out she was nearly four months pregnant (and barely a bump to show for it), she had cried for hours. Their doctor assumed they were tears of happiness – after all those years of trying, miracles do happen – but Fred knew better.

'What will this do to Caroline?' she said to him in the car on the way home from the doctor. 'She's made such progress. This will be a terrible setback. It will make her feel second best, I know it will. The introduction of a sibling is hard enough, let alone this.'

He did his best to reassure her, but that night she woke him from his sleep.

'Fred, I want a termination.'

He was horrified. 'What do you mean?' he said. 'What are you thinking, Martha? This child is a gift. After all you've been through. This is our child.'

'And Caroline isn't?' said Martha.

'You're overwrought, Martha,' he said. 'Come here.' He knew better than to mention hormones or morning sickness. His wife was not a woman to excuse herself on the basis of her womanhood. He held her in his arms until she slept, and in the morning he let it rest. Time, that was what his wife needed.

When Martha gave birth to a healthy seven-pound eight-ounce boy, it was he who brought Caroline to the hospital. They came into the room to find the infant sucking fretfully at his mother's breast, while Martha grimaced and squirmed with pain.

'It's a conspiracy of silence,' she said. 'First the horror of childbirth, now this. No one tells you how much this hurts. Look at the little gobbleguts.' She reached out to Caroline, who was standing near the door. 'Cary, come and give me a hug, sweetheart. Come and meet your baby brother. I've missed you so much.'

Fred took five-year-old Caroline's hand and led her to the bed. Martha detached the child from her breast ('Ow!') and carefully peeled back the white wrap to reveal his pink, squashed face and his pale, mottled flesh.

'Isn't he beautiful?'

Caroline looked doubtful. She reached out to touch the small foot protruding from under the wrap. Her face crumpled.

'Sweetheart?' said Martha. 'What's wrong? Here, Frederick, you take him.'

He fumbled to hold his tiny son, and then stood to attention like a tin soldier. Caroline had been more than two years old when she came to them. He had no experience with the helpless dependence of a newborn.

'Come here, honey, come to Mummy.'

Martha pulled Caroline up onto the bed and wrapped her arms around her. He could see his wife struggling to keep herself in check. She was pale and exhausted from the long labour. He was still recovering from his role as witness – no wonder his father's generation avoided the whole shocking business. Were women meant to feel that much pain? It seemed a terrible injustice.

'You've missed Mummy, haven't you? I'm coming home in a day or two and then everything will be back to normal. Mummy will be home soon.'

Caroline looked up through her tears. 'Is he coming home too?' she wailed.

Martha looked up at Fred and smiled wryly. 'Of course he's coming home, darling,' she said, gently patting Caroline on the back. 'He's your brother.'

He winked at his wife. What else would you expect when a pretender to the throne appears on the scene? Their friends had warned them to be prepared for this. It was all quite normal. But then Caroline pushed herself away from her mother and off the bed. She backed herself up against the washbasin with her fists clenched.

He saw her then as if for the first time, a small girl with honey-coloured skin and a high forehead and a wide mouth who had been flushed out of hiding by the birth of her brother. She was alone and naked, without cover or camouflage.

Then there was the look on Martha's face.

The scallops were perfect, but he had dropped something on his shirt and managed to knock over Jan's water when he reached for his glass of wine. He dipped the corner of his napkin into his glass and dabbed at the spot.

'You should try water for that, not wine,' said Jan. 'We were talking about Callum. How was Caroline when Callum arrived?'

'There were no real issues there. Caroline might have been a little jealous at times, but nothing out of the ordinary, nothing that all siblings wouldn't go through. Am I still spotty?'

'You'll have to soak it when you get home.'

'Mr Lothian?'

Ariel leant over the table, like a cloud. Shoals of silky white breast rose up above the scalloped bodice. Fred thought he might faint. He imagined sinking down into the rift between those soft mounds and swimming away.

'There's an RAC man outside. Would you like me to tell the kitchen to hold your dessert until you've sorted it out?'

'I'll come now,' he said. 'Jan, you have dessert. I can't eat anything else. And if you don't mind, I'm going to have to call a taxi. I'm well over where I should be.'

'I'll drive,' Jan announced, putting her napkin on the table. 'It's about time I got behind the wheel. And I'll pass on dessert too. Could you let the staff know it was a wonderful meal, Ariel? And Fred, thank you for dinner.'

'No. Thank you, Jan, thank you so very much for everything. *Everything*.'

Jan rolled her eyes. 'I'll meet you outside, after I visit the ladies'.'

Fred floated through the restaurant, past the oyster who was peering through his Corbusiers at the label on a bottle of sake; past the sporty seahorses flicking their jaunty tails and jogging up and down their tanks; past Peter, Sanjay and Leila, who tipped their heads towards him; past Lisa Bessell, who was coming back from the bathroom and waved madly and bared her teeth; past the purple coral; past the leather armchair that looked like a clam; right up to the shell beach where the mermaid lived. He was having trouble putting one foot in front of the other. Too much alcohol, or an aneurysm?

Ariel slid his credit card through the machine. He punched in some numbers.

'Oh, I'm sorry, sir.' She turned the machine towards him. Declined. 'Shall we try again?'

'Please.' He paused over the pad. The automatic flow of numbers from brain to finger had been stymied. There was a blockage in the pipe.

'384 3627,' he said. But no, that was his old telephone number. And far too many digits.

2407, but that was his wife's birthday.

0104. Callum's birth.

1701. Caroline's birthday.

1901. The year of his father's birth.

1954. The year his mother died.

1948. Virgil. Virgil.

1994. The phone call.

2901. The day and month of Martha's death.

'It's 2006,' he said loudly.

'I'd keep that to yourself, Mr Lothian,' smiled Ariel, running the card through the slot.

2006. The year he met Jan. He punched with flourish and confidence. The machine beeped.

Ariel peered at the electronic screen. 'Oh, I'm so sorry, Mr Lothian. Do you have another card?'

'Do you take Amex?'

'Of course.'

From the top of the stairs Fred could see the pulsing yellow light of the service van, tracking round and round, like a Ferris wheel. *I think I'm going to be sick*, he thought, then turned and vomited into a giant concrete Triton shell. As he stood up, he tripped and struck the side of his temple on the corner of the lowest concrete step, in full view, he was later informed, of Lisa Bessell, who against her husband's advice had gone after him armed with her mobile phone, just to make absolutely certain she had his number so that he and that lovely lady with the fabulous eyes could come to dinner.

Ariel insisted they call the ambulance. 'Just to make sure, Mr Lothian,' her hand on her pale bosom.

'Of course, Ariel,' he murmured. Anything for Ariel. 'I'm sorry about the clam,' he said. 'I'm so sorry for everything.'

By the time the ambulance arrived, Fred's car battery had been restored and he was fully conscious. He lay on his back with his head on Peter Bessell's jacket and tried to focus on the seagulls circling the lamps, like vultures over a rotting corpse. 'I just want to go home,' he muttered. Why couldn't the monster just go home?

Thank goodness I kept my licence up to date, thought Jan. It had been nearly ten years since she had driven, but even with Lisa Bessell sitting next to her it was not difficult. The ambulance was advancing in a stately fashion – no sirens, no running of red lights – so she had no trouble keeping up with it. It was annoying that Fred's old friends felt they had to come. Lisa Bessell would keep fixing that aquamarine wrap about her bony shoulders and checking the little mirror on the back of the visor to see what was going on in her husband's car. Leila was at the helm of Peter's Porsche, which Jan knew was a less than ideal outcome for all concerned. Both Peter and Sanjay had had far too much to drink, Lisa said – they never should have opened that fourth bottle – and since Lisa had never learnt to drive they had put Sanjay in a taxi home and let Leila take the Carrera to the hospital, even though she had never in her life driven a manual, let alone a six-speed Porsche. 'Or would you prefer to leave your prized possession at the beach for the night, Peter?' That had settled it.

'So, Jan, how long have you and Fred known each other?' asked Lisa, leaning into the mirror to touch up her lipstick.

They were stopped at the lights next to Peter's car. The engine was roaring and they could both see Peter talking in an animated fashion to the driver.

'Just over twenty-four hours,' said Jan.

'Goodness,' said Lisa, 'and you're already going to hospital with him. It must be serious. Look at Peter, would you, telling that poor woman what to do. My husband can be such an arsehole.'

The lights turned green. Jan glanced at Lisa. 'Tell me, Lisa, what was Martha like? Did you know her well? I hope you don't mind me asking.'

'No, of course not. Martha and I saw each other at drop-off and pickup, and when the boys got together. My eldest was Callum's best friend. We talked about all the normal things – school, sport, adolescence, you know, but to tell the truth I always found her a bit reserved. She was very clever, like Callum. I mean Fred is clever, obviously, what with being a professor of engineering and all that, but Martha had more of an interest in things. She was always reading or studying or volunteering. She had strong views, if you know what I mean. Oh, poor Leila, she keeps putting the indicators on by mistake. Peter will be having kittens. I think Martha probably thought we were all superficial.' She laughed. 'Has Fred mentioned Ralph Orr, the architect? His wife Veronica – ex-wife now – was Martha's best friend for years. She's the one you want to talk to. She's been in South Africa, but I just heard she's about to come back for good. They had a problem with their eldest daughter – well, actually, it was drugs. I guess there's no harm telling you now; it was so long ago. We knew the family of the boy involved. His father was in property. The boy's all grown up now. He's on the Terrace with one of the bigger brokers, but the girl just couldn't straighten out. I think it's quicker if you take a left here, Jan, rather than following the ambulance.'

Jan eased into the left lane. What a pity. For a brief moment she had thought she might like Lisa.

'Sneak in here, to the right and then go straight ahead,' said Lisa. 'We have to get to the overnight parking area. She died – the daughter. They were very liberal with their children – Ralph, I mean, not Martha and Fred. I think Ralph was a bit of a ladies' man. I've always wondered if their home life was unstable. Kids don't just start on drugs for nothing. It was a very artistic home. We had dinner there once or twice. Veronica – Ralph's wife – had a degree herself in art or drawing or something. Three girls, they had – two now, of course. I do remember Veronica saying, "Martha is an intellectual without an intellectual sphere" – or something like that. Whatever that meant.'

'Sometimes children choose their own paths,' said Jan quietly. 'Sometimes nothing you do can stop them. Was Martha very beautiful?'

'Oh, would you look at that – Leila's gone and stalled it. Martha was gorgeous. We were all quite jealous of her. She was very lean and vivacious, and she had this wonderful thick, dark hair and a way of dressing without looking like she was trying. She was naturally stylish, but I don't think she spent any money on clothes. She didn't approve of it. She was like that, a real women's libber. She wore jeans – Levi's – which back then was really quite unusual, and men's cotton shirts with the sleeves rolled up. She used to get Veronica to print patterns on them and then she would embroider them with native flowers. One had grevilleas, I think. Her garden was full of them. Such a messy plant, I find. And she always had silver bangles stacked up her arms, like that singer. You know, Joan someone?'

'Joan Baez,' said Jan.

'Martha loved folk music. I think she identified with it. She had that lovely olive skin, and bones to die for. She bought good shoes, I do remember that. I think they were her weakness. We all thought she looked like that actress in that film with Dustin Hoffman – I can't recall her name. Red light ahead, Jan. Why is the ambulance taking this road? The emergency entrance is at the front. Oh, look, is that Fred sitting up and waving?'

Fred's face was pressed against the small glass window at the back of the ambulance. His hair was on end and he was smiling and waving furiously. He disappeared as quickly as he appeared. What was he doing? Wasn't he supposed to be lying down with a strap over him?

'He's drunk,' said Jan. 'It was Anne Bancroft in *The Graduate*. You were saying? Martha?'

'She was devoted to her children, but she went through a difficult time with Caroline. Has Fred told you about Caroline?'

Here we go again, thought Jan. 'You mean the adoption?'

'Yes, and the rest.'

Jan turned into the car park. 'Meaning?'

'Well, she's Aboriginal.'

Dear me. To think she had thought this might just work: Fred and Jan and Peter and Lisa and Sanjay and Leila, and the Porsche Carrera.

An enormous roar to the left. The Porsche careered past them into the car park, accelerated into the speedbump, and was briefly airborne. Jan caught a glimpse of Peter's open mouth. There was a bang, then a terrible screech, followed by silence.

'I think I might leave you with that, Lisa. I'm going in to Emergency.' Jan opened her door. 'If you close the door it will lock by itself. It's got some kind of timer. I think you all should take a cab straight home. Thanks so much for seeing me here safely.'

'Are you sure, Jan? If you need us, please call. Fred has our number. I'd better see how Leila's holding up – and the car.'

Leila was still in the driver's seat, her head resting on the wheel, but Peter was flat on the ground with his head under the front of the Porsche, inspecting the chassis.

'I'll be in touch,' called Lisa.

Jan waved and went in search of Fred.

BOOK 5

Hyperbolic paraboloid

Friday, 20 January 2006

'BOOM! YOU'RE DEAD.'

Morrison was sitting on the blue nylon carpet in the Medicare office, playing with his Hot Wheels cars. He slammed the green one into the yellow one.

'Boom,' he said again, 'you're dead too.'

'Quiet, Morrie,' said Jan. She had a terrible headache, and that barking didn't help. Someone had tied a black and grey kelpie to the bollard outside and it wasn't going to stop its racket until the owner came out.

'Why is that dog wearing a hanky round its neck, Nanna?' Morrison asked when they came in. 'Has it got a cold?' He wanted to pat it, but Jan held him back. It looked friendly enough, but you couldn't tell with dogs. Now that she was responsible for a child again, all the worries were back: pools, cars, bikes, dogs, strangers, viruses.

She looked along the seats. The kelpie with the jaunty red scarf probably belonged to that barefoot girl with dreadlocks and pierced eyebrows. Why did young people want to put holes in themselves? *Stop it, Jan*, she said to herself. She had never been a judgmental person; she had taught all kinds of children from all walks of life and had lived in countries rich and poor, but lately she found herself thinking badly of others, particularly young people. Was that what happened when you got old? Your opinions froze up, along with your joints? But that dog would drive anyone mad.

All morning she had been in and out of offices, first the plush carpeted office at St Sylvan's, where she signed the forms to release her villa back on to the market, then the local estate agent, and now the ticketed queue at Medicare to get the boy on her card. She looked at the electronic board. Only three before her. The estate agent had confirmed what she already knew: if she wanted to buy a two-bedroom place she was going to have to move much further out. 'I'm sorry, Mrs Venturi, but with this budget you'd be lucky to get a one-bedroom anywhere in the area.' She nodded dumbly at the woman with the long red nails and the helmet of dyed black hair. What had she been thinking? She was going to have to start looking at primary schools in other suburbs and getting a feel for neighbourhoods. How do you do that? Stand in their playgrounds and see if they hit their kids, or walk around the local supermarket and see what's in their trolleys? And she would have to buy a car.

Morrie jumped up and dropped the yellow car on top of the green one.

'You're so dead now. Daddy killed you dead.'

The man sitting next to her laughed, but Jan didn't find it funny.

'What are you playing there, Morrie? Why don't you come up and sit with Nan? I've got a banana in here somewhere.' Jan looked in her bag. No banana, but a packet of crisps.

The boy crawled onto her lap. His games set her on edge. They were so intense, and he did the same thing over and over again, as if he were stuck. Morrie grabbed the packet off from her and shoved it down the side of the seat, then put his leg over the crack. He lay still for a moment and then began to scratch his legs. He had been doing that all morning, and now his skin was horribly red and inflamed. She would have to get him to the doctor to see if he was allergic to something.

'Leave that alone, Morrie, or you'll get scars.'

'I already got some,' he said.

He pulled up his long-sleeved T-shirt and lifted his arm. On the soft, white underside she saw red lines. Her stomach turned. She thought of her Grade 1s bent over their desks, ruling up their pads with straight red lines before they began their letters.

'How did you get those, Morrison?' She ran her finger over the raised scar.

The boy pulled his arm away and stared up at her with big, round eyes. He put his thumb in his mouth and began to suck.

'Number 254 to counter 4.'

Morrie was fast asleep in the booster seat when they got back to the house. It was another very hot day, so she couldn't leave him for even a few minutes without the air conditioner. She touched his arm to wake him and then lifted him into her arms. He was a dead weight. She thought about those red lines. His mother? Her son? Some druggie stranger? The boy woke up and she put him down. The garden could do with a good weeding – it wouldn't take much. *There I go again*, she thought. The woman looking after her boy managed to fit five children and an oversized husband into a modest two-bedroom war-service bungalow, and all she could do was criticise the garden.

'We've got bunks,' Margie explained on Jan's first visit. 'My two oldest are in the double bunk on one side, the other three are in the triple bunk on the other, and any extras get the fold-out in the corner. That'll be you, Morrie. Do you like camping?'

She shepherded the boy towards the front door. Thankfully the other children were at school. When she'd picked up Morrison the doorway was jammed with bags and sports gear. Kids were yelling and banging doors. How could anyone cope with such a horde?

Today Margie was waiting inside with the boy's lunch.

'Here's your sandwich, Morrie,' she said, sitting him down

at the kitchen table, 'and don't you get off that seat until all the green, orange and red bits are eaten – and don't go putting them in the bin. I'll be checking in there.' Margie ran a tight ship.

'He's tired,' Jan said, watching Margie fill the kettle.

'I'll put him in front of the TV when he finishes. Milk and sugar? What about *Nemo*, Morrie?'

'I've seen it,' he said. 'It's too scary.' He was lifting up the edges of his sandwich, picking out the grated carrot.

'Then it'll have to be cartoons,' said Margie. 'Come and sit in the lounge, Jan. I'll bring the tea. You look like you need a rest.'

Jan was exhausted, but she didn't want to admit it. There were so many practical things to do before Morrison came to her, but right now it was the other business that was worrying her most. She waited until the door between the kitchen and the lounge room was closed.

'Margie, do you find Morrison very agitated one minute and withdrawn the next? He's either jumping around like a jack-in-the-box, itching and scratching those poor arms and legs, or else he's a million miles away. I've never seen a child get so completely lost in play.'

'We see it all the time,' said Margie. 'Sugar? They've either had no one to give them any attention, or else what was going on around them was too hard for them to take in, so they escaped into their fantasy world. These kids get hyper if they get too much stimulation. They're not used to settling them-selves down. My three were all like that, but the oldest was by far the worst. We still see a psychologist. I guess you haven't got that far yet.'

Jan took a sip of her tea. In fact, she had seen quite a few kids like Morrison in her years of teaching; she just didn't want to recognise the similarities. They turned up in her class and sat at the back. They spent long periods outside the door on the verandah in time-out, or in the principal's office. There would be meetings with the family if they could be found, and the school psychologist if the school had such a person back then. Sometimes there would be a diagnosis, but mostly these children were barely tolerated. They were to be endured, until one day they were no longer in school.

All this time she had been at home with the budgerigars, pretending she was finally having her own life, while Morrison was being damaged. She would never forgive herself. She took a deep breath. 'Have you seen those marks on his arm?'

Margie nodded. 'I was going to talk to you about that. You need to make sure it's on his file or else they might think you've done it – or me. Don't look like that – it happens. I've seen it all. My oldest boy got a look at that arm at the pool the other day. He told us about it. Someone's done that, Jan. He's too young to do it to himself. If it's any consolation, I've seen a whole lot worse than that. I've had dozens of kids through here for emergency care. Morrison has been through a tough time, but he's a good kid. Somewhere down the line someone's tried. He laughs, he cries, he gets angry. He lets it out. You'll get him talking eventually and he'll open up, mark my words. He just needs a routine and lots of love, and now he's going to get it.'

The walls of Margie's lounge room were covered with photographs of children – babies on blankets, teenagers holding trophies, toddlers in plastic cars, and even a set of twins in matching striped T-shirts.

'That's some of our kids. Most of them were just for a few months, a year at the most. Not all of them keep in touch, but we have quite a few call up and come over on Christmas and birthdays. Mike and I always wanted a big family, but I had to have everything out after number two. I was gutted – I mean, really gutted. Sorry, I've got an evil sense of humour.'

'I find it helps,' said Jan. 'Did you ever think about adopting, Margie?'

She laughed. 'You know what they say – rich people adopt, poor people foster. Our three extras came as a sibling group because the department didn't want to split them up so young. Not many people were prepared for three at once, but it was perfect for us. They ranged from four down to eight months, and now the youngest has just started high school. They call us Mum and Dad. And we are Mum and Dad. More tea?'

Jan shook her head.

'We'd love to adopt them legally, but their mum is still in the picture. She's hung in there, and good for her. She doesn't want to give them up. She loves them, and they love her, and she's their mum too. She tries hard, but she's got really bad depression issues and health problems. Basically, she was born poor and she's always been poor, and that's really where her problems come from. She was really young when she had her kids and didn't have any support. She comes over once a month or so, sometimes more often when she's feeling good, and takes the three of them out. Or we have her over for a barbecue and we all sit up and watch *The Biggest Loser*. My kids keep telling me I should go on it.' Margie laughed. 'Have you finished in there, Morrie?' she called out.

Morrie opened the kitchen door and stuck his head out.

'I'm full,' he said. 'Can I watch TV now?'

'Not till you finish all that carrot on your plate. I'll warm the TV up for you.'

Margie reached for the remote and turned on the largest flat-screen television Jan had ever seen.

'What an enormous television,' said Jan. 'It must have cost a fortune.' She saw Margie's face.

'I suppose you think we shouldn't be spending money on things like televisions.'

'Of course not,' said Jan quickly. 'I don't have a television, so I'm out of touch.'

Margie found the cartoon channel and lowered the volume.

'Just to set the record straight, we get paid to foster, but it doesn't come anywhere close to covering what we put out. These kids need a lot of extra support. You can't buy love. We've had special education programmes and psychologists, for a start. The middle one, Jesse, he's dyslexic. We put most of the money into those things, and anything after the essentials goes into a special account for holidays and sports and for things like this television. The kids have their PlayStations and Xbox and they love their movies. They bring their friends over here where I can keep an eye on them all, and it's a lot less expensive than taking them all out to the cinema or those arcades where all sorts hang out.'

Jan nodded. She was ashamed of herself. 'I'm sorry if I sounded judgmental. I've got two dozen budgerigars, so what would I know?'

Margie disappeared into the kitchen. Next to the couch was a basket of washing waiting to be sorted. Folded clothes were stacked in little piles on the carpet. There was some sort of soup simmering in the pressure cooker. On the fridge was a list of chores for each of the children, with a yellow happy face next to completed tasks. Margie was a good person. Fred thought that Jan was a good person, but she wasn't. She lectured Fred about his son and his daughter, but she and Sam had been selfish too. They'd hardly had room for a son. When Paul died she had left Morrison with his mother even though Jan knew she was using drugs. She and Sam thought they had made so many sacrifices to save their son, but perhaps they hadn't really made any of the important ones. They ought to have had more children, for a start. More, or none at all.

She followed Margie into the kitchen, where she was pulling packets of frozen bread rolls out of the freezer and keeping an eye on Morrie's vegetable patch.

'Afternoon tea,' Margie said, nodding at the bread. 'It's a feeding frenzy. Morrison, if you want to watch TV before the big kids come and take over, you'd better get a move on.' She walked back into the lounge room and turned up the volume.

'How can you live without television, Jan?' She began twisting socks into pairs. 'You'll be needing a TV with that one,' she nodded towards the kitchen, 'if you ever want to have a cup of tea again. Do you know how long before you can have him for good? We're supposed to get a call from the social worker, but they're always late. He can't wait to go. It's all he ever talks about.'

'You don't think he'll miss the other children?' Jan picked out two navy school socks and tucked them in together. 'There's only going to be one of me.'

'That kid needs one hundred per cent love, not fighting off my horde to get in my lap. He'd end up the runt of the litter in a large family.'

She hoped Margie was right. 'I'll be here tomorrow morning, to get him for the weekend. I'm hoping that once the department knows my place is on the market, they'll let him come to me until the sale goes through.'

Morrison rushed in and threw himself at Jan. 'I love you, Nanna. I want to eat you up.'

'You don't need to eat me because there's enough food around your mouth for another meal. Go wash your hands and face and then come and say goodbye. Nanna has to go to the hospital.'

'Is everything all right?' asked Margie.

'A friend has had a fall. He's fine, but they kept him in for observation. I'm picking him up.'

'Does this "friend" have a name?'

'His name's Fred, like the chocolate frog. He lives in the same retirement village as I do.' She handed Margie the folded socks and picked up her bag.

'Do you think you could wait a minute before you go?'

'Of course,' said Jan.

Margie took a packet of cigarettes from a drawer under the TV. 'I know I shouldn't,' she said. 'I don't smoke around the kids. I keep quitting and starting again. I've promised Mike I'll give up for good before my fortieth.'

She disappeared through the laundry door. Morrison came back and climbed into Jan's lap. She kissed the top of his head. He smelled young. Morrison would be fine. His scars would fade. There was no need to be afraid.

'I'll be here for you tomorrow morning, okay? You be a good boy for Margie. You're coming to me for the whole weekend. You can help Nanna feed the budgerigars.'

'How do you manage, Margie?' Jan asked her when they were at the front door. 'How do you do it?'

'I don't know, Jan. You just muddle along.'

'But what about your own life?'

Margie pulled a face. 'This *is* my life. I don't have another one. Do you mean, like a career? Or hobbies? I'd like to do more exercise, or join a gym – god knows I need to lose weight – but I guess I don't think it's important enough to *prioritise*. Is that the word? I suppose if I'd had the chance to go to TAFE or university I might think differently. What was your career, Jan?'

'I was a primary school teacher. I loved it.'

'Well, there you go. You helped all those children. I think that's marvellous.'

Jan jangled the keys in her hand. 'I didn't help my son, Morrison's father.'

Margie glanced back towards the house. 'I don't really believe that, Jan. I have to go in. I'll see you in the morning.'

I could live here, thought Jan as she picked her way through the streets of Margie's suburb. Morrison and I could live here with our budgerigars and our books. We could walk to school and do our spelling on the way. He would learn to read and write, to start the small 'a' just before the curve and to run up the straight line and down again to make the strong, straight backbone of the letter. Two big bellies for the capital 'B', and a smidgen of the moon for 'C'. She would show him how to carry those tricky tens across from one column to another, and to borrow from the hundreds to pay back the tens. He would count up in twos, like a little birdie hopping up a path on both legs. Two, four, six, eight, ten. Together they would master time. By turning the small hand and the big hand she would mark out the minutes in the hours and the days of the years, and teach him about day and night and the earth and the moon, and the importance of gravity, how it helps you stay right here on earth where you belong, so you don't just up and float away into a terrible, empty nothingness. She would hold the string tight, so he didn't get away.

She was late for Fred, but it didn't matter now. This was her life, and she was going to do the best she could. Now, was it left at these lights, or the next?

'And how's that tummy, Mrs Jenkins? Let's have a little look, shall we?'

All morning Fred had been sitting on his bed up on the seventh-floor geriatric ward, fully dressed, toothbrush packed, waiting for his doctor to release him from hell, and now Mrs Jenkins had got in before him. The nurse turned down the sheets and rolled up Mrs Jenkins's gown. Poor Mrs Jenkins, all alone with her pale, soft belly. The doctor leant over her and tapped her stomach, as if she were a water tank. The nurse looked up at Fred and whipped the curtains across.

'And how does it feel when I press here?' the doctor said.

From the sound of it, not good.

'And here?'

Even worse.

There were more groans from the bed on the other side. It looked like the old man was finally waking up after his operation.

'What are you doing there?' he said, glaring at Fred. His speech was slurred. 'Where's the girl?'

The man had remarkably hairy eyebrows, just like Pop. Virgil always loved his jokes about Pop's brows. *Watch out for the fireplace, Pop, or you'll be kindling.*

'Would you like me to get the nurse for you?' Fred reached for his buzzer.

'Don't you dare. They'll kill me if they find out I saw them at it. It was one after the other, all night, right under my bed, like dogs. Shameful what goes on with them doctors and nurses. I got no sleep at all.'

The anaesthetic had made the man delusional. The same thing happened with Martha; for two or three days she thought he wasn't her husband and that she was married to Ralph. 'I want Ralph,' she moaned. 'Where's Ralph?'

Fred made sure the old man wasn't watching and then pressed the buzzer. Someone needed to know he'd woken up. The curtains around Mrs Jenkins's bed snapped back and the nurse refilled her water bottle.

'Now, Mrs Jenkins,' said the doctor, 'I want you to tell the nurse when you want to have a number two. Can you do that for me?'

'Yes, Doctor,' said Mrs Jenkins meekly.

Fred gritted his teeth. Mrs Jenkins was one of the true believers, a worshipper of the false god of medicine.

'Excuse me, Doctor?' said Mrs Jenkins.

The doctor looked up from his notes.

'Yes?'

'What about the pain, Doctor? Can you give me something for the pain?'

'We'll write you up some codeine, but that's what got you into trouble in the first place, Mrs Jenkins. You're constipated again. The nurse will give you another suppository, and once we get those stools on the move you'll be almost as good as new.'

'I had the Forte at home all week, and they didn't touch the pain.'

'It's a chicken-and-egg situation, Mrs Jenkins. Let's focus on laying that egg, and then after that we'll worry about the chicken.'

The blonde nurse smiled. The doctor winked at the nurse. My god, the man was a comic – or a sadist. Mrs Jenkins groaned. She didn't look at all well. His mother had suffered for months, dismissing the pain in her abdomen and refusing to go to the doctor, helped along by his father, who hated a whinge-ing woman. 'Shut your glooming, woman,' he said. When they finally took her to the hospital, she was dead in three days.

A male nurse arrived at his bedside. 'Did you call for the nurse?'

Fred nodded towards the old man. 'He's awake,' he said in a low voice, 'but he's delusional and quite agitated. And while you're here, can you tell me when Dr Forster's due? I was told at breakfast they all did their rounds early and it's now nearly lunchtime. I'm supposed to go home today. I'm being picked up at 1 pm.'

The nurse looked at his watch. 'If the doctor doesn't come soon, you won't be going anywhere. Ward 7 is the last stop of their rounds. We don't get that many going home from here, if you know what I mean, and we do all our releases before the handover at two o'clock. It's Friday of the long weekend. The specialists like to get away early so they can beat the traffic down to Eagle Bay.'

First he'd had to endure twenty-four hours downstairs in the Public Emergency Department, where they left him under fluorescent lights in a horrible salmon-pink cubicle, not knowing if it was day or night, counting shift changes and staff turnovers and waiting for some indeterminate event. Between these chasms of boredom was a series of what in other places might be called crises but in the Emergency Department were treated as perfectly normal. Drug addicts were either coming down or going up, old people were strapped up to cardiac monitors, there were drunks who needed dialysis, open wounds and tattoos and limbs broken in fights outside clubs, and cuts to the face when it got out of hand at a twenty-first, not to mention the steady stream of anxious mothers with very hot toddlers who would be sent home with Panadol and an assurance that no, it was not meningococcal, but keep an eye on her and come back if her temperature isn't down by the morning. And then, when he finally got the nod for a bed, he ended up on the geriatric ward.

'But I'm not this old,' he wanted to scream. 'I'm not going to die yet.'

Hieronymus Bosch couldn't have bettered it. The walls were a filthy mint green and the place stank of antiseptic and under-funding. It wasn't Jan's fault; he shouldn't have snapped at her. She had tried to get him transferred to the private hospital or at least to his own room, but there were no beds anywhere. He and Martha always had top insurance cover, and look where it got you. But he was not going to take it lying down. He was not going to be like Mrs Jenkins, suffering in silence over there with Oprah Winfrey on mute. He sat up and directed his concentrated bile at the old man's nurse, who was changing his dressing.

'Who do I have to talk to here? Where's the sister-in-charge? I've been in this hospital three nights, and I've hardly slept.'

The nurse took the chart off the end of the man's bed and initialled a column. How dare he ignore him like this?

'I've had an X-ray, a scan and a suppository. I haven't had a headache since Wednesday, so I have no idea why I'm still here. It's a waste of taxpayers' money – not that any taxpayer's money, let alone a taxpayer, myself excluded, has made it up here in decades.'

Fred could hear his words rattle about him like an old sheet in the wind. It was hopeless. The entire public system was immune to patients' complaints. He had to get out of here. He had to see his son. He had been told that Callum was doing much better, but they would like him to come in to discuss *the situation*.

'The situation?' he repeated on the phone. Things with Callum never changed, and now there was a situation? What did that mean?

He looked at his watch. Jan would be here at any minute. He waited for the doors at the end of the ward to swing open – for the grandchildren carrying helium balloons in the shape of hearts, popping them up and down on their long strings; for the devoted wives returning yesterday's washing to their husbands; for the middle-aged men carrying bunches of red roses to their sick mothers. He strained his neck to peer down the corridor.

No one was coming. Not a soul. The old grey poor people moaned and hacked and gazed into vacant space. An orderly pushed an empty bed into a gap between two patients. A nurse came past with a trolley draped in a white cloth, like the sacraments for benediction.

How long since he had been to Mass? Father McMahon took the altar boys for catechism on Fridays, where he liked to give them what he called 'room for doubt'.

'The Holy Father has room for doubt, lads, but it's a small room, and it's not a room you can stay in for longer than five minutes at a time. Now, are there questions?'

Frederick put up his hand. He needed further clarification on the troubling matter of transubstantiation. It just didn't seem possible that wine and a wafer could be turned into the body and blood of Christ with just a few words in Latin from Father McMahon.

Father listened for a moment to get the gist of the complaint, then cut him off. 'But Freddy, it's a miracle!' he said.

'Exactly how long does it take, Father?'

Father McMahon adjusted the rope on his brown cassock and pushed his glasses up his face. 'It's instantaneous, Freddy. Like that!' He snapped his fingers. 'A clever boy like you has heard of the speed of light, I'm sure?'

'Yes, Father.'

'Well, be thinking of something a million times faster.'

'But it tastes the same, Father. It still tastes like bread dipped in wine.'

'Of course it does! Of course it does, Freddy. You boys don't think God is going to make his flock taste the very flesh and blood of the Lord Jesus? God isn't cruel, Freddy. And he's not stupid. He knows that lads like you would never come back on the Sabbath to receive the Holy Sacrament if it tasted like a piece of uncooked beef and that scab off your knee you keep pulling at. Leave it alone, Frederick Lothian, and get your mother to tape that up before you get an infection and end up with Dr Broadbent, who's got far better things to do than patch up boys who pick. What is it now, Frederick?'

'I need to go to the toilet, Father.'

'Well, off you go now, and don't look down. I've got no more room for doubt, so you'd all better get on the move. It's algebra with Brother Stephen, and don't forget to scrub those nails before you parade down the aisle on Sunday.'

Was it the shock of seeing Tom Chelmsley topple to the ground or the knock on the head? Something had shaken out long-forgotten characters. It was Dr Broadbent who came to the house the morning Mam wouldn't wake up properly. The day was dry and freezing, like the inside of an ice rink. It was Christmas holidays and he was back from boarding school, hiding in his room and dreading every new dawn and wishing – praying even, though by then he no longer believed in prayer – that he could go back to his dormitory, with his books and his slide rule and his compass.

'How long has she been like this, Alexander?' the doctor asked his father.

'I can't say,' said his father. 'It's been a measure of pain in the belly, which I put down to that change women get.'

Fred stood between his father and the doctor as the ambulance pulled away, chewing his nails and wishing he could sit in the van and hold his mother's hand without Dad seeing.

The warm arm around his shoulders was the doctor's, not his dad's. 'Are you coming to the hospital with your mother, Freddy? I'll take him with me if you like, Alexander.'

'No need, Doctor,' said his father. 'The lad will ride with me, if he's not too smart to sit with a man who works for a living, if he's not too grand with his scholarship and his Latin words.'

He held his mother's hand all day while his father was at work. Dr Broadbent came in the mornings and again in the evenings, and brought him soup in a can and chocolate squares in silver foil.

'She ought to have been brought to see me months ago,' he said sadly. 'There are treatments for this, there are operations we can do, but it's too late now, Freddy.'

The doctor must have seen his face because he took up the hand that did not hold his mother's. 'You mustn't blame yourself, Frederick. That dad of yours is a hard man to handle, and she's his wife to care for. Remember that when she's gone.'

All through his fifteenth year, when his mother slipped further and further into the folds of her clothes, right up until Dr Broadbent took his hand in the hospital, he had never imagined that his mother might die. Her illness was a constant in their house, something to touch lightly on weekends at home, where she sat quietly in the corner, knitting and reading, and once or twice, when he caught her, just watching him read and draw.

'I like to see you there,' she said. 'It's enough to see you there.'

Mrs Jenkins had fallen asleep. At least his mother had that feeling, the feeling that something was enough ... your wife, your children, the life you had made.

A specialist came into the ward, followed by a group of medical students who fussed around him, like ducks after stale bread. They pulled up at the bed of an old woman whose racking, murderous cough had kept him awake all night. She was on oxygen, and her compressor pulsed like an underwater sonar. Every half-hour or so she almost choked to death and a nurse would come and roll her on her side and thump her between the blades, tuck in the sides of her sheet, and leave.

The students leant in close to the old woman. Any moment they would open up her gown and press their cold steel instruments onto her frail chest. They would not be using *his* body to hone their diagnostic skills; he had made sure of that. 'NO,' he wrote on the form when he was admitted to Ward 7. *Yes, I know this is a teaching hospital, but NO, I am not happy to have a group of young doctors hovering around my bed while a millionaire specialist in a bow tie talks about me as if I were either already dead or only recently born.* Hospitals were bad enough, but they couldn't hold a candle to some of these doctors. There was always a chance the young ones might turn out differently, but not the chest man over there with his quacking acolytes, and not Mrs Jenkins's gastro man, all out and about gouging the public purse, with their vineyards and their German cars and their carbon racing bikes and their Lycra shorts and their rehydration packs and skiing trips to Whistler – not to mention the so-called holiday houses they rented out three times a year to their brothers-in-law to squeeze out a bit of negative gearing.

When Fred was growing up, Dr Broadbent was the only doctor in the village, and he was too busy looking after people to worry about feathering his nest. He was a Scotsman who suffered himself from the national scourge of psoriasis – not that he let a bit of flaking skin get in the way of his calling.

Nowadays you could hardly find a full-time family doctor in any of these supermarkets they called medical centres; they were full of bony blonde women who punched in a day or two between private-school drop-offs and pickups, and the gym and the shops. Why was the taxpayer subsidising the education of all these people who didn't want to take care of anyone other than themselves? What had happened to the Hippocratic oath?

Was that his doctor coming up the corridor? Finally! He fumbled for his glasses. Where were they? He was suddenly desperate to go to the toilet.

'Mr Lothian?'

Fred looked at the frighteningly young and considerably more competent than most Dr Jane Forster. Clearly, she was an anomaly. How could she be on her way to neurosurgery at her age? Was she married? There was no ring. Did she have children? How could she ever have a family while she was carrying the burden of the brain, with its fragile and ever-so-complicated network of lobes and hemispheres and neural pathways?

Dr Forster looked pale and tired. She smiled wanly. 'I apologise for keeping you waiting, Mr Lothian. I'd intended to do my rounds much earlier. I know you want to go home today. We've had an emergency this morning and I had to go into surgery. It's been a very long day and it's still only morning.'

'A stroke?' He forced himself to say it. The newly renovated Fred would face his darkest fears without flinching.

'A bad road accident – a school bus and a station wagon. You'll hear about it on the news, no doubt.'

'Were any children killed?' asked Fred in as neutral a voice as he could harness.

'Three young people in the station wagon, all under twenty, speeding on the northern interchange. It looks like they ran a red light. Two were killed instantly, the other we lost in the ambulance. She'd only had her licence for six months, so she wasn't supposed to have all those people in the car. I'm for raising the age to twenty-one.'

'And the bus? The children?' He had to ask.

'One killed, two critical, and both of those have trauma to the head. It was one of those old buses without belts. Heads and bones. We were all called in.'

Dr Forster opened her file.

'My son –'

Dr Forster looked up from her notes.

'My son was in a car accident. He has brain damage. I'd like to get out today so I can see him.'

Fred could not endure the physiognomy of sympathy: the knitted brow, the tilted head, the pinching together of the lips. *Ooh, poor little Freddy.* He had left it up to Martha to field sympathy. He stayed up in the stands, from where he could avoid accepting anything at all – sympathy, condolences, the accident itself. But Dr Forster was a professional. Sympathy was not part of her repertoire.

'Does your son live at home with you, Mr Lothian?'

'Oh no,' said Fred, 'he's in a care facility. I could never have managed. My wife has died.' He looked down. The good Dr Forster would help him out here. *Poor Mr Lothian, of course you couldn't manage.*

'When did the accident happen?'

'Nearly fifteen years ago,' said Fred.

'There's a lot more support available now than there was back then,' said Dr Forster briskly. She was sorting through her file. 'We understand it more now. There's still nowhere near enough help, of course. It's still hard on families. I'm part of a lobby group to expand funding for families, and to get some kind of tax concession that recognises their unpaid labour. You're lucky to have a place for your son, and the means to pay for it. But a surprising number of families are choosing to manage at home, at least for as long as they can, and with respite now available many of them do quite well. They have to modify everything, as you can imagine, depending on the level of disability. People put in ramps, pulleys, bridges. It's amazing to see the effort families make to keep their loved ones close to them.'

Fred ran his tongue around his teeth. He tugged at his bottom lip. Dr Forster placed her fingers on his neck. How extraordinary. She was wearing an old watch with a black face exactly like the one his grandfather had given him when Virgil died. It was called a trench watch, with cathedral arms and luminous numbers. He had passed on the watch to Caroline when he moved into the villa.

'That's an interesting old watch,' said Fred.

'I love it. I shouldn't really wear it to work. It's a trench watch from the First World War. It's quite rare.'

'Did you have a relative who fought?'

Dr Forster opened the large grey envelope at the end of the bed. 'Pardon? Oh no, I bought it from an antique shop just over a year ago.'

'In Perth, was this, or overseas?'

'Right here, in the city, on the eastern end of the mall. I think the business has been there for years.'

'It certainly has,' said Fred tightly. 'My wife used to take my daughter there to window-shop.' While Dr Forster checked his eyes he was dying a private death.

'So, Mr Lothian.' She leant in towards him. 'When we look at your pictures we see this.' Dr Forster held up what Fred assumed was a scan of his own brain. It resembled a black-and-white fruit, cut at the equator. Caroline had sold his watch. She had given away the only thing he had left that his granddad had touched.

'Can you see this? It's shaped like a slice of lemon.'

He squinted. 'What is it? Is there a mass?' 'Mass' was a terrible word, an inexact word, but he had to get it out of the way. An even more onerous word forced itself upon him. 'Or a tumour?'

He and Martha had squinted at and peered into sheet after sheet of images that neither of them could understand. 'What is it?' he kept saying to Martha's doctor. 'Where am I supposed to be looking?' All his life he had conjured up three-dimensional spaces from two-dimensional drawings, but these meant nothing to him.

'Nothing as grave as that,' Dr Forster said. 'Can you see that little crescent there between the grey matter and the white matter? That's a small subdural haematoma – a little bleed in the dura mater. It was probably caused by the blow to the head, but we can't be sure. It could have been there a very long time.'

'Tough mother.'

'I beg your pardon,' said Dr Forster.

'*Dura mater.* It's Latin; it means "tough mother".'

The doctor smiled. 'Is that a fact? So, Mr Lothian, the question is, what do we do? This little fellow might resolve all by itself. If we choose the path of least intervention, you'll come in here every month for a scan and I'll have a look at it and see what that tough mother is up to.'

'Or?' Could he live with the idea of something literally hanging over his head? A tiny crescent-shaped gauntlet?

'Or we get a little drill and we make a tiny hole and we let that little mother out. We can do it right here, with a local anaesthetic.'

'What? Here?' *What about the other patients? What about the noise?* He had chills just thinking about it.

'What I propose is this: we send you home right now so you can see your son and rest up. And in one month's time you come in here and we have a look and see what that mother's up to, and we take it from there. How does that sound to you?'

It sounded like a compromise. It sounded like a deferral.

'That sounds very good, Dr Forster,' he said meekly.

'Good. I'll book the scan and you'll get notification in the mail with a time and date. And I want you to take it easy. No deep-sea diving or parachuting. And no driving. Sorry about that, but just for the month. I'll get the charge sister to come down and take the details and get your release forms ready. I'll see you in a month.' She paused. 'And best of luck with your son.'

Dr Forster stretched out her arm. Fred shook her hand. He looked down at Pop's watch. *Give that back*, he wanted to say, *it's mine*.

Dr Forster is racing down the stairs. She is running through the long, white corridors that lead to the operating theatre, the old black-faced watch ticking away like a time bomb, just as it did the day Pop's other arm was blown clean away to the German side. Dr Jane Forster is scrubbing her arms and her hands, and those neat, short nails. She holds out her arms for the surgical gown and lets the nurse tie the tabs. She backs into the swinging doors that lead to the theatre where his beautiful, clever, serious boy lies on a table. He is covered with sheets, as if he were already dead. There is a tube down his throat, and all manner of people are opening up his body. In the distance he hears Martha call.

'Not Callum,' she said on the way to the hospital, 'not Callum.' By the time they reached Emergency, shock had ruptured the two vowels of their son's name and neither of them could speak.

'Lothian,' he said, and followed a doctor through the corridors to Caroline, who was waiting in a room.

Only he had looked inside that theatre; only he had understood from the people in the room and from the costumes they wore and the machines that throbbed in the wings that Callum would never return the same character as he left. Someone led Fred away and put him back with his wife and daughter. He placed his car keys on the cream vinyl seat next to Martha.

'I'll be at home,' he said. 'I'll take a taxi.'

For a short time it was all Martha's fault. If he had not bought the new car he would not have given Callum the old car, and if he had not given his son the old car his son would not have been driving that night. It was all because of the car. But then, if Martha's mother hadn't died and left them money, there would have been no new car. And if Martha had just said, 'No, no, Fred, you can't buy a new car with my mother's money', it would never have happened. It was all Martha's fault.

'What?' said Martha through a haze of grief and fury. 'You're leaving?'

'But you can't leave us, Dad,' cried Caroline. 'We need you here.'

'Mr Lothian?' It was Dr Jane Forster again. What did she want now?

'I just wanted to let you know that they have others.'

'Pardon?' he said.

'At the antique store, they have a few more of these watches if you're interested in buying one. The owner bought them as a lot in an auction in England. We had a long conversation about it. I'm pretty sure they'd still have one or two left. It's not the sort of thing many people want to buy.' She stood for a moment. 'You should be ready to leave within fifteen minutes or so. Best of luck.'

'Thank you,' said Fred. 'Thank you very much.'

'All part of the job,' she said.

A love-heart balloon had escaped from a happier ward and was wandering around the ceiling. Something fried and meaty was coming up for lunch. A man in board shorts and thongs led a woman through the ward. She was weeping into his T-shirt, hiding her face from onlookers.

If not Callum, then who, Martha? It was different for him, because it was all his fault. For Fred there was no accident, and because there was no accident there was no filthy dream of substitution.

He would like to speak to Father McMahon now. *What is the point of pain? How are we supposed to live on with children and death?* But Father McMahon was dead and buried, far from the room for doubt.

And there was Jan, walking towards him on those strong, firm calves of hers. She smiled and lifted a hand. He swung his legs off the bed and picked up his small bag.

'I'm sorry I'm late. How are you feeling? Are you all ready to go?'

'I have to see the sister at the desk, and then I'm free. How was your morning?'

'Exhausting. Yours?'

'I just saw the doctor. I have a subdural haematoma.'

'Is it serious? Do you have to have an operation?'

'It should resolve on its own, and if not they're going to bore a little hole in my skull and let the bugger out.'

'I look forward to that,' said Jan. 'Are you okay to drive?'

'Oh, fine,' said Fred breezily. 'After today I'm all clear.'

'Where to now, Fred?'

'To Callum.'

'To Callum.'

The care facility manager had been on the phone for fifteen minutes, and not even so much as a glance in Fred's direction. He felt quite weak and nauseous. It was partly the smell of mass-produced food stewing in bains-marie, but it was mostly the colour scheme. The place was a sea of salmon pink. Who was responsible for the colour of the walls in public facilities?

Late in his career at the foundry, before the lay-offs and the downturns, when it looked like his father might rise to the top floor, when Alexander could still manage to walk home from the pub instead of being carried, his father took to studying the salmon-pink pages of the *Financial Times*, in preparation for what he called his 'leg-up'.

'Any minute now, Freddy, I'll be getting the leg-up.'

The care facility manager put down the phone and Fred stepped through the door. 'I'm Frederick Lothian, Callum's father.'

She looked up at him from her desk. 'Oh, yes, I thought it was you,' she said carefully. 'We talked on the phone. You were in the hospital. You're obviously feeling better.'

Frederick swallowed. 'It was a minor issue, all resolved now.' All resolved except for the gauntlet.

'I'm Corinne Palmer. You would have spoken to Nicola Masterson on the weekend – it was last Sunday, I think, when we needed approval for the script.' She was going to hammer it in all the way, pound him to pieces. 'Fortunately we were able to contact your daughter. You do realise we can't be calling London just to get a patient on a different antibiotic.'

'I apologised already,' said Fred tightly, 'but I'm here now, and that's the main thing. I want to take over from Caroline. You said I need to fill in some forms?'

The woman went to a filing cabinet at the back of the room and retrieved a large envelope.

'How is Callum?'

'He's much better. The antibiotics have cleared up his chest, but we're worried about pressure sores. We're keeping an eye on him. If you fill these in we'll take it from there.'

'Is he being moved regularly? Are you getting him out of bed? Or is he being left there all day?'

Corinne Palmer's gaze was so fixed and steady there was no doubt she was concealing some very uneven feelings. 'We have a protocol for this, Mr Lothian.'

'Please, call me Fred.'

Corinne Palmer sat back in her chair. She swivelled from side to side, then rocked up and down gently. 'Mr Lothian, we've been managing Callum for years, and many other patients with similar needs.' She paused. 'The staff here were very fond of your wife.'

Frederick bit his tongue. *How dare she? So was I. I was very fond of my wife. Actually, I was her fucking husband.*

'Many of the staff knew her for years,' continued Corinne Palmer.

Frederick did a fair imitation of a smile.

'We were all very sorry to hear about Mrs Lothian's death,' the woman continued. She tucked her chin in to see over the top of her frameless glasses.

Her eyes were shiny and unblinking. Her brown hair was short and fuzzy, like some kind of small feral carnivore, decided Fred.

'A number of my staff planned to go to the funeral, but we were told it was a private function, and then there was no wake. Many of them feel they never got to say goodbye. We did see Caroline afterwards, though. She came in and spent time with the staff, which was a great help. We are very fond of our families.' She rocked back and forth in her chair.

Why did he have to listen to this?

'I understand that the private funeral was your decision, Mr Lothian, and that you didn't want a wake for your wife. I think you should know that we all respected Martha's devotion and advocacy for her son. I'm sure Callum misses her a great deal.'

'We all miss her,' he said. 'Excuse me.'

He stepped back into the corridor, clutching his file. The gauntlet in his brain was swinging to and fro. He would like to push Ms Palmer right off her swivel chair, kick her in the stomach while she was down, and then finish her off with a brick over the head.

A few minutes later a young black woman in a blue uniform came up the corridor and went into the manager's office. Presently they both came out.

'Mr Lothian, this is Anne. She looks after Callum on her shifts. Can you take him across to his room, Anne? Lunch is finished, isn't it? Have all the trays gone up?'

Anne nodded and turned to him.

'Come with me, please,' she said smoothly. Did he detect a second current running under that polite exterior? The whole place was against him. They knew about Martha and Caroline.

They knew about Callum. He followed Anne down the salmon-pink corridor, stepping on salmon-pink tiles. The walkways were lined with empty chairs. Did anyone ever sit in them? Soothing muzak oozed out into the empty walkways, along with scraps of afternoon television, canned laughter and the low hum of the air conditioning.

'Where is everyone?' he asked.

'It's rest time,' said Anne, 'from one in the afternoon until two. On Saturdays and Sundays we extend quiet time until three. We close the doors to all visitors and only those with a security code can come in. You'll have that number in your file there.' She stopped. 'Mrs Lothian was a good friend to me. I only knew her for one year before she got sick, but I heard about the many years she spent caring for her son.'

Fred was alarmed. Were those tears? Surely not? Was this kind of talk permitted between staff and clients?

'I still feel upset that I couldn't see Martha when she was sick. Why wouldn't you let me see her?'

'What do you mean, I wouldn't let you?' Frederick said indignantly. 'I never stopped anyone.'

'But you did,' she said firmly. 'I called and told you I was from the care facility. You said that the family was under a great deal of stress, and Martha didn't want visitors. I asked to speak to Caroline and you said she wasn't there. It was you on the phone, I'm sure of it, with that upper-class English voice of yours, all hoity-toity. I wanted to tell her about my brother. She would have wanted to know.'

Who was this woman? Who was her brother? She couldn't have been more than thirty, but she spoke with righteous conviction. She had no right to talk to him about his wife and family. 'I'm sorry, miss, I really am, but you have to understand, it was a terrible time for us all. My wife was dying. I was struggling myself.'

Her face was implacable. 'It is *Mrs*. I am married. I was so upset when I heard she had passed away and I hadn't seen her.'

What could he say? Stepping into the facility was like falling into toffee. Everywhere he walked he found himself more and more attached. 'Where are you from, Anne?' he asked. Perhaps he could broaden the conversation and shift the focus.

'I'm from Ghana. My husband is here studying for his masters in agricultural management. He has a grant from the government. It was difficult for me here in Australia, and Martha was so kind. She always helped me bathe and feed Callum. She was so devoted, the way she read to him. There are clients here who have no one to care for them. It's so sad. I pray to God for them all.' She paused. 'I am emotional. I was so upset when Dumbledore passed away.'

'Who?' said Fred. 'There's no need to apologise. Now, perhaps we can –'

'I am not apologising, Mr Lothian,' she said. 'I am just telling the truth. I am an emotional person.'

Another African woman walked past in a blue uniform. She slowed down and looked at Anne, then at him. She knew too. They all knew. He had to get out of here, but how could he leave? Jan was not coming back for an hour, and he couldn't just walk out, not with that dragon at the front door, not with everyone knowing. Not without seeing Callum.

'Thank you for caring for Callum, Anne. Now I'd like to see my son.' He spoke in his best colonial English upper-class accent. What choice did he have?

'He's no trouble at all.'

She gave no indication of moving on. Where to now? 'So, Martha knew your brother too?'

'Not personally, of course not, but I talked to Martha about him and all my family. I come from a family of seven children.'

'Goodness me, seven.'

'But only four remain alive.'

There was nothing to say.

'Four girls. I wanted to tell Martha that my youngest brother, the last son, had died. She would have wanted to know.'

'Are they here in Australia? Your family? Your brother?'

'Of course not,' said Anne, as if he were stupid. 'My family are all in Ghana. If my brothers lived here they would not be dead. We could not afford the correct treatments. Martha wanted to pay for medical assistance for my brother, but our family could not accept that. What good can money do? We have an epidemic of HIV.'

As an esteemed professor at a first-rate university he had spoken constantly and with authority to all kinds of people from all over the world. But now he was on the other end of someone's words, and he was speechless.

He followed Anne into a separate wing. She stopped in front of number 29 and pushed open the door. He scanned the room quickly. This was not Callum's room; it was too small and too empty. The last time he was in Callum's room there was a stack of books on a table and folded washing on a chair. There were pictures on the walls. His daughter was crying in a corner. The fan on the ceiling turned around and around, indifferent and implacable.

He looked up. The fan was gone. 'Where's Callum?' Why wasn't he here? *If Callum died this would be all that was left*, he thought. A few clothes, a pair of slippers, a single vase and a small photo on the table by the bed.

'He'll be back from OT very soon, Mr Lothian.'

'When did you move him? Did he have to be moved from

his other room?' Things should not change. Nothing should change.

'We haven't moved him, Mr Lothian. This has always been his room. We try not to move residents. It disorientates them.'

'But it's all different,' he said, unable to express the difference in any way. 'There's no ceiling fan, for a start.'

'All the fans have been taken out. We have ducted air conditioning now.'

At one end of the room, next to the bathroom, was Callum's adjustable bed. The remote controls hung off the back panel. The cotton waffle cover was pulled tight and tucked in on all sides. A series of pulleys hung down from the ceiling above the bed, and there was something on the pillow, something white and fluffy. Next to the bed was a pan in a chair, and a small wooden side table he recognised from home. On it was a vase of fresh pink roses. He could hardly bear to look at them.

'Most of the things you remember were Martha's personal belongings – books, CDs, photographs. We returned them to Caroline when she passed away. You are probably remembering the room when Martha was here. She was always bringing new things to stimulate Callum.'

He picked up the earthenware vase on the table. It was one of Martha's favourites, fire-engine red with geometric incisions at the base. And there was Martha in the photo, smiling her perfect smile, holding a small, fat, bald baby. He picked up the fluffy white bear on the bed. 'This isn't his,' said Frederick. 'This doesn't belong to Callum. He isn't a baby. Take it away.'

Anne crossed her arms. 'He likes it. We put it in his bed at night. Is there anything wrong with that?' She turned and unlocked a small wall cabinet.

Misery.

Callum must have been eight or nine. He was propped up on the couch, poring over *National Geographic* and clutching that damn little bear, or what was left of him. Bunky, the hairless bear. Fred was on his way up to the study when Callum caught him.

'Hey, Dad, look at this! Please, Dad, it won't take a minute. You've got to see this. It's Pompeii! There was this volcano thousands of years ago. But look at this!'

Fred bent over and looked. It was the dog.

'It couldn't have been in a kennel – the Romans wouldn't have had kennels, would they? And a dog wouldn't lie like this with his legs up – he must have been asleep on his back – maybe he was in the sun.'

His left hand cut the air as he spoke, splitting words into short ends. So exact, his son, so keen to break the story down into pieces and put them all back together. So like his father.

'So, the dog is fast asleep, and this hot boiling lava comes pouring down the mountain and flows right over the top of him, and he just freezes, like that!' He snapped his fingers. 'Right? Right, Dad? Is that how the dog got made into a statue?'

Frederick nodded sagely if absently, hoping his boy would move on so he could get back to a troublesome calculation for mechanical resonance, so he wouldn't have to explain the concept of rigor mortis or suffocation, or that it wasn't really a dog, but the space left where a dog had once been, a cavity filled with plaster by an intrepid Italian archaeologist in the 1860s.

Not even the shell of the thing.

Anne was putting capsules and pills into a plastic box, ticking off a chart stuck to the back of the cabinet as she went.

'It says he was a guard dog. That's his collar. He guarded the House of Orpheus. Who's Orpheus, Dad?'

Orpheus is the poet and prophet who tried to bring his beloved wife back from the dead, and then disregarded Hades' warning: 'Do not look back.'

Callum is wedged between them in the bed. They are playing the kissing game – one kiss for Callum, pass it to Mummy, two kisses for Callum, pass them back to Daddy, and when they get to ten they start all over again. Where was Caroline? Why wasn't she in bed with them? It made him anxious, as if he had lost her in a vast shopping centre.

The terror of a lost child. He put the bear back on the pillow.

Anne had finished with the pills and was straightening towels on a trolley at the door. One weekend he took Martha and the children to see a display of skydiving at Toodyay. One of the jumpers began to drift towards the crowd. As he came closer they all scattered, laughing and screaming, unsure if this was some kind of trick or an accident. The man landed awkwardly and rolled on the ground, with a tangle of strings and the red and yellow parachute coming down after him. A gust of wind picked up the chute. The children threw themselves upon it, but every time they managed to hold down a segment, another billowing fold would pop up. That was what it was like now, trying to contain the past.

'He's coming,' said Anne, looking down the corridor.

'I have to use the toilet,' said Fred quickly.

When he came out ten minutes later, Callum was already sitting in a wheelchair facing the full-length window and Anne was wiping down the back of the chair. On the ground just outside the window was the painted gnome that once lived in their front garden. He had always hated that gnome, and was always trying to get Martha to throw it away. 'Why? Because it's bad taste?' Martha said every time he asked her to move it. 'Does it offend your modernist principles? Callum bought it for me at the primary school fete and I love it.' He could not remember when it disappeared from the house, but one day it was gone from under the tree. He thought, *At last she's got rid of it. At last Martha agrees with me.*

The sun was beating into the room and, despite the air conditioning, it was very warm.

'It's a little hot in here,' he said. 'Can we adjust the temperature?'

Anne shook her head. 'It's a centralised system. We like it to be a little warmer because many of our clients have poor circulation. If we make it too cold it's not good for them. I'll leave you alone now. You'll be wanting to talk. He's had his lunch. If you want tea there's a station down the corridor. Please, help yourself.'

She turned to leave, then paused.

'Is Caroline back from her trip to Europe?'

'You've met my daughter?'

Caroline had been living in Melbourne well before Anne started working at the facility, so they could only have met once or twice. How would she know she was in London?

Anne looked at him. Another steady gaze. 'We all know her from her visits. It's wonderful how she comes all the way from Melbourne every month to see her brother. She always calls me before she comes. I tell her if he needs something in particular, and we sort it out together.'

Fred turned towards the wall and looked at a fine hairline crack. Caroline had been coming to and from Melbourne and he hadn't even known. The whole place knew everything. They knew about all those years Martha was here with Callum while her husband was in his study with Marcel Breuer, or in the garage with Dieter Rams.

'She loved her brother very much,' he said through gritted teeth. When would this end? When would this woman leave him alone?

Anne lifted a brow. 'Oh, she still does, Mr Lothian, she still loves her brother. Even when they die you still love them. I know this very well.' She looked at her watch. 'I will check in on you in an hour.'

When Anne was gone, he walked up behind Callum and put his hand on his cheek. It felt soft and warm and bristly. His son needed a shave.

'Callum,' he said quietly, 'it's Dad. I've come to say sorry.'

'But how was he, Fred? I hate people who drive those huge four-wheel drives. These car parks weren't designed for cars like that.' Jan checked the rear-view mirror again. She wasn't used to driving forward, let alone reversing. And she was upset with Fred. He had taken much longer than he said he would at the care facility, which wouldn't have mattered except there was no shade, so she'd had to leave the car running to keep cool and she hated doing that, and now he was giving her absolutely nothing.

'That manager is a disgrace. I'm going to lodge a complaint.'

Fred was pretending to look out the window; he was obviously trying to stop himself crying. It was excruciating to watch. *If only men would learn to weep openly*, thought Jan, *it would be so much easier for everyone.* Sam was had been a very good crier, but then he was Italian.

Fred wiped his eyes and nose. 'Callum is the same, only older. He needs a shave. I had a bit of a run-in with the manager, but it's all sorted now.'

'What about?' said Jan. 'You know, Fred, there's nothing wrong with showing emotion. In some cultures the men do all the crying. Am I clear on the left?'

'After I left Callum I went to the office and I told the Palmer woman I wanted to take him out this Sunday. She refused. "It's a matter of protocol, Mr Lothian" – she won't call me by my first name. She said she had to contact Caroline before these next-of-kin and duty-of-care documents could be processed. "We don't allow our residents to stay with family unless there's been a scheduled home visit from the OT." Can you believe it? A father can't take his own son for a drive! They wouldn't let me take a wheelchair either. I have to get my own chair. I told them I lived at St Sylvan's – everywhere you go there's a ramp or a bar or a handle or a buzzer. And then I have to learn to prepare his food. And there's a first aid course in case he chokes while he's having his food. "And if he's with you for more than a few hours, Mr Lothian, there's the matter of medicine. And the bathroom." I told her he was desperate to get out of there. Jan, it's sixty kilometres here and you're not doing more than thirty. You've got cars banked up behind you.'

Jan looked in the rear-view mirror, then pressed her foot on the accelerator. 'Did he say that?'

'Who?'

'Callum, did he tell you he was desperate to get out?'

'Well, no, of course not, but you can tell.'

Jan sighed. He was not an easy man, not an easy man at all. 'If you think about it, they're right. You've not been around. They don't know you – don't look at me like that, it's the truth. It's the same with Morrison. It's their responsibility to make sure Callum's safe.'

'He's my son, of course he's safe. Anyway, it's sorted.'

'These indicators are on the wrong side of the steering wheel. What do you mean, sorted?'

'In the end the woman rang Caroline and she's emailing the permission. It's all arranged. But I might need your help on Sunday.'

'What kind of help?'

'I might need another set of hands to help get Callum into the car.'

'What? Can't he walk? Surely you should be using a special vehicle? Does the manager know about this?'

'Of course she knows.'

'All right, Fred, but there's no need to snap at me. Of course I'll help. I'll have Morrison with me, though. Guess what I just did?'

'Pardon?'

'Guess what I just did?' She paused. 'I'll say it once more

269

and after that I'm not talking to you. I just bought a television.'
She cocked her head.

Fred looked around at the giant cardboard box wedged in
the gap behind the front seats.

'It's the latest flat-screen. A man is coming to set it up this
afternoon. And I got a new DVD player. I was going to invite
you over to watch a movie tonight.'

'I think I need a quiet night,' said Fred. 'But thank you
anyway. Turn here. Quickly. Right at the lights.'

Jan pulled into the right-hand lane and the car behind her
beeped wildly.

'Don't do that, Fred. I almost had an accident. Why are we
going here? This isn't the way home.'

But it was Fred's way home. They drove past the giant ghost
gum tree that Caroline had ridden straight into on her new
yellow bike on the morning of her eleventh birthday. How she
could have hit it was a mystery, but afterwards there was a split
lip and a trip to the Children's Hospital and a buckled front
wheel to fix. But where was the Maitlands' place? Was that it?
The house was still there, but it was all different. Barry and Lou
must have gone. Where were they? Wouldn't they have contacted him? He had been planning to call them; he was going
to drop in once he got settled at St Sylvan's. Have them over
for a drink. They couldn't have died, could they? He'd been
gone only a year and a half. It would have been in the columns
if they had died.

'Slow down, would you, Jan? Pull over.'

The new owners had pulled up Barry's roses. Barry spent
all his mornings in the front garden fussing over those roses.
Martha came back from her visits with dark-red roses wrapped
in wet newspaper. She would sit at the table and snip off the
thorns before putting them in her vase – her bright-red vase.
When she got sick, Barry walked up every morning they were

in flower and left roses at the front door, and then walked home again.

But of course, that was why they hadn't called him; it was Martha they always loved.

'I thought you hated roses,' he teased her as she snipped the ends and clipped the thorns.

'I like these particular roses,' she said. 'I just don't like roses.'

'That makes no sense.'

'Why? It's perfectly logical. I don't like South Africans, but I've got nothing against Paula.'

Paula was from Durban. She ran the canteen at Caroline's school and she and Martha adored each other.

'You drive me crazy,' he said.

'Ditto,' she replied.

'What are we doing here, Fred? I'd really like to get home. I've been out all day.'

'That house used to have the most wonderful rose garden.'

'It is sad when someone has spent years on a garden and the new owners come along and put a shovel through it all. Gardens take much longer to grow than houses take to build.'

It is awful, thought Fred, staring at what used to be the Maitlands' house. He wondered if any of Martha's grevilleas had survived. The skeleton of the Maitlands' house remained, but it had been rendered and painted and dragged into another era. Martha might have approved of the careful placement of the grass tree and the black kangaroo paws in the recess of the rendered wall, but she would never have banished the roses. They must have added an extension at the back; there was a new skillion roof line and a huge garage on the side to hold the kind of equipment well-off men now seemed to require to balance out their earnings: the paddleboard, the kite surfer, the carbon racing bike.

They drove slowly past the little park where he used to take Caroline and Callum. For years Caroline was wide awake at five o'clock in the morning. When she called out from her bed, he would carry his daughter downstairs to the kitchen, and then, if it wasn't raining or the dead of winter, they would head out into the half-light of dawn while Martha and the baby slept on, curled about each other in the double bed. No matter how many times he pushed that seat of the swing, it was never enough. 'More, Daddy, more!' The swing was no longer rusty grey metal with perilous flaking corners and legs that lifted off the ground if you went too high. The new playground was fire-engine red and sunflower yellow and hibiscus pink. Accidents had been scrupulously modelled then designed away. It was all gone, even the nasty bindies and doublegees had been eradicated with a synthetic surface, yet he could still feel the physical weight of his daughter and son coming back to meet him and being swung away, over and again, like breath.

'That's where Callum fell off the swing,' he told Jan. 'He let go right at the top. I thought he was dead.' The swing came back empty, while Callum propelled himself upwards and out-wards, like a bat, and landed hard on the ground, belly down.

When he saw that Callum could move his head and stagger to his feet, he took his son by the arms and shook him hard. 'What were you doing? Why did you let go? You could have killed yourself, do you hear me? Don't you ever do that again.'

'You're hurting me, Daddy, you're hurting my arms, my tummy hurts. Let go!' he screamed. But Fred could not let go. He pulled Callum along the grass, ignoring the prickles and the bitumen and the screaming and the kicking. His son had almost died and it was all Fred's fault.

'Left or right at the stop sign?'

'Right. Can you stop at that phone booth? I won't be a moment.' He undid his seatbelt and shook his pockets. 'Do you have any fifty-cent pieces, Jan?' Jan found her purse and gave him two. Fred seemed to be in a terrible hurry. She watched him talking into the phone. He lifted his hand as he spoke, chopping the air into pieces. She even saw him laugh. What was he up to?

'All done,' he said when he got back in.

'Is everything all right?'

'I have to go into work in the morning.'

'What work? Aren't you retired?'

'I just called my former student at the department. He's always wanting me to come in. He runs the workshops at the engineering section. I had a favour to ask him.'

'Fine,' said Jan, glancing at him. 'Straight ahead?'

'One more stop and then back to St Sylvan's. What time is it?' He looked at his watch. 'I have to call London when I get home.'

'Your daughter?' She took his silence as a negative.

The corner deli where Caroline and Callum had bought lollies was now just another huge house with a vast black window at the front. The box trees that Martha hated and tried to have replaced were resolutely in situ, but the palette of the suburb had completely changed. When they first moved here it was summer. It was dry and hot and comfortably suburban – what Fred called ordinary and Martha called deadly boring.

'It's so yellow,' she said. 'It's so dead.' But she came to love it. She loved the cool autumn mornings and the sharp pins of light in the night sky. She loved the furious winter fronts that ravaged the city and left it in shreds. She loved the spring, when her garden began to shiver and hum. She loved the large, generous blocks and the lemon-scented gum trees and the hot, empty pavements, and the relief of the sprinklers at dawn and dusk. She even liked the rusty tinge of groundwater that crept up the walls of the blond brick houses. With a fulcrum of money, the horizontal axis of the suburb began to tilt upwards. Now the back gardens had begun to disappear. More and more blocks were being subdivided or battle-axed and sold off for these expensive buff-and-cream two-storey mock-moderns, with their smoky glass and their feature walls and their fake stone facades.

'Just here, Jan, slow down,' he said. 'Stop here.'

Jan didn't want to stop anywhere; she wanted to go home, but Fred was clearly on some kind of mission. She looked out at the plain two-storey box. A red gravel semicircle cut across the front of the house, leaving a half-circle of garden that was a mess of weeds and woody native shrubs. The house appeared vacant and unloved, and out of place among the new mansions.

'What is this, Fred? Why are we here?'

'This is our house,' he said. 'The tenants have quit their lease and I have to have it cleaned. There are bedrooms – five if you count the study – and a pool. There's no fence around the pool, but that can be fixed. You can't have a pool without a fence any more. It's against the law.' He was thinking about four-year-old David Michael from the columns. 'Did I miss Tom Chelmsley's funeral?' he said suddenly.

Jan nodded. 'I went for both of us. I felt so sorry for his sister. You don't want to die with a wall between you and the dead. I made a donation to a charity in his name, and signed it from you and me. I hope you don't mind.'

'Of course not. Let me know what I owe you.'

He rummaged through the glove box until he found a pencil and notebook.

'You seem so busy all of a sudden, Fred. You should take it easy with that head of yours.' Jan leant over to see what he was doing. 'Aren't you a wonderful drawer! Look at the way you've made the house. There are so few lines, but it's all there. Is that a bridge?'

'It's a ramp. Look at the house. See how you have to walk up those steps from the carport to get to the front door? The block's very steep. That's a real problem for a wheelchair. I think we can run the ramp up the left there and swing it around to the right. There might be just enough frontage for a ninety-degree turn, or else it will have to be a switchback. I'll have to calculate the gradient. Ideally you want one in twenty for wheelchair access. Then we have to get him upstairs. If we can't fit a lift in next to the stairwell, I'm going to hang the shaft off the outside of the building, there.'

Jan followed his pointed finger.

'We're going to have to knock through the landing and put the door to the lift flush to the outer wall. That way we get Callum right from the ground floor into the upstairs bedroom next to the larger bathroom. I'll put a monitor in with Callum, so if he needs something in the night I'll be able to sort it out. I hope you don't mind if you and Morrison have the two bedrooms at the back? One of them used to be Caroline's room. There's another smaller bathroom with a shower at that end of the house. Caroline and I will have downstairs.' He stopped drawing and looked at Jan gravely. 'If Caroline ever comes back. Do you think she will?'

Jan looked at Fred. He was absolutely serious. 'You want us all to move here? Into this house? All of us, together?'

Frederick nodded. 'You can pay me rent if you want, but it's not necessary.'

He was out the door before she had a chance to speak. What was she supposed to do now? Turn off the car? Get out? She watched Fred step out the front of the block from boundary to boundary, then scribble in his book. He went into the carport and began to walk backwards, turned ninety degrees and wrote something down, then disappeared around the side of the house.

Jan put the car into gear and drove down the road to the

buildings she had seen as they drove up. It was one of those lovely 1930s primary schools, with high-pitched roofs and wide verandahs, with silver hooks for bags and hoops for balls, with painted lines for handball and squares with the numbers for hopscotch.

She allowed herself for just a moment to imagine standing at the gate with Morrison, zipping up his schoolbag, sending him on his way, then she stopped herself. There were no second chances. You could not live in the same house a second time. Yes, people could change, but there was no returning her son to her side, or erasing those lines on her grandson's arms. How dare Fred impose his mad ideas on her? How dare he get carried away, thinking he could magically solve all their problems with a ramp and a lift and a fence around the pool? Who did he think he was?

As she reversed into the driveway of the school car park, a little girl on rollerblades cut across the road to the empty basketball court. The girl leant to the left and described a perfect arc, then pushed a rubber heel into the ground and came to a sudden stop. She bent down to adjust her shoe, then stood up and took off to the right. *It's so hard to grow old*, thought Jan, *to see the path narrowing. We don't know how to manage so we act as if it's unexpected, like an earthquake or a road accident.* The little girl shot straight forward on both blades. She dipped in both knees and then leapt up into the air to land on one leg. Her supporting ankle tipped and wobbled beneath her weight, and Jan held her breath, certain she would fall, but the girl steadied herself and extended her other leg out behind her. *She's pretending to be a figure skater*, thought Jan. The girl lifted her head to the cloudless sky and stretched out her arms, arching backwards.

Jan beeped and waved and the girl waved back.

At that moment anything was possible.

Monday, 23 January 2006

IT WAS AROUND 6 am when the phone woke her up.

'Dad?' she said groggily.

'Caroline Lothian?'

'Speaking. Who is this?'

'It's Corinne Palmer, the manager of the Sir Charles Court Care Facility.'

'What is it, Corinne? Is something wrong with Callum?'

'That's why I'm calling, Caroline. I'm sorry to trouble you so early in the morning, but we've left a number of messages on your phone.'

'I'm sorry?' she said. 'Is it Callum? Is he –'

'The point is, Caroline, Ms. Lothian, Callum is missing. He's not here.'

'What do you mean, he's not there? Where is he?'

'We believe he's with your father, but we can't locate Mr Lothian. Have you heard from him in the last twelve hours? Do you have any idea where he might have taken Callum? Callum has been gone since yesterday afternoon.'

'He always unplugs his phone. They must be at home. Have you called him at home?'

'We called St Sylvan's Village and the management have been to his villa and checked. He's not there. However, they think he might have been burgled, which is a further concern.'

'Burgled?'

'Apparently there were things strewn everywhere.'

'That's nothing,' she said. 'But where's Callum?'

'Your father's car has gone and he and Callum are missing. Apparently they did not stay at the house last night.'

'Missing,' she repeated. 'Why is Callum with him? How did he get Callum? Why did you let him go? Is this some kind of joke?'

'Caroline, please, calm down and listen. Your father came in on Friday, after he got out of the hospital.'

'What hospital? Why was he in the hospital?'

'I believe it was a minor issue related to a fall he had at a restaurant. He came in on Friday to see Callum and sign the next-of-kin papers, so we don't have a repeat of that business with the antibiotics last week – which you'll have to authorise, of course.'

'I have no idea what's going on,' said Caroline flatly.

'On Friday Mr Lothian said he wanted to take Callum out for the day – that would have been yesterday, Sunday. I told him our policy: until he has proper authorisation and training and has installed safety measures in the home he cannot take Callum. We believe that at around 1.30 in the afternoon your father entered the care facility with another man – an Asian man – and removed your brother from his room with the aid of some kind of homemade wheelchair and took him outside to a waiting car.'

'This is ludicrous. How do you know this? There's a security door. Didn't you see this man come in? It must be someone else. How could my father manage Callum? He's an old man. You have to find out who took Callum. He could die.'

'I'm losing you. Please speak slowly. Mr Lothian was given a folder with the security code for the door when he came in on Friday. We have video of the car park and both your father and his car have been identified by the village. Mr Lothian was in the company of an older woman. She's also from St Sylvan's, and I believe she's now been located. She and an Asian gentleman helped transfer Callum to the back seat of the car, next to the booster seat. Hello? Are you there, Ms Lothian? Caroline?'

'Who are all these people?' Caroline had stopped listening. The situation was beyond her imagining – this had to be some mistake – this woman on the phone was clearly mad. 'What's a booster seat got to do with any of this?'

'There's a child involved – a boy of about five or six who is related to the woman. We've asked Jan Venturi – that's the name of the woman – to come in. Normally we'd call the police, but we do understand that Mr Lothian is Callum's father. It's now Monday lunchtime. Do you have any reason to believe your father could hurt Callum, or place him in danger?'

'No, of course not, other than that he's not at all qualified to look after him, and Callum needs twenty-four-hour care.'

'Is there somewhere they'd go? Where do you think your father might be?'

'It's Monday. He walks by the river.'

'We'd like to call the police, Caroline, but as next of kin you must decide.'

Caroline held the phone in her hand.

'Caroline? Are you there?'

'Don't call the police,' she said quickly. 'Not yet. I have to think. I have a flight to Aberdeen in a few hours. I'll make a few calls and get back to you before I board, and if you hear anything, please contact me. And thank you, Corinne. I'm sure this is all some mistake. I'm sure Callum is fine.'

But she was not sure at all. The sun was coming up. She looked out to the street and saw running shoes, court shoes, flat loafers and lace-ups. It was a day like any other. It was Monday morning.

She listened to the missed calls from the care facility.

The last message was from her father. She sat on the bed while it played, and then she called the airline.

★

Caroline took a sleeping pill at Dubai, but after three hours she was wide awake. She lay in the darkness with the mask over her eyes, trying not to think about what her father might be doing out in the Wheatbelt, in Wandering, of all places. When she heard his message she cancelled her flight to Aberdeen, and then called Nicola Masterson. 'Callum is safe,' she told the woman. She knew where her father had gone. 'I'll be back in thirty-six hours. Don't call the police.'

Was that the right thing to do? Was Callum really safe?

In the lounge at the airport she entered Richard's name into her search engine. He was real. She read reviews of his albums and a short account of the accident. She listened to something he had written for the double bass and cello that was fierce and serious and unsettling, and then she wrote him an email.

> Richard, this is Caroline Lothian, the woman from Australia. I am flying back to Australia today. Something has happened with my father and my brother. I am listening to your music. Please write to me as soon as you can.

Under her name she typed her number, with the international dialling code. She wanted someone serious to talk to, someone else who understood the threat of extinction.

And she wanted to have a baby.

The woman in the seat next to her was snoring. Caroline put on her earphones and turned on the console. When *Rabbit-Proof Fence* came out she announced she would not watch it. She knew the history, and films like that ruin the truth, she told her friends; they overstate things, or fall short. But even then she had felt unsteady in her convictions. After all, what else can any story be, but too much, or not enough?

It was the 1930s; it wasn't her story at all, but from the opening credits she was lost. She was lost when the three children were taken, lost when their mother fell to the ground, lost again when only two came home.

When the film ended she turned off the screen and closed her eyes.

At eleven she told her mother, 'I look like a person that no one would know.' Martha had put this in a notebook, and Caroline kept returning to it. 'To look like' is to resemble; it is to follow the pattern of another. She knew at eleven that she resembled no one. But resemblance was only part of it; without another to recognise her she had felt as if she had no weight in the world. She was an egg in a wooden cabinet, labelled by an unknown hand, emptied of content.

But it wasn't true; she was on her way home right now, and there would be some kind of ending, which was all she might ever have. Which might even be enough.

Last time Fred was in Wandering, the whole family nearly froze to death, but tonight there was just enough cool air to lift the spirits. The moon was rising over the crest of the stubble, and it was so quiet that if you listened carefully you could hear the snap of a fox's jaw on the neck of a rabbit.

Once more Callum was watching the universe, safely strapped into the B3. Roger Wu had done a stellar job welding the axle and harness to the tubed frame, not to mention the improvised footplate. The handles had come off a racing bike. Marcel Breuer would have been proud of Roger. He had picked up the wheels of an old bicycle trailer, and they were perfect. It wasn't all plain sailing at the workshop – there were some sticky questions from his former student. 'Why do you want to ruin a vintage chair, Fred? Can't you just hire a wheel-chair? What's the rush?'

How to explain that he had to do something irrevocable, that he had to leave something behind, *relinquish* something?

'Relinquish', from the Latin, *relinquere*, to surrender. It was not a sacrifice to modify his chair, but a gesture in the true spirit of engineering and modernity. Why cling to the past? But at the care facility, Roger dug in his heels and he'd had to work hard to placate him. 'Can't the staff bring Callum out, Fred? Isn't that their job? Why are we rushing through the corridors like criminals? Shouldn't we be signing him out? Doesn't he need a special van?'

In the end, Fred had to agree to everything Roger wanted, just to keep him quiet. Yes, he would give a series of guest lectures. Yes, he would mentor one or two postgraduate students. And yes, Professor Lothian would even lead a group of structural engineers on a tour of China, South America and Turkey, where they would visit areas in earthquake-prone regions and talk to governments and local councils about pre-stressed concrete solutions. A former student of his had developed a system of embedding wire into concrete and it was proving to be remarkably strong under stress – and cheap. The professor's task was to garner support from the private sector for the university's not-for-profit venture. Yes, yes, yes.

It would not be so easy to appease Jan. He would beg her forgiveness. He would take her back to Le Marin.

At Wandering he was exhausted, but happy. It had been tricky getting Callum out of the car and through the fence by himself. Thank goodness for the wire cutters – he would slip them back into Roger's workshop next time he was there. When he clipped back the barbed wire, he found a compacted channel left by a combine harvester, which made it a little easier to push the chair through the wheat stubble, with Callum piled high with sleeping bags and a thermos and him with a pack of essentials listed in the folder from the care facility.

It was a magnificent evening under the stars. Callum was staring right up at what could be Alpha Centauri. Fred checked the chair. The back wheels were angled so Callum could see right across the field and out into the southern sky. If only he knew what Callum was feeling. When he first got him up here onto the rise he was sure his son was ready to jump out of his chair, climb into a rocket and leave right then and there. 'You're not going anywhere, young man,' he said sternly, as if Callum were nine or ten. Fred smiled. Callum was not young any more, but it was hard not to think of him that way.

The last time Callum was young he was in his final moments of architecture, and he was perfect. He had been invited into the honours programme, and he wanted to go to America to do his PhD. Callum was so much smarter than Fred had ever been. He had his eye on a scholarship at MIT and a bruise on his cheekbone from where a hockey ball had struck him at training. In the last moments of the Grand Final, with the team one-down, he trapped the ball outside the D, dribbled around one, and then two, and, with nothing left to do, shot wide.

Like all perfect children, Callum was unaware of his perfection. Martha liked to say he was born outside of the realms of the ordinary, like a minor god – 'Which doesn't excuse him from the responsibilities of mere mortals, like cleaning his room and doing his chores!' She loved to say those sorts of things – infantilising things. She was never comfortable with either of the children growing up, and if she were here today she would say something like, 'I can't believe you're nearly thirty-four.'

The other Callum had been thin and muscular. The Callum sitting by his side was soft and putty-coloured, and his skin fell away from him as if it were a distant relation to his bones. But never mind; they were coming together again, these two Callums.

For now, just being here together was enough.

It had never been easy with the first Callum.

It was the 10th of June, not the day to be left alone with a four-year-old. He was nursing a fierce hangover from a party at the house of their new friends, Ralph and Veronica Orr. Callum whined, slouched, grumbled and did everything an overtired four-year-old did when he didn't know what to do with himself. Then Alexander called from Lincoln. Drunk, Frederick presumed, although he could never really be sure. He listened to his father sobbing on the other end of the line, then put the phone down, but not before he caught the strangled vowels of his brother's name. 'Virgil …'

His father was calling on Virgil's birthday.

While Fred was on the phone, Callum had managed to get into the cupboard and tip Rice Bubbles all over the floor. Nothing really, but Frederick took Callum's thin arm, squeezed it as hard as he could without breaking it and dragged him into his bedroom, then lifted him up and tossed him onto his bed as if he were yesterday's newspaper. The boy floated down onto the quilt, where he lay perfectly still, looking at his father.

Frederick felt it rising up inside him, like lava, like vomit, generations of loathing for his own powerlessness. He swept the spit from his son's mouth and then he hit him. He hit his four-year-old son on the face with the back of his hand, as his father had hit him and his father's father had hit him, begetting and begetting.

He had hit Callum once and the small head snapped back and forward like a piece of white elastic, returning to him with a red welt clearly visible on his cheek and a trickle of blood bubbling out of the split lip. At that moment he saw his son not as a person, not as a child, but as a space, as the same dark, motherless space in which he himself had been interred as a child, when his own father was master of the void.

He managed to close the bedroom door before his knees gave way. He slid slowly down the corridor wall and dropped his head to his knees. It was a very long time before the door behind him creaked open and one brown eye looked out. Step by step, as if approaching a wild beast, Callum edged forward until he was so close that Frederick could feel his shallow, warm breath. He tried to say something to his son but his mouth had clamped up. Frederick forced himself to look Callum in the face, to let his son see his tears. His shame. When he could, he reached out for the arm that hung limply by his boy's side. He led Callum to the bathroom where he bathed his face and lip in the sink, and then held him in his arms while the bathtub filled. He carried him to the kitchen and found a candle, a match and a chipped Beatrix Potter saucer. He lit the candle and saw Peter Rabbit chasing an eternal orange carrot in Mr McGregor's garden. He undressed his son, then himself, and lowered Callum into the deep, warm bath. He turned off the light in the bathroom, and on that cold, wet winter afternoon Frederick lay in the water holding his four-year-old boy with the yellow light of the old candle catching the white enamel tiles, and tried to wash away the sins of the father.

'Are you thirsty, Callum?' Fred helped him drink some water, then held on to his hand. Callum had long, thin fingers, like his mother.

Frederick was holding on as tight as he could to his mother's thin fingers, as in the distance a man came towards them, pulling his little speck of a brother along with him. He could hear Virgil crying – *snivelling*, his father called it, from an Old English word, *snyflun*, meaning 'mucus of the nose'. His mother's hand tightened on Freddy's, not to reassure him, no; she was terrified of the man approaching like a turbine and she was hoping that if she tossed the boy in front of the man, then the teeth of the machine might catch on him and grind to a temporary halt, giving her just enough time to get out of the way. But the machine was inexorable and it simply picked up Frederick and incorporated him right into its pounding core and continued out of the garden, down the steps and towards the lake.

The small town of Saint-Clair, in a comfortable house by the lake. It was his mother's idea. 'The war is over, Alex, so why not a holiday in France, like other families do?' Grand people, like the owners of the foundry who held his father's fate in their hands. They boarded the train at Victoria Station and took the night ferry from Dover, as if they were a normal family in normal times, as if there were not long sections of the train ride where Mam tried to turn their little heads away from the view, so they would not have to see for themselves the bleeding landscape of France.

Their father laughed. 'Your mother wanted a holiday after the war? Well, here it is, lads.'

But the town was empty, the shops were shuttered and no one was on holiday. After three days spent inside reading *The Hotspur* and hiding from hailstones and their father's palm, the boys were dragged outside, their dad dismissing the high winds and the stormwater pouring down from the mountains, insisting that he, Frederick, get some bloody exercise, and that he, Frederick, row his little brother out to the centre of the turbulent lake.

'But Alex, Virgil can't swim,' protested Mam, and then turned away, giving in for the last time.

No matter. Alexander rolled up his trousers and went to work on the boat, dragging it to the edge, while Mam stood on the bank, worrying her heavy grey wool skirt. His father's strong, pale calves were marbled with cold, half-submerged in the lake's muddy rim, like broken columns.

It was his father who launched them out onto the grey waters, yelling at him to 'be a man', and at Virgil to 'cease his damn snivelling'. Virgil was crouched on the hard seat at the front of the boat, his small mouth wobbling, his face white with cold and dripping with snot, gripping hard the rails of the wooden boat, while Frederick tried to rotate the oars as he had been shown at school, struggling to keep the tips symmetrical in the rough waters. Sport was not his strength, which was why it was always so important to him that Callum excel. Trigonometry, algebra, geometry – this was where Frederick shone. He saw all things in three dimensions, in volumes and cubes, carving deep holes in the graph paper he pinned next to the maps of Europe on the corkboard in his cubicle at school. On his first visit to the British Museum he was allowed to peer into a stereoscopic viewer. He saw a bombed-out cathedral in acute black-and-white, the edges sharply etched. Rouen? Coventry? As he leant in to focus, he understood that this was the nature of his gift: to fold up the ends of flat black lines and equations and drag them off the page and toss them out into the tunnelling depths of three-dimensional space. He would imagine things into being. 'Architecture?' his father responded, incredulous, disgusted. 'No son of mine will be a damned architect.' And so it was to engineering he went, a gift pressed into more practical service.

On the shore his mother's body zigzagged in diminishing zeds until she came to a full stop. When the boat faltered they were far away from her, far from love, unsettled by the high wind and a wave that ripped across the bow as he leant into one oar to turn the boat back. Virgil stood up when he had been instructed to stay seated. He swung around with his arms outstretched, screamed, 'Mummy!' and then tipped like a little teapot over the side and under the stern, never to be seen alive again. Since Frederick thought of a lake as a contained space with a top and a bottom and a volume that could be fathomed, he followed wilfully, purposefully, diving in headfirst after Virgil, until he was thrown to the surface with a mouth full of salty bile and later, vomit. Lost.

Frederick wished he had a Tulip chair, so he could do what he always told his children not to do: spin around until he was dizzy. He was no longer lost. Callum was here. Caroline was on her way back. They were all going home together.

'Did you hear that, Callum? A night bird! A tawny frog-mouth? A mopoke? Your mother would have known. She would have brought her book about birds of the Wheatbelt. All the way to Wandering we would have had to listen to descriptions of their habitats and breeding rituals, and how their nests at Mukinbudin or Burracoppin are under threat from clearing. Caroline would have complained. She's never been interested in any animal unless it's dead and gone. Why is that? How long is it since we saw your sister? A year, fifteen months?

'Callum, don't you go to sleep on me, not yet. I have something in the car for you. Do you know what it is? It's your old telescope, the Dobsonian. You're slipping in the chair, let me help you. I'm worried about those straps. Are they too loose? I know I should have come sooner, Callum. Please, don't look at me like that. I just couldn't see you for a while. Are you angry with me? Are you cross with Daddy? Please don't be angry. Forgive me, Callum. *Mea culpa.* You remember some Latin? When you're settled in, I'm going to get the telescope and you can help us find the constellations. You remember the names, don't you? You always knew the names of things in the sky.

'We're going to have some soup from Jan's flask. She wanted to come with us, because of my head. I'm not supposed to drive, but it's nothing really. It wouldn't have been right for her to come. She's got her grandson to consider – Morrison. You'll like him. He's quite a character. Jan's father used to take her to Kokerbin Rock when she was a girl. Kokerbin Rock is where we went on our last trip together. Did you see Jan in the car? Does it bother you that I've met someone? She's just a friend, Callum. I hope Caroline likes her.'

Fred adjusted the pillow behind Callum's head. 'What do you think of your chair? The last time you saw that chair it was upstairs in my study. It's clever, isn't it?'

It was Jan who gave him the idea. Fred had helped her carry

Oct. 12, 1937. H. A. EVEREST ET AL. 2,095,411

FOLDING WHEEL CHAIR

Filed Feb. 11, 1936 3 Sheets-Sheet 1

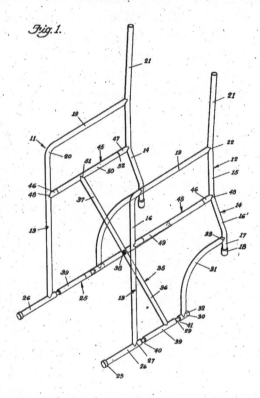

Fig. 1.

Inventors
H.A.Everest
H.C.Jennings.
by Hazard and Miller
Attorneys.

the new TV into her lounge room, and afterwards she helped him with his bags from the hospital.

'I'm not staying,' she said, 'I'm exhausted. And I'm not going to discuss your offer of the house and your ridiculous ideas until I have a really good think, so don't ask me.' She was standing in front of the B3. 'It's like a wheelchair, isn't it?' she said.

The more he looked at the chair, the more he saw that Jan had identified a relationship he had never considered. Perhaps the invention of steel tubing had inspired more than bicycles and the B3? After she left, he looked it up on the internet. Bingo! 'Herbert A. Everest and Harry C. Jennings, Folding wheel chair, US Patent 2095411, 1937'. They were both mechanical engineers, and one of them had broken his back in an accident. The new tubed chair was light and mobile, and revolutionised wheelchair access all over the world. And with their invention of the cross-member – still in use today – you could fold it and take it with you.

'So I called Roger Wu. You met him this morning at the care facility. He wasn't in the best of moods, but he'll come good. The thing is, Callum, from the first cut I had not a single moment of regret. Roger showed me how to weld a seam. You need great heat for high-grade steel, and I had to wear a mask like Ned Kelly and a suit like Neil Armstrong. You know, before that chair I'd never made anything in my entire life, except a boiled egg. And I have something else to confess. I had a maintenance fellow from the university come over one evening and put your telescope together when you were asleep. Remember you woke up that morning and it was all ready in the garage? You were so upset.

'"Daddy," you said, "Why didn't you wait for me? You should have woken me up. I wanted to do it with you. We were making it together. It was our project, you and me. You've ruined it, Daddy." You worked yourself up into a state. You must have been tired from the night before – I think we were at Ralph and Veronica's until late. But you have to see it from my point of view, Callum. There I was, poring over those damn photocopies from America, and driving around with you looking for the right components, but in the end I just could not manage to put the thing together. So I called someone. I was furious at myself.'

Frederick stopped. He tucked the blanket around Callum's legs.

'I was meant to be an architect, Callum. Architects don't have to know how to make things. My grandfather started it, and my father made things his whole miserable life, but I had no capacity, Callum. That's why I taught at the university; my strength was in the theory of the thing. A theoretical bridge is perfect, but a real bridge is a different matter. What if a calculation of load is flawed? I became an expert on disasters. I'm sure I showed you and Caroline that Super 8 film of the collapse of the bridge at Tacoma Narrows?'

A minor oscillation meets a stiff wind, and you have two waves moving closer and closer until they join forces in harmonic motion – or, if you're a stickler, aeroelastic fluttering – with devastating results. It is a tragic convergence. Even with fine weather and an absence of wind, the best design in the world can fail. Even a Saab.

'Do you hear that? I think there's a fox among the sheep in the next paddock. You went straight through that stop sign into the limestone wall. It was a well-lit intersection, there was no rain, no other traffic, and it was clear that you had to stop at the bottom of the hill, but you went through it at over eighty kilometres an hour. They checked the brakes, the tyres, what was left of the engine, but they could find no mechanical faults. Nothing. People said they heard a car going very fast as it reached the bottom of the hill. What if someone had been coming, Callum? What if you'd killed a child? I'm sorry, Callum. This isn't easy for me. We knew you'd been drinking, and that you were over the limit, but not enough for that. All your friends said you were upset about the hockey match, and hadn't talked to anyone at the party. Your mother died not knowing what you were doing, or why it happened. She had no idea.

'Do you know why we're out here under the black sky and not back at my unit? There are no phones here. I'm not going to talk about the accident after tonight. This is the first time I've spoken to you about it, Callum, and once will be enough.

'It was Caroline who called that night. She'd gone to Fleur's house. You remember Fleur? She has those children with ridiculous names. Caroline said you had no idea she was at Fleur's. She hadn't seen you for two weeks or more. It was sheer chance.

'I answered the phone. I've always been glad about that. It would have finished Martha. It was quite late, after 10 pm, and no one ever called at that hour. I picked up the phone and I listened. I could hear sounds, all fighting for attention. The loudest was a kind of choking, or catching in the throat, as if someone was drowning. Underneath that there was a repetitive thump – maybe someone patting the back of the person on the phone, trying to calm them down? I could hear a baby crying, and I thought I heard a dog bark. "Who is it? Is there a dog hurt?" I said. And then I heard some other sound, which I later realised was the ambulance siren. That was when Kate – Fleur's girlfriend – must have taken the phone from Caroline. "Mr Lothian, it's Kate Easton. There's been an accident."

'There was a long pause, although it wasn't really a pause. Pauses can be conscious or unconscious – a lapse in memory, an interruption. I've read books about this. "Pauses work best on the stage when used for dramatic effect." A script might say "Long pause". Between the two parts of a joke they might write "Short pause". Sometimes they use the word "beat". It's years since I learnt French, but a word came to me that night: *un trou*. It translates as "a snag, a hole, a dent, a crack, a gap, a tear". How can you have a word for something that's no longer there? A bridge can fail, and so can speech. Just like buildings in an earthquake, there are some things that the tongue and the mouth and the vocal cords are not designed to withstand.

'And then I noticed Martha. She'd dropped her knitting on the floor and was standing right behind me. When I picked it up the next day, the needles were still in place, neatly folded one over the other, like two hands in a lap. It was a difficult cable pattern Martha was knitting for you, for the long American winters ahead. She loved to go on about "the American winter", do you remember? She was standing very close to me, near the phone, but we were strangers. Have you seen those photos taken after the war in Europe, everyone starving to death but standing patiently in line, waiting their turn? She was pressed right up against me, but her body was pulling away, trying to keep some distance between herself and the stranger in front of her in the queue. "Caroline?" she said after I put down the phone.

'Later the police came and knocked on the front door, just like on television. I wouldn't open it. I said, "I know why you're here. I already know what you're going to tell me. You can go away now. My daughter has called."

'"Mr Lothian, we'd like to speak to you in person. We understand this is a very difficult time."

'In the end I let them in. They wanted to drive us to the hospital. I refused. I shook my head at Martha, and I shook it again at the police. 'No, thank you,' I said. I was polite, but firm. I drove us both, in our own car. I can't remember parking, but I do remember leaving Martha with Caroline in some kind of room and walking down a long corridor to find you.

'And I did find you, Callum. I found you, but I did nothing to preserve you. Martha did it all, with Caroline – the scans, the tests, the prognosis, the daily visits, the physiotherapy and OT. Days and nights and weeks and months and years.

'You remember that Mummy died, Callum? Caroline came and told you.

'I thought that everything I had ever wanted ended with that phone call. For Martha it was different. Her daughter was still alive. But my son was dead. That was what I thought for years, Callum, that you were dead, and that someone else was lying there in the care facility, being washed and fed and toileted. Not someone, but something. An empty egg on a bed of cotton wool.

'I'm so sorry, Callum. I can see now that I was wrong. You're different now, but I can't hold that against you. I'm different too.

'I have one regret. I should have told Martha that I knew why you did it. I should have told her it was not her fault, or your fault, but mine. It was all my fault. Can a young man of twenty-one be so angry with his father that he can drive a car that once belonged to his father – a car that was a gift to his son – into a wall at a great speed? Yes, yes, of course. That's why fathers are such a great danger to their sons. There's no one a boy can hate like his father. I understood the dangers of the relationship, so I held myself apart from you. Martha didn't understand. She said, "Frederick, you have to speak to Callum on his level. He always has to try so hard to come up to you, and he can't manage it. He feels as if whatever he does it's never enough. Stop lecturing him and come out of your office and take him out. He's desperate to see *E. T.*"

'I took you. Do you remember? It was a wonderful film. I'm going to the car now, to get the telescope. I won't be long. It's in the boot. You know, I've kept it under my bed since we moved, wrapped up in a blanket. It's smaller than I remember, but it hasn't gotten any lighter. I'm getting old, eh!'

All the way down the hill Frederick Lothian thought about his house. He would have to find a builder, but he would manage the project himself. He had shown Roger the sketch because Roger was a real engineer. Roger could make things. He had looked at Fred's sketches and taken out a calculator. 'It's all certainly feasible,' he said, 'both the ramp and the lift, as long as the local council doesn't block you, and I don't think you'll have any problems there.'

It would be the first thing he had ever built, something for his children, and he couldn't wait to begin.

Wednesday, 1 February 2006

CAROLINE DROVE NORTH-EAST from Kalgoorlie to
Menzies in a hired car. She thought about her mother flying
down this long road in the back of a ute, with Maureen sitting

next to her. In the report of the trial there was mention of a sister, so it wasn't hard to find Maureen in the phone book.

Maureen was standing outside the house when she arrived, and beat her on the back with her hands when she held her. She made a phone call, and three young men turned up. They were Maureen's sons, Caroline's cousins, and they must have been close by, waiting for the call. They sat in the kitchen at a table, with a howling easterly rocking the walls, holding their cups of tea, while the boys shifted in their seats and played with their cigarette packets. They didn't look much like her, but then Caroline looked just like her mother, Carol, said Maureen, and Carol hadn't looked like anyone else.

'She was the good-looking one,' Maureen said, and the boys laughed.

'Come on, Mum,' they said.

'A thinker, your mother, and she had such feelings. Carol had two moods: laughing and crying. Does that sound right to you?'

'That sounds right,' Caroline said.

'Good at school too, when she went.' Maureen's words were broken by long silences when only the wind spoke. 'She ran off young with a crazy fella and never really came back. You make sure you come back,' said Maureen. 'We'll take you out past Laverton, to Cosmo Newberry. Did you say you got a man at home?'

'Kind of,' she said. 'Almost.' She held her cup to her lips, then put it down. She tried not to look at the boys. 'Maureen, do you know if I have any brothers or sisters?'

This was the question she held on to when she first spoke to Maureen on the phone, and kept with her all the way from Perth to Kalgoorlie, through the long night in the motel, and on the road to Menzies. Martha had said there were none, but now she had to make sure.

Maureen shook her head slowly. 'You came too early. They

took you both to Perth, to King Edward's. Your mum lost a lot of blood and had a big operation, and they put you in one of those incubators. She had to wait weeks to hold you, and then the milk was gone. And there were no more kids after that. She brought you back once, when you were about five months old, and then she went off again. We lost her in Perth, and next we heard you were in foster. We didn't know until later about the adoption.'

Caroline thought, *How could I be talking like this to a stranger?* Her grown-up cousins had dropped their heads, caring enough to feel bad for her.

'We heard later that you got hurt when you were little, and that's why they put you back in the hospital and took you away from her. That was our fault. We should have come down and got you.' Maureen wiped her face. The boys sat still in their seats.

'It wasn't right, what happened to you. Your nan and pop, they were broken up when they knew you were gone. They were well-known around here. You ask anyone. They were big on church and education. I work as a teacher's aide in the local school, with the little ones. Your nan and pop went for the exemption when they brought that in. You know about those laws – we're talking after the war now, late 1940s?'

Caroline nodded.

'Ten years it took them of writing and getting nowhere, until they got those papers letting them go about their business. "Dog tags," they call them now. Some folks looked down on them for doing it, but a lot of people just wanted to put their kids in school, or have tea or go to a movie on a Friday night. We were segregated then. Your pop had to fill in all these forms, and send photos and references, and they had to have a medical certificate to say they had no diseases – things like leprosy, even VD. They had to say they wouldn't mix with Aboriginal people. Your nan and pop didn't want to do that, but they wanted the best for their kids. Who knows if they were right or wrong. It's easy to judge now. Right, boys?'

Maureen got up from the table. There was some history here, something unresolved. Maureen was talking as much to her boys as to Caroline. She brought water to the table and filled her glass.

'Your nan lost her first one. He got taken. She was living out on the Depot then, a real young girl who came in from the desert. She put that little boy on Mount Margaret Mission, and they came and took him in the truck. Real fair, he was. She was out working and she felt it. She knew something had happened to that boy. We've got a word for it. Your cousin Paul here works at the TAFE. He's teaching language.' Maureen nodded at Paul, and then jerked her head at the two other men. They got up and went out the back door onto the verandah. 'It's not a word for men to hear,' she said. 'But Paul's a teacher, so that's different. Tell her, Paul.'

'*Mimipathapathalkiri*,' said Paul.

'*Mimipathapathalkiri*,' repeated Maureen quietly, putting one hand on her breast. 'It means "breast biting", it means the mother feels something's wrong with her baby. An ache. That's what your nan felt when her first was taken.'

Caroline tried the word. '*Mimipatha* –'

'*Mimi-patha-patha-lkiri*,' said Paul. 'It's a Wangkatha word – well, really it's more complicated than that. There's lots of languages round here.'

Caroline wrote it in her notebook with Paul looking over her shoulder.

'You look after that word,' he said, tapping the front of her book with his finger.

Caroline looked at the clock above the fridge. It was a long drive back to Kalgoorlie, and then a late flight to Perth, and on to pick up where she'd left off – London, Aberdeen, and the egg of the Great Auk.

Maureen stood up first. 'Your nan would have loved to see you, with your degrees and your museum job. Don't you go crying on us. You're back now. Go get the boys in off the verandah, Paul, and tell them not to throw their butts on the ground. There's an ashtray for that.'

When Paul left, Maureen put her hand on Caroline's arm. 'I put some photos out for you. You can take them if you want. There's not many.'

'Photos?' said Caroline. She had never thought of photos. Her mother was dead. Why would there be photos?

They were in the kitchen when Martha told her. Caroline was living in a flat with a friend, and she was home for Sunday dinner. She had just met Julian, and she had finished her undergraduate degree and was waiting to see if she had a scholarship. She felt strong.

'I'm going to try to find her, Mum. I need to know if she wants to see me.'

Her mother put the colander down on the board and wiped her hands on a tea towel. 'You can't, Caroline. You can't see her. She died four years ago, when you were in your last year of high school. It was a domestic dispute. It was in the paper.' Martha did not cry. If she had cried, Caroline would have slapped her face.

'Where?'

'Down south, near Albany. You were in Year 12. You were about to have your final exams. Dad thought – we thought ...'

What did they think? 'You said you only knew her first name. That's what you said. You said her name was Carol. Like mine.'

'Her name *was* Carol. They were still taking the mother's name off birth certificates when you were born, but we found out who she was from the matron and from the Department of Native Welfare – it was still called that back then. It was because

301

of the hospital. For some reason the records from the hospital went to the matron, and they had the full name on them. I was reading the paper one day, and I saw her name. I always read the smaller columns, the misdemeanours and convictions.'

'Just in case you saw my mother there?'

'I know how it sounds. But yes, in case I saw your mother. There was a trial and he was convicted. It wasn't your father – your birth father – who did it. It was a man she hardly knew. He already had a record for domestic violence. They met at the pub. I'm so sorry, Caroline.'

Her mother must have known that sorry did not come anywhere near close to it. All of her final year she had stayed after school and studied with the boarders. She sat at a lovely white desk with her books stacked neatly in one corner, her pens in the other, in front of a large window opening out onto a grassy quadrangle. She was going to get top marks. She was going to prove something to all the other girls, but if she had been asked, she would not have known what that something was.

She smashed a plate, then a glass. Her father came down from the study. 'I told you I wanted to find her. In Year 8 and 9 and 10 and 11, I kept telling you and Dad, and you kept saying, 'Wait till you're older, wait till you're older.' And all that time you knew her name; you knew she was living some terrible life while I was wondering what to wear to the fucking school ball? How could you have done that? And then she dies, and you don't even tell me.'

'We didn't know the right time to tell you. We didn't want you to go through all that. We wanted to protect you.' Martha said all manner of things like that, but none of it made any difference. Her father said nothing.

A few months later she made a start. She requested her medical records from the maternity hospital. What she found terrified her. She confided in a woman in one of her classes that she was adopted, and that she had requested her files from the hospital where she was admitted. They were at the Tavern, and after a few beers she imagined this woman could be her friend. 'I was premature,' she said, 'and later I was admitted with burns and a broken leg.'

'How much later?' asked the woman.

'Two and a bit.'

'Lucky you were so young,' she said, 'you can't remember any of it. Do you want another beer?'

Caroline excused herself and left. Was that to be the measure of damage – the things a child remembered?

While Maureen hugged her, Paul stood to one side, holding something in his hand. When she turned to him to say goodbye he handed her a small black Bible.

'Thank you, Paul,' she said.

'Jesus will protect you,' he said gravely.

'I hope so,' said Caroline.

'*Katung-kat-janya* – "the one who is in the above". That was one of the first words we had for Jesus in Wangkatha. You better write that down too.'

He spelt it out as she wrote it in the front of her new Bible. On impulse she held it out to Paul. 'Would you?'

He took the book and pen and sat at the table. 'Here you go,' he said, handing it back.

'Are you a Christian?' Paul asked.

'No,' said Caroline.

'Plenty of time left,' said Paul with a smile.

'And watch for roos,' said Maureen as she closed the car door. 'You shouldn't be driving now, should she, boys? It's getting close to dusk.'

The boys shook their heads and kicked their feet, and stood around the car with their arms crossed.

'You can always stay, you know, Caroline. I like having another woman to talk to. But you got a plane to catch. You're coming back, though. I've got that spare room for you, and I want you back. You hear?'

Paul walked around the car and kicked every tyre. 'Back one's lying a bit low,' he said, leaning in the window. 'Did they check the pressure when you got it?'

'This isn't a country car,' said the youngest cousin. 'It isn't even a four-wheel drive. At least you got a bar.'

'It'll be fine,' said Caroline, smiling. *This is what it would be like to have brothers*, she thought.

It was hard to avoid Slim Dusty songs on the drive back to Kalgoorlie. Slim Dusty and kangaroos. She drove slowly, flicking her high beam on and off. The missions had deep roots in her mother's country. Paul was some kind of preacher, she decided, in some kind of evangelical church. Or perhaps he was just poetic.

> For Caroline.
>
> Getting lost is the easy part,
> it's getting found that's hard.
>> Come back soon.
>
> Your cousin, Paul

Just how did you go about getting found? As she came into Kalgoorlie her phone beeped and she pulled off the road into a truck stop. The text was from Fleur. 'How did it go? Are you okay?'

There was a missed call from her father. No message. Lost for words, as usual. Another set of plans for the house?

She parked the car in front of her motel room and picked up her bag, the Bible, and the photos from Maureen. She couldn't look at the small black-and-white photos with Aunty Maureen standing next to her, pointing and talking. 'I'm about six there, your mother must be eight. See the hair? Your nan was always at it with a comb. There's me and your mother and our lot outside the Methodist Church. Would you look at those dresses? That's your pop and nan, all dressed up. They were big in the church. See how you look like your nan? That's Nan's sister, May. She's gone now. There's your mother at a dance. She's about sixteen. She got that dress specially. Isn't she beautiful?'

She sat on the bed in her motel room and opened the envelope. Maureen had written on the back of each of the photos in pencil. 'At Laverton', 'At Church', 'Nan and Pop', 'Aunty May', 'At the dance'.

At the dance her mother was standing next to a young man in a suit. When she saw him her heart jumped. 'Is that him?'

'Who?' asked Maureen. 'Oh no, that handsome man is Jim, my husband. We all went to school together. He died about ten years ago.'

'I'm sorry,' said Caroline.

'Yes,' said Maureen.

It was almost dark now, and there was traffic on the road. She should get to the airport. Some kind of sign on the street was flashing on and off, flooding her room with light, then plunging it back into shadow. She caught herself in the long mirror on the wall, a thin woman sitting on the edge of a bed, holding an envelope to her chest. She watched the mirror. One moment she was lost, and the next she was found.

Caroline stood up and turned on the overhead light in the room, closed her bag and left.

List of Illustrations and References

p. viii Professor Richard Owen with *Dinornis maximus* (now *D. novaezealandiae*). Plate XCVII in R. Owen, *Memoirs on the Extinct Wingless Birds of New Zealand*, vol. 2, *Plates* (London: John Van Voorst, 1879). Courtesy of the University of Texas Libraries, the University of Texas at Austin.

p. 19 Salginatobel Bridge, 1930. 'An Example of Structural Art: The Salginatobel Bridge of Robert Maillart', David P. Billington, *Journal of the Society of Architectural Historians* 33, no. 1 (March 1974): 61–72.

p. 20 Virgil, *The Works of Virgil*, trans. John Dryden, vol. 2, *The Aeneid*, bk 6.

p. 31 The Wassily Chair, B3. Box 33, reel 5737, frame 543. Marcel Breuer papers, 1920–1986. Archives of American Art, Smithsonian Institution.

p. 33 Plan of Wassily Chair. Box 33, reel 5737, frame 542. Marcel Breuer papers, 1920–1986. Archives of American Art, Smithsonian Institution.

p. 34 Marcel Breuer in the Wassily chair, 1926. Photograph from Heritage Images.

p. 47 Seagram Building, New York, NY, Mies van der Rohe with Philip Johnson. Ezra Stoller, 1958 © Esto. All rights reserved.

p. 49 Postcard, Imperial Hotel Tokyo, 1930s–1940s. Photographer unknown. Wikipedia.

p. 53   The Great Kanto Earthquake Japan of 1923, courtesy of the
        University of Hawaii at Manoa Library (or UHM Library)
        Asia Collection.

p. 62   Braun SK6 turntable and radio, Dieter Rams and Hans
        Gugelot, 1961. Digital image © The Museum of Modern
        Art/Scala, Florence.

p. 70   Trussed Concrete Steel Company envelope, 1909. Courtesy
        Martin Shepard Office Records, Southeastern Architectural
        Archive, Special Collections Division, Tulane University
        Libraries.

p. 72   Reception Desk & Solari Board Sections & Elevations
        – Trans World Airlines Flight Center, John F. Kennedy
        International Airport. Library of Congress, Prints &
        Photographs Division, HABS NY-6371, sheet 29. HABS/
        NPS, Beyer Blinder Belle architects, delineator, 2005.

p. 86   John F. Kennedy International Airport: Trans World Airlines
        terminal. Courtesy of Trans World Airlines, Inc. http://kids.
        britannica.com/comptons/art-126562/The-Trans-World-
        Airlines-terminal-at-John-F-Kennedy-International.

p. 91   Tower, Vladimir Shukhov, 1911.

p. 101 Original Tay River Bridge before collapse, seen from the
        north, 1878–1879. Photographer unknown.

p. 107 Tay River Bridge, middle section collapsed, 1880.
        Photographed by Valentines.

p. 123 Antony Alpers, *A Book of Dolphins* (London: John Murray,
        1960).

p. 124 Alpers, *A Book of Dolphins*.

p. 131 Double egg. Plate XCIX in R. Owen, *Memoirs on the Extinct
        Wingless Birds of New Zealand*, vol. 2, *Plates* (London: John
        Van Voorst, 1879). www.lib.utexas.edu/books/nzbirds/html/
        txu-oclc-7314815-2-22-p-099.html.

Courtesy of the University of Texas Libraries, the University of Texas at Austin.

p. 135 Wood engraving of great auk, by Thomas Bewick. In *A History of British Birds*, vol. 2, *Water Birds* (Newcastle, UK: Sol Hodgson for Beilby & Bewick, 1804).

p. 139 Eggs and bones. Plate CXV in R. Owen, *Memoirs on the Extinct Wingless Birds of New Zealand*, vol. 2, *Plates* (London: John Van Voorst, 1879). www.lib.utexas.edu/books/nzbirds/html/txu-oclc-7314815-2-22-p-115.html
Courtesy of the University of Texas Libraries, the University of Texas at Austin.

p. 156 Martha, the last passenger pigeon, ca. 1957. Photographer unknown. Smithsonian Institution Archives. Image SAI 2010–0612.
W. L. Dawson, *The Birds of Ohio: A Complete Scientific and Popular Description of the 320 Species of Birds Found in the State* (Columbus, OH: Wheaton Publishing, 1903), p. 425.

p. 160 John James Audubon, *Birds of America* (New York: J. J. Audubon, 1843).

p. 164 Men standing with pile of bison skulls, Michigan Carbon Works, mid-1870s. Photographer unknown. Burton Historical Collection, Detroit Public Library. https://digitalcollections.detroitpubliclibrary.org/islandora/object/islandora%3A151477.

p. 171 Quagga, London mare next to keeper, 1864. Photograph by Frank Haes.

p. 177 Newly arrived Mark I Male tank C15 practises for the Battle of Flers. From the collection of Richard Pullen, with thanks.

p. 179 The prototype Mark I tank 'Mother' being tested at Burton Park, January 1916. From the collection of Richard Pullen.

p. 181 Lady workers at William Foster & Co., 1917. Foster's was an agricultural machinery company based in Lincoln, Lincolnshire. The foundry and factory made the first tanks for the British army in the First World War. From the collection of Richard Pullen.

p. 183 New Mark I tank boarding a train at the Foster factory. The Russian script on the side was supposed to fool the Germans into thinking the tanks were water carriers destined for Russia.

p. 202 J. K. Rowling, *Harry Potter and the Philosopher's Stone* (London: Bloomsbury, 1997).

p. 234 Tacoma Narrows Bridge showing man running off roadway during collapse, 7 November 1940. University of Washington Libraries, Special Collections Division, UW20731. http://digitalcollections.lib.washington.edu/cdm/singleitem/collection/farquharson/id/27.

p. 282 'Tacoma Narrows Bridge – Collapse', Wikipedia, last edited 9 December 2017, https://en.wikipedia.org/wiki/Tacoma_Narrows_Bridge_(1940)#Collapse.

p. 290 Folding wheel chair patent. Herbert A. Everest and Harry C. Jennings, US Patent 2095411, filed 11 February 1936, and issued 12 October 1937.

p. 297 *Mr Weaver Bags a Tiger*, 1869. Photographer unknown. https://en.wikipedia.org/wiki/Thylacine.

Acknowledgments

During the writing of *Extinctions* my parents and mother-in-law passed away; the experience of accompanying them through their final years marks these pages. As an engineer, my father would have appreciated the discussion of concrete and bridges, while I think my mother would have rather liked Jan.